To Kate, Mungo, David, Victoria, Duncan, Grainne, Nicholas
and all our brilliant cat sitters.

Mimi says thank you!

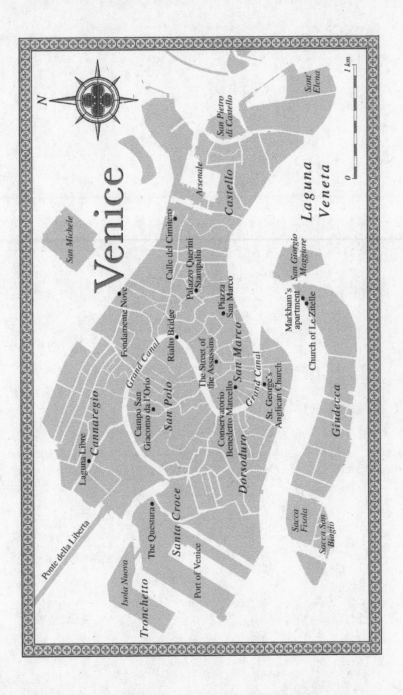

Duri i banchi – Venetian motto, dating from *La Serenissima* at the height of her power.

During naval battles, prior to cannon fire or to ramming an enemy ship, the command would be given to the rowers in the galley to hang on tight to their benches in order to brace themselves for impact.

The most appropriate English translation, therefore, might be *hold fast*.

Prologue

One day the waters are going to win.

That's sad, of course, but inevitable. Now, you may have your own opinions on where the guilt lies for this. Some of you may blame global warming and rising sea levels. Others may point their fingers at the ever deeper dredging of canals by a city ever more greedy to glut itself on the money brought in by ever greater cruise ships. Others might simply blame *moto ondoso*, and the effect of too many motor boats in a city designed for the less destructive effects of the *gondola* and the *sandalo*.

It doesn't matter. There's little point in blaming anyone now. Because the waters are going to win.

Every year they creep just a little bit higher above the impervious stone. Every year, the porous brick crumbles just that little bit more. Every year ground-floor flats are abandoned to the desperate and the gullible, and shop owners begin to wonder just how many more times they can bear to rebuild, repaint and repair their flooded properties.

The relationship between the city and the water has gone wrong. I think everyone knows this. The relationship with the lagoon that once brought protection, and power and wealth, has soured. The waters are creeping back, bit by bit, year on year. And there will come a day when *passerelle* and waders and MOSE will no longer be enough.

Because one day the waters are going to win.

One day. But not today.

Part One

Angels for an Angel

Chapter 1

CPSM 22.50 La laguna subisce gli effetti di non previste raffiche di vento da 100 km orari. Il livello potrebbe raggiungere i 190 centimetri alle ore 23.30

CPSM 22.50 The lagoon is being affected by unforeseen wind gusts of 100 km per hour. The level could reach 190 centimetres at 23.30

– Message from the *Centro Previsioni e Segnalazioni Marea*, Venice, on the night of 12 November 2019.

The wind rattled the windows of the apartment once again, and the lights flickered momentarily. Gramsci howled, and dived under the sofa.

I shook my head. 'Daft cat. He's never cared for storms.'

'I'm not sure I care for this one either,' said Federica.

I peered outside, trying to see how bad things had got, when the windows shook once more and I jumped back, startled.

'*Caro*, just get back from the window, would you?'

'I'm sure it's fine.'

'And I'm not sure it is. Come on. Please.'

I nodded, and stepped back. There was another blast of wind, and, again, the lights flickered.

I shivered. 'God, for a moment there I swear I felt the bloody building move.'

'That's impossible. This place has been here for centuries. It's survived everything the elements have thrown at it. And yet—'

'And yet?'

'I think it moved, too.'

The lights dimmed again before flickering back into life and I heard my phone buzzing away on the table.

'Dario?'

'Nat. Are you okay, man?'

'We're fine. But it's blowing a gale outside and the electricity's on and off. How are you?'

'Well, we're on the top floor. So you think we'd be okay. Except I swear I can feel the building swaying.'

'How's Emily?'

'She thinks it's the most exciting thing ever.' He chuckled. 'Small girls, eh?' Then his voice changed. 'Listen, Nat, I'm calling round all my buddies. Just telling them to stay at home. Don't go out.'

'Don't worry. I've got no intention of getting wet.'

'It's more than that. Have you seen the predictions?'

'Not for a few hours.' The *acqua alta* siren had sounded four notes, an indication that nearly 70 per cent of the city would be flooded to some degree.

'It's worse than we thought. Worse than anyone could have thought. They're saying it's going to be the worst since '66.'

'Bloody hell.'

'So just stay at home, eh?'

'Don't worry, Dario, we're not going anywhere. Just look after yourselves, okay?'

'We will. Take care, *vecio*.'

I hung up.

Fede looked over from her computer. 'Not good?'

'They're fine. But it sounds like this is going to be a bad one.'

She nodded, and tapped the screen of her laptop. 'I know. Messages are coming in from everywhere. Basically, don't go out.'

Her phone buzzed. She half sighed, half smiled and picked it up. '*Ciao, Mamma*. Yes, we've heard . . . no, we're not going out . . . yes, I promise . . . yes, we're fine. I'll call tomorrow, of course. Sleep well. Love you. *Ciao*.'

She laid her phone face down on the table and shook her head. 'Mothers, eh?'

'Everything okay?'

She smiled. 'Yes. Worried of course. I expect *zio* Giacomo will be calling next.' Her expression changed, and became serious. 'But this doesn't sound good.'

'So what do we do?'

She shrugged. 'What is there to do? Nothing. We're the lucky ones, I suppose. At least the power seems to be staying on.' The lights dimmed for a moment. 'Just about.'

I yawned and stretched. 'I guess you're right. Okay, I'm not in the mood for television. Shall we just have an early night?'

Fede shook her head as the windows rattled again. 'Do you think you'll be able to sleep through this?'

'Maybe not. I'm pretty sure you will though.'

She smiled, weakly. 'Maybe so. But, I don't know, it wouldn't seem right somehow. People, friends, all over the city are all living through this. Some worse than others. It wouldn't seem right to sleep through it, somehow.'

I nodded. 'You're right.' I yawned again. 'Okay. Given it's going to be a late night, shall I make us some coffee?'

'Tea for me please, *caro.*'

'Of course.'

I was on my way to the kitchen when the entryphone buzzed. '*Chi è?*'

It's possible that someone replied, but, if so, their words were carried away by the howling wind. I opened the door, and switched the stairwell lights on.

'*Chi è?*' I shouted.

'Nat? It's me, Eduardo.'

I looked down over the bannister. Ed was framed in the doorway, wearing a heavy wax jacket and knee-length rubber boots. He'd only come from next door and yet he looked as if he'd swum here.

'Ed? What the hell are you doing here?'

'Nat, I'm sorry, man, but I need your help. I'm trying to get everything moved out of the reach of the water.' He breathed deeply, and shook his head. 'It's too much for me on my own. Could you—?'

'Of course I could, Ed. Just give me five minutes.'

'Thanks, Nat. You're a lifesaver. I'll see you there, eh?'

I closed the door, and turned to Fede. 'Ed needs a hand down in the bar. I'll be as quick as I can.'

'Of course.' She got to her feet. 'I'll come too.'

'Are you sure?'

'Sure I'm sure. It'll be quicker with three of us.' She went through to the bedroom. 'I've got a waterproof jacket here. What have you got?'

'Just my coat.'

'That's no good, it's too long. Anything below your waist is going to be soaked.'

'Guess I'm just wearing a sweater then.'

'Are you mad? Have you seen the weather?'

'Yeah, but what's the alternative?'

'You've got an emergency plastic mac, haven't you?'

'I haven't worn that in years.'

'Can you squeeze into it?'

'Hopefully. I don't think I'm going to cut a *bella figura* though. Okay, where are the boots?'

'Behind the front door.'

I went to take a look. Two standard pairs of Wellington boots, perhaps knee-length at most. The Street of the Assassins rarely flooded that badly and so they were – usually – enough.

Fede came out of the bedroom, zipped up her jacket, tied her hair back and jammed a woolly hat on to her head. She threw the plastic mac to me, which I struggled into as best I could. It smelled of school trips and disappointing visits to the seaside. It would have to do.

I held up the boots. 'Haven't we got anything better?'

She shook her head.

'So, what does this mean?'

'It means, *caro*, that we're going to get very wet feet.' She patted me on the back. 'Come on.'

***

The wind caught us as soon as we stepped outside, snatching spitefully at our clothing, and we splashed our way to the Magical Brazilians as best we could. Federica had been right. Our boots might have been sufficient for normal flood levels, but were hopelessly inadequate for tonight.

Eduardo had the *paratia* dropped into place, but water was already slopping over the brim. A pump was labouring away uselessly, briefly pushing back outside the water that had already entered, prior to flooding in again.

He was bending over by the refrigerator, pulling out the contents and stacking them as best he could on the bar. He turned around as he heard us enter, and smiled, but exhaustion was etched on his face.

'Thanks, guys.'

'Ed, you should have called us earlier.' I looked around. 'Why were you trying to do all this on your own?'

'I gave the other guys the night off so they could get home. And I didn't think it was going to be this bad. But you're here now. That's all that matters.' He gave me a very tired, very soggy hug. 'Thanks again.'

'So, what do we need to do?'

'We need to empty the fridge. That's probably had it, but we can at least save the contents.'

'We've got space in ours if you like?' I said.

'Yeah, because you're exactly the person I'd choose to look after a refrigerator full of alcohol.' He turned to Federica. 'Fede, can you have a look in the back? In the kitchen. Anything that's still dry, just stick on the shelves, on top of the stove, anywhere you can find that's out of reach of the water. Nat, give me a hand with the tables.'

'What do we need to do?'

'I've got some beer crates from the back. We turn them upside down, and stand the tables on them. Then we put the chairs and stools on the tables.'

'No problem.' I looked at the height of the water outside. 'Are you sure that's going to be enough?'

He shook his head. 'No. I'm not sure at all. But I can't think what else to do.' The lights flickered and, for a moment, we were plunged into darkness.

Ed threw his hands up. 'Ah c'mon, God, give us a break. Please?'

There was a distant rumble of thunder and the lights flickered into life again. He raised his eyes heavenwards. 'Thanks,' he said. Then he turned to me. 'Okay Nat, let's get started.'

Eduardo stood behind the bar, with his head resting on his hands. Then he straightened up, looked around, and nodded.

'Okay. Thanks both. I think this is the best we can do.'

He was probably right. By now we were more than knee-deep in water but everything perishable had been put out of harm's way, and the furniture had been stacked up as best as it could be.

He rubbed his face and ran his hands through his hair. Then he shivered, and pulled his coat around him.

'Ed, you look tired. Dog tired.'

'I feel it.' He looked the two of us up and down. Or as best as he could, given that eighteen inches of us were under water. 'You're soaked.'

Fede chuckled. 'You noticed that?'

'I'm sorry. I'll pay for everything to be cleaned.'

She shook her head. 'No you won't. We're glad to help.'

'Thanks.' He yawned and stretched. 'Well, I think we're done. I'll lock up and then head off home.'

'Are you nuts?' I said. 'I don't even know if any boats are running.'

'Oh, I'll find something. If not, I can always walk.'

'No you can't. Seriously. It's dangerous out there. You can stay with us.'

He was about to protest but then tiredness overtook him and he yawned once more. 'Are you sure?'

'Of course we're sure.'

'He's right, Ed,' said Fede. 'You can't possibly walk in this.'

'Well thanks. Really.' Then he grinned, and grabbed a couple of bottles from on top of the bar. 'Maybe we'll be needing these after all then? Come, let's lock up and go.'

A thought struck me. 'I've never even asked you, Ed. Where do you live?'

'Up in Cannaregio. What, did you think I slept here or something?'

'Well, yes.'

He rolled his eyes, but grinned again. He switched off the useless pump, and stepped over the *paratia* into the street. We followed him outside, and I winced as the icy, filthy water washed even further up my legs. Ed pulled the door shut, struggling against the weight of the water pressure. 'Don't know why I'm bothering to lock up. Nobody's going to be mad enough to try looting the place on a night like this.'

I patted him on the back. 'Come on then. I've got some dry clothes you can borrow. We'll make you up a bed on the sofa. And maybe, for once, I can make you a Negroni?'

He grinned. 'That sounds good right now. Oh man, that sounds good.' Then he stiffened and gripped my arm. 'Christ, did you hear that?'

'What?'

'Breaking glass. Just around the corner.'

Federica shook her head. I could hear nothing over the howling of the wind. 'Are you sure?'

'Nat, I run a bar. I know what breaking glass sounds like.' He jabbed a finger in the direction of Calle de la Mandola. 'It's over there. I'm sure of it.'

I glanced at Fede, who looked as tired as I felt. I think we'd both have been prepared to let it go, but Ed seemed to shake off his tiredness and was away, striding out down the Street of the Assassins as best he could.

We followed in his wake and I cursed under my breath as the waves he was stirring up flooded my boots yet again. The wind caught me as I rounded the corner, and I stumbled for a moment before Federica steadied me. The gale was stronger here, blowing in off Campo Sant'Angelo, and the water – instead of lying dark and stagnant – was roaring like a river in flood. Something I'd never, ever seen before.

Ed was almost up to his waist now. I turned to look at Fede. 'You'll have to go back,' I said.

'Oh, I don't think I do.'

'Look at it. It'll be above your waist. It's too dangerous.'

'And you and Ed will be fine, I suppose?'

'I don't know. But we start from the advantage of not being quite as underwater as you are. Please.'

She looked again at the water sweeping along the *calle*. 'All right. But I'm not leaving. I'll wait here.'

'Okay. Thanks.'

I splashed my way after Ed as best I could, the depth and flow of the water making it difficult to keep my balance. He'd stopped outside a shop halfway up the *calle*.

'Have you got a light, Nat?'

'Only this.' I lit up the torch on my mobile and shone it through the window. 'Christ, I don't believe it.'

The window had exploded inwards, shattered by the pressure of the water.

'I've never seen this happen before,' shouted Ed over the roaring wind. 'I didn't even know it *could* happen.'

I gripped on to his arm to steady myself, as I shone the torch inside. 'Whose place is this, Ed?'

'Fulvio Terzi's. The old bookshop.'

I shook my head. It was one of those places on Calle de la Mandola that I'd walked past hundreds, perhaps thousands, of times without so much as glancing inside.

'His stock's going to be trashed, Nat. Unless we do something.'

'It's hopeless, Ed. There's nothing we can do. Not on our own.'

'He's got valuable stuff here. Antique books, irreplaceable things. We've got to try.'

'You're crazy. How are we even going to get in there?'

Ed took a step backwards, and I reached out to steady him. He looked left and right, up and down, sizing up the window.

'Ed, you'll cut yourself to pieces trying to get through there.'

He reached towards the window and then thought better of it. 'You're right.'

'Leave it. There's nothing we can do.'

He nodded, and then started, gripping my arm again. 'Nat, over there. Just shine your torch.'

I swung my phone from left to right and then back again, the feeble beam of light doing little to illuminate the blackness of the interior.

'There. In the right-hand corner. Just there.'

The beam picked out a dark shape, floating in the water.

'There's someone in there!'

'Are you sure?'

'That's a person, I'm sure of it. How the hell do we get in?'

'If there's someone in there then maybe the door isn't locked.' I checked the handle, noticing that the *paratia* had not been dropped into place. 'It's open.'

I pushed at the door, struggling against the water pressure until Ed added his weight to mine and we forced it open.

The interior looked as if a bomb had hit it. No, the opposite. Everything had exploded inwards, not outwards. Shards of shattered glass and loose-leaf papers swirled in a grotesque kaleidoscope in the knee-deep water.

'Nat, give me a hand here. I've got his shoulders, you take his feet.'

'Should we move him?'

'If we don't, he'll drown. We'll have to risk it.' He nodded towards a desk in the corner of the room, the only thing that wasn't yet underwater.

'Okay, easy now. Let's just take it slowly.'

Between us we half dragged, half floated the body over to the corner, and hauled it, as gently as we could, on to the table. Ed turned the head to one side, and brushed the hair away from the face.

'It's a woman.'

I shone the light closer. Her age was difficult to guess in the dim light from my phone. Thirty-something? There were, I thought, traces of blood on her face and hair. Hardly surprising given the amount of broken glass.

'She's not breathing, Ed.'

'Christ.' He ran a hand through his hair and took a deep breath. 'Do you know what to do?'

I shook my head in despair. 'Kind of. I did a course, years ago. I can try.' I turned her head to the side, allowing water to trickle from her mouth and nose. Then I straightened it again, interlaced my fingers, and started to pump away at her chest.

I opened her mouth and pressed my lips to hers. They were cold and the stink of the foul water on her made me want to gag. I breathed into her lungs, then paused, and then pumped away at her chest again, all the time praying that I was doing more good than harm.

I kept it up for about ten minutes and then slumped, exhausted, over her body. We stood there for a moment, listening to the wind howling through the streets outside.

I raised my head. 'It's no good Ed. She's dead.'

Chapter 2

CPSM 23:35 La marea ha raggiunto i 187 cm alle 22:50. Nei prossimi giorni la marea si manterrà su valori eccezionale. Aggiornamenti su Telegram e Internet.

CPSM 23:35 The tide reached 187 cm at 22:50. In the coming days the tide will remain at exceptional levels. Updates on Telegram and Internet.

– Message from the *Centro Previsioni e Segnalazioni Marea*, Venice, on the night of 12 November 2019.

Eduardo and I stayed with the body for nearly three hours, waiting for help to arrive. It didn't seem right to just leave her there. Eventually, two exhausted paramedics arrived, and took her away on a stretcher to the water ambulance that was waiting by the nearby Ponte de la Cortesia. It had been a brutal, punishing night for them and for all the emergency services. Calls had been coming in constantly from desperate, frightened people in all parts of the city, some areas of which were almost unreachable and many of which were without power. The Giudecca Canal was judged to be almost unnavigable, likewise the area around the Bacino of San Marco and most of the northern lagoon.

Fede had wanted to stay with us, but I'd managed to persuade her that there was nothing to be done except wait. One of us, at least, deserved a proper night's sleep. Ed looked as tired as I'd ever seen him and I was aware that I probably didn't look much better. He splashed his way into the middle of the shop and turned around, looking at the books and prints that were displayed on the higher shelves and at the ones spiralling in the filthy water.

'This is a disaster, Nat. Not just for this poor guy. For the city. I don't know how we're going to come back from this.' He went back to the desk and started opening drawers.

'What are you up to?'

'Trying to find a key. At least if we could do that we could lock the place up. Make it secure.'

'Ed. There's no window left. There's nothing to be done.'

'I know. Doesn't seem right though.'

'It isn't. But we've done what we can.' I patted him on the shoulder. 'Come on. Let's go home.'

Bed was warm, toasty and cosy and I had no intention of leaving it ever, but Federica was slowly and insistently prodding my shoulder.

'Am I snoring again?' I mumbled, my voice thick with sleep.

'No. But I think you ought to get up.'

'What time is it?'

'About six-thirty.'

'Half past six?' I pulled a pillow over my head. 'Give me a call in a couple of hours.'

I'd almost drifted off again when she gently, but firmly,

pulled the pillow away. 'I'm sorry, *caro*, but I think you need to get up.'

'I didn't get to bed until – when was it – the back of two? And I don't have a surgery today.'

'I don't think that's going to matter. It's going to be a busy day. For both of us, I think.' She stroked my hair, and kissed my shoulder. 'Come on. Up you get. I'll make you a coffee.'

Ed sat on the sofa, wearing an old Hawkwind T-shirt of mine that hung rather more loosely on him than it did on me. He hunched over his cup of coffee, unshaven and bleary-eyed.

'Is this a good time to say "You look like I feel?"' I said.

He looked me up and down. 'Funny, that's just what I was thinking.'

'More coffee?'

He shook his head, then got to his feet and yawned and stretched. 'I'd better go and look at the bar. Make a start on cleaning up.'

'Do you want a hand?'

'Nah, you've done enough already. I'd say stop by later and I'll stand you a drink but,' he sighed, 'I don't know when we'll be open again. I'll see you whenever, eh?'

'Okay, Ed. Mind how you go.'

He stretched again, wincing slightly and made his way downstairs, waving to Federica, who was talking animatedly on the phone.

I made myself another coffee and promised myself it would be the last. I was waiting for the Moka to stop bubbling, when Fede kissed me on the back of the neck and slipped her arms around my waist.

'How's it going?'

'Not good. I've been on the phone to the Querini Stampalia. They asked if I could come in.'

'Why?'

She shook her head. 'No idea. They just need volunteers. To do what, I don't know.'

'Are the boats running? I mean, are they running as normal?'

'No idea.' She yawned and stretched, and then started to pull on her boots and waterproof jacket. 'I'll see you later, okay?'

I heard my own phone starting to ring. A British mobile number, and one, I suspected, that belonged to one of the numerous expats in Venice. Surgery or not, it was, I suspected, going to be a long morning.

I lost count of the phone calls. Desperate people whose lives, up until now, had been comfortable ones, suddenly finding themselves in need of somewhere to stay because their apartment was uninhabitable. Or wondering who to contact to get their electricity back on. Or wondering why their boats had vanished from their moorings overnight. Or who had worried relatives back in the UK trying to get hold of their loved ones.

And, of course, the press were there; with requests for radio interviews, articles for newspapers, even television. Usually, I'd have been flattered. But right now all I really wanted was for the telephone to stop ringing.

Federica had called as well. Or, at least, she'd left a message for me, her voice sounding tired and shaky. Things were bad at the Querini Stampalia, she'd told me. The archive on the ground floor had completely flooded. She wasn't sure quite what she could do to help but neither did she feel like coming home just yet.

I sat behind my desk, with my phone in front of me, and stared at it, daring it to ring. Gramsci hopped up and gave it a swat with his paw, sending it spinning, propellor-like.

'Hello puss.'

He miaowed.

'Haven't seen you for a while. Were you under that sofa all night?'

He miaowed again.

'That's not like you.' A thought struck me. 'You didn't even come out for breakfast, did you?'

He'd missed a meal for the first time since he'd moved in. He must have been genuinely scared. Snowflakes were one thing but storms, being something that couldn't be physically attacked, were another.

'Come on then, eh? I'll make myself another coffee and then I'll get you breakfast.' I reached out to stroke him but he snatched at my hand. He was, evidently, feeling better. 'Or, and here's another idea, I'll get your breakfast and then I'll make my coffee?'

I flicked through the pages of notes on my desk. An unfortunate number of the expat community had next to no Italian and so I'd promised them that I'd make some phone calls on their behalf to try and get their power back on, or at least find them a hotel room. It wasn't going to be easy and was likely to take me the rest of the morning. But it would all seem that little bit more manageable after yet more caffeine.

I yawned and got to my feet. 'Come on then, Gramsci.'

Inevitably, the phone chose that moment in which to ring. I looked at the screen, thinking I'd call them back, and cursed. A Rome number. One that I recognised. A call that couldn't be put off.

'Mr Ambassador, *buongiorno*.'

'Naaathan, good morning.' William Maxwell, a man who would never use one syllable if two were available, stretched out my name to its maximum possible length. 'How are you?'

He sounded friendly. Did that mean it was an 'Excellency' day or merely a 'Mr Ambassador' day? Would there ever be a 'William' day?

'I'm not so good,' I paused, 'Ambassador Maxwell.'

'I'm sorry to hear that, Naaathan. Things sound a bit grim up there. What's the situation on the street?'

'No idea,' I said, without thinking.

'I'm sorry? You what?'

I held the phone away from me and gently banged my head on the table, under the eyes of a watchful Gramsci.

'In all honesty, Ambassador, I haven't been outside the apartment this morning. I've been on the phone constantly, fielding queries from what seems like every British resident in the city.'

'Oh. Well, yes, I can imagine that. I'm told the phones have been ringing quite a bit in the office here.'

'I imagine they have.'

'I don't understand though. Aren't the telephones out?'

'No. Just the electricity, in some areas. But most of the Brits here are only resident for a few months of the year. Which means most of them don't have landlines. Which means, if there's no electricity, you find yourself watching the charge on your phone go down and wondering if it's more important to call an electrician, a hotel or your kids back in the UK.'

'I see. Well, I'm sorry, Nathan, but we've been telling everyone to contact you for the most up-to-date information. Is there anything we can help you with? Share the burden a bit, you know?'

'I don't think so, Ambassador.'

'Anything at all,' he paused, 'press, that sort of thing?'

I leafed through my notes again. 'Depends. Do you feel like a video-link interview with Sky News?'

'Oh. Well, I hadn't really thought. I suppose I could. If it would help at all.'

I smiled to myself. 'Oh, I think it would, Excellency. BBC "World at One" okay?'

'Yes, of course.'

'"This Morning with Richard and Judy"?'

'Good heavens. Really?'

'No, I made that one up.' I yawned. 'Sorry.'

Maxwell wasn't a man entirely without a sense of humour, and he chuckled, gently. 'You sound tired, Nathan. Try and grab a bit of shut-eye when you can. In the meantime, send the media queries to the press office here. We'll take those off your hands.'

'That's most kind of you, Ambassador.'

'Not at all, Nathan. We're all in this together, after all. Keep in touch.'

He hung up, and I placed my phone back down on the desk, spinning it around as Gramsci would have done. I smiled for a moment. Maxwell wasn't such a bad sort, really, but I could imagine him visibly preening at the prospect of being able to drawl his dark-brown tones all over the airwaves.

Then I shook my head. There really wasn't much to feel good about. God knows what kind of state the city was in, but it had been enough to almost reduce Federica to tears. And a young woman had been found floating face down in a pool of filthy water only metres from where I lived.

I yawned and got to my feet. 'Come on, Gramsci. Let's get you fed, eh?'

Chapter 3

'Fede? Where are you? Is everything all right?'

Her voice was ragged. 'I don't know.' Then she paused. 'No. I'm not all right. Nothing's all right. I'll be home in a couple of hours. Maybe more.'

'Okay. Do you need to take a break? Should we meet somewhere for a late lunch?'

She paused for a moment. 'Are you serious? Have you been outside? There's nowhere to go, Nathan. Nowhere.'

'I'm sorry. I've been indoors all morning. The phone keeps ringing.'

'I'm sorry too. I know you must have been busy. I'll be back late afternoon. But you should go outside and take a look at the city.'

'I will do. I could do with getting some air, to be honest. But don't you want me to wait for you? I'll make you something to eat, and then we could go out together.'

'No.' Her voice broke yet again. 'I don't think I can bear to see much more of it. Not right now.'

I decided I'd walk down to the Rialto. It would be too late to pick up some fish for dinner, even if the market was open, but it would give me some idea of the state of the city.

Ed tapped on the window of the Brazilians as I passed by. I turned to give him a wave, but he beckoned me to come in.

'How's it going?'

He shook his head. 'Nat, I'm dog tired. All I want to do is go home and sleep. And yet,' he spread his arms wide, 'all this. It's all got to be cleared up.'

'Do you have to do it now?'

'If we want to open later.'

'Ed, I don't know what you've heard but I don't think any-one's going to be along later. Not today, not tomorrow, maybe not the day after.'

He laughed, hollowly. 'Probably just as well.' He clicked the light switch on and off. 'No power. Christ knows when that'll be on again. So I've got food rotting away in the kitchen. And then there's that.' He nodded his head towards the large refrigerator lying face down on the floor. 'It must have floated and then toppled over. Come on, can you give me a hand with it?'

'Sure.' The two of us gave it a heave, and hauled it upright, water pouring from its insides and sloshing across the floor.

Ed gave me a nod. 'Just drag it into the corner. That'll do for now.'

'Okay.'

We stood there in the cold and the damp, staring at a fridge that was never going to work again.

'I'm so sorry, Ed.'

He nodded, and patted me on the back. 'We'll be all right. Give us a couple of days and you won't even notice. It's just,' he sighed and looked so very, very tired, 'it's hard work you know?'

'I understand.'

'Where are you off to?'

'I thought I might head up to the Rialto. See if anywhere's open. Maybe pick up something for dinner.'

He laughed but, again, there was no mirth in it. 'Good luck with that.'

'Are you going to be much longer here, Ed? You look like you need to sleep.'

'I think that's about as much as I can bear to do for now. I'll lock up, go home. Maybe sleep for a week.' He turned the sign on the door around so that it read *Chiuso*. He locked up, patted me on the shoulder again, and we headed off; me in the direction of Rialto, and Ed towards Cannaregio.

I'd always disliked the way *acqua alta* was covered in the foreign press. There seemed to be no understanding, for example, that Piazza San Marco was the lowest point in the city and, therefore, would flood even with the most modest of tides. Pictures of bare-chested tourists pretending to swim in the Piazza made for a striking image, but did nothing to reflect the reality of the situation for most residents.

The actuality, of course, was that Venice had got used to living with *acqua alta*. It was just something that happened. You checked the news for predicted levels of flooding, you installed the meteorological app on your smartphone, and, above all, you listened out for the sirens. A mournful wailing drone, followed by a variable number of plinging sounds. A single pling might mean nothing more than 'avoid the Piazza'. Four plings strongly suggested that you should stay at home.

Similarly, you dropped your *paratia* into place and hoped, in the event of being unfortunate enough to live on the ground floor, that would be enough to protect your property. You put your furniture and electrical equipment on top of bricks. You instinctively knew the best routes around town. You knew which streets would stay dry, whilst ones only metres away would flood. You knew where the system of *passerelle* would conduct you above the waters. In the morning, you washed your shop out with fresh water to carry the stink away and life went back to normal, until the next time. High water was something that Venice had become used to living with.

The waters had yet to recede fully, and the wind was still blowing a gale along the street. I turned into Calle de la Mandola, bracing myself for what I was about to see. And immediately I realised that this was something different.

Water was still flowing along the streets, almost up to my knees. Some windows – like Terzi's – had cracked or caved in with the pressure of the water. Rubbish was being swept along by the current, and desperate-looking shopkeepers were running pumps at full stretch in a useless attempt to empty their properties of the filth that had been swept in overnight.

I walked on through Campo Manin and into Campo San Luca, where the same scenes were repeated. Everywhere, pumps running, properties being swept out as best they could, rubbish being piled up in the *campi* for *Veritas* to collect. Fridges and other electrical goods, now useless, had been dragged outside for collection at some unknown point in the future.

I turned down one of the narrow *calli* that led to the Rialto Bridge. The water was still deep here – Rialto being another of those areas that flooded easily – and I took my time wading through it, taking care not to set up any waves with which to splash those passers-by coming in the opposite direction. Then I turned on to the street facing the Grand Canal and stopped dead in my tracks.

Three gondolas had been washed on to the *fondamenta*. There were few pedestrians around, and they seemed to be outnumbered by press and camera crews. The Grand Canal itself was almost devoid of traffic, although an occasional police or ambulance boat would speed past, sending up great waves that splashed on to the already flooded *fondamenta* and setting the gondolas rocking. The canal itself was thick with the flotsam and jetsam that had been washed in as the waters receded. Every shop was occupied, as the exhausted proprietors did their best to clean up, yet nothing was open.

There seemed little point in attempting to go any further.

This wasn't just flooding. Neither was it something the city could just live with. I turned and splashed my way back to the Street of the Assassins, wondering how, if ever, the city was going to recover from this.

Chapter 4

I don't know.

I'm sorry.

Those two phrases pretty much defined the latter part of the afternoon.

I don't know.

I'm sorry.

Yes, I can put you in contact with a plumber. Or an electrician. But no, I don't know when they'll be able to come round.

Yes, I can give you a list of numbers for hotels and bed and breakfasts. But no, I don't know if they'll have room.

No, I don't know of any working bancomats in the city.

No, I don't know if any supermarkets are open.

I don't know.

I'm sorry.

I switched off my phone and put my head in my hands. Just to give myself five minutes' rest. My most recent conversation had been with a woman who lived in a ground-floor flat on Giudecca. What had previously been a very desirable property was now going to need a complete redecoration. When, of course, somebody could be found to do it.

But was it worth it, given the likelihood of having to do the same thing again – when? In a year's time? In a month? In a couple of days? Oh, and the chances of insurance covering flood damage to a ground-floor property in Venice? Round about none.

I don't know and *I'm sorry*. She'd been crying by the time she'd hung up, and I felt like joining her.

I reached out to – carefully – scratch Gramsci on the top of his head. 'Ah, you're a lucky cat, aren't you? Heat, light, comfy sofas, perhaps more than the regulation amount of food. And, of course, you live on the second floor. Yes, I think you're a very fortunate cat indeed.' He nipped at my finger, perhaps to show that he wasn't one hundred per cent convinced.

I heard keys rattling in the lock, and the door opening. Federica. She hung her coat up and gave me a weak smile, but her eyes were red.

'Fede?'

'Hi.'

'Do you need a drink?'

She shook her head. 'Maybe just a cup of tea. I'm not sure anything stronger would be a good idea.'

'Is it bad?'

'As bad as I could imagine. Worse, probably. The archive has flooded. There are hundreds of books waterlogged. Maybe thousands. The entire ground floor is still under water. No electricity. The lifts are out. They're already talking about half a million euros' worth of damage.'

'God.'

'And that's one *palazzo*, Nathan. Just one *palazzo* in the whole of the city. How much is this going to cost? How much of it can be put right? How much of it has been lost for ever?'

She slumped down next to me, put her head on my shoulder and, for perhaps the first time since I'd known her, cried ever so gently.

We sat there in silence, listening to the sound of the ever-present wind outside. Then I became aware of the rain starting to patter against the windows.

Fede raised her head. 'That's all we need.'

I sighed. 'Come on then. I'll make you a cup of tea.'

'That'd be nice.'

'I'm not sure what to do about dinner. I'll have to see what's in the fridge.'

'Whatever we've got in will be fine. How's Ed?'

'He's gone home. I think he realised there was no chance of any customers tonight. And besides, he needs to properly rest. The bar's going to need some serious work.'

She shook her head. 'Poor guy. And there's thousands of people like him tonight, throughout the city. What are they all going to do? Some of them won't have heating. Some of them won't have lighting. Just sitting there in the cold and the dark. Waiting for help that's going to be a long time coming.' I was about to speak, but the entryphone buzzed. Fede looked at me. 'Maybe it's Ed, after all?'

'Maybe so. Or maybe a hapless Brit in need of help. Oh well.' I got to my feet and went over to the door.

'*Chi è?*'

'Nathan. It's Vanni from the *Questura*. Can I come in?'

'Sure.' I buzzed him up.

He looked cold, wet and very, very tired, but he smiled at me and then at Federica.

'*Dottoressa*.'

'Hello, Vanni. And you haven't got to call me *dottoressa* every time.'

'My apologies.'

'No need to. It's very sweet. I might even ask Nathan to start using it.'

He beamed at her and then patted me on the shoulder. 'Ah, what a lucky man you are, Nathan.'

'Oh, I know. You look tired, Vanni. What brings you out here on a night like this? Can I get you a coffee or something stronger?'

He shook his head. 'I'm sorry, Nathan, but this is official. I need your help.'

'Of course. What's the problem?'

'The woman you found last night. In the Calle de la Mandola.'

'Yes?'

'She's a British citizen, Nathan.' He sighed. 'But more than that. We're treating this as a suspicious death.'

'You're kidding!' Vanni shook his head. 'I don't understand. Eduardo and I found her floating in the water. We thought she'd drowned.'

'So did we, when you called. And when we brought her in.'

'There was no sign of violence, though.'

He raised his eyebrows. 'Are you sure? Quite sure?'

'There was some blood on her hair. That's all I saw. I assumed that was from the window bursting inwards.'

He shook his head again. 'That's what the ambulance crew thought when they brought her in. But no. Can't blame them, they'd been out all night. They must have been on their knees by the time they got your call. But she had a fractured skull.'

'Couldn't she just have fallen? The window bursts in, the shock sends her falling back. Something like that?'

'Pathologist says no. The force of the explosion would have been nowhere near strong enough for that. And there were small fragments of glass in her hair.'

'From the window?'

'No. Fragments of coloured glass. What we're talking about is a blow to the back of the head with a heavy glass object. Now we found a broken glass paperweight on the floor, so we're assuming that was the weapon. There's also a strongbox set into the rear wall that somebody had attempted to force open. We don't know if she surprised a burglar, or if she was already there when they entered.'

'God. That poor woman.'

'So, I'm afraid, Nathan, I'd really like you to come out with me. It seems there's another party to inform.'

'Okay. Tell me more.'

'She had an Italian ID card. So she was resident here, long-term. Dr Jennifer Whiteread. Profession listed as *Professoressa*.' He shrugged. 'I know that doesn't narrow it down very much.'

He was right. *Professoressa* was a title vague enough to mean whatever you wanted it to mean, from having a Chair at Ca'Foscari to giving English lessons to bored, recalcitrant teenagers.

'Her address is in Castello. The Calle del Cimitero. There's another *straniero* resident at the same address. Another one of yours. Mr Matthew Blake.'

'Husband? Boyfriend?'

'Who knows?' He paused. 'I guess that's what we're going to find out. I'm sorry, Nathan, I wouldn't normally ask on a night like this but it needs to be done as soon as possible.'

Informing next of kin was my job. And, given the circumstances, it was now Vanni's as well. The wind rattled the windows again, and the rain was stronger now. Inside was cosy, and warm, and the prospect of spending the early evening cooking over a warm stove was a pleasant one. But someone in Venice had lost a loved one and didn't even know it yet. Perhaps they'd spent all day dialling her number, leaving increasingly frantic messages. Calling friends and work colleagues in the hope that they'd seen her. There wasn't, really, any choice to be made.

'Of course I'll do it, Vanni.'

'Thank you, Nathan. I mean it.'

I pulled on my coat and turned to Federica. 'Sorry, *cara,* I need to do this.'

She hugged me. 'I know you do. Just be careful, okay?'

'I will. I'll cook when I get home, promise.'

'No you won't. Just give me a call when you're on the way.'

'But the *pizzeria* won't be open.'

'No, I mean I'll cook.'

'But you never cook.'

She smiled. 'There's one thing I can do. *Fagioli alla Bud Spencer*'.

'What?'

'I used to cook it for *nonno*. You remember I told you how

much he loved Bud Spencer? So it was the one thing I learned to cook properly.'

'Well, I'm honoured. And thanks.'

Vanni raised his eyebrows. '*Fagioli alla Bud Spencer*, eh?'

Fede smiled. 'I can cook for three as easily as two, Vanni.'

'Hmm.' He stroked his moustache. 'It's a pleasant thought. But Barbara will be cross if I'm home later than I need to be. Besides, Mr Blake's apartment is in my direction.'

'Next time.'

'Most certainly.'

I gave her a hug and a kiss. 'Okay, see you later. I'll call you as soon as I can.' And Vanni and I stepped out into the wind and rain.

Chapter 5

'Where's the boat, Vanni?' We'd almost reached Campo San Luca by the time the question occurred to me.

'The boat?'

'I assumed you'd have a police launch?'

'Oh, I see. Sorry, Nathan, they're a bit thin on the ground at the moment. And besides, if we were to use a boat, we'd need a pilot. And that didn't seem fair given the sort of day they've all had.'

'Oh. Right.' Another thought struck me. 'Vanni, I've been on the phone all day with anxious Brits. Nobody's called me to report a missing person.'

'Perhaps they went straight to Rome or Milan?'

'No. I spoke to the ambassador earlier. Somebody would have called me.'

'Maybe Mr Blake just doesn't know that Venice has its very own Honorary Consul?'

'He hasn't called the *Questura* though?'

'Who knows? It's been a hell of a busy day. Phones have been ringing non-stop. He might just have been in a queue. Or perhaps he tried the *carabinieri*? Who knows?'

The streets were dark, shadowy and devoid of people except

for a small group of tourists miserably splashing through the water in cheap emergency waterproofs. They stopped me to ask if we knew of any restaurants that would be open. I gave them directions to a place I knew near the Rialto Bridge that had an upstairs dining room. I wasn't at all convinced it would be open, but it was at least a possibility.

We walked down past Rialto and through Campo San Bartolomeo, where Carlo Goldoni – or at least his statue – strode forth above the waters, utterly unperturbed by the rain pouring from his tricorn hat. Then on through the network of narrow *calli* that led deeper into Castello, and away from the tourist areas. Into Campo San Francesco della Vigna, over-shadowed by the *campanile* of the eponymous church, and the frames of the great, disused gasometers that overlooked it.

I stopped to look at a sign fixed to the door of the church, where a handwritten notice announced that tomorrow's early morning Mass had been cancelled. There were, I knew, irre-placeable works of art inside and I wondered what condition they might be in now.

Blake's apartment was in the Calle del Cimitero, which led away from the church and towards Celestia. The name 'Whiteread' on a shiny horseshoe doorbell plate stood out among the Venetian names of Masiero, Zorzi and Scarpa.

I pressed the bell. No one answered and I gave it thirty sec-onds until I tried again. Still no answer. I stepped back into the street, and shielded my eyes as I gazed upwards through the rain. The lights on the top floor were still on. That didn't necessarily prove anyone was home but – I looked around from left to right – neither did it seem very likely that anyone would be out tonight unless they really had to be. Vanni gave me a glance, and I shrugged. Having come this far, we'd try once more. I leaned on the buzzer for thirty seconds, took my thumb away, counted to ten and leaned on it for thirty more.

The speakerphone crackled and a voice thick with sleep spoke. 'Hello? Yes?'

'Mr Blake? I'm Nathan Sutherland. I'm the British Honorary Consul in Venice.'

'Oh thank God, thank God.' The sleepiness vanished, to be replaced with a note of desperation. 'Come up, please. Top floor.'

The intercom buzzed and the door clicked open. We stepped over the *paratia* into the hall. The level of water inside appeared to be the same level as outside, and the place stank of stagnant water and an unhealthy damp that I could feel sinking into my bones.

The lights in the stairwell came on. Looking up, I could see the shadowy figure of a man craning over the bannister to look down at us. 'Top floor,' he repeated.

I'd thought I'd been in better shape since I'd quit smoking, but I was panting by the time I reached his apartment, and struggled not to gasp as I was speaking. In normal times, I imagined, this would have been funny.

'Mr Blake? Mr Matthew Blake?'

He nodded.

'I'm Nathan Sutherland.'

'So you said.'

He stretched out his hand for me to shake, giving me a few more precious seconds to get my breath back.

'You've found her then? Where is she? Is she all right?'

I looked at his face and read in his expression the desperate need to convince himself. Hoping against hope that I was going to say she was recovering in hospital and would be home in a few days.

Blake looked at Vanni, as if realising that there were two of us for the first time, and clutched the doorframe for support as he realised what that meant.

'Mr Blake. This is Commissario Girotto. Could we come in perhaps? I think you might need to sit down.'

We let him cry, curled up in his chair and resting his head on a pink sweater that hung over the back. Occasionally, he closed his eyes and pulled it to his face, breathing deeply.

We sat there in silence, his body shaking from time to time, as I looked around the room. It was a small apartment, with the sort of *terrazzo* floor tiles that looked factory-produced as opposed to being the product of an artisan workshop. Furniture, similarly, was modern rather than *signorile*. A small portable television stood on a coffee table in the corner of the room. A variety of non-matching bookshelves lined one wall.

I decided first names might be good. 'Matthew, I don't know if this will help at all, but can I get you something to drink?'

He nodded. 'There's a bottle of whisky in the cupboard next to the fridge. Have one yourselves.' I went through to the kitchen. J&B. Budget whisky but, to me at least, ever so slightly cool given its guaranteed appearance in every 1970s Italian thriller. I searched around for a glass and found three on the draining rack. I poured us out generous but not, I thought, excessive measures, took them through and sat them down on the table between us, next to a framed photograph of Blake and a young woman.

'May I?' I said.

He nodded. I picked it up. The two of them, in thick padded jackets, were hugging each other and smiling at the camera. They stood against a background of a bright blue sky, and a range of white-capped mountains.

'That was us, last year. In the Gran Sasso. A walking holiday. Anything to get Jen out of a church or a museum.'

'She's pretty,' I said. In all honesty, I couldn't really make her out under her woolly hat and dark glasses, but I thought that was probably what he needed to hear.

He nodded again. 'Yeah.' He took a deep breath and looked over to Vanni. 'So, I guess you want to ask me some questions?'

'Nothing too much tonight, Mr Blake. We just need a few things for our records. If you could tell us what time Dr Whiteread went missing. Or, at least, if you remember what time you started to become concerned.'

Blake shook his head. 'I don't remember exactly. It was about nine o'clock, perhaps. She said she just needed to go out for five minutes, maybe ten. Said she wanted to take some photos. And I suppose that makes sense in a way. Once-in-a-lifetime opportunity, that sort of thing. And I said,' he screwed his eyes shut and drew in a shuddering grasp of air, 'oh Christ, I said it was a great idea, and maybe even the papers would be interested and we'd get a few quid. And then she didn't come back. And I thought, well, she's been gone for an hour. So I called her. Again and again.'

I imagined him sitting there, listening to the wind and

the rain, with the lights flickering on and off. Dialling and redialling the same number. Sitting alone in a strange country, wondering where the person he loved most in the world could possibly be. Wishing he'd said something else to her. *Don't go out. Not now.*

Vanni nodded. 'I understand,' he said. 'Could you just tell us when you reported her as missing?'

Blake looked confused. 'I didn't. Well, at least I don't think I did. I mean, I wouldn't know how, I don't really speak Italian. I just kept calling Jen, again and again. And then the power kept going off and I wondered what I'd do if I lost power in my phone, if she was trying to get hold of me.'

'I understand,' I said. 'A number of people in the city have been telling me the same thing today.'

Vanni scribbled away in his notepad. 'Okay. There's not much more we need to know for the time being.' He raised his head and smiled encouragingly at Matthew. 'I see her job description in her *Carta d'Identità* just says *Professoressa*. Could you tell us the name and address of her employer?'

'It's something called the Markham Foundation. They're on Giudecca. I don't know the exact address, I'm sorry.'

The name meant nothing to me, but Vanni merely smiled and nodded. 'No problem. We can find out the address easily enough.' He snapped his notebook shut. 'That's all we need for now.' He turned to me. 'Mr Sutherland, is there anything else you need to know?'

I nodded. 'Matthew, unless I'm mistaken, you're not the next of kin?'

He shook his head. 'She has a dad. He lives in South Wales. He, well, he doesn't like me very much.'

'I'm sorry.'

'I'm not quite sure why. I think he thinks I'm a bit of a waster.'

I took a closer look at him. He had shoulder-length hair in a centre parting, and wore black square-frame glasses. He looked tired, his eyes were, of course, red with crying, and he clearly hadn't shaved that morning, yet he was evidently a good-looking guy in a politely bohemian way.

'I'm a writer,' he said, as if reading my thoughts. 'Well, a children's writer to be precise.' Then he chuckled, and looked awkward, as if he'd confessed to something a little embarrassing. 'He thinks that isn't a proper job.'

'A writer?' I said. 'Let me guess, you went into it for the money?'

He laughed again, but then his face dropped immediately as if he'd remembered he had no place being happy.

'Jen and I had a project together. She's really talented, you know?' He winced. 'She – was – really talented, I mean. She was going to illustrate a book of my stories. Well, that's half the work with children's books really, isn't it? So I had this idea for a series of books about a cat who lives on a gondola, and I kept thinking of ways to get her involved with that.'

'Uh-huh.' I took a sip of whisky, and closed my eyes and sighed as I felt its heat spreading through me, warming the chill away.

Vanni took a deep breath. 'Mr Blake, as you said, you're not the next of kin. But you knew Dr Whiteread, I imagine, better than anyone else in the city. And so there is something which you need to do. We'd like you to identify the body.'

'What?' He sat bolt upright, his knees banging into the table and setting our glasses rocking.

'I'm sorry. If there was anyone else, I'd ask them. But there isn't.'

He shook his head, violently. 'I can't. I just can't.'

'I know it's difficult. But we have to ask you this.'

Blake slumped back into his chair, tucking his chin into his chest in order to hide his face, and pulling Jenny's sweater around his shoulders for comfort.

'Matthew,' I continued, 'I'll come with you so you won't have to be alone. And, if you like, I can inform Jenny's father.'

'You'd do that?'

'If you like.'

'Thank you.' He took a deep breath. 'Okay. I'll do it. Is it – how does she look?'

'It won't be horrible,' said Vanni. 'It's not like in the movies. We'll just show you a photograph, that's all.'

Blake looked unsure for a moment, but then nodded. 'Okay. When and where?'

'I'll be in touch with Mr Sutherland tomorrow. He'll then phone you and we can arrange to meet at the *Questura*.'

Blake nodded once more. 'I understand.' He got to his feet. 'Let me give you my number.'

His jacket was hanging on the back of the door, and he went through the pockets. He took out a wallet, flicked through it, and then passed me a business card.

I took it from him. It was an image of a beautiful young woman, dark-haired and bare-shouldered, dressed in pink and gold. 'Well, this is lovely,' I smiled.

'Jen designed them. She said if I was going to be a writer,

it would be good for me to have them. More professional, she said.'

'I don't recognise it, I'm afraid.'

Blake managed a weak smile. 'It's Calliope. The muse of epic poetry. Jen said she was sorry, but there was no muse of cats on gondolas, so it would have to do until I'd actually written the book. It's a copy of a picture in the National Gallery, I think. I know she told me who it was by but,' he scratched his head, 'I can't remember now.'

'My goodness,' said Vanni. 'She really was a very talented young woman.'

'She was. She'd sit there for hours in the gallery, she told me, sketching away. She was just an amazing woman, you know?' His voice trembled.

'Matthew, is there anyone you know who you can call? Who can come over and be with you for a bit?'

He shook his head. 'No. Jenny was the person who knew everyone. I've got friends back in the UK but I don't really know anyone here.'

'I understand. Maybe you should call someone back home. I'm sure that would help.'

He nodded. 'I will.'

'Thanks, Matthew. I'll see you sometime tomorrow, then?'

'Okay. Thank you, Mr Sutherland.' He nodded at Vanni. 'And thank you, Commissario.' He poured himself another glass of whisky and, for a moment, I regretted the fact I'd suggested it. But then again, *se non ora, quando?*

Vanni and I took our leave, and I closed the door behind us. I was halfway down the top flight of stairs when the lights flickered and then cut out completely. I missed my footing in the dark and half slipped, half slid down the steps before Vanni was able to grab my arm and steady me. I was unable to stop myself crying out with the shock, and my heart pounded as I stood there clutching the bannister, waiting for my eyes to adjust to the dark.

'You all right, Nathan?'

I took a deep breath. 'I think so. Close though. If you hadn't been there I'd have fallen.'

I heard the noise of a door opening on the landing below us, and saw a figure framed by the pale, flickering light of a candle.

'I'm sorry,' I called out. 'I didn't mean to disturb you.'

'Jenny?' It was a woman's voice, Italian. 'Jenny, darling.'

Much of her face was hidden in shadow but, from the light of the candle in her left hand, I could see she was an old woman, with her hair drawn tightly back in a bun.

'Jenny, darling. Have you come to see the angels?'

'I'm sorry?'

I heard a noise from behind her. 'It's not her, *signora*. Come inside.'

'The angels, darling. Is that why you're here?'

I saw a figure in shadow behind her. 'It's not her, *signora.*' A woman's voice, tired and exasperated, and perhaps with a hint of an East European accent. 'Come away from the door. Please.' She put her hand on the old woman's shoulder and pulled her back. Then she closed the door, and we were once more in darkness.

I heard a voice from inside, higher-pitched now and distraught. 'I thought she wanted to see the angels.'

'Please, *signora*. No angels tonight. Go to bed now. Please.'

There was a hum of electricity, and the lights flickered into life.

I turned to Vanni.

'Angels?' he whispered.

I shrugged. 'What does that mean?'

He frowned. 'I don't know.' He yawned. 'Ah, it's late now, Nathan. Way too late. We'll talk tomorrow, eh?'

I nodded, and we made our way downstairs as carefully as we could, expecting the lights to go again at any moment. Then we splashed our way through the hallway, and out into the street, steeling ourselves for our respective journeys home.

It was close to midnight by the time I arrived back at the Street of the Assassins, cold and wet through. But Federica was still awake and a great steaming pot of *fagioli alla Bud Spencer* was simmering away in the kitchen. It was little more than sausage meat, borlotti beans and a tin of tomatoes, and Fede would have been the first to admit she wasn't the greatest cook in the world. But at that moment, feeling the cold slowly leaving my body and the damp leaving my bones, it felt like the best meal I'd ever had.

Chapter 6

I slipped my arm under Blake's shoulders, afraid for a moment that he was going to topple from his chair. I held him there, listening to him dragging great, deep breaths of air into his body. Then he nodded, as if to indicate that he was okay, and bent over, placing his hands on his knees for support.

He closed his eyes, and breathed deeply. For a moment I was worried he was going to vomit. Then he shook his head, as if he could read my mind. 'I'm fine.'

'Are you sure it's her, Matthew?'

He nodded. 'I'm sure.'

I turned to Vanni, who nodded at me before scribbling a few lines in his notebook. Then he slid the photograph from his desk, and tucked it away inside an envelope.

Blake straightened up and opened his eyes. I really had tried to be honest with him. It wasn't horrible to look at. But then it wasn't my partner photographed lying cold and grey on a mortician's slab.

'Can we go now, Nathan? Please?'

'Of course we can. We're finished, aren't we, Vanni?' He nodded, but said nothing, tucking his notebook back inside his jacket. 'Come on, Matthew, let's get you out of here, eh?'

***

Blake leaned back against the wall, and lit a cigarette, his hands shaking. I hadn't noticed him smoking before. My surprise must have been evident as he caught my expression and gave me a weak smile.

'Jen didn't like me smoking in the apartment. Come to that, she didn't like me smoking at all. She quit as soon as we arrived here. New start, she said.'

He closed his eyes, and exhaled slowly, the smoke curling up around his face. Vanni took out one of his small cigars and joined in. Great. Now there were two of them.

'Are you okay, Nathan?' asked Vanni.

'Yes. Fine.' I switched to Italian. 'Two years without a cigarette now. You aren't making it easy.'

Vanni laughed a rumbly, smoker's laugh. Then he caught sight of Blake, his head still leaning back against the wall, and immediately stopped. Blake dropped his cigarette to the pavement, and ground it underfoot. He rubbed his red eyes, and looked at us both.

'So. Can I go now, then?'

Vanni nodded. 'You can. Thank you so much, Mr Blake. I know it can't have been easy.'

'There's nothing more you need?' He shuddered. 'I won't have to do this again?'

'Nothing more. There will be some papers to sign. In Italy there always are. But you needn't wait around for that. I was thinking perhaps Mr Sutherland here might take them round to you?'

'That'd be good of you. Did you contact her dad?'

'I did.'

'Thanks for that. How is he?'

'Not good.'

He shook his head. 'Sorry, that was a stupid question. Is he coming over?'

I thought back to that morning's horrible telephone call, a conversation punctuated with choking sobs and tears. 'He was ready to jump on the next flight, but I managed to persuade him not to. Just take a day or two to think it over, I told him. There's no point in coming at the moment. Not with the city like this.'

Vanni nodded. 'Sensible. Well done, Nathan.'

'He shouldn't come at all.' Blake almost spat the words out.

'I don't understand,' I said.

He lit another cigarette, his hands shaking. 'Why?' he said. 'What's the point? His daughter's dead. It's not going to help.'

'I think I understand,' I said. 'He's grieving. He's lost his daughter. What can he do? Nothing. But getting on a plane makes him feel as if he's doing something. It gives him back a little bit of control.'

'But he shouldn't come now. Not just now. Look at the place. It looks like death. It stinks of death.' His voice trembled. He caught the expression on my face. 'Don't worry. I'll be okay. I'm not going to do anything stupid.' He took a deep breath. 'Thank you for all you're doing.'

Vanni extended his hand.

'Mr Blake.'

'Commissario.'

'Thank you for everything. As I said, I know it must be difficult.'

Blake nodded and turned to go, grinding his cigarette underfoot and lighting a third to accompany him on his way. We watched him make his way along the *fondamenta*. Poor guy, I thought. Soon he'd be alone in his flat, accompanied by just a bottle of whisky and a packet of cheap cigarettes.

Vanni patted me on the shoulder. 'Thank you for this, Nathan.' He checked his watch. 'And now I think we have time for a late breakfast and then, perhaps, we can have a little chat.'

Vanni shook his coat out, brushed the rain from his hat and settled himself behind his desk. I hadn't paid much attention to his appearance earlier, being more concerned with Blake, but under the unforgiving lights of his office he looked tired and drawn. There was a Newton's Cradle on his desk. I hadn't seen one of them in years. He caught my eye and smiled. 'It was a birthday present from Barbara.' He set it in motion, the balls rhythmically clacking.

'So,' he said. 'Suspicious death, Nathan. Which means it might be some time until we can release the body for burial. And as she's a British citizen.' He smiled apologetically at me. 'Well, I imagine you'll have people to inform.'

I sighed, and rubbed my forehead. 'Is there no other way? Really?'

'I'm sorry.'

'Then I'll have to telephone her dad again. That's not going to be an easy conversation. And I'll have to tell Blake, he'll need to know as well.'

'Ah yes. Mr Blake.' Vanni set the Newton's Cradle in

motion once more. 'Nathan, your English is better than mine, of course. I miss things in conversation. What's your impression of him?'

'He seems like a nice enough guy. Obviously devastated. Don't you think?'

He shrugged. 'He's convincingly devastated, let's put it that way.'

'Where are you going with this, Vanni?'

'I'd just like to know a little more about him.' He tapped a pencil on the table. 'He says he was at home on the night of the *acqua granda*?'

'Well, you'd have to be nuts to have been outside.'

'You would, indeed, have to be nuts. Nevertheless, Dr Whiteread decided to go out.'

'To take photographs, according to Blake. That's possible.'

'Oh, it is. But then walking halfway across the city in order to visit an antique bookshop? That seems less possible.'

'So what was she doing there?'

Vanni shrugged. 'Perhaps Mr Blake would know. We didn't find much on her. A purse with her ID card. No bank notes or cards. Presumably stolen. There were the usual things in her handbag. And then there was this.'

He turned his monitor to face me. It was a photograph – no, not a photograph, but a drawing – of five delicately beautiful faces, caught in a shaft of golden light against a background of dark, stormy clouds.

'Where was this, Vanni?'

'In a plastic envelope in her bag. Which was on the desk, out of reach of the water.'

'What is it?'

He shrugged. 'Five faces. Five little girls. Is there anything more to it?'

'Maybe so. Can you expand it?'

'Sure.'

He clicked on the image with his mouse, expanding it to twice the original size.

'That's too much. A little less,' I said. He zoomed out a little. 'That's it. Now do you see it? Five faces, yes, but look around their shoulders. Difficult to see at first, but when you know they're there you'll wonder how you ever missed it.'

Vanni peered closer at the screen, and then leaned back, screwing his eyes up. He took his glasses off, and held them in front of him, moving them back and forth as if playing the trombone.

'Ah,' he said, finally.

'What do you see?'

'Wings.'

'So they're not just little girls but—'

'Angels.'

'Angels. *Cherubim. Seraphim. Putti.* I'm not really up to speed with the nomenclature of angels, but I'm sure Fede could tell us exactly what they are.'

Vanni slipped his spectacles back on to his nose, and drummed his fingers on the desk. 'Angels. Like last night. The old woman in the apartment.'

'*Have you come to see the angels?*' I said.

He nodded. 'There's something else. This isn't just a drawing or a print, Nathan.' He clicked the mouse, and the image changed. 'It's a greetings card of some kind. A home-made one. That picture has been stuck on the front. With this message on the inside.'

I leaned over to take a closer look. *'Angels for an angel. With all my love, Jenny xx'*

'Now then,' said Vanni. 'I wonder who this angel might be?'

'Matthew Blake?'

'Could be. Or—' He paused.

'Or?'

'Well, I'm wondering what she was doing in Fulvio Terzi's bookshop late at night?'

'Oh. You mean—?'

'Sex or money, Nathan. It's always one of those.'

'And where is the good *signor* Terzi to be found right now?'

'We've spoken to him. Dr Whiteread had a key to his bookshop. She used to go there for research occasionally. And sometimes she'd just help run the shop for him in her spare time.'

'Right. How did they know each other?'

'He also does consultancy work for the Markham Foundation. Where Dr Whiteread worked. Do you know Giles Markham, Nathan?'

'I've heard of him,' I said. 'Might even have met him once or twice. Part of the expat Brit set. Does some fundraising for the city, as I remember. Posh bloke, isn't he?'

Vanni sighed. 'Yes, Nathan. Mr Giles Markham, Businessman and Philanthropist is, indeed, what you might call a "posh bloke".'

'Right. So what's the Markham Foundation?'

'Some sort of charitable fund. Apparently he's raised

hundreds of thousands for restoration projects throughout the city over the past five years.'

'"The Markham Foundation". Blimey, there's a bit of an ego thing going on there, eh? So what do you want me to do, Vanni?'

'Well, as I said, I'd appreciate it if you could let the appropriate people know that there'll be a delay before we can release the body. But could you also speak to Mr Markham? Seeing that he was her employer. We'll be speaking to him ourselves in good time, of course, but it might be nice if you saw him. Given he's one of yours as well.' I nodded. 'Oh. And there might be one more thing . . .' He set the Newton's Cradle in motion again.

'What's that?'

'That image. The angels. Do you know what it is?'

I shook my head. 'I keep thinking I ought to, but no.'

'A pity. Could you ask your wonderful wife?'

'I can try. Doesn't anybody here know?'

'We're just the humble police, Nathan. Not the *Guardia*, not the *carabinieri*. We don't have specialist art experts. Well, there's the young Boscolo lad. He went to art school. But that's not quite the same.'

'Okay. I'll do my best. Or, rather, I'll ask Fede to do her best. Email me a copy, eh?'

Vanni grinned. 'Always knew I could depend on you, Nathan. Just find out what you can. What is it and why did she have it?'

I nodded. 'As I said, I'll do my best.' I yawned and stretched. 'Blimey, somehow it seems I've got quite a lot of work on. How about you?'

Vanni stopped smiling. 'That's a joke, right, Nathan?'

'Sorry, I wasn't thinking. Still helping clear up?'

'That's right, you weren't thinking. And it's going to be weeks, months, Christ knows how long until we even begin to clear the worst of this.' He rubbed his eyes. 'I'm sorry. Didn't mean to snap. I'm just tired, that's all.'

'No worries, Vanni. My fault.' I got to my feet. 'I'll see what Fede has to say about this. I'll be in touch, okay?'

Chapter 7

Giles Markham was, evidently, a very busy man. Too busy to answer his phone, at any rate. And, despite giving every appearance of being very rich, it seemed he didn't stretch to employing a secretary.

Phone calls from distressed Brits had, thankfully, slowed down. Or did that just mean that nobody had any charge left on their phones? Fede had left me a message telling me that she wouldn't be home for lunch. Ed showed no sign of opening up the Brazilians.

I needed something to do.

I had a thesis on *The Decameron* to translate but there was plenty of time for that and, moreover, plague-ridden Tuscany was not where my head wanted to be at that moment.

I looked at the front page of *Il Gazzettino* with its headline of *L'apocalisse della città sommersa!* For once, I thought, they were not exaggerating. I flicked through the first few pages. Everywhere, images of damage, of devastation that nobody could have imagined forty-eight hours previously. Reports and photographs of the emergency services and ordinary citizens working away to get the city back on its feet.

Everybody, it seemed to me, was doing something. I

needed to be doing something too. Lying on the sofa with a lunchtime spritz would seem dishonourable.

Okay then. We had a bereaved British citizen in the city. There were documents he'd need to sign, and there was more information I could give him. Not much, perhaps, but it was something productive that I could do. I printed off the necessary files, and then filed them in an official-looking folder with 'British Honorary Consulate in Venice' stamped on the front. It was time for another meeting with Matthew Blake.

Blake looked at me with tired eyes and, I thought, just a touch of irritation.

'Mr Consul. I wasn't expecting to see you again so soon.'

'Sorry, is now a bad time?' The words were out of my mouth before I could take them back, but Blake did his best to smile.

'There's not really a great time at the moment.'

'I understand. Look, none of this has to be done now but I thought it might be useful if I brought some documentation round for you.' I took out the folder. 'May I—?'

He nodded. 'Let's sit down, eh?'

'Now then, there are a few things you'll need to sign which will relate to getting a death certificate released. Like I said, this isn't something you need to do now. As well as that, I've got a few handouts just detailing what we – that's the FCO and the Consulate here in Venice – can actually do. And I've also got the Memorandum of Understanding between the FCO, the National Police Chiefs' Council and the Chief Coroner. In England and Wales that is.'

Blake frowned. 'So what's that, exactly?'

'It just describes the way all three departments co-operate in the event of – something like this – and what services we can provide. To be honest, it's a bit long, and a bit dry.' I moved it aside. 'I've put together a more concise version.' I slid it across the coffee table.

He ran his eyes over it. 'Thanks for that. I see there's a list of English-speaking priests. Is that really what you think I need?'

'Some people appreciate it. Especially if they don't have anyone to talk to.'

He shook his head, but smiled. 'Jen always had more interest in that sort of thing than I do. I suppose that explains the angels. But no, I don't want to be trapped at home with a priest. Don't worry. There are people I can call back in the UK if I need to. Friends of Jen. Friends of mine. I'd rather deal with this sort of thing on my own, to be honest.'

'I understand.'

He read further and his expression changed. '*Interpreters and English-speaking lawyers.* I don't understand. Why would I need those?'

'Well, almost certainly you won't. This is just a general list of services as I said.'

'*Almost* certainly?'

'Well, yes. It's just that her death is being treated as suspicious and so they might want to talk to you some more.'

'So what you mean is, they think I had something to do with her death?'

'Matthew, that's not what I'm saying at all.'

'Christ almighty.' He ran a hand through his hair. 'This is how it works, isn't it? I've read about this before. Whenever something like this happens, it's the foreign guy who's under suspicion. What about Fulvio Terzi, eh? It was his bloody shop that she was found in. Why aren't they speaking to him?'

'They have done, as I understand.'

Silence hung in the air, as Blake slowly got to his feet. 'So it was him? That's what they're saying?'

'No, they simply needed to talk to him. Jenny had a key to his shop. She was a frequent visitor there. There are any number of reasons, I understand, why she might have been there.'

'You know, it'd have been better for him if they'd arrested him. Because it's not going to be pleasant when I catch up with him.'

'Matthew, you need to calm down here.'

'I don't have to do anything, Mr Consul. Nothing you tell me at any rate.'

I got to my feet, slowly, and attempted to put my hand on his shoulder, but he knocked it away. 'Don't touch me.'

'Okay. Okay. I'm sorry.' I sat back down. 'Look. There are things we need to talk about. I know it's difficult, believe me. But both of us need to be calm here.'

He opened his mouth, as if he was about to shout at me some more, but then took a deep breath. He held his hands up, palms outwards, and sighed. 'I'm sorry. You're right, of course.' He sat down, slowly. 'So let's talk. What happens next?'

'Well, I don't know much more than you do. Under normal circumstances, the police would be pretty good at keeping me up to date with the progress of the investigation. But,' I jerked my thumb in the direction of the window, 'out there?

Very much not normal circumstances. So I'm not expecting to hear very much until some sort of order has been restored.'

He nodded. 'Okay. What else?'

'Well, as I said, the police might want to talk to you again.'

He grinned, a wide crazy smile. 'To ask me if I killed Jen?'

I thought about lying, but decided I had to be honest with him. 'They might do. At the very least, I expect them to ask where you were on the night that she died.' I waited for his answer, but there was none forthcoming. 'And so?' I prompted.

'I was here. All night. As you know. And awake for most of it, like half the city. And no, nobody saw me.' He paused. 'Are you my lawyer now?'

I shook my head. 'No. But, as you know, I can get you one.'

'Thanks. But no thanks.'

I took a deep breath. 'Matthew, they're going to ask you – again – why Jenny went out that night.'

'Do you mean, "Did you have a row?".'

'No, that's not what I mean.' I paused, and then sighed. 'Actually, yes, that is what I mean. If you want me to help you, you have to let me ask questions like these. Because the police are going to ask them and they're not going to be as polite.'

'Okay. Well, the answer is, no, we did not have a row.' His voice was tight, controlled, as if he was on the edge of shouting.

'And don't get angry. The police won't like that. I'm trying to help, remember?'

He took a deep breath, and then forced a feeble smile on to

his face. 'You're not really doing a great PR job for the Italian police, Mr Consul.'

'They're okay.' I paused. 'Most of them. But now everyone at the *Questura* is tired and stressed and pissed off. Just remember that. If they want to speak to you, be nice to them.'

'I will be.'

'So. Did Jenny tell you where she was going?'

'Just out, to take photographs. As I told you.'

'Did she mention Terzi's bookshop?'

He reached for a fresh packet of cigarettes, scowling as he picked away at the cellophane wrapping. 'No.'

I rubbed my forehead. 'Okay. So just why – and, again, this is something the police are going to ask – why did she decide to go out on the worst night in fifty years when even a glance out of the window would have told her it was crazy verging on dangerous to do so?'

'And my answer to that, Mr Consul, is the same as before. She said she just needed to go out for five minutes, maybe ten. Said she wanted to take some photos. And I suppose that made sense in a way. Once-in-a-lifetime opportunity, that sort of thing.' He sighed. 'Okay. So until the police come knocking at my door, what should I be doing?'

'Nothing. Absolutely nothing. Get on with your life in the most normal way you can. I'll let you know as soon as I know anything.'

'Isn't there anything else you can do?'

I pointed at the sheaf of papers on the coffee table. 'This is what we can do. And right now the *very* best thing we can do is to step back from this. Let the police do their job. That's our best hope of this being sorted out. I'll be in touch, okay?

But in the meantime,' I paused, 'don't do anything daft. You understand?'

He nodded, but I wasn't at all convinced that he did.

I'd made my way past the door on the landing below, when I heard it creak open behind me.

'Jenny. Jenny darling?'

I stiffened, and stopped, my hand resting on the bannister. I turned around, slowly.

It was the woman from the night before. Her face was clearer in the electric light than it had been by candlelight. Her grey hair was drawn up into an untidy bun, and her features, although fine, were deeply lined with age. She reached out her hand towards me.

'Jenny. Is that you?'

I took a step towards her, as gently as I could to avoid frightening her. I could see her face more clearly now, and her eyes were milky-white. She was blind.

'I'm not Jenny, *signora*. My name's Nathan Sutherland. I'm the British Honorary Consul. I've been visiting Matthew, Jenny's boyfriend. Jenny is – well, Jenny is . . .'

My voice trailed off. A figure appeared behind the *signora* and shook her head, slowly waving her finger from side to side. She put her hands on the old woman's shoulders and gently turned her around, moving her back inside.

'No time for angels now, *signora*. No time for angels now.' She turned her head to smile at me. 'Good afternoon, *signore*,' she whispered in that light East European accent, before making to close the door.

'I'm sorry,' I said. 'Can I speak with you for a moment?'

She scowled. 'It's not a good time.'

'It really won't take long. Or I can come back later if you prefer?'

She sighed, a little theatrically, and then turned to her elderly companion. 'One moment, *signora*.' She pushed her hand towards me, as if to indicate that I should move back from the door, then stepped outside and closed it behind her. 'What do you want, *signore*? I shouldn't leave her alone too long.'

'My name's Nathan Sutherland, *signora*—?'

'Oksana.'

'The couple upstairs, Oksana. Jennifer Whiteread and Matthew Blake. Do you know them?'

'No, *signore*.'

'Are you sure? It's just that *signora*,' I craned my head in order to see the nameplate on the door, 'Masiero seems to know Jenny's name.'

'She knows her name, *signore*. They would say hello to each other. That's all.'

'Okay. It's just that she said something about "coming to see the angels"?'

Oksana lowered her voice. 'The *signora* is confused, Mr Sutherland. It's something she says from time to time. It doesn't mean anything.'

'Are you sure? Does the phrase *Angels for an angel* mean anything to you?'

She shook her head. 'It doesn't. I'm sorry.' She leaned her head back against the door. 'Now she's calling for me. I must go.'

I hadn't heard anything. Nevertheless I was about to thank

her for her time, when she closed the door in my face. From inside I heard Oksana's voice.

'There are no angels, *signora*. Not now.'

Chapter 8

Walking home suddenly seemed like it would be a bit of an effort, and I wasn't confident that there'd be any bars open along the way in which to break the journey. I could, I supposed, stop off at the Querini Stampalia to check in with Fede, but I was pretty sure that they didn't need me getting in the way.

I decided to walk down through Castello in the direction of Piazza San Marco. I was horribly fascinated to see what it might look like. And afterwards I could get a boat up to Sant'Angelo. It was raining more gently now, but it still seemed like the driest solution.

I splashed my way along the narrow *calli* that led down to the Riva degli Schiavoni, with the intention of walking along the *fondamenta* in the direction of the Ducal palace and Piazza San Marco.

Then I emerged on to the front, looked out upon the *bacino*, and realised that I was going to be walking home.

The *fondamenta* near Vivaldi's church of the *Pietà* was half blocked by a *vaporetto*. It lay there like a beached whale in the low winter sun, where it had been thrown up by the waves and the wind, and stranded as the tides retreated. Shallow waves lapped around its great bulk.

'Christ almighty.'

I stood and stared at it, scarcely able to believe what I was seeing. A gondola was one thing but a boat capable of transporting over one hundred people? The *vaporetto* pontoons, from what I could see, were all taped off. A handwritten sign outside the nearest one informed me that this was for 'essential safety work'.

'Christ,' I repeated. I shook my head, and walked over the Ponte de la Paglia, empty of people for perhaps the first time since I'd arrived in the city. I stopped at the halfway point, and looked towards the Bridge of Sighs, wondering what the condemned would have thought if this had been their very last view of *La Serenissima*.

I looked at the graffiti sprayed on a nearby shop wall: *Venezia NON è Disneyland*. Somebody had already taken a spray can to it and changed it to *Venezia è Floodland*.

I continued walking in the direction of the Piazza. The water was still high here, and I had to take it slowly to prevent it lapping over the top of my boots. I hadn't expected to find any *passerelle* in the square – these, I knew, would have been the first things to float away – but was pleasantly surprised to see that they'd already been replaced. Then I remembered that both the Patriarch and the mayor had been scheduled to make a statement to the press from outside the Basilica that morning. Obviously, it would never have done for God's Representative in Venice and the man who saw himself as God's Representative for Mestre to have got their feet wet, and so emergency *passerelle* had quickly been moved into position.

The Piazza itself didn't look quite as bad as I'd feared. I wondered how many newspapers throughout the world had featured the Basilica reflecting perfectly in the floodwater in recent days. Shop owners had cleaned up as best they could. Chairs and tables stood again outside the great *caffès* of Florian and Quadri although neither showed any sign of opening.

The only sign of life came from outside the Caffè Lavena. Closed as it was, a group of tourists in bathing costumes were sitting outside it on a stray *passerella*, their feet dangling in the water, and drinking beer straight from the bottle.

I looked at them in disbelief, and made my way along the *passerelle* to the edge of the Basilica, and stood there for a moment, looking at them, and wondering just where the hell I was going to find the words to tell them what I thought.

'Hey man,' one of them shouted in an American accent. 'Come on in. The water's lovely.'

This, evidently, was the funniest joke in the world and his friends howled with laughter, one of them spraying beer out through his nose.

'Seriously, come on. We'll even give you a beer. Think how cool this is gonna look on Instagram.'

I simply didn't have the words. I'd spent a lot of time arguing with Fede and Dario that tourists, for the most part, were not such a bad bunch and that the stories we read of bad behaviour were surprisingly few given the huge numbers of visitors the city attracted. And then you came across something like this.

I shook my head in disgust, and swore under my breath. I was about to move on, when I felt the *passerelle* moving behind me, almost bouncing, as if someone was not just walking but running along them.

I turned around and jumped to one side as a young woman barged past me, leaned over to stare at them, and unleashed a stream of impressively creative swearing.

I looked at her more closely. She had pitch-black back-combed hair, and thick eyeliner, and was wearing a long black leather coat which, I couldn't help thinking, must have been impractical in the flooded streets. She reminded me more than a little of Siouxsie Sioux. The guys looked at her for a moment, then at each other in mock surprise, and burst out laughing.

I looked from the boys to Siouxsie and back again. Laughing, I thought, didn't seem like such a great idea.

'Can you say that in English? I'm sorry, we're just dumbass Americans and we don't understand.'

'Hey baby, you wanna join us for a drink?'

'Yeah, she looks better than he does. Come on, come and sit down.'

Her fists clenched, and for a moment I thought she was going to jump down off the *passerella*, stride through the waters and start punching them. Part of me dearly wanted to see that. The other part of me realised there was a chance of someone getting hurt. I moved towards her, and stretched out my arm in front of her being ever so careful not to actually touch her.

One of the Americans whistled. 'Look out boys, seems we might have some competition here.'

She swatted my hand away. 'Don't touch me.'

'I wasn't going to.' I dropped my voice to a whisper. 'Look.

They're just a bunch of stupid kids. They don't know what's happened here. They'll get back home, read all about it and realise they were behaving like a bunch of jerks. It's not worth getting involved.'

She rolled her eyes and turned away from me, although not before jabbing me in the chest as if to suggest, ever so politely, that I should move the hell back.

The three lads looked at me and jeered.

'You're out of luck, buster!'

'Looks like she prefers Americans.'

'Come on, baby, we've still got some beer left.'

She looked at them and shook her head. She smiled in a way that reminded me of Federica when I'd done something that I should be apologising for.

One of them got to his feet and splashed his way, slightly unsteadily, towards her, causing great ripples to spread across the water.

'Come on, eh? Join us for a beer.'

Siouxsie crouched down, her long black coat spreading out on the *passerella* behind her and bent her head until it was very close to his.

'Maybe I will. But first there's something I'd like you to do for me.' Her English was perfect, although there was no disguising her Venetian accent.

He took a swig from the bottle, and bowed exaggeratedly.

'Anything *the signora* desires.'

The smile never left her face. 'I'd like you to fuck off out of my city and never, ever come back, you bunch of entitled little pricks.'

'Wha—?'

'This isn't Disneyland. This isn't a theme park. People live here. People work here. So why don't you piss off home, burn your neighbour's house down and have a barbecue in the ashes. Because that's what you're doing here.'

The young man's face flushed red, a mixture of embarrassment and anger. 'Jesus Christ, you know how much we've spent in your crappy city? You should be grateful we're here.'

'I know. I know.' She continued to smile. 'We are grateful. We're very grateful for a bunch of pig-shit ignorant tourists coming over here and screwing our city.' Then, in an instant, she whipped her arm out and punched him in the face. There were skull rings on two of her fingers and I winced.

He staggered back, clutching his face. 'You crazy bitch.'

She drew herself to her feet and looked down at them all, flexing her fingers.

'You still want to offer me that beer?'

'Crazy bitch,' one of them repeated, 'we're gonna call the police.'

'Go right ahead.'

I reached my arm out towards her again. 'Look. They're drunk and stupid. And I hate these people as much as you do. But just leave it.'

She turned to me, still flexing her fingers, and sighed heavily. 'You're starting to bore me,' she said, and shoved me in the chest.

It wasn't much of a push, but it was enough. I stepped back, only to discover there was nothing solid behind me. I whirled my arms furiously in the hope of regaining my balance, but it was too late and I toppled backwards into the water.

I dragged myself to my feet, and swept the wet hair out of my eyes. She was already away, the heels of her boots tik-takking their way along the *passerelle*. I opened my mouth to shout after her, and then thought it would be better to save my breath.

The three young Americans were pointing and laughing at me, one of them grinning through the blood that was trickling from his nose.

I splashed my way to the edge of the Piazza with what little dignity I could muster, their jeers ringing in my ears, before disappearing into the blessed anonymity of the back streets.

'*Ciao, tesoro*,' said Fede, as I opened the door. Then she saw me, and raised her eyebrows.

'So. What happened?' she said, in the tone of voice she reserved for when she was expecting me to deliver disappointing news.

'I've been beaten up by Siouxsie Sioux,' I said.

Fede sighed. 'Okay. Have a shower, get changed and then you can tell me all about it. Oh, and Nathan?'

'Yes?'

'Try not to drip on the floor.'

Chapter 9

'So,' I said, almost sighing with pleasure at the luxury of dry socks, 'how has your day been?' I looked more closely at her. 'Oh, Fede, you look tired.'

She attempted to smile, and failed. 'I am. And as for my day, well, it's been horrible.'

'Okay. Tell me about it. Shall I fix us a spritz?'

She shook her head and yawned. 'Do you know, all I really want now is a nice hot cup of tea.'

That wasn't a good sign. 'Sure,' I said, and went through to the kitchen.

I heard Fede flop down on to the sofa behind me, disturbing Gramsci and drawing an irate yowl out of him. I wondered if it would be disloyal to make myself a spritz if we weren't both having one? What was the right thing to do here? It seemed a bit late in the day to be making coffee, and tea had never been my thing. In the event, I poured myself a prosecco as the best 'not really drinking' option I could think of.

I sat her mug down in front of her. 'Go on then. Tell me all about it.'

She yawned. 'Not much more to say than yesterday.

Nothing electrical is working. The place still stinks of damp. The manuscripts,' she shook her head, 'are a disaster area. But we'll carry on. There's nothing else we can do.' She patted me on the knee. 'Tell me more about your day. Maybe it'll cheer me up.'

'Well, as I said, it ended with me being pushed into a lake in the middle of Piazza San Marco by a girl who looked like Siouxsie Sioux.'

She smiled, and gave me a peck on the cheek. 'There we go. I feel better already.'

I flinched. 'God, you're still freezing cold!'

'I know. The heating's still not back on at the *palazzo*. And we're standing in water all day.'

'You're going to catch your death like that!'

She smiled. 'Mr Nathan Sutherland, Honorary Consul in Venice, currently possessed by the spirit of my mother.' She wrapped her fingers around her mug of tea, breathing in its aroma. 'That's better.'

'So tell me more,' I said.

'As I said, it's a disaster area. The manuscripts on the ground floor are waterlogged. All of them. Some of them date back to the fifteenth century. Irreplaceable.'

'I don't understand,' I said, 'why are these things kept on the ground floor in the first place?'

She sighed. 'It was the easiest place to store them. The most practical place to store them. So everyone thought. Nobody expected the water to ever reach a level like this. They were locked away securely but water always finds a way.'

'So why does it have to be you who sorts it out?'

She looked puzzled. 'It doesn't.'

'I mean frescoes and mosaics are your area. Don't they have people who deal with rare books and manuscripts and that sort of thing?'

She laid her head on my shoulder. 'They do, but everyone has to help in whatever way they can. What else is there to do? I know I don't know anything about conservation of manuscripts, but I can still fetch and carry. You take each and every volume out of the water, you lay it out flat, and that is pretty much all you can do until the experts take a look at it.'

'That's a good thing you're doing,' I said. 'Seriously.'

She shrugged. 'Somebody has to do it. You'd be amazed how many people are involved. Everybody wants to help. Students, the security guards, the people who work at the bar.'

'And you. I'm so proud of you.'

'I just feel that I have to. I don't know how many hours I've spent researching in the Querini Stampalia. I owe it a lot.' She drank a little more of her tea, placed the mug back down on the table, and sighed. 'Oh, this is helping. Thank you.'

'Shall I make dinner?'

She shook her head. 'I don't really feel like eating.'

'Fede, have you eaten today?'

She opened her mouth and, for a moment, I thought she was about to lie to me. Then she shook her head again, and, once more, I was troubled by how dreadfully tired she looked. 'There's nowhere to go,' she said, 'everywhere is closed.'

'Okay,' I said, 'then you need to eat something.'

'I really don't feel like it. I'll be fine.'

'I don't care,' I said, 'and you're very much not fine. And I don't care if I am being your mother, you do need to eat something.'

She smiled. 'Okay then. But you really are spending too much time with her.' She yawned. 'Come on then,' she said, 'talk to me while you're cooking. Take my mind off it. Tell me more about your day.'

Federica shook her head. 'So, what does Vanni think happened?'

I shrugged. 'He doesn't know. I mean, their main theory is that Whiteread either disturbed or was disturbed by a burglar. Somebody tried to force the safe, and she had no money or cards on her. But then he asked me what I thought of Blake.'

'Really?'

'Yes. I mean, it seems unlikely to me, the guy is distraught. But you can never tell, I suppose. And then there's the bookshop owner.'

'Fulvio Terzi.'

'That's the fellow. Vanni was wondering just what might have drawn Jenny Whiteread out to his shop on a foul night.'

Fede looked at me and rolled her eyes when she realised the implication. 'God, you men. You really all do have a one-track mind, don't you?'

'Sex or money, *tesoro*. It always comes down to one of those two.'

She frowned. 'Nathan, have you ever met Fulvio Terzi?'

I shook my head. 'No. It was always one of those shops I meant to go into and never got round to. Why?'

'Well, he's an attractive enough man of a certain age, yes. But if you were to ask me if his blazing, white-hot sexuality was sufficient to draw a young woman halfway across the city through a raging flood in the hope of having sex in a book-shop – well, I'd have to say no.'

'Okay, it was just a theory. Evidently a rubbish one,' I huffed. 'Anyway, there's something I need you to check out. Something they found in her bag.'

She nodded. 'Uh-huh. Tell me more.'

'It's a greetings card, with a picture of angels on the front. Come on, I'll show you on the computer. Vanni emailed me a copy.'

Fede smiled. 'Ah, I always dreamed that married life would be like this. Spending a cosy evening looking over my husband's pictures of angels.'

'It's ever such a good picture,' I said, pretending to be hurt.

'Oh, I'm sure it is, *tesoro*. Let's have a look then.'

I logged on to my email, and found Vanni's email at the top of my inbox. I clicked on the attached image. 'Here we go.' I expanded it to fill the screen.

Fede rested her hands on my shoulders as she leaned over to look at the screen.

'Oh, *that*,' she said.

'You know what this is?' I said, spinning my chair around to look at her.

'Of course.' She looked confused. 'Don't you?'

'No.'

'Are you quite sure?' She looked genuinely puzzled.

'Seriously, I've got no idea. What is it?'

'Joshua Reynolds. *Angel's Heads*.'

'Reynolds. Oh, I've heard of him. One of ours, wasn't he?'

'One of yours, yes. You've never seen this before?'

'I suppose I must have done. Don't ask me where, though.'

'I'm amazed. I thought the English were crazy about Reynolds.'

'Well, we were, but then we had this thing called Rock and Roll, and a popular beat combo called The Beatles, and so I think poor old Sir Joshua got a bit left behind.'

'I'm being serious. The Victorians loved him.'

'I'm sure they did.' I frowned. 'Hang on, how old do you think I am?'

'Old enough. I've seen your record collection, remember?'

'Hmmph. I'll pretend I didn't hear that.'

'Come on. Let me drive for a moment. I'll show you.'

She sat herself down on my knee, and I put my arms around her as she typed away.

'Here we go,' she said. 'Take a look at this.' She brought up a Wikipedia page.

Joshua Reynolds' *Angel's Heads*. Fede was right. The Victorians had loved him. The image had been used over and over again in almost every conceivable context. Bars of soap and biscuit tins. The National Society for the Prevention of Cruelty to Children. A Student Midwife organisation.

'I still don't really recognise it,' I said, kissing the back of her neck.

'It's on biscuit tins, for heaven's sake.'

'Maybe I bought the wrong type of biscuit?'

'Anyway, you understand now how highly the Victorians thought of him?'

'I do.'

She expanded the original image still further. 'But there's something else that's interesting about this. The original is an oil, but this is a watercolour. So this isn't an image that's been clipped from a magazine, or printed off the internet.' She tapped the screen. 'You can see brushstrokes here. It's a hand-painted card.'

'By Whiteread?'

'Perhaps so. It really is very good. This little card is quite a precious gift.'

'No kidding. She seems to have had quite a thing about angels.'

'*Angels for an angel*,' said Fede, 'I wonder who that particular angel is?' She yawned. 'But now I really am going to bed. Come on. I think we both need a proper night's sleep.'

I nodded. 'I'll be along in a moment. Promise.'

She kissed the top of my head, and made her way to the bedroom whilst I tapped away at the keyboard, searching for more information. Fede was right. Reynolds seemed to have caught the Victorian *zeitgeist* perfectly, although it was a shame he hadn't been around to enjoy it, having died in 1792.

The full title of the work was actually *A Child's Portrait in Different Views: 'Angel's Heads'*. I looked closer and smiled. They were not five different angels as I'd first thought but, rather, the same young girl – the five-year-old Lady Frances Gordon – painted from five different angles. *Not angels, but angles*, I smiled to myself. It wasn't my sort of art at all. But, I had to concede, it really was a very pretty image.

Angels for an angel.

Poor Jenny Whiteread, I thought. The angels, sadly, had not been watching over her.

Chapter 10

You run. You run and you run and you run, the thick grass whipping at your bare legs, the precious bag clutched to your chest. Your lungs should be burning with the effort but right now, on this bright sunny day, you don't care.

You trip and almost fall, but just about recover your balance, and you laugh with sheer happiness.

Again you stumble, and this time you roll as the world turns from green to blue and green again, as you keep your bag tight against you. You sit up, and think for a moment about crying, but there's no time for that. You get to your feet, and shake your head the way Rufus the spaniel does, as if trying to shake the dizziness out of it.

And then you're away again, remembering to stop at the busy road in front of your house, forcing yourself to Stop, Look and Listen. Dad won't be home, but Mum will.

She's watching television, with a cigarette in her hand, and that, for a moment, makes you sad. Then she smiles when she sees you, and all that is forgotten.

Mum stubs out the cigarette and, for a moment, looks guilty as she sees the expression in your eyes. She keeps saying she'll give up soon, she promises you.

'Hello, angel.'

'Hello, Mum!' you say, because you're not a little girl any more, and 'Mummy' sounds too babyish. Sometimes you wish she wouldn't call you 'angel'. You tell her not to, but you worry that she'll forget and call you it in front of your friends and then that'll be the most embarrassing thing ever and there'll be teasing at school.

So you open your bag, and take out your drawing. And for a moment you feel embarrassed, like the first time you took home a drawing of a house and Mum and Gran made a big fuss of you and told you what a clever girl you were and stuck it to the fridge door. But this is different.

You show her the drawing. A winged figure carrying a sword. You're not quite sure what the sword's doing there, to be honest. It just felt right.

You hang on to Mum's neck as she oohs and ahhs over it. For a moment, you feel a bit awkward. Looking at it again, you can see things that aren't quite right. Things that need to change. It's still, perhaps, a little girl's drawing. But inside you, deep inside, you know this one is a bit special. And you remember how Mrs Jones didn't give you a gold star or anything like that; she just pulled you close to her when you were looking at it together and told you that one day, maybe one day, you were going to be an artist.

Mum hugs you, and ruffles your hair.

'My angel,' she says. And you both smile.

Chapter 11

I put the phone down and grimaced at Federica.

'I don't think I'm going to like this bloke,' I said.

She rolled her eyes. 'Let me guess. 'Rich? Handsome? Successful?'

'Oh all of those, I'm quite sure.'

'You can't base a dislike of someone you've never met just on that.'

'No, but it'll do until I get some supporting evidence.'

'Do you think you've spent too much time in the communist bar, *caro*?'

'I haven't been there for ages. But I gave the boys a call this morning. Just to check how they were.'

Federica smiled at the mention of *the boys*. Sergio and Lorenzo had over a hundred and fifty years between them.

'How are they?'

'They're fine. But the bar is in a bit of a state. I might try and drop by there later. See if I can give them a hand with clearing up.'

'You're going to be over on Giudecca?'

'That's where Markham lives. Over by Zitelle.'

'Neighbours with Elton John then.' She smiled. 'Okay. I'll

be at the Querini if you need me. In the meantime, try not to get into a fight with anyone.'

There was, I was disappointed to find, no bell with the name 'E. John' on it. Markham and Elton, then, were not quite neighbours. That was a shame. I'd hoped I might find them gathered around the piano.

Markham's apartment formed part of a seventeenth-century *palazzo*, separated from the *fondamenta* by a hefty barred gate. There were, it appeared, three other apartments in the same building, all evidently tourist leases judging by the secure key boxes fixed to the wall.

I rang the bell and waited. Nobody answered and I wondered how much time I should give it. Giles Markham, the briefest of searches on the internet had shown me, was a very important and busy man. On the other hand, a young British woman had been murdered and, as the Honorary Consul in Venice, was I not entitled to lean on someone's doorbell for as long as I wanted?

I rested my thumb on the bell once more, and the speaker-phone crackled into life. From the other end of the line came a desperate, hoarse panting.

'*Chi . . . è . . . ?*'

I almost jumped back with the shock. 'Mr Markham?'

There was no sound from the other end, save that of the relentless gasping. I reached for my phone, wondering if I should call the police, the ambulance or both.

'Mr Markham? It's Nathan Sutherland. The Honorary Consul. Are you all right?'

'Sutherland?' He panted again. 'Thank God you're here.'

The doorbell buzzed and the gate clicked open. 'It's the second floor. I'll see you there.'

I ran through the gates and into what would normally have been a neat and well-maintained *cortile*, dirty and muddy now from the the flooding. A staircase directly ahead of me ran up to a first-floor *loggia*, with a heavy bronze door at the far end, and continued upwards to a more modern *porta blindata*.

I took the steps two at a time, phone in hand and poised to call the emergency number. I laid my hand upon the lion's-head knocker but, as soon as I did so, the door opened inwards and there stood a middle-aged man in a tracksuit with a sweatband around his forehead.

'Mr Markham?'

He panted, and leaned on the doorframe, pushing his damp hair back from his brow. 'The very same.' He grinned, and extended his hand for a moist, sweaty handshake.

'I thought you were being murdered!'

He laughed, which turned out to have been a bad idea, as it developed into a coughing fit which left him purple-faced and breathless.

'Come in, come in,' he gasped and led me to the kitchen where he poured out a large glass of water and held it against his forehead.

We stood there until his breathing had returned to normal, and then he smiled once more. 'My apologies. This is all doctor's orders. Blood pressure too high, cardiovascular risk really not good, cholesterol levels bit of a disaster area. So, out go all the fun things and in comes ten kilometres a day on the running machine. I was about seven k in when you rang the doorbell. That might have saved my life.' He drained his glass and refilled it. 'I'm being very rude. Can I offer you something to drink?'

'Just a coffee, if that's okay?'

He looked disappointed. 'Oh. Do you have to? I'm afraid that's something else that's been taken away from me.'

'I'm sorry. Water will be fine in that case.'

'With lemon and ice?'

'Oh, I don't know. That practically makes it a cocktail. I'll take mine straight.'

He grinned, and poured me out a glass from a bottle of San Pellegrino on the brushed aluminium counter. Then he rolled his shoulders and rotated his head with an unpleasant crunching sound that I did well to suppress a wince at.

'I'm told this is doing me good. Hope so. Do you run, Mr Sutherland?'

'Well, I have done. On occasion.'

'The doctor tells me I should aim for the Venice Half-Marathon. Have you ever done that?'

'Well, I suppose if you add up all the running I've done in the course of my life, it might add up to a half-marathon. If that counts?'

He looked puzzled for a moment, and then chuckled. 'Ah, you're a man after my own heart, Mr Sutherland. Let's go and sit down eh? I think I'm still allowed to do that. Hanging around in the kitchen like this makes me feel like we're at a particularly unsuccessful party.'

He led me through into what seemed, to my eyes, to be the most un-Venetian living room in the whole of Venice. An enormous wide-screen TV hung on one wall. Two large black leather sofas formed an L-shape around a glass coffee table the approximate size of Wales. The room was otherwise bare of furnishings, with the exception of a running machine that had been placed directly in front of the floor to ceiling windows, offering a panoramic view of the Bacino of San Marco. To the left of the window stood a glass lectern on a black steel frame, holding what seemed to be an expensive coffee-table art book.

'Wow,' I said.

He smiled. 'Some view, isn't it? I could do without having that wretched machine in here, but it does make the morning jog that little more bearable.'

'I can imagine.' I was about to walk over to the window, but he raised his hand.

'Sorry to be rude, but would you mind taking your shoes off? It's a bugger trying to keep this floor clean. There's a box of slippers there by the door. There should be some in your size.'

I'd only come across this sort of thing in the smartest of contemporary art galleries before. But it was, I had to admit, a most wonderfully polished floor and it would be a shame to spoil it. I searched through the box until I found a pair that looked about the right size and slipped them on. Markham smiled and gestured towards the window.

I made my way over to him, sliding for a moment and almost losing my balance.

'Sorry.' He reached out to grab my arm. 'The floor can be a little perilous, I'm afraid. You do get used to it.' He gestured with his free hand. 'How long have you been here, Mr Sutherland?'

'Over ten years now.'

'Longer than me then. Much longer. Strange we've never

run into each other. But do tell me you never get tired of looking at a view like that?'

I shook my head. 'I never have. And I don't think I ever will.'

'That's good to know. Good to know.' He chuckled. 'I was a bit worried.'

I stared out through the windows, flecked with raindrops, across the slate-grey lagoon towards the Doge's Palace and the Basilica, which appeared to have had the colour leached out of them. I moved a little closer, and could see the faint image of myself in the window. A ghostly figure in a room made up of greys, blacks and whites. A room utterly without decoration.

It was one hell of an apartment, no doubt about it. But it seemed devoid of warmth and the weather outside only contributed to the chilliness of the atmosphere. There was no hint of a breeze making its way through the impeccably double-glazed windows yet I shivered, ever so slightly.

'You're cold?' Markham must have noticed.

I shook my head. 'It's still brutal outside. But I'm warming up nicely thanks.' Indeed, I could feel heat starting to creep gently up from my toes, and I looked down at my gallery-issue slippers. 'Is there—?'

'Underfloor heating. Yes.'

I whistled. 'Lovely.' I turned around. 'You must have done one hell of a lot of work here, Mr Markham.'

'Oh, I have. The place was little more than a shell when I bought it. The floor was a disaster area. Some fragments of *terrazzo* but nothing that could be saved, unfortunately. So my architect recommended just covering it with a layer of waxed concrete. Not very Venetian, of course, but I like it.'

'It's wonderful,' I lied. A thought struck me. 'What are the neighbours like?'

'Neighbours?' He looked puzzled.

'Yes. I noticed the three secure key boxes fixed outside. I just wondered what it was like having tourists come and go all the time.'

His expression cleared. 'Oh, they're not for tourists. Those flats are mine. In case people want to come and stay.'

'I see.' I smiled. 'Lucky people.'

'Well, up to a point. They haven't got quite the same marvellous view, I'm afraid.'

'I'm sure they're still very lucky.' I paused. 'I'm sorry, I haven't told you why I'm here.'

Markham's expression changed. 'I think I can guess. This is about poor Jenny Whiteread, isn't it?'

I nodded. 'I'm afraid so.'

'Poor Jenny,' he repeated. 'Let's sit down, eh?' He looked at my empty glass. 'Let me get you another and then we can talk.'

Chapter 12

I sat down on the nearest sofa, which swallowed me up until my knees were above the level of my head. I allowed Markham to twitch the glass out of my hands.

'Back in a moment. Make yourself comfortable.'

Short of being horizontal I wasn't sure it was physically possible to be any more comfortable. I took another look around the room as best I could, constrained as I was by the comfiest black leather sofa in the world.

Clean. That was the word. Giles Markham had moved to an ancient, crumbling city and had buffed and polished his little corner of it to a mirror finish. I sighed contentedly and leaned my head back, breathing in the smell of the leather.

Markham coughed, gently, and I opened my eyes. He pressed a glass into my hand, and slid a slate coaster towards me. One would not, of course, be so vulgar as to leave a ring on Giles Markham's coffee table. He sat down on the adjacent sofa, resting his hands on his knees, and looked at me across the abyss that separated us.

'So, I've been in touch with Jenny's father.'

'You have?' I tried to keep the surprise out of my voice.

'As her employer, it seemed appropriate.'

'I'm not sure every employer would do the same. That was kind of you.'

'Well, Mr Whiteread said he'd already spoken to you, of course. It sounds like you've handled everything very professionally. You should be proud.'

I wondered if this was how he spoke to employees during Performance Reviews, just before telling them they were about to be made redundant. 'Thank you. It's never the easiest thing to do, as I'm sure you can imagine.'

'I'm not sure I can. In business one frequently has to be the bearer of bad news. But nothing like this. Anyway, I've arranged a flight for him. My expense, of course.'

'I'm sorry?'

'He seemed quite set on coming over.'

'Oh.'

'I hope I haven't done something wrong,' said Markham, in a tone of voice that suggested he really did not care whether he had or not and was challenging me to say otherwise.

'Well, it's just that I told him that the city was chaotic at the moment and that perhaps he should wait. Maybe even until next year. Think about it.' I nodded my head at the window. 'Cold. Wet. The streets running with water or caked in mud. That's not an image he'd want of the city where his daughter spent her last days. Better to come back in the spring, when it's all come back to life. And then he'd understand why she loved it so much, and maybe he'd love it too.'

'That's rather lovely, Mr Sutherland. There's something of the poet about you. But perhaps he'd had time to think things over before I spoke to him. Grief works in strange ways, you know.'

'I suppose so.'

'Anyway, it's most useful you being here. Many hands making light work, that sort of thing.'

'Oh yes?' I said, wondering where this was going.

'Well, it'd be useful if you could sort out a hotel for Mr Whiteread. You probably know about this sort of thing better than I do. I'll pay, of course.' He chuckled. 'I mean, get him somewhere nice, but perhaps not the Gritti or the Bauer. I get the impression Mr Whiteread's from quite a modest background and he might find that sort of thing a bit intimidating.'

'Right. Yes, perhaps he would,' I said, wondering just why the hell I was agreeing.

'And if you could meet him at the airport, that'd be wonderful. Bit of a long, lonely journey in for the poor fellow otherwise. Get a water taxi. Again, I'll cover it.'

I nodded. 'Of course.'

'Good man.' He smiled. 'I know your boss a little. Maxwell. Next time we speak I'll tell him what a great help you've been.'

'Why, thank you. Perhaps I'll make Consul of the Month at last.'

He raised an eyebrow. 'Oh, is that a thing?'

'I'm afraid it isn't. I thought about suggesting it though, and that perhaps we could have badges as well.' He looked confused. 'I'm just joking,' I explained.

'Oh. I see.' He gave the politest of little laughs.

'Anyway, this is kind of you. Thank you. I think it'll make it easier for Mr Whiteread. As much as anything can.'

'I hope so.' He leaned forward, slightly. 'So, Mr Sutherland, is there anything else I can help you with?'

'In all honesty, I don't really know. There's nothing more – officially – for me to do. Unofficially – well, maybe there's more.'

Markham put his head to one side and raised his eyebrows. 'Tell me more.'

'It's just there was something about her death. Something that seems strange to me. And maybe it's nonsense, maybe not. I'm wondering if it could be anything to do with her interest in angels. Well, angels in art, I mean. Was this anything to do with her work for you?'

He chuckled. 'My goodness me, no. I suppose there might be someone with a need for a dedicated angels specialist but not me.'

'Oh right. Would it be terribly rude for me to ask you what her work for you involved?'

He laughed, properly now, and clapped his hands in delight. '"Would it be terribly rude?" You can take the Englishman out of England but you can't take England out of the Englishman, eh? No it wouldn't be rude at all. Jenny's job was to spend my money.'

'I'm sorry?'

'There you go again. "I'm sorry." I can see how you became a diplomat, Mr Sutherland. But, seriously, that was Jenny's job. To spend my money. The Markham Foundation gets hundreds of requests for funds every year. We can't, unfortunately, help everyone. So Jenny's role was to identify what we might class as the most deserving cases. Or at least the ones where we were in a position to make the greatest difference.'

'Wow.' I laughed. 'I have to say, that sounds like a brilliant job. I can't believe you didn't want to do it yourself.'

He looked serious for a moment. 'I wouldn't know where to begin, to be honest. My Italian's not great, and I don't really know how things work over here. More than that, I don't know all that much about art.'

'You don't? That surprises me, to be honest.'

'No, I'm strictly of the "I know what I like" school. And so, I thought it wouldn't be fair or appropriate for me to make any sort of judgement on deserving or undeserving cases. So I needed people to go through every application and decide which ones would be a good use of our money. And as it turns out I was blessed with two of the very best.'

'Jenny Whiteread and Fulvio Terzi?'

'Indeed.' I couldn't be sure, but I thought his expression darkened at the mention of Terzi's name. Then he smiled, sadly, and spread his hands wide, gesturing towards the window and that spectacular view across the city.

'Look at it, Mr Sutherland. Every year, it crumbles away a little more. Every year, the water does that little bit more damage. The very thing that kept this city safe for over one thousand years is now the thing that's destroying it.

'Every year we get more requests than we can possibly hope to deal with. A painting or a mosaic that needs restoring. But that's just the sexy stuff, the thing that gets you the headlines in the glossies. Most of it's far more banal than that. Exteriors that need replastering. Electrics that need to be replaced. Major structural damage caused by hundreds of years of rot. It's everywhere. And it's not going to get any better.' He shook his head. 'Especially not after this.'

He checked his watch. 'That reminds me, I'm due to speak to the mayor again this afternoon. He's interested in broadcasting an appeal from the crypt of St Mark's next week.'

Markham, I felt, was not trying to boast. It just seemed perfectly natural to him that, in the midst of a crisis, his number would be on the list of those that the mayor of Venice would call.

'Does he speak English?'

'The mayor? Not a word. Worse than my Italian. But he has "people", you know?' He paused, and then smiled as if an idea had just occurred to him. 'Actually, why don't you come along next week?'

'As your plus one?'

He laughed. 'Not exactly. But I think it might add something if you were there. It would add a little bit of weight to it. Englishmen standing with their Venetian brothers and sisters. And not just businessmen but the Consul as well. Would you think about it?'

'Well, I've never been invited to a crypt before. But I'd be honoured.'

'Good man. Any chance you might give a bit of a speech? Doesn't have to be anything too long. "Britain stands with Venice", that sort of thing.'

'Of course.' I paused. 'It's good of you to do this, you know? All this work, I mean.'

'Kind of you to say so.'

'Why Venice, in particular?'

'Because of my father. He came here as a young man, just after he left university. He always joked that he was born in the wrong time and that he'd have been better suited to the days of the Grand Tour. He returned home, he said, with a suntan and an Italian wife and neither of them lasted very long. But,' he tapped his chest, 'at least the second of them led to me.

'I think I was probably in my early teens when I first came here with him. I've got to be honest, I found it terribly boring. Church after bloody church and museum after bloody museum. But it was the first time we'd gone away together. I'd always been left with Nanny before that. So it was our first holiday together as men, if you like. And so, no matter how dull I found it, I wasn't going to let him down by complaining. So, year on year we came back to Venice and, eventually, I found I loved it too.

'And then, of course, came our final visit together. I remember how he was so quiet on the water taxi back to Marco Polo. He hardly said a word during the flight. Just sat there, with his head resting against the window, so he could look out. It was only later that I found out he was ill.

'He loved this city so much, I thought I should try and put something back. In his memory. Now, I could have called it Save Venice or Venice in Peril but,' he smiled, 'other people had got there before me. There's so many of these organisations with the word "Venice" in their name that I honestly couldn't think of anything new. So the Richard Markham Foundation it became. And Jenny and Fulvio help me to spend its money.'

'As I said, it sounds like a great job.'

'I hope so. She seemed to enjoy it. And it gave her time for her other work.'

'I don't understand? Her other work?'

'She was working on an art book. About Venice. Such a tragedy we'll never see it. It wasn't just going to be a coffee-table book. She wanted it to be a scholarly work as well.' He sighed. 'Angels really were her passion, you know?'

'I wonder why?'

'Oh, she believed in them. Absolutely. That's what she told me. And I don't think she was teasing.' He smiled. 'Do you believe in angels, Mr Sutherland?'

'Well, I met an Archangel once. He tried to kill me.'

He grinned. 'And now I think you're definitely teasing me.'

I smiled back. 'I assure you I'm not. But it's a long story. For another time perhaps.'

'Well, that's something to look forward to.' He paused. 'I have to say you seem very dedicated for someone with an honorary position, Mr Sutherland. Do you take such an interest in all your clients?'

'Perhaps not with the lost passport bunch. Of which there are many. But this is different. Jenny's death is being treated as suspicious, which means we can't get her home quickly. Which is partly my responsibility.'

'And so you're sleuthing? Is that your responsibility as well?'

'It isn't. And I wouldn't call it that. I'm just trying to find out anything that might be useful to the police.'

Markham stared at me, and then nodded. 'Okay.' He clapped his hands together in front of him. 'So. What else do you need to know?'

I hadn't really thought that far ahead. 'Well. Anything really.'

He shook a finger at me and grinned. 'No. That won't do. If somebody did that to me in business, I'd call them out for wasting my time. Be precise.'

'Why not start by telling me what she was like?'

'She was,' he frowned, 'decent. Nice. A good person, you'd say.'

I smiled at him. 'Okay. Now I'm asking you to be more precise.'

'She could appear scatty. In a bit of a dream world. But that wouldn't be fair. When she was talking about something that genuinely interested her, she was absolutely precise. Forensic, even. She used to say that she could tell if an application was worth our time from the first paragraph of the covering letter.'

'Ruthless, then, would you say?'

'Some might say that. I'd prefer to say she didn't suffer fools gladly.'

'What else?'

'Drank too much coffee. Didn't like seafood – which is a bit of a problem in Venice. Would just walk for hours. Probably knew every priest in the city. Slightly disappointing boyfriend.'

'Matthew Blake? You've met him?'

'Just a couple of times.' He pursed his lips and frowned.

'You didn't like him?'

'Not so much that. I just thought that perhaps he didn't like people very much. Very quiet. Laid-back. Perhaps just a bit too laid-back. I don't want to be cruel, but I wondered if he was quite worthy of her.'

'Well, sometimes opposites attract. I mean, my wife's beautiful and intelligent and I have a regrettable record collection and an unfriendly cat. These things can work out.'

'I think you're teasing me again, Mr Sutherland.'

I grinned. 'I'm really not.' I reached for my phone, and brought up the Reynolds image. 'There's something I'd like to show you. It's probably nothing but for some reason I can't quite get it out of my head.' I showed it to Markham. 'Do you recognise this?'

He frowned. *'Angels for an angel*. No, I'm sorry, that means nothing to me. Where did you find this?'

'It was inside her bag. It was found with her. In Fulvio Terzi's bookshop.'

Markham nodded. 'Well, she spent a lot of time there. They were great friends. She'd often go over there for research or even to keep the shop open if he was away. He actually got her the job with me, you know? He was on holiday in London and literally ran into her. Well, I'd mentioned the fact that I needed somebody else to help – we had an intern, but that wasn't working out – and Jenny seemed ideal.'

'I see.' I paused. 'Has he come back to work yet?'

He shook his head. 'I told him to take a couple of days off and to return when he felt like it.' He drummed his fingers on the table. 'Can I see that picture again?'

'Sure.'

I passed it to him, and then he smiled and snapped his fingers. *'Angels for an angel*. Still don't understand that. But I have seen that image before.' He got to his feet. 'Come on.'

I struggled out of the embrace of the black leather sofa. 'Where are we going?'

'Just down to the office. I think I can sort this out for you.'

Chapter 13

'The office?'

'Yes. I turned one of my apartments into a work space. It's nice to know I can just come down and see what's going on. Or that they can just pop up and see me any time. Or simply if we all want to go out for coffee or for lunch. It's all very relaxed.'

He led me down an external flight of stairs to the *loggia*, and the heavy bronze door. He took out a bunch of keys and unlocked it, then pushed it open and grunted with the effort as it shuddered and grated along the stone floor.

'I really should replace this, you know. Get a proper *porta blindata* installed. Anyway, in you come.'

There was no view across the lagoon from here. The only light came from a window looking into the *cortile* below. And whereas Markham's apartment seemed to be a conscious attempt to scrub away the *Venezianità*, this, in all its slightly cramped, slightly crumbling glory, seemed more like the homes and offices I'd seen throughout the city. It smelled of old furniture and cigar boxes. In a good way.

Markham read my expression correctly. 'I know, it's not quite like my apartment, is it?'

'You didn't feel like remodelling it?'

'Oh, I thought about it. But it would just have been a needless expense. Besides, Fulvio wouldn't have it. If he was supposed to be spending three days a week working over here, he said, he wanted it to be somewhere he felt comfortable.'

'I can understand that,' I said. I nodded at the floor-to-ceiling bookshelves. 'Quite a collection you've got here.'

'All Fulvio's. It's only a fraction of what he's got at home and in his shop. But he tells me every building in the city is catalogued here. Makes it easier to assess a project, having as much information as possible directly to hand.'

'I wonder if my house is here?'

Markham chuckled. 'You'll have to ask him that. But it wouldn't surprise me.'

I took another look around the room, and then it was my turn to laugh as my eyes fell on a small leather-topped coffee table in the corner of the room, with three crystal-glass tumblers and a bottle of J&B whisky on top.

'This seems like a fun place to work,' I said.

'Well, I blame Fulvio for that. That's how he likes to end every Friday.'

'With a glass of J&B?' I said.

'That's what his dad used to drink, he told me. Apparently it was quite popular here in the 1970s.'

There was a gentle cough from behind us. 'Are you taking my name in vain, Giles?'

I turned to see a tall, grey-haired man wrapped up against the elements in a heavy Venetian *tabarro*.

Markham looked surprised. 'Fulvio. I didn't expect to see you in today. Or for some time.'

'I thought it would do me good to come in, Giles. It gives me something to do.'

He brushed past me, spraying me with a fine cloud of cold water from his coat. He hung it up and then turned around, as if noticing me for the first time. 'Oh, I'm sorry,' he said, and brushed the droplets of water from my sleeve with his hand.

'Quite all right,' I said.

He turned to Markham with a quizzical expression on his face.

'Fulvio, this is Mr Sutherland. He's the British Honorary Consul.'

Terzi gave me a thin smile and offered an icy hand to shake. 'The British Consul. My goodness. I thought we hadn't had one of those since Napoleon marched in here.'

'Well, the key word is "Honorary". I'm not really even a diplomat, let alone an ambassador.'

He nodded. 'Mm-hmm. I imagine you've come to talk to Giles about poor Jenny.'

'That's right. One of the more difficult aspects of the job is that you have to be the bearer of bad news.'

'I can imagine.' He rubbed his hands together. 'Dear God, it's icy out there. So, Mr Sutherland, has Giles been able to put your mind at rest on everything? He's good at that.'

'He's being most—'

Markham interrupted me. 'I've arranged for Jenny's father to come over, for as long as he likes. Mr Sutherland is kindly helping me out with the donkey work.'

Terzi nodded. 'Good of him.' He turned to me. '"Donkey work", eh? That's something else Giles is very good at.

Organising things. And people. I imagine you've already realised that.'

I didn't know quite how to respond and decided it would be
best to treat it as a little joke. But neither Terzi nor Markham
were smiling.

'Fulvio,' said Markham, 'I said you should take some
time off. I don't expect you to be here so soon given what
happened.'

Terzi rubbed his forehead as if in pain. 'Giles, my bookshop is both a disaster area and a crime scene. I'm not even
allowed to go in there in the vain hope I might just be able to
rescue some of the stock. I'd rather be here and get on with
my work. If that's all right with you, of course?'

Markham nodded. 'It's quite all right, Fulvio, of course it
is. I'm sorry, I didn't mean to upset you.'

Terzi took a deep breath. 'I'm fine. Really, I'm fine. All
I want to do is work. That's all.' He clicked on his monitor,
and then leaned back in his chair and laughed, with traces of
genuine humour this time. 'Windows update. Well, of course
there is.'

And then I noticed the photograph on his desk, in a simple
black clip frame. Reynolds's *Angel's Heads*.

I picked it up, almost without thinking. '*Angels for an
angel*,' I said.

Terzi stiffened, and yanked it from my fingers. He glared
at me, his hands trembling. Then he placed it back down on
the desk, turning it this way and that as if trying to find the
exact position I'd moved it from. He shook his head as if
trying to shake the anger out, and then patted me on the arm.
'I'm so sorry. That was a gift from Jenny.'

'It was thoughtless of me. I do apologise. Obviously that image meant something important to her.'

'I believe her PhD thesis was on Reynolds. So, yes, it meant a lot to her.' He took a deep breath. 'Well, it's been nice to meet you, Mr Sutherland, but – if you don't mind – I should probably get on with my work.' He looked at his monitor. 'At least, when Microsoft and Mr Gates decide that I'm allowed to.'

'We'll leave you to it, Fulvio,' said Markham. He paused. 'The police. Is everything okay?'

Terzi nodded. 'They've been civil, at least. It hasn't quite been the third degree.'

'Well, I'm glad about that,' I said. 'Do they have any ideas?'

Terzi shrugged. 'Jenny had a key for my shop. I told her she could use it any time she needed. For research, you know. I have quite a collection of books. And while she was doing that, well, she would keep the shop open for me as well.

'And so I asked her, on the day of the flood, if she could perhaps make sure that all the stock had been moved to the higher shelves. Just if she happened to be there. And then someone passed by, late at night. The streets were empty. Nobody else was around. Just a young woman, alone.'

He closed his eyes and rubbed the bridge of his nose. 'There's a strongbox set into the wall that I'm told they tried to force open. Not that there would have been much to find.'

Markham nodded. 'Okay. Thanks Fulvio, we'll get out of your hair.' He turned to me. 'Nathan . . . ?'

'Of course. I'm sorry we had to meet like this, *signor* Terzi.'

Terzi nodded without looking at me, and went back to staring at the spinning circle of death on his PC.

Markham took me by the elbow and steered me outside. He shook his head as the door closed behind him. 'They were good friends, Nathan. The shock must have been terrible for him. He's not normally like this.'

'I understand. I'm surprised he's back in work so soon. Anyway, many thanks for your time, Mr Markham.'

'Giles, please.'

'Giles. I'll make the arrangements for Mr Whiteread and I'll be in touch.'

'Good man.'

'Well, thank you once again for all you've done.' Even as I was speaking, I was wondering just why I was thanking him for all the work I was about to do on his behalf. But Giles Markham had an air about him that suggested he was used to being thanked for things.

I made my way outside to the rain-slicked *fondamenta*, and looked out over the Giudecca Canal, wondering just why somebody might have chosen the worst night in fifty years to attempt to loot a bookshop.

Chapter 14

A tall thin girl was struggling to drag a fridge along Calle de la Mandola.

As far as I was aware, there had been no looting. Indeed, Venice hadn't really gone in for that sort of thing since the Sack of Constantinople. But the shops weren't open, so I assumed she hadn't bought it. And even if she had, I assumed there'd be some sort of 'home delivery' option as opposed to a 'drag it home yourself' one.

Still, there she was. A tall, thin girl trying to drag a fridge along the Calle de la Mandola.

I walked over to her, wondering if I should offer to help in some way, and then stopped as I caught a proper sight of her face. There was no mistaking her. The long black coat and that shock of dark hair, backcombed to within an inch of its life.

'Siouxsie Sioux!' I said.

She turned to look at me, and seemed confused for a moment as if she was trying to recall where she'd seen me before. Perhaps she pushed complete strangers off *passerelle* every day?

'What did you call me?' she said, a warning note in her voice.

'Siouxsie Sioux. Look, I'm sorry, but I don't know your name and I didn't think you'd like "Abusive Girl".'

'You what?'

'"Abusive Girl" or, I don't know, "*Passerelle* Pushing Woman". I couldn't decide what was best. So I stuck with Siouxsie Sioux. She's—'

'I know who Siouxsie is. There's no need to be patronising.' She looked me up and down. 'I'm surprised you've heard of her though.'

'Oh, don't be fooled by my bourgeois exterior. I saw her once, you know.'

'You did?' She failed to keep the surprise out of her voice. Her eyes narrowed. 'When?'

'1995. With the Banshees. "The Rapture" tour.' I smiled. 'Probably before you were born?'

'You know, you can stop patronising me any time you like.'

'I'm right though?'

She glared at me, but nodded. 'Well, yes.'

'Anyway, you're the one who pushed me into a lake in Piazza San Marco. I think you're the one who should be apologising.'

'It was your fault.'

'MY fault?'

'You came along trying to do your big Alpha Male thing and stopping the little woman from getting involved.'

'Oh yes. That's absolutely right. When I look in the mirror in the morning, all I see looking back at me is one great big Alpha Male-shaped ball of testosteroneyness. Believe it or not, all I was trying to do was to stop something unpleasant from kicking off.'

'Well, there was no need to.' She folded her arms and put her head to one side. 'Anyway, it was nothing to do with you. Nothing that a *tourist*,' she lingered over the word, 'needed to get involved with.'

I rubbed my forehead. This, it seemed, was going to be one of *those* conversations.

'I'm not a tourist. I live here. I've lived here for over ten years.'

'You do? That's nice. Venice is a great place to live.' She paused. Ever so slightly. 'If you don't have to work.'

'I've got a job, you know.'

'You have?' She sounded both surprised and disappointed.

'I'm an Honorary Consul.'

'That's a job?'

'Sometimes I wonder that myself. Look,' I said, 'could we maybe not fight? I'm not having a brilliant day, to be honest, and I could do without it. And this is my emergency coat, so I could also do without being pushed into any pools, or anything like that.'

She patted the top of the fridge. 'Okay then. Are you going to give me a hand with this?'

'I don't know. What would you like me to do with it?'

'Help me drag it into the *campo*.'

'Sure. Any particular reason why?'

She sighed, 'Because, Englishman, the old *signora* who lives here is not going to be able to do it herself.'

'That I can understand. Why not just leave it outside the door for *Veritas* to collect?'

She looked at me and shook her head in disbelief. 'Because every house in this street has a ton of crap to be thrown out.

If they leave it outside the door, the whole *calle* is going to be blocked up. So we drag this out into the *campo* and then, maybe within a couple of days, *Veritas* will arrive, find everything in one place, take it all away and the city will start to look just a bit less crap again.'

'You thought of this?'

She shrugged. 'Me and a couple of my friends. Students, you know?'

'You're a student?'

'Sure. At the *Conservatorio*. Italian Baroque studies.'

'Oh right.' I tried, and failed, to keep the surprise out of my voice.

She noticed immediately. 'What does "oh right" mean?'

'Sorry. I didn't mean to be rude. It's just with all this,' I waved my hands in what I prayed was a relatively neutral and non-offensive way, 'you know, the hair and the coat and the long dangly jewellery. Well, I mean, you don't look like a Baroque music student.'

'Oh really. Well, you don't look like an honorary consul to me either.'

'What are we supposed to look like?'

'That's kind of my point, Englishman. Now, are you going to be a bit less useless and give me a hand here?'

I sighed, and tugged up the sleeves of my coat in the hope that would make me look a little more like a man who was used to shifting heavy electrical goods.

'Okay, Siouxsie. Let's do this.'

'I've got a name you know.'

'Oh right. Which is . . . ?'

'Lucia. Lucia Frigo.'

'Well, it's nice to be introduced at last, Lucia. My name's Nathan Sutherland. I sometimes answer to Nat. But both of those are better than "Englishman".'

I think she might have smiled. Just a little. 'Okay then, Nathan. Shift your arse and give me a hand with this.'

I gave a little bow. 'It'll be my pleasure, *Lucia*.'

Chapter 15

Federica was lying fast asleep on the sofa by the time I returned, with Gramsci curled up in her lap.

I was prepared to let them both sleep on, and closed the door as quietly as I could. Not quietly enough. It was the slightest click, but still sufficient for Gramsci to open one eye, yawn, stretch and dig his claws into Federica's knees.

She woke up with a start, yelped, and pushed him off her.

'Little bastard.'

'Don't say that. You'll hurt his feelings.'

'I think he's drawn blood. And these are my second-least grotty jeans.'

'I'm sorry. My fault. Have you been back long?'

She checked her watch. 'Only about an hour.' It was her turn to yawn and stretch. 'Oh, but it's been a long day.' She frowned. 'I'm surprised I'm back before you.'

'Well, I've just been helping Siouxsie Sioux drag a fridge into Campo Manin.'

'That was kind of you. Considering.'

'Ah, she seems all right. She's a bit scary but I think her heart's in the right place.'

'She didn't push you into anything this time?'

'No. That's not the sort of thing you do to people who help you move fridges.'

'So, Siouxsie Sioux's one of the Mud Angels then?'

'The what?'

'The Mud Angels. That's what the papers are calling them. Young people. Students. Some of them still at school. Just helping out, trying to clean the place up.' She sat upright on the sofa. 'There's something lovely about it, you know. For years people have been doing nothing except bitch and whine and complain about this city. And then something like this happens, and it's as if people have finally realised what Venice means to them. People from everywhere, just volunteering to help. Plumbers and electricians are coming in from Mestre. Students are dragging the debris out of houses and cleaning up as best they can. It's lovely.' She smiled. 'So tell me then. How much did you dislike Giles Markham?'

'You know, at the risk of being told "I told you so", I quite liked him.'

'There we go.' She smiled again. 'And I told you so.'

'I mean, he seems like a nice enough bloke. Quite normal. And yet there's something about him. No matter how nice he might seem to be there's always this feeling that he's telling you what to do. And he does seem a little bit blasé about the fact that one of his employees has been murdered.'

'He's a businessman. An English businessman as well. He's probably just being, well, very *English* about it. And I don't suppose you get to be very rich by asking people nicely. Was it useful though?'

'Maybe.' I rubbed my chin. 'At least I found out about the Reynolds image. It was the subject of her thesis. But, get this, Fulvio Terzi has a copy of it on his desk. It was a present from her.'

'Does he now? *Angels for an angel* then?'

'I wonder. Markham was kind of dropping hints that there might have been something going on between Jenny and Terzi.'

'Going . . . *on*?' Fede lingered over the last word.

'You know, having a relationship, something like that?'

'Hmm. It's possible. I could imagine him being the sort of person that has both *goings* and *ons*.'

'I wonder if Matthew Blake knew about it?'

'Well, that would need some top diplomatic ability from you, *caro*. "Excuse me Mr Blake, but did you know your partner was having a relationship with a man old enough to be her father?"'

I adjusted an imaginary bow-tie. 'Well, what job could be better suited to the top British diplomat in Venice?'

She smiled and ruffled my hair. Her phone plinged.

'Oh, leave it,' I said. 'I'll fix us some drinks, eh?'

She yawned. 'No, it might be important. Maybe the Querini want some of us to go in tomorrow.' She tapped away at the screen, and then her expression darkened.

'Bad news?'

She nodded. 'The worst.'

'Tell me.'

'It's the *previsione* for tomorrow. It's another high tide. A hundred and forty-eight centimetres this time.'

'Christ, really?'

She nodded. 'Bad enough at any time. But now, after all this.' She shook her head. 'That's devastating.'

I got to my feet and rubbed my forehead. Then I sighed and went to get my coat.

'Where are you going?'

'Downstairs. I think Ed's going to need a hand again.'

I took a look around the Brazilians. Everything that could be raised, had been raised. Everything that needed to be stood on top of something else, had been stood on top of something else. The useless fridge stood in the corner, waiting to be taken away.

Ed chocked the *paratia* into place, and put his hands on his hips, breathing deeply.

'Thanks, Nat.'

'No worries, Ed.'

'No, I mean it. This is the second time in how many days, four, five? I'm losing count.' He shuffled over to the bar, pulled up a stool and sat down. Then he laid his head gently on the counter. 'Christ, I'm so tired, man.'

'There's a sofa at ours, you know, Ed. If you can't face the walk.'

He raised his head, and shook it, wearily. 'Thanks, Nat, but if I leave now I'll get home in time to sleep in my own bed. And I could really do with that.' He checked his watch. 'But I suppose I've still got a bit of time. Fancy a beer?'

I nodded.

He took two down from a shelf above the bar. 'The fridge doesn't work but it's cold enough not to matter,' he said, flipping the tops off and passing a bottle to me. We clinked them together and drank in silence for a while. Ed was hunched over, making it difficult to see his face.

'Ed, why don't you leave me the keys, eh?'

He raised his head. 'Why?'

'Take tomorrow off. Leave me the keys. I'll come down and clear the place out tomorrow afternoon. Hell, I can even ask Dario to come and lend a hand. I know what I'm doing by now.'

'You'd really do that, Nat?'

'Sure I would, Ed.'

He rubbed his eyes, but then grinned. 'You sure this isn't just a clever way of getting the keys to the bar?'

I snapped my fingers. 'Ah, the one flaw in my cunning plan!'

He grinned again, and reached into his pocket. 'Here you are. That's the spare set. You can hang on to them. You sure you know what to do?'

'Sure.'

'Thanks.' He sighed. 'Because I think I'm going to go home and sleep right through till Monday.'

'Hey, take Monday off as well. I'll cover for you.'

His eyes narrowed. 'What have you got in mind?'

'Look, you're shattered. You need time off. In the meantime, I'll cover for you. I can be the genial host. The stout yeoman of the bar. It's always been a bit of a dream, to work in one.'

'Nat, I think you mean it's always been your dream to *live* in one.'

'Well. Yes.'

'You know, maybe that wouldn't be such a bad idea.'

I shook my head. 'I don't know. Gramsci would miss me. And I'm not sure Federica would be that keen either.'

'No, seriously. Maybe you should take the place over?'

'Ed, I was joking. Really. There's no way I could do that.'

He sighed. 'But maybe somebody needs to.'

I put my bottle down on the bar. 'Ed, what are you saying?'

'I'm saying I think maybe I've had enough, Nat. I'm tired of this shit happening all the time. Every year, autumn to spring. Sweep out the bar, make everything look good, and then do the same again just a few weeks later. Regular as clockwork. Except now it's not every couple of weeks, it's every couple of days.'

'Ed, this is a one-off. Surely?'

He shook his head. 'I'm beginning to wonder, Nat. Beginning to wonder if it's just too difficult. My cousin's got a place out in Mestre. He could do with a bar manager. Then maybe I could start looking for a place of my own.'

'Ed, you're just tired. Don't say this.'

He forced a weak, tired smile on to his face. 'Don't worry, Nat. There'll always be someone here to make you Negronis.'

'Oh, Ed,' I said, 'it's never been about the bloody Negronis.'

He smiled, weakly, and we clinked bottles again. Then he shook his head, once more. 'I'm just so tired of all this, you know?'

And I could only nod in agreement.

Chapter 16

I found it hard to sleep that night. It was not, I kept telling myself, because I was worried about having to make my own Negronis.

I kept tossing and turning until Federica, still half asleep, dug me in the ribs in a 'please stop tossing and turning' kind of way. I got the message, and slipped out of bed as quietly as I could, and into the living room.

I looked out of the window. Still dark outside. The dawn was a few hours off. I could watch a film, I supposed, but I wasn't sure that would help me to drop off.

I'd put a record on. Then I heard the sound of gentle snoring coming from the bedroom and reconsidered. No, first of all I'd put some headphones on, and then a record. Tangerine Dream. *Zeit.* I hadn't played it for a while, but it was definitely a headphones album. Good music for dozing off to, I hoped, despite the famously apocalyptic image of a solar eclipse on the sleeve. I slipped it into the machine, adjusted my headphones, and pressed 'play' as I stretched out on the sofa.

I woke to the early light of dawn streaming through the windows, and found my headphones on the floor from when I had torn them from my head whilst assailed by the blackest of nightmares. There was, perhaps, a reason why I hadn't played this one for years.

I got to my feet, stiffly, as my back groaned in protest. Gramsci lay on top of the radiator, his paws thrown over his eyes, but further sleep for me seemed out of the question.

I pulled on my coat and a pair of Wellington boots. A walk, I thought, would help to blow away the cobwebs.

I walked through the grey half-light of dawn, down Calle de la Mandola, and past Terzi's shop with its boarded-up window. Daniele Manin's statue in the square that bore his name was surrounded by piles of detritus, dragged there by the Mud Angels. I shook my head. If *Veritas* didn't pick this up before the next flood, this was all going to float away. I checked my watch. Not long now until the next siren. Was it really going to be as bad as predicted?

I walked on through Campo San Luca, past the Goldoni theatre and on towards San Salvador. I stopped to look in the window of the Borsalino shop, wondering, as I always did, if I'd ever have sufficient money to treat myself to a hat from there. And then, as ever, I wondered if my head would ever be quite the right shape to deserve something so splendid to put on top of it. Then I was heading towards Piazza San Marco, the streets no longer lined with cheap tourist shops but expensive international boutiques, where large men would wait on the doors sizing up the potential size of your wallet should you attempt to cross the threshold.

Passerelle still criss-crossed the area directly in front of the Basilica. Pools of water were already beginning to form, as water rose up from beneath the ancient stones. This, I knew, was always going to happen. There was no need to panic. Not just yet.

Quadri, Florian and the Gran Caffè Lavena were all closed. Were they still cleaning up after the *acqua granda*? Perhaps so. It didn't matter how grand you were, the problems of cleaning up would be just the same, whether you were one of the most historic sites in the city or the Magical Brazilians; although I imagined Quadri probably had more people to help clear up than Eduardo did. Neither, I imagined, had the owners of Florian needed to knock on the door of the bloke upstairs to ask them to help move the refrigerator.

The only signs of life came from the Bar Americano where a tired-looking *barista* was polishing the counter. I wondered if I should have a coffee in solidarity. Then I remembered what I'd read about the prices and decided that perhaps Ed could do with my money instead.

I walked to the centre of the Piazza, and yawned. I turned through a full circle, stretching my arms wide in an attempt to get the kinks out of my back. Piazza San Marco. 'The most beautiful drawing room in Europe', devoid of people. Just me, the *barista* and the pigeons, all wondering what the day was going to bring.

And then I heard it. The mournful wail of the *acqua alta* alarm. I remembered how exciting it had seemed when I'd heard it for the first time after arriving in Venice. Now I was just sick of the sound of it. Everyone, wherever they might be in town, would be listening right now, hoping against hope that it wouldn't be as bad as predicted.

One pling. Going to be wet out. Watch where you go. You might want to think about wellies.

Two plings. One hundred and twenty centimetres or more. One third of the city will be flooding in four hours' time. Get that *paratia* in place.

Three plings. Seventy per cent of the city under water. Manageable. Horrible but manageable.

I looked towards the grey skies, feeling the drizzle on my face. *Come on, Lord, give the old place a break, eh?*

And then – and then – there was no fourth pling. It was going to be a tough day, a grim day. But the city would cope. Ground-floor apartments would have to be swept out once more. Business owners would curse as they stacked their goods on to tables, and shifted anything electrical out of the reach of the waters. But it would be manageable. And right now, I felt, the city would settle for that.

Once more, I spun through a full circle, stretching my arms wide and shouting 'Yes!', my voice echoing in the empty square and startling a group of pigeons into flight.

'Yes!' I shouted again, and started to laugh. And then, feeling the rain beginning to fall more heavily, I made my way back to the Street of the Assassins.

Chapter 17

The waters were predicted to reach 130 centimetres. Manageable, yes. Short of catastrophic, most definitely. But every shop, every house that had been cleaned out would be flooded again. Worse, all the rubbish that had been gathered and piled up awaiting collection would start to float. In about three hours' time.

I entered the apartment as quietly as I could. I thought about making Federica a cup of tea, but she'd had a tough couple of days and so I decided to let her sleep on.

I went through to the kitchen to make a coffee, automatically reaching down to refill Gramsci's bowl with kitty biscuits. I heard the heavy thump on the floor as he jumped down from the back of the sofa, and waddled through.

'Morning, Fat Cat.'

He ignored me and settled down to munching.

'So did you hear how many plings there were?'

Munch. Munch. Munch.

'Maybe miaow once for three plings, twice for four plings?'

Munch. Munch. Munch.

'Blimey. The conversation never stops in this house, does it?'

I took my coffee through to the living room, and stood by

the window. It was raining outside, gently now, but there was no sign of water creeping up the alley. There wouldn't be. Not for an hour or two yet. But I wondered how many people, like me, were staring through windows, wondering and waiting. Father Michael, I knew, would already be up and about, preparing a sermon for a congregation that might not feel like turning up, and wondering if he'd be having to sweep the water out of his church for the second time in five days.

I opened the window, and stuck my head outside, the better to look down into the Street of the Assassins. The cold air made me catch my breath, and drew an aggrieved yowl out of Gramsci, who'd followed me through without my noticing.

I couldn't see directly into the Brazilians from my position, but neither could I see any lights on. Good. Ed, it seemed, had taken me up on the offer. Or had he decided that there simply was no point, and was going to let the floodwater do its worst? Had he just given up? I shook my head. That was something I didn't want to think about.

I noticed *signor* Gabriele, the elderly owner of the bookshop opposite, opening up. How long had I been here? Almost ten years? I couldn't remember ever speaking to him. I'd never even been inside his shop.

Well, today that was going to change. I was going to make up for lost time. I was going to be a good neighbour.

'*Signor* Gabriele,' I called out.

He looked around, unsure as to where my voice was coming from.

'*Signor* Gabriele,' I called again.

He turned around and peered up at me. 'Who are you?' he said.

Fair enough, I supposed.

'I'm Nathan Sutherland. We're neighbours. Well, sort of.'

He adjusted his spectacles on the end of his long, thin nose. 'Oh yes. I know you.'

'That's right!' I smiled at him. 'It's me, Nathan!'

'That's right. Ten years you've been here. Never said a word to me. Never once come into the shop. Spend all your time in the bar downstairs, is that right?'

'Er. Yes.'

'So. What do you want? Some cheap books, is that it?'

'No. Really. I just wondered if I could help?'

'What do you mean, can you help?'

'Look, you're always closed on Sundays—'

'Nice of you to notice.'

' —and so I thought, well, with the *acqua alta* and everything, you might need a hand.'

'And then I give you some free books, is that it?'

'No. I don't care about the free books. Although that'd be nice, obviously. I just wondered if I could help?'

He sighed, removed his glasses, and rubbed his nose. 'Okay. Yes. Maybe you can.'

'Great. I'll be right down.'

He looked up at me and shook his head. 'You'll freeze to death. Put some proper clothes on first.'

'All right.'

I walked back into the bedroom as quietly as I could. Fede was still fast asleep. Gramsci, fleeing from the icy draught, had squirmed under the duvet, leaving only his tail, twitching with annoyance, to be seen.

I pulled on the heaviest pair of jeans and the thickest

sweater I could find. Then I bent over Federica, brushed the hair away from her face, and kissed her.

'See you later, *cara*,' I whispered. 'I'm off to do my bit as a socially responsible citizen.'

I'd never been into Gabriele's shop before but, from what I'd been able to see from outside, it was a labyrinth of mass-market paperbacks, first editions, expensive exhibition catalogues and coffee-table books all piled high in great tottering columns. Now, however, almost everything had been boxed up and piled on shelves and tables in an attempt to keep them out of reach of the waters.

It hadn't worked.

The place had the familiar smell of old books and leather, but mixed now with the unmistakable odour of damp.

Gabriele looked at me and shrugged, as if he hadn't really expected me to turn up. 'Okay, my friend.' He gave the faintest of smiles. 'Let's get started. What do you know about books?'

'Well, I've read a few.'

'Do you know anything about conservation?'

'Next to nothing. My wife would, though.'

'Oh. Couldn't you send her instead?'

'She's been at the Querini Stampalia all week. I thought she deserved to sleep in.'

'Ah. Okay.' He nodded, and then sighed. 'We'll do the best we can.'

'So what can I do?'

'I've divided the stock into three.' He gave a short, mirthless laugh. 'We could call it triage, I suppose. These here,' he tapped the table to his left, 'are dry. So we're going to move them up to the top shelves. Should be safe enough there. Those at the back of the shop are damaged but might be okay with some work and are worth spending time on. They go into the room in the back. All these at the front,' he swept his arms in a wide circle indicating the mass of sodden books that had yet to be boxed up, 'these were soaked through the other night. They're junk. Trash.'

'So, what, do we just bag them up and wait for *Veritas*?'

He shook his head. 'No. Can't bear to do that. Hate throwing books away. We'll put them on the shelves at the front of the shop. People can just take them away free or pay what they want.'

'I understand. So what do you want me to do?'

'First of all, put the boxes on the highest shelves.' He smiled, with a touch more warmth this time, and patted me on the arm. 'I'm not as young as I used to be. You'll be better at that.'

'No problem.'

'If you want to be really good, come back in a couple of days and take them all down again. At least if it looks as if all this might be over. For now.'

'I will. Promise.'

He grunted. 'I'll go through the stock at the back. Sort through the damage. Find what we can save. That needs an expert. No job for you.' He was, I thought, not trying to be unkind.

'I understand.'

'That'll take some time. So when you've finished shifting stock to the higher shelves, you can make a start on putting out the water-damaged ones on the tables at the front of the shop. I'd do it but,' he sniffed, 'like I said, I don't like throwing books away. Or seeing damaged ones.'

'Of course.'

'Oh, and there's one more thing.'

'Yes?'

'You could make me a cup of coffee. There's a kitchen in the back. Actually, make us both a coffee. I think we're going to need a lot of it.'

I heard the bells of Santo Stefano chiming midday and realised that the highest tide had now passed. The second wave, mercifully, had not been as bad as expected. Yet water was sloshing over the *paratia*, and the shop was flooded to the height of our Wellington boots.

Gabriele sighed, and patted me on the shoulder. 'And we're finished. A job well done, Nathan. Thank you.' It was the first time he'd used my name. 'I think I owe you something for this,' he continued.

I waved my hands. 'No. No, you really don't.'

He blinked at me. 'I'm not talking about money.'

'Oh.'

'Of course not.' He went into the back of the shop and returned with our coffee cups and a dusty bottle of grappa. 'Something better than money.' He poured us out a generous measure. 'Cheers, Nathan.'

'Cheers, Gabriele.'

It was supermarket grappa. Cooking grappa. Served in a used coffee cup. Standing in a cold damp room, surrounded by ruined books, with the smell of paper and leather and damp everywhere, it was perhaps the best grappa I'd ever had. I felt its heat radiating out from my stomach, to my hands and feet, and smiled.

'Good, eh?'

'Best drink of the day.'

He drained his cup and refilled us both. He sighed. 'You know, Nathan, they tell us they have computerised weather centres now. Control centres throughout the province monitoring the weather, the atmospheric pressure, the moon, the tides – whatever. Sirens throughout the city telling us how bad it's going to be. But in the past, all they had to do was ask a Venetian. We could tell, you know?' He tapped his nose, and sniffed. 'We could smell it. Feel it. Too much salt in the air, or too little. Just a little colder, or a little warmer than it should be. And now,' he shrugged, 'it's gone. I can't feel it any more. Something's not right. With the lagoon, with the weather. I don't know what it is. But I can't feel it any more.' He chuckled, and turned away from me. 'Or maybe I'm just losing my sense of smell.'

He looked up at the upper shelves with my neatly stacked boxes, and then at the water outside. Gabriele would be sweeping his shop out with fresh water in a few hours' time; something, I was sure, he was well accustomed to. But this, unlike the night of the *acqua granda*, was something manageable.

'It seems you didn't need to move those after all,' he said, gesturing upwards.

'Ah, it's no problem.'

'Well, if you hadn't, you can guarantee the whole damn shop would have gone under. That seems to be the way the world works now.'

'I'll come back tomorrow. Take them down again.'

'There's no rush.' He shrugged. 'I don't think I'm going to be busy any time soon.'

Gabriele's shop was perhaps just fifty metres from Fulvio Terzi's. They sold – at least to my eyes – almost identical things. Surely, I thought, they must know each other. Were they friends or rivals? I'd done a hard morning's work in his shop for nothing more than a deconstructed *caffè corretto*. I figured I was allowed to ask him a question.

'Gabriele, can I ask you about Fulvio Terzi? Do you know him?'

He looked surprised at first, but then shrugged and nodded. 'Sure I know him. Same line of business. I wouldn't say he was a friend exactly.'

'You heard about the young Englishwoman who was found in his shop on the night of the *aqua granda*?'

He nodded. 'I did. Terrible business, of course. She was there quite a lot. They had some sort of arrangement, I think. She was researching a book, wasn't she?' I nodded. 'Well, Fulvio's got a pretty good collection of rare books. Stuff that's never actually put on sale. I understand he told her she could use them for reference any time.'

'That's one thing I don't understand. Why is he working for Giles Markham as well?'

Gabriele rubbed finger and thumb together. 'Why does anybody do anything my friend? Money.' He sighed. 'And there's no money in this business any more.'

'There always seem to be people in here.'

'Sure there are. People come in all the time and wander about and tell me what a lovely bookshop I have. And then they leave without buying anything. Or maybe an old Mondadori *giallo* for a couple of euros.' He shook his head. 'We'd make more money selling masks. Or fake Murano glass.'

'I'm sorry.'

'It's okay. I'll just do another couple of years and then I'll sell up. Then maybe move out to the mainland.' He sighed. 'Not sure I can be doing with this for much longer.' He looked around his shop. 'How many times a year do I have to do this? I'm not so young any more. I never thought I'd leave Venice. But maybe it's time to say enough is enough.'

'Don't say that. There's always MOSE.'

He looked at me for a moment and then we both burst out laughing. Construction work on the MOSE system of flood barriers had started back in 2003 and was still about twelve months away from completion. As, indeed, it had been for most of the last fifteen years. Along the way it had sucked in just over five billion euros, twenty million more had gone missing, and a mayor of Venice had been arrested and later resigned in the hope that people would just agree to let bygones be bygones and say no more about it. People had given up wondering or even caring if it would ever be finished, and the whole project now exuded the same horrid fascination as a traffic accident.

'Anyway, Terzi's a smart guy. He's seen which way the wind is blowing. So he gets another job on the side. Maybe this one has a bit of prestige as well, you know? And if he can get the *bella signora* to keep an eye on his place as well, then so much the better.'

'Did they, er, see much of each other?'

Gabriele laughed again. 'You English. You never, ever get to the point do you? *Did they see much of each other.*' He mimicked my accent. 'Well, yes, I think they did. She seemed like a smart young woman, you know? They probably had a lot to talk about.' He paused. 'He took her out on his boat a couple of times.'

'He has a boat?'

'Sure. Near San Giacomo dell'Orio, I think.' He paused, and his gaze became cautious, shifty even. 'I think I might have seen her, you know? The night she died.'

'Seriously?'

'I think so. It was dark and she'd fallen over and so her hair was plastered everywhere but I think it was her.'

'Did she say anything?'

'She did. I mean my English isn't so good, but she said something to me.' He paused. '"*If he's done this, I'll kill him.*" That was it.'

'Bloody hell.'

'Then she ran on. Down the *calle*. I called after her, told her to go home. And that was it.'

'Bloody hell,' I repeated. 'But thanks.' A thought struck me. 'You've never asked me what my interest is?'

He shrugged. 'I walk past your apartment every day. There's a nice shiny brass plate on your door. British Honorary Consul in Venice, it says. I figured that was something to do with it.'

'Oh right. Well, it's nice not to have to invent a story for once.' I smiled. 'I'll see you in a couple of days then, Gabriele.'

I was about to haul my leg over the *paratia*, and then

paused for a moment to take in the rows of ruined books. For passers-by to take away, or just to leave what they felt was fair.

I sighed.

'Look. Maybe I'd like a few of these.'

Chapter 18

'You've been out a long time, *caro*.'

'Sorry. I've been being a responsible citizen. I've been help-ing the chap over the road get his shop *acqua alta*-proofed.'

'That was kind.' She kissed me. 'Proud of you.'

'Well, I keep thinking about you being at work every day, and I feel a bit useless much of the time, and it's not like I have a nine-to-five job. So I thought I ought to help.'

'Even on a Sunday?'

'Even on a Sunday. What's the alternative? Stay in and watch from the comfort of the apartment as the guy's life's work is slowly swept away?'

She smiled, and hugged me. 'Okay then. I think you've earned a lazy afternoon. I could even cook you lunch if you like?'

I looked at her. 'You sure?'

'If you're okay with *pasta al pomodoro*? I'm sorry, I know it's not the sort of thing you'd usually do.'

'That's fine.' I yawned and stretched. 'Right now *pasta al pomodoro* sounds like the best thing in the world.'

'Great. Go and sit down and keep Unfriendly Cat com-pany. You look tired.'

I yawned again. 'I am.' I paused. 'Oh, there's one thing I need to do first.'

I opened the front door. There were four large boxes outside, almost blocking the entrance.

Federica looked at me, and her eyes narrowed. 'What have you done?'

'They're, erm, Casanova's memoirs. And his letters as well. I've always wanted to read them. Well, quite wanted to read them.'

'And so you decided today was the day to start?'

'Absolutely!'

'I see. How much did that all set you back?'

'Oh, hardly anything. Because . . .' My voice trailed off as I realised what I was going to have to say.

'Because?'

'Because Gabriele – he's my new pal – has a lot of water-logged stock. And so he's kind of giving them away to anyone who'll have them.'

'Giving them away?'

'Well, I *say* giving them away, but donations are always welcome.'

'Right. So not so much "giving them away", more sort of "selling them"?'

'Well, yes.'

'So you've bought a collection of waterlogged books? Is that what you mean?'

'Erm, yes. That's exactly what I mean. Look, it's the guy's whole life. I thought I needed to help.'

She sighed. 'You're right. And I suppose it was a nice thing to do. Come on then, let's get them inside and see if we can make space for them.'

'Great. Oh and could you give me a hand downstairs as well?'

'Downstairs?'

'Yes.' I paused. 'I've got the complete *Decline and Fall of the Roman Empire* down there.'

Gramsci stared down at us from the top of *The Decline and Fall of the Roman Empire,* now taking pride of place in the hall.

'See,' I said, 'he likes it. Educational and practical!'

Fede looked up at the cat. 'Please tell me they aren't staying there,' she said.

'No, no. Absolutely not. I'll move them, I promise. He'll get bored of them within a couple of days.'

She sighed. 'Anyway, I've had a productive morning as well. Tell you what, why don't you make me a cup of tea, and then we'll have a talk about angels.'

Fede tapped away at her computer, and then grabbed my elbow to pull me over to her. 'This is it,' she said, tapping the screen with her glasses. 'It was published three years ago.'

I looked over her shoulder. '"*From the Realms of Glory: Two thousand years of the angelic in art*",' I read. '"Dr Jennifer T Whiteread. Foreword by John Julius Norwich." Wow. She knew some heavyweight people.'

'It seems she did. Now, take a look at that cover.'

'Reynolds.'

'The very same.'

'As we know, it was an image that meant a lot to her.' She scrolled down the page. 'It got very good reviews.'

'I wonder how it sold?'

Fede shrugged. 'Who knows? It's expensive. Too expensive just to have as a coffee-table book. But it does look lovely.'

I reached over to move the mouse, clicking on the image of Jenny in order to expand it. At first glance I found it hard to recognise the woman I had found in Terzi's shop. Pixie-like, her reddish hair cut in a Louise Brooks bob, she smiled out at us from the steps of the National Gallery.

'Pretty, wasn't she?' said Fede.

'Uh-huh,' I said, trying to keep my voice non-committal.

She sighed. 'You're allowed to say you find another woman attractive, Nathan.'

'I am? Oh good.'

'Well, you don't *have* to, of course. But I won't be offended.'

'Right. Well, yes, she was very pretty.' I scrolled through her biography. 'Just thirty-four. And just look what she did. Undergraduate, Christ Church College, History of Art. Research degree at the Courtauld Institute. Then she worked for the Ashmolean for a while. Then UCL. That's a lot packed into just thirty-four years.' I looked over at Federica. 'What were you doing at thirty-four years old?'

She frowned. 'I'm not sure I can remember.'

I smiled. 'Well, that's understandable.'

She slapped my wrist. 'It's not that long ago, you know. What about you?'

'I think I was struggling with an unhappy marriage. It was long before you turned up, anyway.' A miaow came from on top of the stack of books. 'And him, of course.'

Fede turned back to the computer. 'Anyway – get this – her biography says that she was working on a follow-up. *The*

Angels of Venice: One thousand years of the angelic in Venetian art.'

'That's a lot of angels.'

'And a hell of a lot of research. Maybe that's what led her to the Markham Foundation? The chance of living in Venice whilst spending somebody else's money, and working on her book.'

'You know, that does sound pretty good.'

Fede smiled and patted me on the arm. 'Come on. I think I could actually manage a spritz now.'

'Oh good. A spritz it shall be!' I said.

There was a miaow from on high, followed by the sound of heavy, soggy books falling to the floor.

Fede sighed. 'After you've picked those up, of course.'

Chapter 19

Marco Polo airport, 10.15. I scribbled the word 'Whiteread' on a sheet of blank paper, tucked it inside a plastic sleeve, and stood at the arrivals gate waiting for the father of a dead woman to arrive.

I'd taken the *vaporetto* to Piazzale Roma, and then the mainland bus out to the airport. But that, as Markham had said, would not do for the return journey. The thought of having to make polite conversation with a grieving parent as the bus made its way through anonymous suburbs under dark grey skies felt beyond me. Moreover, everyone else on the bus would probably be a tourist. No matter the weather, no matter the season, no matter the state the city was in, people would be smiling, and chatting and happy, and that, I felt, would be unbearable to William Whiteread.

My phone rang. Dario's number.

'*Ciao, vecio*. How are things?'

'Still waiting.'

'How are you doing?'

'Not good to be honest. Stressed. I've not done this before. Not person to person.'

'You'll be fine, Nat. And everything's sorted out, okay?

You just go to the water-taxi dock and Davide will be there. He says he's watching the arrivals on his phone so he'll be there right on time. No queuing, nothing. Nobody else to pick up, just the two of you.'

'Thanks, Dario. And he knows I'll settle up with him, yeah?'

I could almost hear him shaking his head. 'Nat, he's not going to ask for anything.'

'Dario, I'll cover this. Markham will pay me back anyway. Seriously. I don't want the guy to be out of pocket.'

'And Davide doesn't want to be making money out of something like this. Seriously.'

'Wow. I wouldn't have expected this from a water-taxi driver.'

'Neither would I, to be honest. I think it's the *acqua granda*. It's made people act a bit differently, you know? Maybe we're just being nicer to people?'

'I hope so. That'd be good, wouldn't it?'

'Just don't talk to him about politics. He's basically a good guy, but he's a bit right-wing. But he'll be sensible, and won't hoon around at all. He got into trouble a few months ago. He picked up some rock star guy and let him take control for a while . . .'

'Wow. Well, thanks again, Dario.'

'No worries, buddy. Take care, eh?'

I hung up. People were starting to file through arrivals. I held my sign up, but I needn't have bothered. I recognised Whiteread immediately.

Most of the arrivals were happy and smiling, joking and relaxed after having had an eight o'clock beer in the departure lounge. Some of the others were suited, carrying briefcases and already on the phone, looking around in annoyance if their pick-up was nowhere to be seen. But William Whiteread just looked lost. Alone in the sea of humanity that surged around him, joking, laughing, shouting, waving, pointing; he simply looked . . . lost. And alone.

I'd imagined him as being old and frail, but he wasn't. He looked like someone who listened to the same music as me, watched the same films as me, read the same books as me. If my life had taken a different path in Aberystwyth or in Edinburgh, then twenty years down the line I could have been him. I could have been the one talking to my friends about my lovely girl. My lovely daughter. Showing them photographs from childhood, from university. *My girl's doing well for herself. She's in Venice now, you know?* Asking about boyfriends. *Is he the one?* When will you be walking up the aisle, when will you be the one making the speech where she blushes and says *Oh, Dad* and slaps you on the arm?

I'd never had that. And, at that moment, I felt so lucky. Because neither would I ever be faced with the prospect of losing it.

Whiteread noticed the sign, and walked over to me. I went to hug him but thought better of it and turned it into an awkward handshake. He grabbed me anyway and pulled me to him, patting me on the back.

'Mr Whiteread?'

He nodded at me, and did his best to smile. 'Call me Bill, please.'

'I'm Nathan Sutherland. The Honorary Consul. If you just

come with me.' I reached for his wheelie bag, but he shook his head, and I led him off in the direction of the water-taxi stop.

I'd never been in a taxi before. I'd seen plenty of them, of course, mainly on the Grand Canal, as happy tourists stood up at the back photographing the city. Strictly speaking, they were supposed to avoid the Grand Canal unless they were actually taking someone directly to a hotel but . . . well, visitors seemed to like it, and blind eyes, as ever, were turned.

Whiteread sat opposite, neither speaking nor looking at me, as I wondered what on earth to say. It didn't seem appropriate to point out any of the islands or areas of interest as we passed by them. In the grey and the rain there wasn't much to look at anyway.

Would he feel happier just being left in silence? Or perhaps he'd like to talk, instead of just sitting there wrapped in his own dark thoughts. I checked my watch. 'We won't be long now. The bus journey can take some time, but we'll be there in about ten minutes.'

Bill nodded.

'Then I'll take you to your hotel. It's the Tintoretto on Fondamente Nove. I thought – well, I thought you might like to be somewhere near to where Jenny lived. So you could see the things she'd have seen every day.'

He smiled, weakly. 'That was thoughtful of you.'

'Have you been to Venice before?'

'No. I was going to visit Jenny next spring. Wait until April or May, she told me. And now—' He broke off, and we sat in silence for a moment. 'Do we have to go straight there?'

'No. No, of course not. If you'd prefer to go for lunch first or just take a walk around, that's fine. I can check your luggage into your hotel for you if you like and then—'

He shook his head. 'No, that's not what I mean. I think I'd like to see where she lived first of all.'

'If that's what you want.'

'I think that's what I'd like to do. Can we do that, Mr Sutherland?'

'Yes, of course.' I took my phone from my pocket. 'Although I don't have the keys.'

'You don't?'

'No. I'll call Matthew. Hopefully he'll be at home.' I tapped at the keypad.

There was silence for a moment as Bill stared at me.

'He's still there?'

The question surprised me. 'Well, yes.'

He was about to speak again, but then Blake picked up my call.

'Hello.'

I pressed the mute button, and smiled at Bill. 'I'll take this outside,' I said, nodding to the double doors that led out to the deck. He looked confused and a little concerned. 'It's difficult to get a signal in here,' I lied.

The wind whipped at my coat as I stepped outside, cold rain blowing in my face. The driver looked at me and raised his eyebrows, not understanding why I was leaving the warmth of the cabin. I pointed at my phone, and he shrugged before turning his eyes back to the lagoon.

I unmuted. 'Matthew, it's Nathan.'

'Nathan? Mr Sutherland?'

'That's me. Are you free now? Are you at home?'

'I am. Do you want to meet? Just give me half an hour, eh? I've not been up long.'

'Matthew, I'm sorry to spring this on you but I'm on a boat from Marco Polo with Bill Whiteread.'

There was silence on the other end of the line.

'Bill Whiteread,' I repeated. 'Jenny's dad.'

'Oh, right.' Silence again. 'I guess he wants to meet up some time, right?'

'Matthew, we're on our way now. He wants to see where Jenny lived. Before he even checks into the hotel.'

'Now?' I heard him swear under his breath. 'Look, I'm sorry, but now's really not a good time. I've only just got up and, to be honest, the flat's in a bit of a state. Maybe give me a call tomorrow morning, yeah?'

'Matthew, I don't think you understand.' I was aware I was raising my voice and turned around to reassure myself that Whiteread hadn't heard anything. He gave me a quizzical look and I gave him a smile and a thumbs up. 'We're coming round. Now.'

'So, what, I have to let him in, is that what you're saying?'

'What I'm saying is that I'm on a boat with a distraught father coming to visit the city where his daughter was killed, and he'd like to see the place where she lived. I can understand that, can't you?'

'Sure, yeah, but—'

'But nothing, Matthew. Open the windows, have a last-minute sweep up. Brush your hair, whatever. Just be there when I arrive or, trust me, you're going to look like the bad guy in all this.'

There was silence on the line for a few seconds followed by 'Fuck', as Blake hung up.

I hoped that meant yes. I turned around and made my way back into the cabin, sweeping the rain from my hair.

Blake hadn't been lying when he'd said the apartment was in a bit of a state. He'd had something resembling a quick clean-up, although with limited success. The air was chilly, suggesting he'd opened the windows to try and clear the room of the fug of stale cigarette smoke whilst a saucerful of butts lay on the table next to the sofa, together with the bottle of J&B.

Bill took a look around, and shook his head. I could feel the disappointment radiating from him. He took a deep breath, and grabbed Blake's arm tightly, making him wince.

'Hello, Matthew,' he said.

Blake nodded. 'Mr Whiteread. William.'

We stood there in a silence thicker than the smoke.

'Look,' I said, 'shall I go and make us all a cup of tea? Coffee if you'd rather?'

Bill put his hand on my arm, gripping it with surprising strength. 'No thanks, Mr Sutherland, I'd prefer you to stay here.'

I nodded.

Blake spoke. 'I'm so sorry.'

'I am too, Matthew.'

'I don't know what to say, William. I just don't. I wake up every morning hoping this has all been some horrible dream and then—'

Bill screwed his eyes shut, and waved his hand. 'Please

stop, Matthew. Just stop, please.' He took a deep breath, opened his eyes and glared at him. 'Where were you, boy?' His voice was low, little more than a whisper.

'I don't understand.'

'Then I'll repeat it. Where were you? The night my girl was killed. Where were you?'

'I was here, all night. Just waiting for her to come back.'

Bill nodded. 'So you let her go out on, what, the worst night in fifty years?'

Blake clamped his eyes shut. 'I know. And you must know how much I regret that.'

'Had a row, had you?'

'No. It wasn't like that. She wanted – well, she wanted to go out and take some photographs.'

'I thought photography was more your thing? Oh no, that's writing, isn't it? Oh, hang on now, isn't it "event management" or "party organiser" or something like that?'

Blake shot me a glance that said *see what I have to deal with?*

'I do a lot of things, Bill. You know that.'

Bill nodded. 'So I understand. I'm just wondering what you've been doing here in Venice. While Jenny's been out at work. Because the last I heard she had two jobs as well as working on her book.'

'She was very busy, I know. I was very proud of her.'

'And, of course, I was helping her out with the rent. Helping both of you out, of course. Just for a year. Because it was her dream to live here, if only for a while. And so, again, I wonder what you've been doing all this time.'

'I've got lots of projects on the go, Bill. I contribute whatever I can.'

'Oh, I'm sorry, perhaps I was imagining all those phone calls when she was almost in tears, telling me she was finding it difficult to cope.'

Blake threw his hands up and turned away. 'Oh, for Christ's sake.'

'Enjoyed your little ride on my daughter's gravy train, have you? Well, it's over now.' He took a deep breath. 'I want you out of here.'

Blake spun around, jabbing his finger at him. 'This is not fair. And you can't do that.'

'I don't have to do anything. Because there'll be no more money coming from me. Not a penny. So don't come to me next time the rent's due.'

Blake shook his head, and swore under his breath.

'What did you call me?'

'You heard.'

I held my hands up. 'Look, everybody's a bit on edge. Everybody's tired. Why don't we all sit down, eh? I'll make us a coffee.' I tried to lighten the atmosphere. 'Decaff perhaps?'

Nobody laughed. I laid my hand on Whiteread's arm. 'Bill, Matthew's upset as well.'

He shook my hand off. 'Don't say that.'

'Come on, let's sit down and I'll make us all a cup of coffee.'

'I don't want to sit down. I don't want a cup of coffee. What I want,' his face crumpled, 'what I want is my little girl back.' His legs almost collapsed under him and he would have fallen had I not been there to catch him. I lowered him into a chair, where he sat, his body wracked with great, choking sobs.

Blake turned away from us, and rested his head against the window, staring outside at the rain. 'I know you think I'm a waste of space, Mr Whiteread. But I loved her too, you know,' he said, without turning round.

'Come on, Bill,' I said. 'Let's get out of here, and get you settled in to your hotel, eh?'

He nodded, and pulled himself to his feet.

'Goodbye, Matthew,' I said. 'I'll be in touch.'

I clicked the door behind us, leaving Blake standing in silence by the window.

Chapter 20

Bill stopped to look out at the lagoon as we were walking along Fondamente Nove. I wondered if I should suggest he step back a bit from the edge but that would have broken the silence, and I had the impression that he was happy, or at least happier, being alone in his thoughts. So we both stood there and stared out at the grey lagoon, a soft rain falling gently upon us, until he broke the silence.

'What's that?' he asked, pointing towards the nearest island, where cypress trees towered over the walls.

'That's San Michele,' I said.

'Lovely, isn't it?'

I nodded.

'Looks like there's a church there as well. So how many people live there?'

'No one lives there, Bill. It's – well, it's the cemetery.'

'Oh.'

We stood there for a few more minutes, just listening to the sound of the wind and the waves.

'It looks lovely, doesn't it? Peaceful. But I want to get her home. To be with her mam.'

The rain was falling more steadily now, and I turned up

the collar of my coat. Bill seemed oblivious to it, and continued staring out towards the island. Then he shook his head, and snapped out of it.

'You're getting soaked there, Mr Sutherland. You'll catch your death.'

I looked up at the ever-darkening sky. 'It's all right, Bill. Take all the time you want.'

'No, we should be going. Best to get myself checked in and then—' He fell silent.

'Have you got any plans, Bill? Is there anywhere you'd like to go?'

'Well, to be honest, Mr Sutherland, I hadn't really thought.'

'I can meet you any time. If you need someone to show you around.'

'That's kind. Thanks. But I think maybe I'll just check in and have a lie-down for a bit.'

'Is there anyone you need to call? Family or friends?'

He shook his head. 'Well, there's a few people back home of course, but nobody I need to speak to right now. That'll wait.'

'I understand.' We walked on, skirting an abandoned washing machine on the *fondamenta*. 'I'm sorry you're having to see it like this, you know?'

He stopped walking. 'Like what?'

'Well, you know, with it chucking it down with rain and it being grey everywhere. And the streets being full of rubbish.'

He grabbed the lapels of my coat and spun me around, dragging me closer so he could look straight into my eyes. 'Mr Sutherland, my little girl is dead. Never going to see her again. Never going to speak to her again. She won't be

Skyping next Sunday afternoon, or turning up for Christmas. And when my friends ask how Jenny is doing, I won't be able to say she's doing great, or that she's got some posh job in Venice or even that her boyfriend seems like a bit of an arse but at least he seems to make her happy. I'll have to say that my little girl is dead. And then, after a while, they'll just stop talking about her. Trying to be kind, they think. Same as it was after her mam died. But it's not being kind, not really. It means there'll always be a Jenny-shaped hole in things. So, you see, I don't care about all this. I don't care if it's raining or if people are leaving their washing machines in the streets or not. Because my little girl is dead.'

He released his grip, and dropped his hands to his sides. 'I'm sorry,' he muttered.

'No. That was stupid of me. Thoughtless.'

He patted me on the back. 'No, boy, not stupid at all. You're still young, you see.'

I gave a half-laugh. 'I don't feel it, you know.'

'Well, you're young enough, anyway. It's the way we measure our lives out, isn't it? First there's invitations to weddings. And then a few years down the line, there's invitations to baptisms. Then you get asked how your kids are getting on at school. Then about how your parents are. And then, finally, you get asked how *you* are.' He stopped, as if suddenly struck by a thought. 'Must be strange for your parents, though. With you being all the way out over here. They must be dead proud though, I'll bet. Do they come and visit often?'

I shook my head. 'Mum's dead. And Dad – well, I don't know. We haven't spoken in years.'

He patted me on the back again. 'Well now, looks like I'm

being the thoughtless one.' He looked up at the sky. 'And like I said, we'll catch our deaths. Come on.'

We walked on, past the abandoned white goods that lined the *fondamenta*, in the direction of the Hotel Tintoretto. And that's where I left him. Trying to be brave, but alone in the middle of a city where his little girl had met her end, face down in a pool of water.

And I knew, right then, that I was going to find out who had done this.

Part Two

Four Avenging Angels

Chapter 21

Vanni was a good cop. An honest cop. But he, like every other cop in the city, was working at breaking point right now. If I were to help out then, perhaps, Bill Whiteread might be able to take his daughter home sooner rather than later.

What harm could there be in it?

'Opportunistic thief finds young woman alone in a shop late at night with the streets empty. They enter, there's a struggle, and the young woman is killed. Her assailant steals her money and cards before trying, and failing, to force the safe open. They flee, and some time later – we don't know exactly how long – the flooding causes the window to cave in thus attracting the attention of Eduardo and myself.'

I looked down at Gramsci. 'Makes sense, doesn't it, puss? A simple tale of a robbery gone wrong. Makes perfect sense.'

He leapt on to the back of the sofa and scratched away half-heartedly.

'Except, when you think about it, it makes no sense at all, does it? Who sets out to rob a bookshop on the worst night in half a century? For that matter, who sets out to rob a bookshop at all?'

Gramsci curled up and crossed his paws over his eyes.

'Look, stick with me on this, okay? So, who else do we have? Who did she really know in the city? Giles Markham, Fulvio Terzi and Matthew Blake. Oh, and Markham said she knew every priest in town as well, but that might take a while to check out.'

There was no answer from Gramsci, just the regular rise and fall of his chest.

'Yes, you sleep on it. Probably a good idea. I'll work on it in the meanwhile, eh?'

Sex or money, Nathan. It's always one of those.

Well, Giles Markham had plenty of the latter and had seemed to express no particular interest in the former. Matthew Blake, of course, was in need of money. And Fulvio Terzi – well, Markham had described his relationship with Jenny as 'close'. How close?

Nothing about Terzi's online presence made me think he was capable of murder, however. In his early sixties, possessed of slightly raddled good looks that reminded me of the elder Gian Maria Volontè, and perhaps just a little bit too fond of the cravat, he'd graduated in art history from Ca'Foscari University in the late 1970s. He'd been expected to pursue a career in academia, but had turned his back on it in order to take over his father's shop in Calle de la Mandola, buying and selling old books and manuscripts. He thought it was important to continue in the family tradition, he'd said, in an interview with *La Nuova*. And besides, he joked, having a proper job would at least ensure he got out of bed in the morning.

He'd been married, and divorced, twice. Well, I thought, that could happen to anyone. Would it be fair to say that

Fulvio Terzi had an eye for the ladies? He was a good-looking fellow. If you liked that sort of thing.

Jenny Whiteread would have been thirty years younger. Still, Terzi, I imagined, would have been seen as a bit of a catch. Whereas at home was good old Matthew Blake, an aspiring children's writer with all the glittering prospects that being an aspiring children's writer brings with it.

If he's done this, I'll kill him. But what? And who? Terzi? Blake?

Gramsci, to my surprise, hopped up on to the desk.

'I don't call that much of a sleep, puss.' I waved a finger at him. 'Does this mean you've thought of something?'

He pounced on my fingers, drawing an *ow!* from me. He relaxed his grip, just ever so slightly. I knew what this meant. Snatching them back was the challenge. Do it too quickly and his claws would sink in. End result, pain. The trick was to pull them back almost imperceptibly. So slowly that he wouldn't even realise they were moving, until it was too late.

I stared deep into his unblinking eyes, narrowing like Lee Van Cleef's, as I slowly drew my hand back. In my head, I could hear the chimes of the watch from *For a Few Dollars More*.

Almost there.

"Ciao, caro!"

I looked up at the sound of Federica's voice. Only a moment, but it was enough, and I howled as Gramsci's claws sank in. He sat there for a moment, gazing at me in triumph, before propelling himself off the desk like a rocket from a bottle and scattering papers across the room.

'Sorry, were you playing?'

I sucked my fingers. 'It's never playing. Not with him.'

'Sorry,' she repeated. 'Are you working on something?'

'Sort of. I'm working on Fulvio Terzi. Tell me about him, again.'

She shrugged. 'I met him once or twice but I don't really know him. There are people at the Querini who might. I think he's advised them on acquisitions in the past. Old manuscripts and the like.'

'Anything else?'

She shrugged. 'He's probably Venice's most eligible twice-divorced man. But that's a pretty narrow field.'

I nodded. 'Mm-hmm.' I tapped away at the website for the *Pagine Bianche*. 'It seems he lives over near San Giacomo dell'Orio.'

'Oh right. Do you think Dario knows him?'

'Possibly, but he's not been back in Venice that long.' Then I clicked my fingers and got to my feet.

'Where are you going?'

'First of all, I'm going to buy a modest but inoffensive bottle of wine. And then I'm going to have a chat with *zio* Giacomo.'

Federica's sort-of-uncle, Giacomo Maturi, had lived for most of his life in Campo San Giacomo dell'Orio in the *sestiere* of Santa Croce, which technically made him a neighbour of Dario, Vally and Emily. However, whilst he was happy to take a coffee with Dario should they happen to meet in the street, he maintained a respectful distance from them, possibly fearing that he might be called upon, one day, for babysitting duties. He seemed pleased to see me, although surprised and possibly a little suspicious as well.

'My boy, what brings you over here?'

'Oh, *zio* Giacomo, I was just passing by and thought it might be nice to drop in.'

'Hmm.' He sniffed. 'This isn't something that Federica's made you do, is it?'

'No, no. But she's had a tough week. I told her just to put her feet up and relax.'

'I can imagine. Well now.' He checked his watch. 'It's a little early in the day to start drinking, surely?' He took the bottle from me and unwrapped the tissue paper. Gratifyingly, he raised his eyebrows. 'On the other hand, I'll fetch us some glasses.'

Zio Giacomo swirled his wine. 'Not bad. Not bad at all. Now, my boy, what can I do for you?'

'Well now, can't a fellow pay a social call without wanting something?'

Giacomo peered at me over the rim of his glass and twinkled at me – I hoped – just ever so slightly. 'Come on now, out with it.'

'It's about a man called Fulvio Terzi.'

Giacomo nodded. 'I see. And about the young British woman who was found in his shop?'

'That's right.'

'Hmm. Now, might I ask why you're interested in this, Nathan?'

I took a deep breath. 'Well, it's been suggested to me that Terzi might just have been conducting some sort of relationship with her. And so I thought perhaps that was something worth investigating. After all, that might supply a motive and—'

He waved his hand in order to cut me off. 'I see. So you're interfering again.'

'Well, yes.'

He sighed. 'Leave it to the police, my boy, they deal with this sort of thing every day. Well, not every day, one would hope, but my point stands.'

'It's not as easy as that, Giacomo.'

'No?'

'The police will deal with it, yes. But what they don't have to deal with is a distraught father, alone in a foreign city where his daughter was killed, wondering when he'll be able to take her home and bury her. And so I think I've got to interfere.'

'You could end up making things worse, you know?'

'I know. But I'll be careful. I promise.'

'Oh dear, oh dear.' He sighed once more. 'So, go on then. What can I help with?'

'Well, you used to work in the bank in Campo Manin near Terzi's bookshop.'

He closed his eyes as if in pain. 'My boy, I worked at the bank as an archivist. Saying "I worked in the bank" might suggest to people that I worked in high finance. And I think that's a misunderstanding we all want to avoid these days.'

'Sorry.'

'And what have I told you about apologising?'

'I'm— Look, okay, you worked near Terzi's shop for a number of years. He also lives in the *campo*. Do you know him? What's he like?'

'Well, he does live nearby, that's true. Just two buildings down. But I have to say I don't know him.'

'You never went to his shop?'

'No. There were two bookshops on that street. *Signor* Terzi's and Gabriele's. Terzi's was the one I didn't go to.'

'Oh. Any reason?'

'The coffee was better at Gabriele's.'

'So you don't know him at all?'

'I'm afraid not. I know he's well spoken of on the whole, but I'm afraid that's all.'

'On the whole?'

'Indeed. But let's talk about that later. How have you both been this past week, my boy?'

'Oh, we're fine. We're on the second floor as you know, so we got away with it. The entrance hall downstairs needed sweeping out but that was it. We might need to think about replastering it but,' I shrugged, 'what's the point if it has to be redone every twelve months?'

Giacomo nodded, and his eyes filled with sadness. 'Ah, you know, my boy, I was here in 1966. I was a young man then. Very young, I suppose. But I remember wondering if that was the very end of the city.

'It rained for three days, you know? It seemed that it would never stop. For twenty-four hours nothing could get in or out. The city, truly, had never been so cut off since before the construction of the Ponte della Libertà.

'I remember myself, and the other young men in our apartment block, helping to gather up all the children from the surrounding buildings. And we made sure they were all wrapped up warm, and we put them all on a *vaporetto* to sleep. Somewhere we knew they'd be safe. And we made it all a big adventure for them.' His eyes grew misty with the recollection. 'I remember how people came from all over Italy – all over the world – to help. It was, I have to say, profoundly moving. To realise how much this city was loved. And then, of course, there was the shame. We, the Venetians, had let this happen. Over a century of neglect had led to this. *La Serenissima*, the most beautiful city on earth, where the canals now flowed black with the heating oil from flooded buildings. We had let this happen. Through inaction, through greed. And then,' he sighed, 'then we let it happen all over again. And again, I imagine, we'll tell ourselves that something must be done. And nothing will be done. Until it happens once more. Until that day when the water finally wins.' He shook his head. 'So, tell me. How's that benighted bar of yours?'

'The Brazilians? Not so good, I'm afraid. It flooded pretty badly. Eduardo's thinking of perhaps getting out.'

'Ah, I'm sorry to hear that. Do give him my regards. I know it must be difficult.'

'Thanks. I will.' I smiled, trying to lighten the mood. 'Does that mean you'll be popping by for a *tramezzino*?'

'It certainly does not!' He refilled our glasses. 'You know, it's been good to see you again, my boy. It's rather cheered me up after the past week. I've found all this terribly distressing. The same cycle of mistakes. The same excuses we all made half a century ago. "History repeats itself, first as tragedy, second as farce."' He shook his head. 'I think Marx got that one wrong. The second time is tragedy as well.'

'I think you're in danger of becoming morose again, *zio* Giacomo.'

'I am, aren't I? Come on then, tell me more about this ridiculous investigation of yours. That should cheer me up.'

'Well, okay then. Terzi has a boat, I understand.'

'He does, yes. Why the interest?'

'Well, Gabriele – from the bookshop – told me he'd been known to take Jenny out on it.'

Giacomo winced, as if in pain. 'Ah. Something terribly sordid then. I thought it might be. Anyway, yes, he does have a boat and that brings me back to that matter I mentioned earlier.'

'Oh, about *generally* being well thought of?'

'Indeed. There was some unpleasantness a year or two ago. His boat's moored very near here. You head over the bridge towards the Calle del Savio, and it's moored in that colonnaded passage on the Rio de San Zan Degolà. Now that's not an easy place to get a mooring. Not at all.'

'Because in just two minutes you're on the Grand Canal?'

'Exactly. Now a mooring became available two years ago. I believe the previous occupant had died. As you can imagine, there was a great deal of interest in getting that space. But, in the end, it went to Fulvio Terzi.'

'Uh-huh.'

'It wasn't long, though, until rumours started to spread. That Terzi had bribed an official to make sure the mooring went to him.'

I raised my eyebrows. 'I see.'

'More than that. *Signor* Terzi has a very fine boat. Very fine indeed.' He paused. 'Who would have known there was such a good living to be made from bookselling? But this, of course, might merely be malicious gossip.' He smiled at me in a way that said *this is not merely malicious gossip*. 'I hope that's been helpful?'

I got to my feet. 'Immensely. Thank you so much, *zio* Giacomo.'

'A pleasure. Now give my love to lovely Federica. And I hope it won't be too long until the next time.'

'Absolutely. I'll cook.'

'You will?' His face fell. 'Oh well, if you must. Now then,' he wagged a finger at me, 'you're not going to do anything silly, are you?'

'Me? Oh no, absolutely not.'

'Good. Good. You're a married man now. Responsibilities and all that.' He patted me on the back. 'It's been good to see you again, Nathan.'

'It's been a pleasure.' I paused for a moment. '*Zio* Giacomo, you have a boat, don't you?'

'I certainly do.'

I kept my voice as light as possible. 'And is it moored nearby?'

'Oh no.' He smiled at me. 'As I said, it's very difficult to get a mooring around here.'

Chapter 22

It was starting to get dark now, but not quite dark enough for what I had in mind. I thought of calling Dario, on the off chance he might be free for a quick beer, but he would, I knew, try to talk me out of it.

I walked around the outside of the great church that gave the square its name, and over the bridge that led to the Calle del Savio. Terzi's boat was not difficult to spot. Nineteen-sixties, Riva-style, a gorgeous thing in polished wood that stood out amongst the barges and rough-and-ready boats that, I imagined, were used for business rather than pleasure. I looked back over my shoulder. Terzi's apartment was perhaps two minutes away. And two minutes in his boat would take him out on to the Grand Canal.

No wonder Jenny Whiteread had been out with him. If he'd asked me I'd have said yes as well.

The nearby *Al Bagolo* did the best *cicheti* in the campo and a more than reasonable spritz. They usually had the newspapers as well so I could while away a bit of time there. I texted Federica. *'Might be back late. Love you.'* My phone plinged back almost immediately. *'Me too. And you too.'* Followed by another one. *'PS Do not do anything stupid.'* I smiled and tucked my phone away, confident in the knowledge that I would not be doing anything stupid for at least an hour.

Two children were riding their bikes in circles around the *campo* under the watchful eye of Dad who, yawning and checking his watch, decided that that was probably enough for today.

'Simone! Alice! Come on, time for dinner!'

'Aw, Dad, do we have to?'

'Just five more minutes?'

'Oh well, looks like I'm getting your pizza tonight as well then.' He patted his stomach. 'Lucky me!'

He started to make his way across the *campo*. The two kids exchanged a glance. He was, in all likelihood, bluffing. But could they take that risk? Then, as one, they sped off after him.

I smiled. Campo San Giacomo dell'Orio, where kids still played football in the street and rode bicycles. Dario had chosen a good part of town to live in.

I was thinking about what *cicheti* I might have without spoiling my dinner or, more importantly, making Federica jealous, when the door to Terzi's apartment block opened and Matthew Blake came out.

He looked quickly to the left and then to the right before deciding there was no point in pretending he hadn't seen me. Silence hung in the air between us for a moment.

'I suppose this means we're going to have a difficult conversation,' he said.

I nodded. 'Looks like we are.'

'Spritz?'

Blake nodded.

'Campari or Aperol?'

'*Select*, if they've got it.'

I nodded. I'd never got on with *Select*. A Venetian *aperitivo*, I'd always felt it suffered in comparison with the more famous Campari. To my taste, it lacked something of an edge, and whilst the purists might have claimed that it made the most authentic spritz, that wasn't enough for me. Crucially, it was an *amaro* that wasn't quite as *amaro* as you might like. Federica, of course, told me I was overthinking this.

'Jen always preferred it. So I kind of got into the habit as well,' said Blake, as if he could read my thoughts.

'Oh,' I said, and tried to smile. 'Would you like anything to eat?'

'I might have a *tramezzino*. Just tuna and egg. Or are you going to disapprove of my choice of sandwiches as well?' I was about to speak, but he smiled and waved my apologies away. 'No, it's all right. I'm very good at body language.'

'One of the things about being a writer, I suppose?'

'Exactly. It's not all clouds and daffodils you know.'

'Shall we take these outside?' I said, nodding towards the door.

'It's a bit cold.'

'Oh, awkward conversations are always best held outdoors. Besides, I thought you might like to smoke.' I smiled. 'I'm quite good at body language as well.'

We made our way outside, under the gaze of the barman who might once have been incredulous but had long since become used to foreigners who were seemingly impervious to the cold.

'So,' I said, as I pulled my coat around me. 'Why don't

you start by telling me exactly what you were doing at Fulvio Terzi's apartment?'

Blake gave a very thin smile. 'Well now. Why don't you start by telling me what you were doing there?'

'Me? I was on my way here.'

'This isn't exactly your part of the city though, is it?'

'No, but my best friend lives here and so does my sort-of uncle-in-law.' Matthew looked confused. 'It's complicated.'

Blake reached for his cigarettes and lit up. I'd have pushed my chair back, but then remembered what he'd said about body language. He dragged on his cigarette and then turned away to exhale in a failed attempt to keep the smoke out of my face. His hand was shaking, just ever so slightly, but that could, of course, have been the cold.

'So what were you doing there, Matthew?'

'I just wanted a chat with him.'

'That's really not a smart thing to do.'

'It isn't?'

'Look. It's just that,' I took a deep breath, 'I've heard stuff about Terzi and Jenny and, basically, well, what I've heard, and I don't know if any of this is true, is—'

He saved me the trouble. 'That she was shagging him?'

I winced.

'I think I knew.'

'I'm sorry.'

He shrugged. ''S'all right. It's something else to forget about this poxy city.'

'Look at it this way, Matthew. You're the guy whose girl-friend was having some sort of relationship with Fulvio Terzi. It doesn't matter whether she was or not. What matters is that people think she might have been. Do you see where I'm going with this?'

Blake said nothing, but exhaled slowly, this time making no effort to blow the smoke away from me. I pushed my chair back. To hell with body language.

'Which is why,' I continued, 'going round to his house for a little chat is a really bad idea. Especially given that you said it wouldn't be pleasant if you caught up with him. So, do I take it *signor* Terzi is still alive and well and in good spirits?'

'He wouldn't answer the door to me.'

'Good. Well done, sensible *signor* Terzi. And lucky for you that nothing kicked off and he didn't make a complaint leading to the police starting to think that Jennifer Whiteread's boyfriend seems to be prone to violent behaviour.'

'I wouldn't have done anything. Really. You know how you just say things you don't mean at times. Under stress, when you get emotional.'

I nodded. 'I know. As I said, I'll do what I can for you within the limits of what the Consulate is actually authorised to do. Which, I'm afraid, is not very much. So right now doing nothing would be the smart thing to do. Let the police deal with this. Be a good guy. If they want to speak with you, fine. Give me a call. I'll get you a lawyer and a translator.'

He nodded. 'Why are you doing this?'

'You're a British citizen, Matthew. Which means I'll do what I can to help you. But you need to help me as well.'

'Okay. So where do I start?

I smiled. 'I guess you can start by paying for these.'

Chapter 23

I checked my watch. Six-thirty. Federica would be home in about two hours. This gave me approximately thirty minutes to do something illegal, followed by a leisurely walk home, time to start preparing dinner, a spritz, and a suitably tactful response to the question, 'So, what have you been up to today?'

Fulvio Terzi, I reminded myself, had almost certainly done nothing wrong. And so, I thought, I really shouldn't be breaking into his boat. Yet there was the card found in her bag that matched the photo on his desk. 'Angels for an angel.' And Jenny, according to Markham and Gabriele, was a 'close' friend of Terzi and had spent a lot of time on his boat.

It wasn't much to go on. And there were better ways – more *legal* ways – of spending a cold, wet November evening. Nevertheless, Fulvio Terzi had a close relationship with the murdered woman who had been found in his shop. It might just be worth checking out.

I've never known much about boats but it seemed to me that Terzi was a man of more than a little wealth and some considerable taste. The *Leopardi* had a pleasingly retro look to it, reminiscent of the days when boats still looked like proper boats.

There was no tarpaulin in place, which seemed strange given the weather and the fact that the boat was evidently expensive. I stepped on board, a little clumsily, setting it rocking. I stretched my hand out to try the handle on the cabin door, and then froze.

Someone was moving inside. Terzi, of course. That explained the missing tarpaulin. Should I call out to him, or just beat a hasty retreat?

'*Signor* Terzi,' I called out.

The movement stopped.

'*Signor* Terzi,' I called again.

The door suddenly flew open, hitting me in the face and sending me staggering backwards. A hooded figure leapt out of the cabin, a black briefcase in his hand, and made to jump on to the *fondamenta*.

I managed to grab his foot, sending him sprawling on to the ground and the briefcase skittering towards the edge of the canal. He kicked backwards, enough for him to free himself from my grasp, and was up and running before I could catch my breath.

The kick must have thrown him off balance as he fell once more and slid across the *fondamenta*, stretching for the briefcase but succeeding only in tipping it into the canal. He didn't even pause to see if he could rescue it, but got to his feet and pelted off around the corner before I could even get to my feet.

I sat there in the wildly rocking boat, trying to catch my breath, then brushed myself down and stood up, a little shakily. Nobody seemed to be around. The weather was keeping everyone indoors.

This hadn't gone as expected. I'd thought I would have a quiet look round on deck for God knows what, and then return home for dinner, satisfied that I had done some 'investigating'. But this now felt serious. If I went in – given the cabin door was unlocked – was I actually committing a crime?

I shrugged. Stupid to stand here in the rain and not do the one thing I'd come out for, especially now that someone had gone to the trouble of doing my work for me.

I pulled the cabin door open and stepped inside. My hand hovered over what looked like a light switch. Should I turn it on? Perhaps not. Better not to draw any more attention to myself than necessary. I switched my phone light on instead, shielding it with my hand.

The cuddy was small and cramped, as expected, and barely high enough to stand in. Nevertheless, it was well equipped, and held two banquettes that looked as if they'd convert into beds, with a cabinet between them. A stove stood near the cabin entrance, with a kettle on the hob.

I smiled to myself. I'd never stayed overnight on a boat before, but Fulvio Terzi's made it look as if it might be fun. As long as I remembered to be careful whenever I stood up.

Nothing seemed to be disturbed. But somebody had been here before me. And for what? I sighed. This was pointless. I don't know what I expected to find, but there was nothing here, nothing that looked as if it shouldn't be.

I opened a couple of drawers in the cabinet and then swore as I realised that I'd have left fingerprints. Multiple fingerprints, now I thought about it. Where else had I touched? The door? The light switch? Or had I actually touched that, I couldn't remember? I would, I reflected, have made a particularly rubbish thief.

Whatever. It was too late now. I might as well carry on. Vanni, I was sure, would understand. Well, probably understand.

I tried another drawer in the cabinet. There was a half-empty packet of cigarettes inside, and a few papers stuck together with a folded Post-It note.

The top sheet was an image of a woodcut or an etching, possibly cut from a book or magazine. The details weren't easy to make out in the darkness, and I wondered once more if I should risk the light. I decided against it and persevered as best I could with the light from my telephone.

In the background of the image stood the figure of God, flanked by two angels. The foreground was harder to make out. A battlefield, perhaps? A battlefield, or at least a field of the dead and dying, laid waste by four angelic figures wielding swords. The style looked familiar to me, yet the name of the artist wouldn't come to mind.

Angels . . .

I picked away at the Post-It with my nails, prising it apart carefully, and peered at the message scrawled upon it.

Dearest Fulvio. Take a look at this. Please let me know what you think. J xx

Jenny? Of course.

I re-tacked the Post-It around the papers as best I could. I was about to replace it in the drawer when the thought struck me that it might be good to take a copy of the image. I snapped off a quick photograph and then cursed when the light flared in the enclosed space. Too quick though, surely, for anyone to notice? Time, then, to make my way home, admit to Federica what I'd been up to and attempt to cook something spectacular by way of apologising.

I got to my feet without thinking, and cracked my head on the roof of the cabin.

'Shit,' I cried out, and slumped back down on the sofa, rubbing my head as I waited for the pain to ease.

Then the cabin light flicked on, revealing a figure in the doorway.

'I hope you haven't hurt yourself, Mr Sutherland,' said Fulvio Terzi.

Chapter 24

'You know, I can probably explain this,' I said.

Terzi didn't move. 'Why not explain it to the police?' he said.

'I'd rather explain it to you if I could. It'll save everyone a lot of bother.'

He nodded, made his way inside, and sat down on the banquette opposite.

'So. Go on then.'

'I was passing by and noticed the boat was uncovered. That struck me as being a bit strange, given the weather. And there was an intruder on board. Whoever it was ran off down the *fondamenta* with a briefcase in their hand. Anyway, we had bit of a fight and it ended up in the canal. I'm sorry, but if that was yours, you've lost it.'

He frowned. 'A briefcase? I wouldn't keep anything valuable on here. A boat isn't that difficult to break into. As you've just discovered.'

'You don't seem too worried?'

He shrugged. 'Nothing in here worth stealing. Anyway, Mr Honorary Consul, why don't you tell me why you happened to be in this part of town and how you just happened to recognise my boat?'

'I was visiting my wife's uncle. He lives a couple of doors along from you.'

'Oh yes?'

'Giacomo Maturi. Perhaps you know him?'

He shook his head. 'I don't know him. I know of him though. So I suppose I can believe that. Strange, though, that it happened to be my boat you were passing by.'

'I'm interested in boats.'

'And that I don't believe.'

'Okay then, I'll be honest. Gabriele from the bookshop on the Street of the Assassins told me you'd been known to take Jenny out on the boat a number of times.'

'I'm allowed to do that.'

'I know. I just found it interesting, that's all. I also found it interesting that Matthew Blake was calling on you earlier this evening.'

'Mr Sutherland, you seem to make a habit of being in the right place at the right time.'

'I guess I'm just lucky that way.'

'Anyway, if you really want to know, Mr Blake's business with me seemed to be the shouting of abuse through the door. I didn't think it was necessary to let him in. I could get the gist of it from my sofa.'

'I'm sorry. He's been through a lot.'

'Of course. I am sorry for him, you know?'

'But you were seeing his girlfriend.'

He sighed. 'Well, that just kind of happened. I don't think anybody plans for these things. But if you really want to know about it, I suppose there's no harm in telling you. Drink?'

'What, here?'

'Oh yes. I don't think this is a conversation to have in a bar. Whisky okay?'

I nodded and he took a half-empty bottle down from the bottom of the cabinet, along with two plastic cups. J&B again. 'It started in London two years ago.'

Chapter 25

Running again.

The alarm didn't go off because you decided to have just one more with the girls and forgot to set it, and now you're going to be late and Idiot Boss is going to be cross and you haven't even got a cup of coffee inside you to make it even vaguely bearable.

And to make it worse, to make it just that little bit worse, the bloody bus is pulling away from the kerb, and if you miss that it's another fifteen minutes until the next one which will most certainly mean the Disappointed Eyes of the Idiot Boss, possibly escalating to a Sad Shake of the Head and perhaps even a Pursing of Lips.

But you might, just might, be able to make it, if you get a bit of a head of steam on. So you run and run and run, your coat flapping and briefcase swinging at your side.

And then, suddenly, you're airborne and, for a moment, you're the little girl flying through the air in a field again. But this time the sky is grey, and the ground is cold and hard; enough to draw a shriek out of you as you land and your briefcase goes skittering across the pavement.

A woman screams, thinking you're about to fall into the traffic, and you try to raise yourself to your knees, to tell her that it's okay, but the breath has been knocked out of you and the words won't come.

'Are you all right?' A man's voice. 'Take it easy. Can you stand?'

You nod. 'I think so.' The palms of your hands are grazed and your knee is throbbing. You look down at your coat. It's seen better days. If your phone still works, you'll call in with a sickie, and Idiot Boss can find someone else to be disappointed in.

The stranger hooks a hand under your elbow and helps you to your feet. Stars dance in front of your eyes for a moment, but then everything clears. 'Thank you.'

He smiles. 'No problem. Look, your stuff's gone everywhere, just give me a moment.'

You look down and see that your briefcase has flown open, strewing papers, pens, packets of sweets, yesterday's unread news-paper and a near-empty packet of cigarettes across the pavement. Passers-by make great show of stepping over or around them, but Guardian Angel – as you've decided to call him – scurries around collecting everything that he possibly can. A sheet of paper is carried away by the wind but he chases it along the street until he's able to retrieve it.

He holds them together as best he can and makes to pass them over to you. Then he pauses, and nods at the image on the top sheet. 'You're an artist?'

You laugh. It hurts a bit so you decide not to do it again. 'No, I just like to draw.' You make air quotes with your fingers, before remembering that you really hate people who do that. 'I'm a Visual Resource Curator.'

'My goodness. I'm impressed.'

'You know what that is?' In spite of yourself, you laugh once

more. *'I think you must be the first one. I've been telling my dad what I do for a living for about five years now and I still have to re-explain it every time we meet.'*

'Yes, I know what it is.' He smiles. *'So tell me, where do you curate your visual resources?'*

'UCL.'

He whistles. *'I'm impressed.'*

'Well, don't be. It's not quite as glamorous as that.'

'Looking to change?'

'Love to. But,' you shake your head and that hurts a bit as well so you decide not to do that again either, *'I've got a BA in Art History and a PhD in Joshua Reynolds. That kind of limits what I can do.'*

'Reynolds.' He nods to himself. *'Look, I'm not saying I can do anything, but here are my details.'* He reaches into his coat and takes out a business card. *'Give me a call any time.'* He checks his watch. *'And now I really do have to run.'* He gives you a gentle pat on the shoulder, turns, and makes his way along the street. Then he stops, and turns once more. *'Oh, and you really should take the day off. That coat needs dry-cleaning if nothing else.'*

You look down at his business card.

Fulvio Terzi. Fine Art Consultant. London and Venice.

You tap the card against your palm before dropping it inside your handbag. Your mobile is buzzing. Idiot Boss, already. But that can wait.

Venice . . .

Chapter 26

Terzi drained his glass. 'We met each other a number of times. I liked her. I could tell she was smart. And so I got her the job with Markham.'

'You gave her a job because she was smart and you liked her?'

He shrugged. 'Sure. What better way to do it? Markham said he needed somebody else to help out with the Foundation. And I found somebody by accident. Jenny was keen. Really super-keen. She had this idea for a book about angels which she was going to work on at the same time.'

'Always angels,' I said.

'It happens, in the art world. People specialise in the most minute things. Angels aren't really all that special. I've met authorities on halos for example, but,' he smiled, 'try telling a publisher you want to write an art book about halos and you'll be waiting a long time until you retire on the royalties.'

He topped my glass up again. I would have refused, but I was facing a long walk home on a cold, wet evening and figured the J&B would take the edge off.

I shivered. 'Any chance we could have some heating on in here?'

Terzi shook his head. 'Too dangerous. The heater needs servicing. Risk of carbon monoxide poisoning. It happens every year, you know. People forget, go away for the evening, put the heater on to keep warm. And never wake up again.'

I pulled my coat around myself. 'So anyway. Venice. How did Matthew feel about it?'

'Who knows? But I don't imagine it's a hard sell if someone asks if you'd like to live in Venice for a couple of years.'

'Do you know him?'

'Not really.'

'Never taken him out on the boat?'

'No.'

'Any reason why not?'

'Because I didn't want to have sex with him.'

There wasn't very much I could say to that. I shook my head. 'Christ.'

'So then, Mr Nathan Sutherland. British Honorary Consul in Venice. Have I answered all your questions to your satisfaction?'

I shrugged. 'I guess there's not much more to say.'

'Oh good. Well now, I've had some dealings with the Italian Consular Service in the past and private sleuthing doesn't seem to be one of their responsibilities. May I ask why it's one of yours?'

I sighed. 'It isn't. Not really. But her father is here, right now, in this city. He doesn't know when he's going to be able to bury his daughter. It could drag on for weeks. Months. And yes, I know I'm not a cop. I'm not even a proper consul. But if there's anything I can do to at least give him some closure on this, then I'm going to do it.'

Terzi closed his eyes, and rubbed them, ever so gently. Then he nodded. 'I understand,' he said. 'Look, I don't know why I'm telling you this. Maybe I should just go straight to the police, but there's no proof of anything at all.' He took a deep breath. 'I think there's a problem with Markham. I don't know exactly what it is. But I think Jenny had found something. There's something not right about the way that organisation is being run.'

'Such as?'

He rubbed his forehead. 'Jenny thought there was money that couldn't be accounted for. Now, I can't be sure about that. Neither could she, to be honest. But there seemed to be irregularities. Money coming in not equalling money going out. As simple as that.'

'Admin costs? Staff costs? I assume you and Jenny get some sort of payment from Markham.'

'Not enough to cover the differences we're talking about. And there were other things. Projects that never quite came to completion or that seemed to have been done on the cheap.'

I nodded. 'Fulvio, did Markham know that Jenny knew any of this?'

He sighed. 'I don't know, Mr Sutherland. I just don't know.'

Chapter 27

Bill Whiteread knocked on my door at eight the following morning.

'Hello, Nathan,' he coughed, awkwardly. 'Sorry if I'm being any bother. It's just I thought there's, well, there's something you might be able to help me with.'

I didn't usually hold surgeries on Monday mornings, and never at eight o'clock, but neither was I going to turn away a bereaved father on his own in the middle of an unfamiliar city.

'No problem at all,' I said.

Fede smiled at him, and kissed me on the cheek.

'I need to go, okay? See you later, *caro*.'

'Have a good day, *cara mia*.'

'What have you got planned?'

'Dario phoned. He wants me to go over and help him clear out his *magazzino*.'

'Does he? Or does he just want his pal to come over for a token amount of clearing, followed by beers?'

'Well, yes, it could be that.' She was, I noticed, wrapped up in multiple layers. 'Is the heating back on at the Querini yet?'

She shook her head.

'You'll be frozen. I'll make us *stufato di vitello* for dinner. With polenta. It'll get some warmth back into you.'

'Thank you, *tesoro*. See you later.' She turned to Bill. 'Nice to meet you, Mr Whiteread. I hope everything goes as well as it can over the next couple of days.'

He smiled, as best he could. 'Thank you, *signora*.'

Fede bent down to scratch Gramsci behind the ears. He made to scratch her, but succeeded only in snagging his claws in her mittens. Frantically, he wrenched them this way and that, rolling over in an attempt to free himself. Then, as if to indicate that this was, of course, precisely what he had intended to do, he stalked from the room.

'Bye-bye, unfriendly cat,' said Fede, and waved goodbye to us.

Bill smiled at me. 'Been married long?'

'Just over a year.'

'I thought so. I can tell, you know. Good years.'

'Can I get you a coffee, Bill? Moka or capsule?'

He looked a little embarrassed. 'I don't suppose you have any instant?'

I shook my head.

'It's just I don't think I'll ever get used to these tiny cups everyone uses.' He frowned. 'Sorry, that sounded rude.'

'Not at all. Tell you what, Bill, what if I take you out for a late breakfast? I'll find somewhere that'll serve you a proper British-sized cup.'

'Sorry. Is this a bit pathetic?'

'Not at all. But if you don't mind, I'll stand at the other end of the bar and pretend I don't know you.'

He looked worried for a moment, but then got the joke and smiled.

'Now then, Bill. You didn't just come out here for breakfast, did you?'

He took a deep breath. 'No.'

'Okay. What can I do for you?'

'It's just—' His voice caught in his throat, and I instinctively pushed over to him the box of tissues that I kept on the desk for these occasions. He blew his nose. 'Thank you. It's just that I'm starting to wonder why I came over here. I mean, it was nice to see where Jenny lived. And then I went for a walk last night. I didn't feel like dinner. Then I just went back to my hotel and – well – I wondered what I should do next.'

I could imagine. The loneliness of a hotel room for one, surfing through the TV channels in a language you didn't understand, in the hope of finding something you recognised.

'Anyway, I was thinking . . . maybe it would be good to see where, you know, where it happened.'

I nodded. I'd wondered as much. 'Are you sure, Bill?'

'No,' he half laughed. 'I'm not sure at all. But I am sure that if I don't see it and then I go home, I'll regret it. But, um,' he drummed his fingers on the table, 'I'm not sure if I can do it on my own. And so I was wondering if you'd come with me.'

'Sure. Of course I will. And then we'll find somewhere for breakfast, eh?'

He blew his nose again. 'I'm sorry, I'm probably taking up so much of your time. I'm sure you've got better things to be doing.'

'Well, I'm working on a translation for a PhD student. *Fate versus Free Will in* The Decameron. But, given that Boccaccio hasn't been with us for over six hundred years, I'm sure it's nothing so important that it won't wait until after breakfast. Come on.'

There was, of course, little to see. Terzi – or someone – had arranged for the windows to be boarded up, and black and yellow 'Do not cross' tape had been fixed across the door by the police.

Bill placed the palm of his right hand on the door, and rested his forehead there, murmuring something under his breath. I stood back to give him some space. The street was busy, even at this hour of the morning, and passers-by would occasionally turn their heads to look at him before moving on.

He straightened up again, rubbing his eyes. 'Sorry. Not quite sure how I expected to feel, to be honest.'

I nodded.

'You were here, weren't you? You found her?' he continued.

'I did.'

'How was it? I mean, how was she?' His voice was shaking, just a little.

'It was dark, Bill. There wasn't much to see. There were two of us. Me, and Eduardo from the bar downstairs. And she was just floating there. Face down. I tried giving her the kiss of life but it was too late. I'm sorry.'

'Yes, I know. But how was she?'

I took a deep breath. 'She was just cold. We thought she was just unconscious at first.'

'Cold,' he murmured, and shivered, pulling his coat tight around him. He closed his eyes for a few moments, nodding to himself.

He opened his eyes again. 'So it could have been an accident? That's what you're saying?'

I shook my head. 'I'm sorry. That's what we thought. But the police are certain that,' I fumbled for the least horrible words, and failed, 'she was attacked.'

'But if they're wrong? Couldn't she just have fallen?'

'I'm sorry.'

'You keep saying that.' His voice was rising, and one or two passers-by turned their heads for longer than felt comfortable. 'Because if she'd just fallen or something, then we could have her back home, couldn't we? I could have my little girl back again?'

There was no point trying to dance around this any longer. 'Bill, she was hit on the back of the head with some sort of blunt object. That's what killed her. Not the fall. I am so sorry, but your daughter was murdered.'

'Then I'm never going to get her home, am I?' He was crying now. 'I've read about this in the papers. Italian police, Italian bureaucracy. I'm never going to get her home, am I?'

'We will, Bill. I promise you that. We'll get her home.'

He shook his head, and then his face crumpled. He clutched at the door and, for a moment, I was afraid he was going to fall.

I slipped an arm under his shoulders and hugged him, and held him there as he wept on my shoulder. I became aware that people were staring at us.

'*Signori.*' The speaker was a young man. 'Is something wrong? Can I help?'

I shook my head. Because, of course, there was nothing to be done.

Chapter 28

'Sorry about that. Sometimes, I'm okay, you know. Like when her mother died. I could go for hours, maybe longer, without even thinking about it. And then it happens.

'I still go swimming, you know? Every day if I can. And you've got to be careful. It might only be the Gower, but you've got to watch out for rip tides. And I remember one day – wasn't all that long ago now – being pulled out to sea. And you fight and you fight against it, and the shore is getting further and further away. So much so, you can't even keep your eyes on it any more. All there is is the sea, just the water around you, and you panic that if you stop moving it'll drag you down.' He paused. 'Surfer saw me in the end and got me to land. Young fellow he was, of course, and I felt like a silly old fool. But that's what it's like. Grief, I mean. It comes out of nowhere on a sunny day, snatches you away from land and that's it. Can't breathe any more. You're drowning.' He tapped his spoon against his coffee cup. 'God, listen to me, eh?'

I'd walked Bill back along Calle de la Mandola, to the Street of the Assassins and into the Magical Brazilians. I'd sat him down in the corner and let him cry to himself whilst I walked over to Ed and ordered two *caffè corretti* with grappa.

I wasn't sure it was the sort of coffee that Bill would enjoy, but I was pretty sure it was the sort he needed. Neither was I sure of the advisability of giving alcohol to someone in a fragile emotional state, but I couldn't think of anything else to do.

'This is pretty good, you know?'

'Is it helping?'

'It is. For now.'

'Would you like another?'

'Do you advise it?'

'Right now, I think it's a good idea.'

'Okay then. Just the one, mind. I know how this stuff works. Brings all the sunshine back for a while, and then it brings the black dogs a few hours later.'

I turned around and held two fingers up to Ed. He mouthed the words 'Is everything all right?' at me, and I mouthed 'I think so' back at him.

'Tell me about Jenny, Bill.'

He raised an eyebrow. 'Well, I will if you want. But why?'

'Because I want to know?'

'Is this part of your job, Nathan?'

'Not at all.'

'I mean – and I'm not being nasty here, don't misunderstand me – do you do this for everyone? Not just the daft, lonely old men?'

'No.' I sipped at my coffee, enjoying the sweetness of too much sugar and the burn of the alcohol. 'It's just that you're my first one.'

'Sorry?'

'You're my first one, Bill. You know, I've lost count of the number of people I've had to deliver bad news to. Someone's been hospitalised, been robbed, been arrested. And,' I sighed, 'sometimes worse things than that.

'But all of this was over the phone. Suddenly you're here. In person. And so I don't really know what to do, Bill. I'm finding my way here. So, as I said. Tell me about Jenny.'

His eyes were still red, but he was smiling now. 'What is there to say? Pain in the neck, sometimes, to be honest, but then I'm told they can all be. She had to grow up fast. Her mam died when she was barely thirteen. Now, when something like that happens you can do one of two things. You can go to pieces, and maybe crawl into a bottle.' He nodded to himself. 'I thought of that, more than once or twice. Or you just carry on, one day at a time. Holding yourself together for your little girl. And, of course, she did the exact same thing for her old man.

'She was always a bright little thing. Never worked too hard at school because she didn't have to.' He grinned. 'We usually hate people like that, don't we? And she always wanted to be an artist, which is where I went a bit wrong with her to be honest. Telling her it wasn't a steady job. Wasn't even a proper job. I regret that now, of course.'

'She got there in the end, though.'

'She did, but maybe if she'd done what she always wanted to do she wouldn't have found herself in a job that she never tired of telling me she hated. And we wouldn't have had this conversation that started with "Dad, I'm going to Venice to write about angels."' He took a deep breath. 'And so we wouldn't be having this conversation now.'

'You thought it was a mad idea?'

'Of course. I told her it was crazy, and she was throwing

up a perfectly good job and that nobody expects to like what they do for work anyway. That's why it's called work. But then,' he took another deep breath, 'I asked her what she was going to be earning. I asked her what it would cost to spend a year in a city like Venice. And then I looked at the difference and decided I could cover it for a year. If that was really what her heart was set on, then I'd do it.'

I nodded, and smiled. 'Bet she was thrilled, yeah?'

He grinned. 'You should have seen her face, Nathan. Made it all worthwhile. They say money can't buy you happiness, but maybe it can buy you a few moments like that.'

I paused, swirling the dregs of my coffee. 'What about Matthew?' I said.

'What about him?'

'You don't like him, evidently.'

'I just think he's a waste of space, that's all. But then I suppose nobody's ever good enough.'

'To be fair, I don't think anyone makes much money as a writer.'

He laughed, hollowly. '"Writer" this week, is it? Let me see, I think when we met he was a photographer. Then a "party organiser", if that's a job. I think he might have been writing some poetry at some point, but I don't think that lasted more than a week. Anyway, my hopes of him contributing to the household budget were not high, shall we say? I did hope, perhaps, that she might meet a nice Italian boy but it seems that wasn't to be.'

'How long had they been together?'

'Couple of years, now. She went to an opening of his. Yes, he had an exhibition of his photographs on, at a proper gallery and everything. Drinks, snacks, jazz band playing in the corner. *Vernissage*, they call it. Of course, it turned out he'd paid for it all himself. Just a vanity project. Anyway, that was his hobby of the week and he moved on to other things.

'The thing is, he's a good-looking swine in his own way. I know that. And he can be charming and he can be funny. But he's a chancer.'

'He must be getting money from somewhere?'

'Trustafarian, as I understand. Only thing is, Mummy and Daddy aren't around any more. So having burned his way through their cash, he moved on to mine.' He sniffed. 'And there seemed to be no way to help Jenny out without helping him out at the same time. But that's over now. When this month's rent has gone he can do what he likes.'

'He's grieving as well, Bill.'

'Is he now?'

'It hits us all in different ways.'

'I know that. Oh, I know that. And in a way, I hope he is. Because if he's hurting – really hurting – that would at least mean he's being honest with us. Because, I tell you this, I would really, really like to know what happened that night and where the hell he was.'

I nodded. 'I know that, Bill. And so would I.'

Chapter 29

Matthew is shooting things again.

You close the door, a little louder than necessary, just so he knows you've arrived.

'Hi babes!' he says, without turning around.

You kiss the top of his head, and slip an arm around him.

'Good day?' you say.

He nods, but his eyes don't move from the screen and his fingers are moving furiously over the control pad in his hands.

'Good? Great! I've been following this guy around all day and now I've shot him and stolen all his magic items!'

'That's nice, Matty.'

'Sorry? Too much information?' He taps away at the controller and the action on screen freezes. 'Sit down, I'll make you a cup of tea.'

You smile back at him, and hold up the Oddbins bag in front of you. 'I thought maybe we'd have something stronger. Something to celebrate with.'

'You don't mean?'

You can't hold it in any longer and jump up and down on the spot. 'I got the job!'

'You're kidding?'

'Absolutely not. I heard at lunchtime and so this afternoon I went straight into Idiot Boss's office and told her where she could stick her rotten job.'

He takes the bag from you. 'Champagne, then?'

You laugh. 'No, prosecco of course.'

'More appropriate?'

'No. Just cheaper.'

'So when do we leave? I've always wanted to go to Florence.'

You pick up a cushion from the back of the sofa and clout him around the head. 'Venice, silly! V E N I C E. Remember?'

'I'm only joking. So, remind me again, what's this job all about?'

'Spending other people's money!'

'Fantastic. That sounds like my ideal job.'

'Yes, I thought that too. Come on, help me find some glasses.'

You find two champagne flutes that just about match. They'll do. You pick and tug at the foil wrap on the bottle with your fingernails, worrying away at it until it comes free. There must be a knack to this, you think, and then you smile thinking about how much time you'll have to acquire it.

The bottle isn't as chilled as it might be and so the cork explodes upwards, bouncing off the ceiling, whilst warm prosecco sprays everywhere. Neither of you care, as you clink glasses and hug as best you can.

'Come on then, tell me more.'

'It's an organisation run by a man called Giles Markham. His father died about five years ago and he set up a charitable foundation in his memory. Basically they give money to people for restoration projects. Only, of course, they can't just give money to everyone, so each request has to be properly analysed. Is this a *good use of the foundation's money, is it feasible given the amount of money available? That sort of thing.'*

'And that's a full-time job?'

'Well, not quite. Giles deals with fundraising, that sort of thing. That does sound like a full-time job. But I'll just be working for him a couple of days a week. I filter out those requests that seem feasible, talk it over with him and then he signs the cheque.'

'Wow. You really are going to be spending a rich man's money.'

'I know.' You sip at your prosecco.

'This is one of the jobs they don't tell you about at school, isn't it?'

'It absolutely is.'

'So what are you going to do with the rest of your time?'

'Well, this is what's so perfect. I'll have all that time to work on my book.'

'Oh yes. Your Angels of Florence *thing.'*

'I'll clonk you again as soon as I get my hands on a cushion. The Angels of Venice. *Although, if it sells well, maybe I'll do an* Angels of Florence *as a sequel.'*

He grins, and then a thought strikes him and he looks serious. 'Venice is expensive though, right? Can we manage on you just working a few days a week?'

You had, in all truth, been expecting this and make light of it. 'Well, if I'm going to be a famous struggling author, I'm going to need you to keep me in the style to which I'm accustomed.'

'Oh. But I don't speak Italian.'

'You'll pick it up. And I'm sure there's lots of things you can do. Teaching English, maybe. Or bar work. They must need lots of English speakers during the summer.'

'Bar work?'

'Or – and I did think about this – Giles has a couple of rental properties in the city. He said perhaps you might be able to help him out in managing them.'

'What does that involve?'

'Oh, showing people around, picking up the keys when they leave. Maybe a little light cleaning.'

'Cleaning? Seriously?'

'Don't go all precious on me, darling. You can't just lie around on the sofa drinking prosecco for a year.'

'I can't?' He pretends to sulk, but you can't be one hundred per cent sure if it's just an act.

'No, absolutely you can't.' You pause, and then smile. 'And besides . . . well, I've spoken to Dad and . . .'

'He came up trumps?'

You nod. He puts down his glass, then picks you up and spins you around. He kisses you hard on the lips, holding your face in his hand.

'I bloody love you, Jenners!'

'I love you too, Matty.'

'But I tell you what, I think I love your dad even more.'

'Don't be silly.'

'No, I'm serious. He might just have saved me from twelve months of indentured servitude.'

'I'm serious about you working, though. Seriously serious. Dad's giving me an allowance.' You frown. 'Oh God, I'm in my thirties and I'm getting an allowance from the Bank of Dad. But anyway, it'll only go so far. You are going to need to get some kind of a job.'

'Don't worry. I absolutely will. Anyway, I've kind of got a project as well. I'm going to write a children's book. About a cat on a gondola!'

You must have frowned, as he catches the expression on your face and looks cross for a moment. 'What, you're the only one who's allowed to write, is that it?'

'No, of course not, don't be silly.' You kiss him on the cheek. 'It sounds wonderful.'

He kisses you again, harder this time, and slides his hand slowly up under your skirt. 'Shall we just go to bed then?'

'Oh, I think so.'

He leads you towards the bedroom, and then stops. 'No, tell you what. Let's save that for later.' He grabs his coat. 'Let's go and spend some of your dad's money. There's that new Italian place at the end of the road.'

'Matt, that's supposed to be expensive.'

He laughs. 'Call it research, then.'

'Oh, come on. Let's just go to bed and then we'll order pizza. That's Italian enough, no?'

'No, there'll be plenty of that where we're going. This place is supposed to be great. Champagne and oysters, what do you say?'

You roll your eyes. 'Okay then. But don't think we'll be doing this sort of thing every night.'

'That's my girl. And then we'll come back and make love through to the morning because you won't have to go in and see Idiot Boss tomorrow and then . . . well, we'll have to get online and start looking for somewhere to live. Or didn't you say your new boss has flats to rent? Maybe we'll end up staying there? Maybe he'll do us a good rate? Hey, maybe he'll let us stay there for free?'

You're tired now and coming down from the emotional high of the afternoon. In all honesty, pizza in bed sounds like the better option, but Matt's puppyish enthusiasm, his words tripping over each other in his excitement, is endearing.

'*All in good time, Matty.*' *You hardly ever call him that, but he seems so childishly excited it seems appropriate. 'And anyway, I've found us a place.*'

'*You have? Where?*'

'*It's in Castello. One of the parts of the city where the real Venetians still live. In the Calle del Cimitero.*' *You smile.* '*Cemetery Street.*'

'*Wow. There's a name. Why there, though? I thought we'd be doing all this planning together?*'

You shake your head. '*No. It has to be there. It just absolutely has to be.*'

'*I don't understand.*'

'*You will.*' *You put your coat on and pull him towards you to kiss him. 'I promise. Now come on then. Champagne and oysters it is.*'

Chapter 30

'Thanks for coming over, Nat. I told Vally everything would be sorted by the time she got back and, well, it's going to be too much for me on my own. Especially with *her* in tow.' Dario looked down at Emily, and ruffled her hair. The little girl smiled, and threw her arms around his knees.

'You mean you've not finished already?' I smiled.

He shook his head, and I was struck by how tired he looked. 'Been rushed off my feet with work over the past few days,' he said.

'I don't get it. Surely nobody's looking at buying houses at the moment?'

'They aren't. But we've got any number of tourist flats with angry landlords demanding to know what the damage is, and what needs to be done before they're in a fit state to let out again. I tell you, Nat, I'm just tired of telling people that, no, we don't know when their electricity's going to be back on again.'

I nodded. 'Yep. Same here.'

'I think maybe I need to find a less stressful job. Maybe roadying for Ozzie Osbourne. Something like that.' He yawned and stretched. 'Come on then. Let's have a look in the cellar.' He took me by the hand, realised he'd got it wrong, then took Emily's hand and led me downstairs.

'I didn't know you had a cellar,' I said. 'Come to that, I didn't know anyone in Venice did.'

'Well, plenty of houses still have them. Whether they can use them or not is another matter. Our neighbour said ours hadn't flooded since '66.'

He pushed the cellar door open and toggled the light switch up and down, to no effect. 'The electricity's still off down here, then. You know, I'm kind of glad Vally's away at the moment.'

I nodded at Emily. 'And what about—?'

He sighed. 'Got to be honest, Nat, I did think that maybe she should go and see her grandparents along with her mum. But then I thought, she's Venetian. I think she needs to be here for this. To see what's going on. And I know maybe she won't remember much. But perhaps she will, and then when she's our age she'll be telling her kids about the great flood of '19, and about how their granddad took her to see the city, to watch how everybody came together to help out.'

'And how he got his mate to come round to clear out his cellar.'

He smiled. 'Yeah. That too.'

He toggled the light switch again, evidently more in hope than expectation, and sighed. 'Okay.' He pushed the cellar door open, and wedged it with a fire extinguisher. 'There'll be enough light to see by. I just want to see what the damage is.'

We walked down a couple of steps into the cellar itself. The light was barely enough to see by, but as my eyes slowly adjusted to the darkness, I could make out the dimensions of the space. We were in a narrow corridor, lined on one side by a series of wooden, padlocked doors. Faint daylight streamed in from narrow windows set into the top of the far wall. A child's bicycle lay on its side, its front wheel turning gently with the movement of the shallow water that it lay in. The air was stale, and stank of damp.

Dario reached into his pocket and took out a key. 'This one's ours,' he said, as he fumbled with the padlock. Water was still pooling around our ankles. This was slightly more serious for Emily – being, as she was, only about three feet tall – but she was taking it in her stride.

Dario smiled, thinly. 'Having a cellar in Venice. We thought we'd got lucky. We had all sorts of stuff – too much for the flat – that we thought we could stash down here.'

He removed the padlock, and gently moved Emily aside. He tugged at the door but the swollen wood refused to budge. He swore, and then winced at having done so in front of his little daughter. He put both of his hands on the door, braced a foot against the wall, and yanked at it with all his strength. He pulled again, and again, until it suddenly sprang open, sending him stumbling back into the wall. At the same time, the door set a wave moving through the basement, and I hauled Emily into the air just before the water reached the top of her wellies.

'Thanks, man.' He looked inside the cellar and took a deep breath. 'Okay. Not good.'

I stood on tiptoe – not easy whilst wearing wellies and carrying a small girl – to peek over his shoulder.

Dario shook his head. 'Not flooded since '66 they told us. And now it floods again. Two years after I thought it was a smart idea to move back to Venice. What was I thinking, eh Nat?'

I patted his shoulder with my free hand. 'Come on, Dario. It might not be so bad.'

I was starting to find Emily heavier than I remembered. 'Can I put you down, sweetheart?' I asked. She nodded. Dario stepped aside, and I carried her through to the *magazzino*, setting her down gently on a coffee table, which raised her to about the height of Dario's shoulders.

He looked around, and nodded. 'Okay. You're right, it's not that bad. The furniture might dry out.' He looked up to a narrow window set into the top of the rear wall. The cement was stained and discoloured directly below it. Dario splashed his way through the cellar, and reached up, gently probing it with his fingers. Fragments of cement crumbled away and splashed into the water pooling around his feet. He brushed his fingers clean, almost absent-mindedly, on his coat.

'Okay. That's going to need fixing up. And the windows are going to need resealing. Everybody's are, I suppose. Something to talk about at the next condominial meeting.' He turned around in a full circle, taking in the rest of the damage, creating a gentle whirlpool as he did so.

'You're right, Nat. It's not so bad. The furniture might have had it, but it's not as if it was worth much anyway.' He looked down at his feet, and tapped his boot against a small portable television. 'Never found space for that. Guess we're not going to now.' Then he rested his hand on a large mattress leaning against the wall. 'And that's had it of course.' He shook his head. 'It's not even ours. Belonged to the previous owner. Should have thrown it out when we moved in but never found the time. Funny how much crap you just end up with over the years, isn't it?'

A terrible thought crept into my head. 'Dario, the boxes aren't down here, are they?'

He looked confused. 'The boxes?'

'The stuff I helped you move from Mestre. Your vinyl.' I paused. 'And the Pink Floyd tablecloth.'

He looked at me with utter astonishment on his face, and then laughed. 'No. Do you think I'd leave that in the cellar? In a city below sea level? I don't care if it's been over fifty years since the last time it flooded, there was no way I was going to risk that. No. It's upstairs. On top of a wardrobe. Just to be extra secure.'

'I'm glad. I really didn't want to be here in the event of anything bad having happened to it.'

'I know what you mean.' He looked serious again. 'You know, the guy who lives downstairs from us is maybe eighty-something. His wife died a few years ago. His kids live in Rome and they don't visit as often as they once did. He had stuff in his cellar – old photos, even some of the kids' favourite toys. Things he kept in case his grandchildren visited. All gone.'

He rubbed his nose. 'This is an ageing city, *vecio*. Sometimes I feel like we're amongst the youngest people here. And the older you get, the more important memories are.'

I nodded. Especially in a city like Venice, I thought. A city built on memories as much as it was built on mud and petrified wood.

He continued. 'Maybe every house in this city has someone like him. Someone realising that all those memories have just been washed away by the lagoon.' He shook his head. 'Ah, look at me. I'm getting all miserable. You'd think I'd been listening to *The Wall* or something.' He splashed his way back towards us and picked Emily up, squeezing her hard enough to get a happy little *meep* out of her. 'Good thing I've got you to keep me happy, eh sweetheart?' He kissed the top of her head and then turned to me. 'We're the lucky ones, I know.'

I looked around. 'What are we going to do with all this stuff?'

He shrugged. 'I thought we could just leave it here until it dries out, but I see the kids are out – the Mud Angels, you know – piling up all the crap in the middle of the square. Maybe we should just take the TV out. And the mattress.'

The television, I was pretty sure, I could manage. Manoeuvring a water-soaked mattress up a flight of stairs and out into the middle of the *campo* seemed more challenging.

'Are you sure?' I said. 'Wouldn't it be easier just to call *Veritas*?'

Dario nodded. 'Well, it would. But we're not gonna do that.'

My face fell. 'No?'

'No.' He patted Emily on the head. 'Remember what I said? I want her to remember this. How the whole city came together to help out.'

'Are you sure?' I said.

He nodded.

'What about you, Emily?' I said, trying to keep the desperation out of my voice.

She looked at me, and said nothing. But she smiled.

Oh hell.

'Great,' I said. 'I've been emotionally blackmailed by a five-year-old.'

Dario grinned, and patted my arm. 'Welcome to DarioWorld, *vecio*. Come on then. Television first, and then we'll see what we can do with the mattress.'

Dario, I knew, was in better shape than me. So when he suggested taking a break for a minute, I knew we were in trouble. I bent over, panting, resting my hands on my knees. The mattress took that as a sign to start leaning over, and I grabbed it and hauled it upright again before it could topple over. Sodden and heavy with water, it had taken all our strength to drag it up the cellar steps and out into the street. Emily had done all she could to help but, despite her good intentions, a five-year-old was not well equipped for this sort of work.

'I hope that's not your best coat,' said Dario.

'It's my second best one. The other needs a clean. Someone pushed me into a pond in San Marco the other day.' He looked confused, and I shook my head. 'Long story.' I closed my eyes, and rested my forehead against the mattress, my limbs shaking from the effort. 'Just give me a minute, eh?'

I felt someone tapping my shoulder.

'Mr Consul?'

My eyes flicked open. 'Siouxsie? I mean, Aggressive Girl? I mean, Lucia?'

'Any of those are fine, Mr Consul. And yes, it's me. How're you doing?'

I closed my eyes again. 'Not so good, if truth be told.'

'Can we give you a hand with that?'

I nodded. 'That'd be very good indeed.'

Dario bristled, slightly. 'I think we can manage this ourselves.'

I shook my head. 'No. We really can't.'

Lucia put her fingers to her mouth and whistled, making me start. 'Alessio! Bruno! Over here, guys.'

Two young men were manoeuvring a washing machine into the middle of a pile of junk in the centre of the *campo*. They looked over at us, then nodded at each other, and jogged over. One of them grabbed my end of the mattress. 'Here mister, let me give you a hand with that.'

'Thanks.'

The other took Dario's end. He made a token show of protesting, but I could tell he was secretly quite pleased. They dragged it off at a faster rate than we were ever likely to have managed.

I turned to Lucia. 'So are you covering every *campo* in town?'

She shrugged. 'It feels like it, some days.' She held her phone up for me to see. 'We have a WhatsApp group. If somebody needs a bit of help, they message the group and whoever's nearest goes to help.' She looked over at Dario and Emily. 'I'm Lucia, by the way.'

'Dario.' He looked down. 'And this is my lovely girl Emily.'

Lucia knelt down, and smiled at her. 'Hi, Emily.'

The little girl looked taken aback at first, as if not quite sure what to think. Then she smiled. 'You have funny hair,' she said.

Lucia laughed. 'I do, don't I?' She reached out her hand. 'Come on, sweetheart, let's go and help Alessio and Bruno. Give your dad and Nathan a rest.'

Emily looked up at Dario. Dario looked at me. I nodded and his face relaxed, and he smiled at Lucia who led Emily off by the hand.

'Do you know, she looks a bit like Siouxsie Sioux?'

'Yeah. We've had that conversation.' I yawned. 'Okay. Is there anything else left?'

He shook his head. 'I don't think so, *vecio*. As soon as Emily's finished here I think we can take a break and we can all go to the bar.'

As if on cue, Lucia and Emily returned. The little girl was half carrying, half dragging a black leather briefcase. Lucia shook her head, but she was smiling. 'Emily thinks she's found something important.' She lowered her voice, 'Sorry. I tried to stop her.'

Emily held it up towards Dario, who looked confused for a moment. Then his expression cleared, and he grinned. He knelt down to give his daughter a hug.

'Ah, you're a clever girl, aren't you?' He looked up at us. 'See, she sees me leaving for work every morning with a big, black briefcase. Just like this one. So she sees this in the middle of that pile of junk and thinks it must be mine.' He hugged her again. 'What a clever girl you are,' he repeated. He held the case up in front of her little face. 'But I don't think it's mine, darling. Do you want to put it back?'

Emily nodded happily and took it from his hands, skipping over to the pile of refuse before throwing it as hard as she could into the middle.

Dario clapped his hands, and then smiled at Lucia and me.

'Right then. I think we've earned a spritz, eh?'

Chapter 31

Lucia leaned her head back against the wall, and sighed.

'Better?'

She took a long draught of her beer. 'Better now,' she said.

'You're knackered, Lucia. You should go home and take a break.'

'I will do. After this. Dad will be wanting his dinner as well.'

Dario spoke up. 'Your dad? He must be about my age.'

Lucia nodded.

'Tell him to make his own bloody dinner. That's what I'd do.'

She closed her eyes and shook her head. 'I know. But he's just my dad, you know. Never cooked in his life and then when mum upped and left, he just seemed a bit lost. So somebody has to do it.'

'You should take a break anyway, Lucia. You can't save the city on your own, you know.'

She yawned and shrugged. 'Like I said. This is something Venice has to do for itself. Otherwise it's just left to rich guys like Giles Markham.'

'You know him?' I couldn't keep the surprise out of my voice.

'I don't know him, but he joined our WhatsApp group this morning. Said he'd read about the Mud Angels – Christ, I hate that name – in the papers and wanted to be part of it all.'

'Blimey.'

'But what's he going to do? Roll his sleeves up and clear all the crap away? Or just appear on TV with the mayor and ask for money?'

I coughed. 'Actually that's exactly what he's going to do.'

She rolled her eyes. '*Dimmi.*'

'There's going to be a broadcast from the crypt of St Mark's in a couple of days. He's appearing with the mayor and the Patriarch. Appealing for funds.'

Lucia swore under her breath, but not softly enough to avoid the attention of Emily, who raised her head sleepily at the mention of a potentially exciting new word. Dario frowned. 'I don't want to have to explain that to her mother, you know?'

'Sorry.'

'Anyway,' I continued, 'what's so bad about that? It's the crypt of San Marco. It's a beautiful place. If it's damaged, it needs restoring and if that means some rich British guy has to go on TV and ask for money, I say good for him.'

Lucia shook her head. 'You don't understand. It's beautiful, sure, but it's not real life. It's just Venice under glass. Tourist Venice.' She jabbed a finger towards the *campo*. 'That's what's real. Out there. People whose houses are full of mud and filth, where nothing works any more.' She drained her glass and set it down on the table with what I thought was unnecessary force. 'If *Mister* Markham wants to be useful, tell him to do something other than just throwing money around. Give us a hand shifting dead refrigerators or televisions. Because right now that'll make more difference than appearing on TV with the Patriarch and the mayor.' She spoke the final words as if trying to keep them physically distant from her.

I nodded. 'Okay. I'll do that.'

'You what?'

'I'm a guest as well. At the broadcast. And before you roll your eyes—'

'I was not!'

'Yes you were. Before you roll your eyes at me, I'm there in my diplomatic capacity as British Honorary Consul and representative of Her Majesty's Foreign Service.'

There was silence around the table.

'All right, that didn't sound quite so pompous in my head. But the point is, I'm not going as a fundraiser or anything like that. More as a representative of the British community in Venice.'

'Still quite pompous, Nat,' said Dario.

'Whatever. Anyway, I'll be seeing Markham then. And you know what – I'm going to ask if he'll roll up his sleeves and get involved. Because I think he might.'

'And the mayor and the Patriarch?'

'That might be more difficult.'

Dario grinned. 'Not impossible for the Consul to the Most Serene Republic though? So what's he like, this Markham guy?'

'I thought I was going to hate him.'

'Why?'

'Well. He's very rich. And has a better flat than I ever will.' This time it was Dario's turn to roll his eyes, and Lucia's

to laugh. 'And, yes, he has this kind of "get it done atti-
tude" which grates against my intrinsic laziness. But it has
to be said, his heart's in the right place. I think he walks the
walk, you know? The young woman who was killed – Jenny
Whiteread — well, he arranged for her dad to come over.
Actually, that's not quite right. I arranged for him to come
over. But he paid for it.'

Lucia shook her head. 'There we go, you see. Everything's
easier when you have the money. That's just the way these
people work,' she said, with a certain studied weariness.

'Okay, Lucia, I get it. You don't like him, fair enough.'

'No I don't.' She paused. 'He's got you doing his dirty
work for him, hasn't he? All he has to do up is turn up and
wait for everyone to tell him what a great guy he is. I bet he
was the same with that poor English woman. God help anybody who has to work with someone like that.'

'Don't be too sure.' I managed to restrain myself from wag-
ging a finger. 'I've spoken with one of the people who works
for him and he hasn't had anything bad to say.' Well, not
about working conditions perhaps, although Fulvio Terzi had
suggested that not all was as it should be in Giles Markham's
philanthropic empire.

Terzi.

I half dropped my spritz on to the table, waking Emily
from her doze.

'Bloody hell.'

'What is it, Nat?'

'That briefcase. The one Emily found.'

'Yes. Is it important?'

'I don't know, but it might be.' I drained my glass and

crashed it down on the table again. 'Order me another one. I think I'm going to need it.'

I ran back to the mountain of rubbish in the middle of San Giacomo dell'Orio, and stood there scanning it, as the rain fell ever harder. I looked to the left, and then to the right. Refrigerators, fridge-freezers, television sets. Black plastic bags full of rubbish. Waterlogged sofas, and ruined computers.

It had to be there somewhere.

I could go back and ask Emily, I supposed, but trusting the powers of recall of a five-year-old might be pushing it.

I climbed up on top of a dead freezer and looked around. Then I knelt down and started pulling black bags from the pile in the centre. My coat was starting to soak through and mud, I was aware, was going to cling to everything. I pulled up each bag in turn, checked beneath them, and then replaced them. Nothing.

'Hey!'

It had to be there, somewhere. Unless someone had walked off with it.

'Hey, mister!'

I turned around. The speaker was a middle-aged man in a long coat, holding up a briefcase.

'Are you looking for this?'

I sighed with relief. 'I certainly am.'

'You want to be careful. I was just taking it to the police. It didn't look like the sort of thing that ought to be left lying around.'

'Thank you. Thank you so much. I was giving my pal a hand to clear out his cellar. I must have put it down for a moment and the next thing I knew,' I gestured behind me at the pile of rubbish, 'it must have got thrown here.'

He smiled. 'Good thing I was passing.' He looked me up and down. 'But you ought to get back inside. You'll catch your death.'

'I will. Thanks.' I stretched out my hand and he passed the briefcase to me. Then he tipped the brim of his hat, and turned and walked away.

I returned to the bar, holding the briefcase above my head in triumph. Dario and Emily looked at me in confusion. Lucia, merely as if she wished she was anywhere other than here.

I sat down at the table, and put the briefcase down by my side. 'Come on then,' I said. 'I think this deserves a drink. And then, I think, there'll be some work to do. Emily, you haven't got anything to drink there? Another hot chocolate?'

Dario's eyes widened. 'Two in one day? That much sugar? I'll never get her to sleep.'

I clapped him on the back. 'Oh, you'll be fine. Just sing a little bit of *Dark Side of the Moon* to her and she'll be off in no time.'

'Okay then.' He put his finger to his lips. 'But don't say a word to her mother!'

Lucia looked from Dario to me and back again. 'I don't think I'll ever understand married people,' she said.

'Oh, you will, Lucia, you will.' I turned to Emily. 'Another hot chocolate then? For being a brilliant girl?'

Emily looked up at me, confused for a moment. Then her expression cleared and she smiled and nodded.

Chapter 32

Lucia checked her watch. 'I should be home, you know. Dad's going to need me.'

I placed the briefcase in the middle of Dario's living-room table. 'Won't be long,' I said.

'I don't even know why I'm here.'

'Because we're having an adventure. Isn't that reason enough? And don't roll your eyes!'

She rolled her eyes.

'Nat, man, you're soaked,' said Dario.

'I know.' I leaned against the radiator, feeling the warmth seep back into me and I smiled as I felt it scorch the small of my back.

Dario drummed his fingers on the table. 'So, *vecio*. Can I ask why you've brought an old briefcase which you retrieved from a pile of rubbish and put it down in the middle of my living room?'

'Because I didn't want to open it in the bar.'

I moved – not without some reluctance – away from the radiator, and ran my fingers over the case. It was closed with two thick leather straps and two shiny combination locks.

'See,' I said, 'it's relatively new. This isn't junk that's been thrown away.'

I felt I was dry enough to risk the sofa, and sat down in front of the case, running my fingers over the dials. I undid the straps, then tried, and failed, to click the locks open. I hadn't really expected them to. I put my glasses on and peered at the numbers. Then I took them off my nose and moved them closer to the dials. Then further away. Then back again. I bent closer in, straining my eyes, trying to make out the tiny numbers.

'You know what you're doing, Nat?' said Dario.

'No. But I thought if I could make out which numbers are the most discoloured, that might give us a clue as to the code.'

Dario nodded. 'That's quite clever.'

'It is,' said Lucia. 'Never going to work though.' She was standing by Dario's CD racks, with her head on one side, the better to scan the titles. She straightened up. 'You must really like Pink Floyd.'

Dario smiled. 'Of course. How about you?'

'It's more my dad's music to be honest.' She scanned the rack further. 'Genesis. Led Zeppelin.' She laughed. 'My god, you actually are my dad!'

'Oh thanks. You might not have noticed but I'm old enough to be.'

'Only just.' She smiled. 'What about you, Mr Consul?'

'More of a Hawkwind man myself.'

She looked puzzled. 'Who?'

'Pivotal English space-rock band of the 1970s and . . . oh, never mind. Anyway, what do you mean by "never going to work"?'

'It's never going to work, that's all. It's a clever idea, I suppose. Just look for the numbers that are the most tarnished. Put them all in line and,' she snapped her fingers, 'click. But it doesn't work. Think about the way you lock a case like this. You just spin the numbers. The difference in how tarnished they are is going to be next to nothing.'

I sighed. 'Okay. So what do you suggest we do? Take it in turns to check every combination from one to nine hundred and ninety-nine?'

She shook her head. 'That doesn't work either. At some point you stop concentrating and click over two by mistake. Or just forget where you are.'

Dario and I stared at her.

'You sound like this is something you've done,' said Dario.

'I did a gig with my band a year ago. It was a free festival in Pordenone.' She smiled. '*Anarchy in Pordenone*, they called it. Anyway, I had a new guitar case and I was a bit pissed and forgot the new number. Mauro the bass player showed me how to get it open.'

She riffled through her bag and brought out a Swiss army knife. She unfolded the smallest blade. 'This'll do. Hopefully.' She looked at me. 'Budge up.'

I shuffled along the sofa to make space for her. Then she leaned closer in to me, turning her head this way and that and staring into my glasses.

She nodded. 'They'll do,' and twitched them off my nose. 'Oi!'

'Sorry. I don't have mine.' She frowned. 'Not quite right.' She pulled them down to the end of her nose. 'Better.'

She took the knife in her right hand, and gently pushed it

into the gap between the leftmost dial and the edge of the case. She clicked the dial over, one digit at a time, back and forth, back and forth as if feeling for something. Then she smiled. 'That one.' She moved to the centre dial, and repeated the operation. And then to the right-most one. She pulled the latch to the left, and the lock sprang open with a satisfying clunk.

She turned and smiled at us, and then got to work on the right-hand lock. Thirty seconds later she clicked it open, smiled, and pushed my glasses back on to my nose.

'Thank the Lord for helpful bass players,' I said.

'So. What do we do now?' said Dario.

'I guess we open it. Bit like the end of *Pulp Fiction*, isn't it?'

'You like old movies as well?' said Lucia.

Dario and I looked at each other, both of us suddenly feeling very old. 'Go on then,' I said. 'Let's have a look.'

Dario waved his hands. 'Whoa. Let's just wait a minute, shall we? Why are we doing this exactly?'

'Because I was passing by the *campo* the other night and saw somebody running away from Terzi's boat with a briefcase. A briefcase that then fell into the canal. Now it might just be that somebody fished it out and threw it into the pile of junk in the centre of the *campo*. So I'm guessing that whatever's in there is of interest.'

Dario nodded. 'And I'm guessing that – even if it's the same one – whatever's in there belongs to *signor* Terzi. So why not just take it round to him?'

'He told me it wasn't his. So we're at liberty to open it up, aren't we? And we're going to because there's something strange about Jenny Whiteread's death and I'm seeing angels everywhere.'

Lucia looked at Dario.

'It's okay,' he said. 'He just does this kind of thing from time to time.'

'Seriously. There was a card in her bag with "Angels for an angel" written on it. Her downstairs neighbour asked me if "she'd come to see the angels". And then on Terzi's boat, there's a woodcut or an engraving of some kind – again, with angels on it. So, let's open it up. And if there's nothing in there relating to angels then I'll accept I've got this all wrong and we'll take it to the police and they can stick it in lost property. Deal?'

Dario nodded.

Lucia rolled her eyes. 'Some adventure this is. We've got as far as almost opening a briefcase. Let's get on with it.' She clicked it open, reached inside and took out a small hardback book. She turned the pages, but cautiously. 'It's wet through, but not too bad. I've seen worse things at the Conservatorio in the past few days. Ooh, what are these?' She dropped a bunch of keys on to the table, where they landed with a clatter.

'House keys? Office keys?'

'Maybe both. But let's have a look at that book, eh?'

Lucia passed it over to me. It was cloth-bound, in a faded red. The title, in gold, had almost flaked away with age.

Auf Dürers Spuren.

Eine Reise durch Italien.

Friedrich Wilhelm Syberberg

'German,' I said. 'I don't suppose either of you speak German?'

They both shook their heads.

I leafed through the pages as carefully as I could. 'Printed in 1911,' I said. I continued paging through. There were a number of attractive pen and ink drawings of Venice and a number of other cities unfamiliar to me.

I continued leafing through, and then stopped at a chapter heading.

Apocalipsis cum figuris

'Wahey. Something I can actually read.' I turned the page, and smiled. There, in front of me, was a woodcut of four angels with swords. 'This is it. I saw this image on Terzi's boat. Angels. Always angels. You see?'

Lucia and Dario looked at each other, uncertainly.

'Are you sure about this, *vecio*? It doesn't seem much to go on.'

'There's a pattern here, Dario. I'm convinced of it. First of all I'm going to ask Gabriele to look at this book for me. Maybe he speaks German, who knows? Even if he doesn't, he might be able to tell me something about it.'

'And then?'

'And then if there's anything interesting, and if it isn't something that I think should be reported to the police immediately then—'

'Yes?'

'I don't know. I hadn't really thought that far ahead.'

Lucia shook her head. 'Call this an adventure? We've opened a briefcase and found a book about angels. I was expecting a bit more.'

I rubbed my forehead. 'Look. Can we just reset the parameters a bit? Can we at least start from the premise that I don't know what I'm doing but I'm kind of trying to be well intentioned?'

Dario nodded. 'He means well, *signora*.'

Lucia nodded. I smiled at Dario.

'But it took me a while to work him out as well.'

I stopped smiling.

'Okay,' I sighed. 'If we're all in this together, what else is in there?'

'A mobile phone. And a portable charger. And a laptop.' She laid them on the table.

'Why keep a mobile phone in your briefcase?'

She shrugged. 'It was plugged in. Who wants to carry around a mobile phone with a charger in your pocket? And besides, this is a smart briefcase. There's a special slot for a mobile. Waste of money buying a case like this and then not using it properly.'

I reached for the phone, and weighed it in my hand. 'So what do you think? Should we switch it on?'

Lucia snatched it back. 'Give that here! It's wet through, like the laptop. If we switch it on we could fuck it up.'

'Okay. So what do we do?' I looked over at Dario. 'Your pal Franco?'

He shook his head. 'He's good at passwords and things. I'm not sure if he'd know how to go about repairing a water-logged phone and PC though.'

'Lucia?'

She chuckled. 'Yeah. I know someone who could take a look at them. Mauro's good at this sort of thing.'

'Mauro the helpful bass player?'

'That's him. But you'll need to do us a favour.'

'Sure. No problem.'

She laughed again. 'You haven't heard what it is yet.'

Chapter 33

Matthew's been gone a few hours now. He says he wants to walk the streets on his own for a while 'just to get a feel for the place'. He has another project now, a book of black and white photographs of Venice together with some of his stories. You're not sure if there's a market for that, but decide not to say anything. He's been spiky recently, constantly on edge.

'We never spend any time together any more.'

'I'm at work all day. It's a good opportunity, I've got to make an impression here.'

'And when you're not there? You know, the rest of the week?'

'There's my book. I'm sorry. I know it's taking up a lot of time. Just give me a few weeks.'

'A few weeks?'

You sigh. 'Okay then. A few months.'

'Right.' He pauses. 'Tell me about the people you work with again?'

'Well, there's only really the two of them. Giles — that's Mr Markham of course — and Fulvio.'

'What are they like?'

'I don't really see too much of Giles. Fulvio's lovely, though.'

'Lovely.'

He mimics your tone of voice, but you decide not to rise to it.
'You'd like him. We should all go out together sometime.'

'What's he do, then? When he's not – I don't know, what's the word – consulting?'

He drawls the word out, with a languid wave of his hand and, for a moment, you hate him.

'He has a bookshop. In San Marco.'

'A bookshop. How lovely.' *He stresses the word again. He wants an argument. He wants a fight. But you're not going to give him one.*

'Yes. An antiquarian bookshop. He's got an extraordinary collection.' *You pause for a moment, unsure if you should say what comes next. You know it'll make him angry. And then rage stabs at you like a hot knife and you decide that you'll give him something to really be angry about. You slow the words down, ever so slightly. Just to add that extra little bit of emphasis.* 'I'm finding it immensely useful in research for the book.'

He nods, and smiles a little. Just enough to show you that he knows what you're trying to do.

'You've been over there?'

'Of course. I could hardly keep asking him to bring rare books over to Giudecca, could I?'

'So he's been there with you?'

Now it's your turn to smile. 'Only the first time.'

'You've been there more than once?'

'Yes.' *The smile doesn't leave your face.* 'He gave me a key. Told me I could let myself in whenever I liked. As I said, he's been very helpful.'

'Oh, it seems everyone wants to help you. Mr Terzi, of course, and then there's Daddy.'

You flush with anger. 'We wouldn't be able to live here if it wasn't for my dad. You know that. I don't earn enough money for the two of us and you – well – you don't earn anything at all.'

'Oh Christ, how often do I have to say this? I. Don't. Speak. The. Language. Sweetheart.'

He's in your face now, and his features are twisted with anger as he over-enunciates every word, as if speaking to an imbecile. You take a step back. Then he shakes his head and turns around.

He walks to the door, and pulls on his coat. He turns back to you, and wags his finger. 'Tell you what, though. Be nice if Mr Terzi or Daddy decided to be ever so helpful to me. If they decided they could help me with one of my projects. That'd be good, eh?'

And then he's gone. He slams the door. Of course he does. His tread is heavy on the staircase, measured; wanting you to hear every last step. Then you hear the front door slam, and you're left in silence.

You can feel the tears starting to prickle, but you choke them back. You won't let him do this to you. A scream builds in your throat and you force yourself to breathe deeply. The temptation is to throw something, to break something, but you settle for half-heartedly punching a cushion, and that makes you smile.

You go to the bathroom, and splash cold water on to your face. You rest your forehead on the tap, and feel every last drop trickling from your skin. Then you raise your head, brush your hair back from your face with your damp hands and stare into the mirror.

I am Dr Jennifer Whiteread. I am thirty-four years old. I live in Venice. I work for the Markham Foundation as a researcher. I am writing a book about angels.

I also have a shit boyfriend.

You nod your head, and the face in the mirror nods back at you. You smile, and so does she.

Jenny with the shit boyfriend would spend the evening on the sofa with a box of hankies and a bottle of wine, watching whatever seemed to be the least unbearably awful thing on RAI. But Dr Jennifer Whiteread doesn't do that sort of thing.

You take another look in the mirror. Your eyes are a little red, but not embarrassingly so.

Let's do this. The face in the mirror sets her jaw in a firm line. Let's do this.

You make your way downstairs and knock at the door with the name 'Masiero' on it.

There are voices from inside, and then light shines out from under the door. You hear a chain rattling and a bolt being pulled back.

'Yes?'

The speaker is a young blonde woman, about your age, in T-shirt and tracksuit bottoms.

'Good evening. My name's Jenny. I've just moved in upstairs.'

She smiles. 'Oh yes. I've seen you around.' She extends her hand. 'Oksana.'

'Hello Oksana. Nice to meet you. I was wondering – is the signora *in?'*

She looks confused for a moment. Almost suspicious. But then her expression clears. 'Yes of course. Come on in. Signora Masiero,' *she calls, 'we've got a visitor.'*

The old lady is seated at a table, with her back to you. She turns to you and smiles. You catch sight of her eyes and almost gasp, but then realise how rude that would be and so you smile back at her and Oksana.

You'd planned the speech out in advance but now the words won't come. And then, laughing at the silliness of what you're about to say, you come out with it. 'Signora Masiero, my name's Jennifer Whiteread and I'd like to talk to you about angels.'

Chapter 34

'You look tired,' said Fede.

I yawned. 'I am tired. But I'm dry and I'm warm again, so all in all, no complaints.'

'What are you working on then? The *Decameron* thesis?'

'That'll wait. Besides, it's very boring. No, I've been thinking about something Terzi said to me the other day. About the way Markham does business. So I've been doing a bit of a search on him'

'Hmm. Found anything?'

I gestured at my laptop. 'Not much, to be honest. Oh, there are features about Markham in the glossies. "My Fabulous Life", that sort of thing. And lots about the Markham Foundation. It just seems difficult to find evidence of anything they've actually *done*. But there are a few churches that have approached them, so I've been telephoning round.'

'But no luck?'

I shook my head. 'It's been more difficult than I expected. The few people I've managed to get hold of weren't interested in talking about it.'

'I can kind of understand that. Everyone's busy clearing up at the moment.'

I rubbed my nose. 'I think it's more than that. I'm getting the impression that people really don't want to talk about it.'

'You're a foreign guy calling them just after the biggest disaster in fifty years. It's not all that surprising.'

'Maybe not.' I yawned and drew myself up to my full height. Then I wagged a finger at her. 'But I am Her Majesty's Honorary Consul.'

'Times have changed, *caro mio*. It's not like being the Ambassador to *La Serenissima* any more.'

'Evidently not.' I sighed, and sat down behind my desk again. 'Oh, this is going nowhere. I'm starting to feel I could ring round every church in the city and still get no answer. What about the Querini? It's possible he might have been involved there.'

She shook her head. 'I did ask. But nobody has any memory of Markham pledging any money to them.'

I sighed. 'Okay. I guess we're a bit stuck then.'

She rubbed my shoulders. 'You've done all you can, *caro*. I don't think there's much more to be done. It's up to the police to decide what they want to do now.'

'I know. I know. But there's something that isn't quite right. If only we could see it.' I clicked my fingers. 'I've got it.'

'You have? Oh, good.'

'The Tall Priest. Father Michael at St George's. He's worth a go. And if he hasn't had any dealings with Markham, he might know people who have.'

'Are you sure?'

'Well, why not?'

'It's just, well, it's not exactly St Mark's is it? It's not going to get his name on front pages back in the UK.'

'Hmm. Maybe that's the point.' I tapped my fingers on the desk for a moment, and then nodded to myself. I picked up the phone.

'*Padre*. It's Nathan.'

Father Michael Rayner, the Tall Priest, was waiting for me at the doors of St George's Anglican Church.

'Nathan? How are you?'

'Cold. And damp.' I looked around at the square. 'Sometimes I wonder if I'm ever going to feel warm and dry again. And the city – just look at it. Apart from the detritus piled up everywhere, I'm starting to feel like we're living in black and white. Grey canals under a grey sky. It's like the colour's been leached from everything.'

'Mm-hmm.' He nodded. 'Have you quite finished?'

'I have.'

'Good.' He passed me a mop and bucket. 'You can give me a hand with this. If you're cold, this will warm you up. And if you're wet, well, then you won't mind too much about getting wetter.'

'Hang on, you've got me out here to work?'

'Absolutely.'

'Don't you have people to help out with this sort of thing?'

'Nathan, let's just say that the age profile of our congregation makes me something of a spring chicken and you a positive youngster.' Then he looked serious, and shook his head. 'Besides, some of them still have problems of their own. But I imagine you know about that?'

I nodded. 'I've spoken to a number of them. The electricity's back on in most places now, so at least nobody's going cold. But redecorating – well, that's going to take months.' A thought struck me. Rayner's house was near the Zattere, and flooded easily even in the best of times. 'What about you, Michael? How are things?'

He sighed. 'Not great, I'll be honest. Downstairs is – well, let's just say that for a few hours on the night in question we could have advertised the chaplaincy house as having a desirable integral swimming pool.'

'Oh hell. Did nothing work? You put the *paratia* in place, right?'

'Nathan, well-meaning parishioners kept calling me just to check that I had, indeed, put the *paratia* in place. And I had. But—' he trailed off.

'Not enough?'

'Useless. Complete waste of time. The water just came up through the floor.'

I shook my head. 'I'm sorry, Michael. What did you do?'

'Sat on the stairs and watched the downstairs furniture floating around. Curiously hypnotic after a while.'

'You've got insurance though, right?'

'Yes. If they pay out. But *forza maggiore*'s normally what they call this sort of thing. Who knows what they'll do? And if they don't,' he shrugged, 'I guess we go cap in hand to the Diocese for a loan. But at least we can do that. Not everybody has that option.'

'I'm sorry.'

He clapped me on the back. 'Thank you, Nathan. Evidently you think it's serious enough to call me Michael instead of *padre*. That's a little miracle in itself. Come on then, let's get to work.'

'What are we doing?'

'We're mopping out the church. Yet again. I've done it once already, but that foul water just seems to be clinging everywhere. I'm hoping one more go will do it.'

We went inside. The smell of old churches and damp. An interior devoid of light and colour.

'Any chance of putting the lights on?'

He shook his head. 'None at all. That still remains to be sorted out.'

I shivered. 'I assume that goes for the heating as well?'

'It certainly does.' He smiled and clapped his hands together. 'Many are cold, but few are frozen, Nathan.'

We swabbed and mopped the floors all morning until the sun made a half-hearted attempt at breaking through the clouds, sending thin beams of light shining through the stained-glass windows. It wasn't much, but it was enough to lift our spirits. Rayner leaned on his mop, and gave a great, deep sigh.

'Okay, Nathan. I think we're done.'

'You're sure? You don't want me to, I don't know, give the pews a good polish or anything?'

'Well, that would be nice. But that can wait until tomorrow if you like.'

'Don't push it.'

Rayner took out a thermos from a canvas bag on one of the rearmost pews. 'Coffee?'

I was about to accept, but then I remembered the quality of his coffee. 'I'm fine, thanks.'

'Biscuit?' There were only a couple left, and I was about to refuse when he saw the expression on my face. 'Go on. The poor will always be with us, but biscuits we have for only a short time.'

I did wonder if he was really supposed to say things like this but that, evidently, was between him and his boss. He sipped at his coffee, and closed his eyes. 'You know, we had a report on TripAdvisor the other day complaining that we had the most uncomfortable pews in the city. I can only assume they'd never been to San Salvador.'

'People leave reviews of churches on TripAdvisor?'

He opened his eyes. 'Oh yes. It seems rather strange to me, but I suppose it helps keep us on our toes. Make sure everyone's nice and smiley to visitors. Choose hymns everyone will know. Keep the sermon to a bearable length. That sort of thing.'

'I had no idea.'

'It seems even the Church must move with the times, Nathan. As to the pews, well, there's not much we can do about those at the moment. Limited funds available and what we have—' He broke off.

'What is it, *padre*?' He was staring over my shoulder but, when I turned around, I could see nothing. 'What are you looking at?'

'That crack in the plaster. Over there, look. Just under Robert Browning's window.'

Rayner pointed towards the stained-glass window dedicated to the great poet, and I followed his gaze. There was, indeed, a thin lightning-shaped crack leading down from the window to just above the floor.

'What about it?'

'It wasn't there this morning.'

He got to his feet, grunting with the effort, and I followed him as he made his way over to the wall. There was no mistaking the fact that the plaster in that area was dark and discoloured.

Rayner looked upwards. 'That window. It's not sealed terribly well. We've been wanting to fix it for years, but it costs a fortune to repair stained glass.' He raised his hand to the wall, and touched it, ever so gently. 'Sweating,' he murmured.

'About the only thing that is,' I grumbled.

I followed the line of the crack upwards to where it began, just below the level of the window, which was heavily blackened and stained with mould. The low winter sun was now shining brightly through the glass, making it difficult to see clearly. As I shielded my eyes, I couldn't help thinking that the crack seemed to be widening.

I looked away, waiting for my eyes to adjust, and then back again. There was no doubt. Thin, spidery cracks were slowly radiating outwards from the original. The plaster, ominously, was starting to bulge outwards.

Oh, bloody hell.

Rayner appeared quite oblivious to the danger, so I threw my arms around him and dragged him away as best I could. I caught my foot on the edge of the nearest pew and toppled to the floor, bearing him with me. Behind us I could hear a great, wet *crump* as the sodden plaster slid from the wall and crumbled to the floor of the church.

We lay there, for a moment, in the sudden silence.

'Are you all right, Nathan?' said Rayner, sprawled on top of me.

'I think so.'

He raised himself to his feet, brushing white fragments of plaster from his clothes. His hair and moustache were dishevelled and dusted with white, giving him a half-comic, half-ghostly appearance that I could only assume mirrored my own. Tiny white particles spiralled in the light streaming in through the window.

I hauled myself to my feet, and we went to inspect the damage. As we made our way over, another fragment fell from the wall, as if it had grown tired of clinging on.

A huge area of plasterwork had crumbled away, smashing into hundreds, perhaps thousands of fragments and coating the entirety of the narthex in a layer of fine white dust and chunks of wet plaster.

'Oh Christ,' I said. I looked over at Rayner. 'Sorry.'

I'd been expecting to be told off for my casual blasphemy but Rayner appeared not to have heard me. He merely shook his head – shaking a fine layer of dust from it – and patted me on the back, raising a similar white cloud from my shoulders. Then he went and sat down in the nearest pew, closing his eyes and putting his hands together. His lips moved, silently, as I stood there, wondering what on earth to say.

Eventually, he opened his eyes. He smiled at me. 'You know, you can speak if you want, Nathan?'

'Sorry. I don't like to interrupt you while you're praying.'

'I wasn't praying. I was having a bloody good swear and hoping His attentions were elsewhere.' He raised his eyes to the ceiling, and shook his fists. 'You know, You don't make it easy for us, do You?' he shouted. As if in response, another slab of plaster dropped from the wall.

'So what do we do now?' I said.

He shrugged. 'I think we go home and have a very large drink. I'll be back tomorrow.' He nodded over towards the pile of rubble. 'I'll make a start on that.'

'That's a hell of a lot of work, Michael.'

'I know. But I can't ask any of my flock to help out.'

'I'll help.'

'That's kind of you. Thank you.'

A thought struck me. 'Better than that,' I said. 'I can get some help in.'

'Are you sure?'

'Absolutely I'm sure. Look.' I took my phone out of my pocket. 'There's a WhatsApp group for the Mud Angels.'

'The what?'

'The Mud Angels. They're a bunch of students who're helping to clear up the city. One of them's a friend of mine.' I paused. 'Well, at least I think she is. At least she hasn't pushed me into any ponds recently.'

'I think you've lost me, Nathan. I'm not sure what this WhatsApp is of which you speak.'

'Trust me. This'll work. Look, it'll take the two of us forever to shift that,' I nodded at the pile of plaster, 'but I'll leave a message on the app and some fit young people will come round at some point and help us sort it out.'

'Really? Just like that?'

'Absolutely like that. It's kind of amazing. And, well, a bit humbling really.'

He nodded. 'It is. This sort of thing can bring out the best in people, I find. One might even say it restores one's faith.' He looked upwards and wagged a finger at the ceiling. 'Just as well for You,' he shouted.

I paused for a moment, half expecting a retaliatory bolt of lightning, but Father Michael and his employer had, it seemed, the sort of relationship where one party could be one hundred per cent honest without the other side taking offence.

He put his hands on his hips. 'Well now. Does that mean we can call it a day?'

I nodded. 'I think it's best. I imagine we both need to clean ourselves up.' I tapped away at WhatsApp. 'There we go. I've left a message for Lucia. I'll let you know when they're coming round.'

'Okay. Thanks again, Nathan. Oh, I'd completely forgotten. There was something you wanted to ask me? About Giles Markham?'

'It'll wait until tomorrow, Michael.' I made my way to the front door and turned to find him sitting in one of the pews, his head bowed. 'Are you not coming?'

'I'll stay here for a while, Nathan. Don't worry, I'll lock up. There's just someone I'd like to have a chat with first.'

'There is?'

Rayner raised his eyebrows heavenwards and smiled.

'Oh. I see.'

'Go on, Nathan. I'll see you tomorrow.'

The winter sun broke through the cloud again, sending a shaft of light through the windows and catching Father Michael in its rays. The Tall Priest, his clothes dusty with plaster, sitting in prayer in the middle of his ruined church as fine white dust swirled around him. The effect was curiously angelic.

Chapter 35

'*Ciao, cara*, I'm home.'

'*Ciao, caro*.' Fede smiled at me from the sofa, and then did a double take. She got to her feet, and looked me up and down. 'Okay, I imagine you know what I'm going to ask?'

'If I did the shopping?' I asked, as innocently as I could.

She gave me a playful little punch in the chest, the effect of which was to send a cloud of fine white powder into the air. I coughed, which dislodged a larger piece from my hair, which Gramsci immediately pounced upon, batting it across the room.

'Oh. You mean *this*?' I said, running my fingers down my body from shoulders to kneecaps.

'Uh-huh. What happened?'

'Bits of church fell on me.'

'I might have guessed. But seriously, are you all right?'

'Oh, I'm fine. Second-best coat is going to need a bit of a clean of course.'

'Does that mean moving into third-best coat?'

'There is no third-best coat.'

She laughed. 'My husband, Her Majesty's Honorary Consul in Venice. Look at you, eh?'

I laughed and went to kiss her but she held her hands up.

'No. Second-best coat isn't the only thing that needs cleaning up. You have a shower, and I'll fix you a spritz.'

Federica put her pizza box down on the table and leaned her head on my shoulder.

'Sorry,' I said, 'I should have cooked really.'

She shook her head. 'No you shouldn't. You've had a tough day. And besides, *Rosa Rossa* will be glad of the custom. It's the first day they've been open since the *acqua granda.*'

'So we're performing a valuable social service, is that what you mean?'

'It is.'

'Well, I guess we're the right people for it. Spritz?'

'Do we need another?'

'We don't *need* another. But the Campari people would probably like us to.'

'Oh, very well then.'

'Two spritzes coming up.' I got to my feet, and grunted.

'Are you all right? You sure you didn't get clonked by something this afternoon?'

'No, I'm fine.' I stretched and yawned. 'This is just middle age.' My phone buzzed and I saw a WhatsApp message waiting for me. 'It's Lucia. Good news. Some of them are going to come round to St George's tomorrow morning and give us a hand.'

'Brilliant.'

'I'll give the *padre* a call.'

'Uh-huh.' She looked up at me. 'Do you think Markham will turn up?'

'I hadn't thought of that. He was very keen to be involved but I don't know – is he really the sort of person to help with sweeping a pile of wet plaster out of a church on a winter's morning?'

She smiled. 'I didn't think you were, *tesoro*.'

'Ah well. Old Nathan might not have been. But New Nathan is the socially responsible citizen who does this sort of thing for his friends and his adopted city.'

'And I'm very proud of this New Nathan. Don't lose too much of the old one though.'

'Oh, I won't, don't worry.' A thought struck me. 'So, does that mean we should listen to a bit of Hawkwind then?'

She wrinkled her nose. 'Maybe not.'

I was at the church by nine o'clock, resplendent in my plaster-covered second-best coat. There was precious little point in wearing something clean given what we were about to do.

'Nathan.'

'Morning, *padre*.'

He sighed. 'I suppose it's too much to hope that – having gone through the bonding experience of a large section of church fall on us – we could move on to first-name terms all the time.'

'I'm sorry. I'll try to remember.'

I saw Lucia making her way over the bridge into the *campo*, with two burly youths behind her. I gave her a wave.

Rayner raised his eyebrows. 'Good heavens.'

'That's them,' I said. 'Three of our mud angels.'

'My goodness.' He lowered his voice. 'I'm not sure she looks terribly angelic.'

'Lucia? Oh, you'd be surprised. She's got a heart of gold. Well, probably.'

'Do you think she'll actually be able to enter on to holy ground?'

'I don't think she'll be struck by lightning, if that's what you mean. She's a good sort. She just has too many black clothes.'

'Evidently.' He smiled. 'I was joking, you realise?'

'You were? I'm sorry, I thought you were just being middle-aged.'

Rayner, I thought, was on the verge of digging me in the ribs, Federica-style, but changed his mind, perhaps considering this an unpriestly thing to do.

Lucia nodded at me, and patted Rayner on the shoulder. 'Hello, Nathan. Morning, *padre*.'

'Michael, please.'

'Sorry. Morning, *padre* Michael. This is Alessio and Bruno.'

The two lads nodded. Both of them were red-eyed and unshaven and looked as if they could have done with another couple of hours in bed.

'Thanks for coming out,' I said.

One of them yawned. 'No worries. Let's have a look, eh?'

We stepped aside to let them enter.

'Hmm. Nasty,' said Alessio.

'Bit of work that,' said Bruno.

Lucia looked at us. 'I worry that they're overcommitting a bit. They might not want to go back to student life . . .'

It took a good few hours' work but, by midday, most of the solids had been piled up in the *campo*, awaiting a collection from *Veritas*. All that remained was to shift the fine layer of dust that now clung to everything inside the church. Alessio and Bruno looked dead on their feet.

'You know, Lucia,' said Rayner, 'Nathan and I can probably finish this ourselves.'

She shook her head. 'No, it's okay. It'll be quicker with five of us. Besides,' she looked us both up and down, 'we're younger than you.'

'Just a bit.'

'Just a bit. Of course.'

'I seem to have missed all the excitement.' The voice came from the front of the church, where Giles Markham stood in the doorway.

'Giles. Thanks for coming,' I said.

'Sorry I'm late. I really would have been here first thing, but I've been on the phone to the mayor all morning. He's very excited about this broadcast from San Marco. "Spirit of the City", all that sort of thing. And, of course, we might hopefully raise a bit of money as well.'

I nodded. 'Giles, this is Father Michael Rayner. And Lucia, Alessio and Bruno. They've done a brilliant job for us this morning.'

Markham ignored them and went to shake Rayner's hand. 'Father Michael. Good to meet you at last. We seem to keep missing each other.'

'I'm here every Sunday morning,' said Rayner, drily.

'Anyway, we should talk. Later.' He patted Rayner on the chest and nodded at the others. 'A brilliant job. Indeed. Well done everyone.' He looked around the interior. 'Not quite done yet though. Bit of sweeping out to be done, and then we can all go home, eh?'

***

Lucia and I stood in the *campo*, brooms clutched in our frozen hands.

She nodded towards the church.

'Is this prick who I think he is?' she said.

'This is indeed the famous Giles Markham.'

She shook her head. 'Prick,' she repeated.

'He's trying to help, Lucia.'

'He is?'

'Come on. Look at him. He's a middle-aged guy like me and the *padre*, but he's doing his best.'

Lucia looked me up and down. 'The difference is that you and the *padre* both look like shit after all you've done this morning. Look at him. Not a hair out of place. Turns up after the hard work's been done, in order to do five minutes' sweeping. Just to feel good about himself.'

'I think you're being uncharitable.'

'I think I'm being over-charitable. Look.' She grabbed my arm, and nodded towards the steps of the church. Markham was leaning on his broom and directing the two lads. He made a couple of sweeping motions, as if to demonstrate that there was perhaps something lacking in the way they were cleaning up.

'Alessio and Bruno didn't finish until nearly midnight yesterday. They were dragging dead televisions out of a shop on Via Garibaldi. I think they know how to operate a broom without being shown how to.'

I was finding it increasingly hard to stick up for Markham, but thought I should at least try. Perhaps it wasn't his fault. The guy had spent all his life telling people what to do and

I imagined it might be hard to break the habit. I opened my mouth to speak, but he caught sight of us.

'Here! Nathan, over here! Give us a hand, eh? Don't go keeping the pretty girl all to yourself.'

I was about to shout something back, but the words would not come.

'Come on. Don't stand around like that all day, you'll swallow a fly or something.'

I closed my mouth again.

'Prick,' I muttered under my breath.

Lucia smiled, and clapped her hands together. 'Come on, Nathan,' she called out. 'You heard the man. Get to work.'

I swore under my breath once more, and stomped off towards the church where Giles Markham was about to instruct me in the finer points of how to use a broom.

Markham put his hands on his hips, and sighed with satisfaction. 'Good job, everyone.'

If he was aware of the chilliness emanating from the three young people, he seemed unaware of it. He reached into his jacket and took out his wallet.

'I think you need something of a reward for that.'

Lucia shook her head. 'Forget it.'

'No, I insist. You've worked hard.'

'We're not doing it for the money. We're not the Boy Scouts.'

'I know you're not. That's what I think is so commendable about it.' He took out three one-hundred-euro bills. 'Please. If not for yourselves, then for the group. You should do something nice when all this is over.'

Lucia shook her head, but looked uncertain now. Markham

stretched out his hand towards her. She half snatched the notes from him, and passed one to Alessio and one to Bruno. The other she tucked away inside her jeans.

'Thank you,' she said, but couldn't meet Markham's gaze. She stared at the ground, as if feeling guilty. As if she'd just done something dirty.

Markham smiled. 'A pleasure,' he said, softly.

'*Signori*?' A man cosily wrapped up in a Gore-Tex anorak was standing at the church door. 'We're looking for Mr Markham?'

Markham smiled. '*Signor* Marangoni?'

'*Si*,' he nodded. 'My companion is outside – we thought that would be the best place for photographs. And then perhaps you and I can go for a coffee and a chat.'

I looked at Markham. 'The press?'

He nodded, and clapped me on the shoulder, raising a fine cloud of dust. 'Absolutely, Nathan. Get them on your side and you'll soon see things start to move.' He smiled at Rayner. 'A bit of publicity for you as well. And, like I said, we should definitely have a talk some time. Come on then, let's go. Brightest smiles everyone.'

He chivvied us outside, and lined us up in front of the church.

'Okay, Father Michael, perhaps if you stand in the middle there. You're the important one, after all. Maybe hold that broom. Actually, perhaps we should all do that. Makes us look down to earth.' He called out to the photographer. 'Sorry, not trying to do your job for you.'

The photographer gave a smile that doubled nicely as a grimace.

'You to the left of Michael, Nathan. I'll go to his right.'

'Giles, what about the students?'

'Oh yes.' He looked around. 'Maybe later, though. The narrative here is that the Brits are rolling up their sleeves as well.'

'Erm. Right.'

I looked around for our three mud angels. Then I spotted them on the bridge, heading out of the *campo* and in the direction of the Accademia.

'Lucia,' I called out.

She turned and stared at me.

'Lucia, wait up. You need to be in this as well.'

She shook her head. I couldn't see the expression on her face, but I didn't need to. Then she turned and walked away.

Chapter 36

Fede took off her glasses and stared at me over the top of her laptop.

'This is becoming a little irritating,' she said.

'Sorry,' I said. 'I'm just finding it hard to settle.'

Since I'd got back home I'd had a shower, drunk two cups of coffee, resisted the temptation of an early spritz and even tried to interest Gramsci in playing with a ball. None of it had worked.

'So what would make you feel better?'

'I think punching Giles Markham in his stupid punchable face would help.'

Fede sighed, and closed her laptop. 'Okay. But, given that the diplomatic service aren't really supposed to do that sort of thing, why don't you just have a good old rant and tell me all about it?'

She allowed me a good five minutes of invective, in which the words 'smug', 'arrogant' and 'entitled' featured prominently. Eventually, I had to pause for breath.

'Better?'

'Much. Thank you.' A thought struck me. 'I'm sorry, I haven't asked you how your day's been. Why aren't you at the Querini?'

'Nothing more that I can do there. I can help with drying out manuscripts. Getting the lifts going again is beyond me. Anyway, *La Repubblica* have asked if I'd contribute a short piece on the effect of salt water on the mosaics in the Basilica. So that's what I'm working on.'

'Ah. Sorry. Have I been getting in the way a bit?'

'No, not at all. Nothing aids my concentration more than you being in one of your bear-with-a-sore-head moods.'

'Sorry.'

She tapped her laptop. 'Oh, it'll wait. Anyway, would it put you in a better mood if I told you what I discovered in that book you found the other day?'

'You've found something? Why didn't you tell me?'

'It was difficult to make myself heard over the ranting.'

'Hmm. Okay. Point taken. So . . . ?'

She beckoned me over. 'Take a look at this.'

The book was still damp, and she took great care in turning the pages until she came to the image of the four angels.

'Albrecht Durer,' she said. '*The Battle of the Angels*. Sometimes called *The Four Avenging Angels*. It's from his series of woodcuts on *The Apocalypse of St John*. In this image, four angels are loosed upon the world to kill a third of mankind.'

'That's the image I saw on Terzi's boat,' I said.

'Are you sure?'

'Absolutely I'm sure. That's not the sort of image one easily forgets. A third of mankind eh?'

'Well, that's the thing about St John. He's very apocalyptic. So let's take another look at that photograph you took, shall we?'

'It's on my phone.'

'That'll be too small. Email it to me, would you, *caro*?'

I tapped away on my phone and, a few seconds later, her laptop *plinged* as the email arrived. She clicked on the attachment.

'There we are.' She turned the monitor so I could see it more clearly. 'Now, it's not a brilliant photograph but, given you were covertly breaking into *signor* Terzi's boat at the time, that's only to be expected.'

'Technically, I was not breaking in.'

'Anyway,' she continued, 'that's the image you saw, yes?'

'Yes.'

'Now take a look at the book. What do you see?'

'It's the same.'

She sighed. 'Look properly.'

'I am and it's the same and,' I adjusted my glasses, 'it's not the same, is it?'

Fede grinned at me as she shook her head. 'No. Not at all. Because what we have here,' she tapped the screen again, 'is a photograph of a woodcut. Whereas what we have in the book is a reproduction of a pen and ink drawing.'

'So somebody copied it?'

'Perhaps so. But there is one other possibility.'

'Which is?'

'That this drawing is by Durer himself and it's a study for the final work.'

'Wow.'

'I can't be sure of course. It might just be that the author of the book did it himself. Impossible to tell without being able to read the text.'

'You're right.' I picked the book up and closed it, gently. 'Okay. Let's see what Gabriele has to say about this. And let's hope he studied German as part of his degree.'

I pulled on my coat and opened the door. Federica didn't move.

'You're not coming?'

She folded her fingers together and rested her chin on them. 'Is this likely to take some time?'

'I don't know. If he does speak German, it might do. If he doesn't, I guess I'll be back in five minutes.'

'Okay. Well, hopefully he does.' She smiled, and turned back to her computer. 'That way, at least, I might get a little bit of work done today.'

'*In the Footsteps of Durer,*' Gabriele read. '*A journey through Italy.* Friedrich Wilhelm Syberberg. Mm-hmm. Where did you get this?'

'Would you believe it ended up in a pile of rubbish in Campo San Giacomo dell'Orio by accident.'

He whistled. 'Then we're very lucky.'

'You mean it's valuable?'

'Oh, I'm not saying that. But it's certainly of interest. Come with me.'

He led me through to the back room, where a laptop was balanced on a packing case. A large black and white cat looked down at us from a shelf lined with books.

Gabriele smiled. 'This is Ariosto. He moved in about seven years ago. I don't imagine that's his real name but he seems to like it.' He chucked him under the chin. Ariosto purred and gave him a playful swat with his paw. 'And if he didn't like it,

I'm sure he'd have let me know by now. So, let's have a look at this book of yours.'

He tapped away at the keyboard. 'There's a database of rare books that I subscribe to. Invaluable for scholars. And also for someone in my line of business. Now, here we are.' He read from the screen. 'Syberberg, Friedrich Wilhelm. Born Nuremberg 1889, died London 1947. Known works *In the Footsteps of Durer*. Nothing else listed. Poor *Herr* Syberberg doesn't seem to have left us much of a footprint himself.' He chuckled at the little joke.

'But you can read it?'

Gabriele took off his glasses and gave me a hard stare. 'Of course.'

'Oh good. Now, there's one particular part I'd like you to translate for me. It's the chapter with the photograph of the *Avenging Angels*.'

'Mm-hmm. You're a translator as well, aren't you, Nathan?'

'That's right.'

'Do you do this stuff for free?'

It was a fair point. 'No. Of course, I understand. I'll pay for your time.'

'Okay then. Well, you can start by going across to the bar. Get me a beer and a *tramezzino*. Have one yourself if you like. I can't work on an empty stomach.'

I returned five minutes later with two beers and a plate of sandwiches. Gabriele took his, and then motioned for me to sit down on top of a packing case. Ariosto showed rather too much interest in my *tramezzini*, and so I decided the solution was to eat them as quickly as possible. Following which I regretted not having bought more, but Gabriele looked as if he would not appreciate being further disturbed.

And so I sat there, as still as I could, and sipped at my beer whilst Gabriele worked his way through the chapter, punctuating his reading with the occasional whistle or harrumph and pausing occasionally to tap away at his keyboard. Finally, just as I was wondering if I could risk asking him if I should go and fetch us another round, he took off his glasses and gently closed the book.

'So,' he said. 'Albrecht Durer. What do you know about him?'

'Not much. My wife knows more.'

'You should have brought her over then.'

'She's a bit busy at the moment. I didn't think she'd like being asked to sit on a box and watch someone else read.'

'Hmm. Fair enough I suppose.' He tapped the cover of the book. 'Durer was born in Nuremberg in 1471. Even as a boy, it could be seen he had a rare talent as a painter and so, of course, his father found him an apprenticeship. Following which, young Albrecht was expected to leave Nuremberg for his *Wanderjahre.*'

The word was close enough to English for me to guess at its meaning. 'Is that kind of like our Grand Tour?' I said.

'Similar in some ways. Only with more formal study and fewer prostitutes. Now we don't know very much as to what our Albrecht did on his *Wanderjahre* or, indeed, where he went. Perhaps he came to Italy – Nuremberg had strong links with Venice – but we cannot be sure. At any rate, we know he returned home in 1494, and got married. Then, just a few months later, the plague struck Nuremberg and Albrecht struck out for Italy once more. On his own.'

'He left his wife behind in the middle of a *plague*? Blimey, Federica would have had something to say about that.'

Gabriele shrugged. 'Not the happiest of marriages, it would seem. Anyway,' he tapped the cover of the book again, 'this is where our story really starts. *Herr* Syberberg seems to have set out to recreate Albrecht's travels throughout Italy. Durer went to Bologna to study perspective, and then to Padua and on to Mantua to meet Andrea Mantegna. Who, unfortunately, died before he arrived. But most of his time was spent in Venice.

'Now – and this is where *Herr* Syberberg is really interesting – Durer's *Apocalypse* woodcuts were first published in 1498. But general critical theory accepts that he probably started work on these in Italy.'

Gabriele paused for a moment, and grinned at me. 'And Syberberg claims that in Castello, the Masiero family have kept a pen and ink sketch of the *Avenging Angels* ever since Durer's visit to the city back in 1495. Over five hundred years ago.'

'Seriously?'

'Who knows? It's possible, I suppose.'

'But why don't more people know about this?'

He shrugged. 'It's a small press book. There were only ever a few hundred copies printed. And who knows what happened to the drawing? It could easily have disappeared during the occupation in World War Two.'

A pen and ink sketch by Albrecht Durer. Yes, I thought, that would certainly be something worth killing for. I wondered how many Masieros there could be in Venice?

And then I remembered the conversation with Oksana. And the nameplate on the door.

Masiero. It couldn't be. Could it?

'Have you come to see the angels?'

'Are you all right, Nathan?'

I shook my head. 'I am. Lots to think on, though. Thanks, Gabriele.'

'It's been helpful?'

'Invaluable, I'd say.'

He pressed the book into my hand. 'Well, it's been a pleasure. It's been a good workout for my German if nothing else. Come back some time and I'll read you the next chapter.'

'Maybe I will.'

We shook hands and I made my way to the door. Gabriele coughed and I turned around.

'You do remember what I said about translating for free, Nathan?'

He nodded at a stack of books on the floor. *The Collected Works of Carlo Goldoni.*

I sighed and reached for my wallet.

Chapter 37

Matthew snaps the cover of his laptop shut as soon as you come through the door. You've noticed him doing this more and more often recently.

'Ciao, babes!'

'Hello, Matty.'

'How's your day been?'

You sigh, and flop down on the sofa. 'Frustrating. We had a nice little application in from a church on the mainland. The Cappuccini in Mestre. They have an icon in need of some work. It wouldn't take much, but Giles knocked it back. "Not box office enough," he says.'

'Well, maybe he's got a point. Restoring something in Mestre isn't going to lead to many column inches in the rest of the world.'

'I know, but I thought the whole point of the foundation was to give something back to the city. Not just to get Giles Bloody Markham on the cover of La Nuova every couple of weeks.'

'Oh dear. Does this mean you've got another Idiot Boss?'

You sigh. 'It's beginning to feel like it. This was supposed to be my dream job and it just feels like it's going wrong, or that I'm just there to be some dolly bird at press junkets.' You pause for a moment, unsure as to whether you should continue. 'And there's something else.'

'Oh yes?'

You take a deep breath. 'We've had a, well, I suppose you could call it a complaint. From Don Giovanni at the church of the Zittelle. Well, not really a complaint, he was being far too nice about it for that. But the Foundation funded some work for them over a year ago. The whole of the interior was replastered. It turns out it's crumbling away already.

'I took a look at the original application. And then at the architect's report. The work should have been good for at least five years. So I went to Giles. I thought he should know. I said I was a bit worried that we might have used the wrong contractors and perhaps it had been done on the cheap.'

'So what did he say?'

'Well, he seemed angry at first. I can understand that. But then he just smiled, and told me not to concern myself and that he'd sort it out. It was almost like he was telling me not to worry my pretty little head about it.'

'Well, it is a very pretty little head.'

You sigh. 'Wrong thing to say, Matthew. Wrong thing to say.'

'Sorry.' He gets to his feet. 'Prosecco?'

'Oh, that'd be lovely.' You yawn and stretch. 'Thank you.'

'And then afterwards I think we should go out for dinner. What's that really good place? The one where Markham took us just after we arrived?'

'Ai Gondolieri?'

'That's the one.'

'Oh, Matty, it's a lovely thought but it's expensive. That's only for special occasions. Besides, we really do have to start keeping an eye on money. Dad's allowance isn't going to last forever.'

He leans over and kisses the top of your head, rubbing your

shoulders. 'I know, but if my lovely girlfriend has had a tough day at work, then I think we should do something to cheer her up.' He stands up. 'Just give me a couple of minutes to fix the drinks, and then I'll give them a call and see if they've got a table free.'

You nod, tiredly. A quiet night in would do you just as well, but Matty, it seems, is in one of those moods where he's determined to be the best boyfriend in the world, even if he's having to spend other people's money in order to do so. You lay your head back on the sofa, and close your eyes for a moment, listening to him beavering away in the kitchen.

Then you open your eyes again. His laptop is on the table, closed up. And you wonder precisely what he's been keeping secret from you. You challenged him about it once before and he laughed and said it was a secret, a surprise for your birthday. But your birthday has been and gone, marked by nothing more than a pair of fake Murano glass earrings.

And so you get to your feet and pad over to the table, listening all the while for sounds from the kitchen. You flip up the lid of the laptop.

The browser is open at the webpage of a major London auction house, displaying the outcome of a recent sale. It's a woodcut. A woodcut of a rhinoceros. One of a set of eight, extraordinary opportunity to purchase. Estimated price £75,000–£125,000. Price realised, £530,000.

Over half a million pounds. For a woodcut by Albrecht Durer.

You close the laptop and sit down again. You close your eyes, feeling the tears prickling.

You should never have told anyone about this.

Fulvio and Giles had been the same. Excited at first, yes, but then unable to stop talking about the publicity this would generate or how much money it would fetch.

You remember their faces. Fulvio, disbelieving and patronising at first; followed by his growing excitement as you showed him the documents. Then he called Giles in and the two of them huddled over the results of your work – your work – oblivious to your presence. Hunched down over the images and the papers. Vampire-like.

And now Matthew. Always, always coming back to money.

Why does everything have to be so vulgar? So ugly?

You should never have told anyone about this.

Chapter 38

'Naaathan.'

'Ambassador Maxwell. Good morning, Excellency.'

Hmm. Was *Excellency* too much, first thing in the morning? Still, best to take no chances.

'I've seen the newspaper report. Well done, Nathan. Very well done.'

'Thank you, Excellency.' I paused. 'Erm, could I ask which newspaper report? I haven't seen the papers yet.'

He chuckled. 'You and the English priest outside the church with Giles Markham. Brits rolling up their sleeves and helping out. Very well done indeed.'

'Oh good.'

'Seriously, it fits the narrative wonderfully. *Britain's leaving the EU, but not Europe. Still the best of friends and supportive partners.* It'll go down very well indeed.'

'I'm glad.'

'I know I said pass any media work on to us but you seem to have handled this very well.'

'In all honesty, Excellency, I really didn't have all that much to do with it. It was Giles Markham who arranged all the press.'

'Ah well, I can imagine he's very good at that sort of thing.'

'He certainly seems to be. Do you know him?'

'I've heard him speak a couple of times. Once in London, once in Rome. Quite inspiring in his way. He can be a little – *overpowering*, is that the word?'

'Yes. I think that's exactly the word.'

'But I suppose that's what he thinks he needs to do in order to get things done. I met a few of them in my previous life. In business, you know.' He chuckled again. I didn't think I'd ever heard him laugh so much. 'God knows, I don't miss those days. Anyway, mustn't keep you. Enjoy the rest of your day, Nathan. You've earned it.'

'Thank you, Excellency.'

'Oh, I don't think there's any need for any of this *Excellency* nonsense, Nathan. William will be fine.'

'Oh right. Well, in that case, thanks, William.'

He hung up, and I spun round in a complete circle in my chair.

Gramsci sat on the desk, staring at me. I picked him up at arm's length.

'How about that, Grams? Do you not have a brilliant owner?'

He miaowed, and his paws scrabbled furiously through the air.

'Okay, okay. I know owner isn't quite the right word.' I put him down, and he scurried away. 'But I am quite brilliant, aren't I?'

'You are, *caro*? What have you done now?' Federica came out of the bathroom, towelling her hair.

'I seem to have been brilliant by accident.'

'Oh?'

'Yes. Ambassador Maxwell's very pleased with me.'

'You mean that photoshoot yesterday?'

'Exactly that. Markham arranged it all and,' I coughed, modestly, 'I seem to be looking quite good on the back of it. Mind you, he didn't have a church wall collapsing on him, so perhaps it's only fair.'

She smiled. '"Church wall collapsing". I can see this is a tale that's going to grow in the telling.'

'Well, it sort of did.'

'Sort of did, in that you got a bit dusty when some plaster dropped on you. Did you tell him how you pulled Father Michael out of the way a second before the masonry came crashing down on him?'

'No. Well, not yet anyway.'

She smiled, and hugged me, and I breathed in the smell of her hair, damp against my cheek. 'I'm glad you're happy, though.'

'Well, I am. Early morning calls with the Ambassador don't usually end this well. I'll be called to the Palace next. Honoured for Diplomacy in the Service of Her Majesty. That sort of thing.'

'How lovely. Will I get to come as well?'

'Oh, I'll insist on it, *cara*.'

I heard the doorbell ringing. Once. Then twice. Then a continuous buzzing as the mystery caller leaned on the bell.

'All right. All right. I'm coming,' I muttered.

Federica looked out of the window.

'Ah,' she said.

'Ah?'

'I'm sorry, *caro*, but it might be that not everybody was so thrilled with the press coverage.'

I picked up the entryphone and had time to say the '*Ch*' in '*Chi'è?*' before I yanked the phone away from my ear, in an attempt to escape from the torrent of abuse at the other end.

Fede looked at me. 'Angry girl?'

I sighed, and pressed the buzzer to let her in. Then I opened the apartment door in order to save her the trouble of knocking it down.

Lucia Frigo was the first person I had ever met who was adept in the use of a rolled-up newspaper as a deadly weapon.

I backed away from her, step by step, as she jabbed the rolled-up *Gazzettino* into my chest, time and time again.

'*Cazzo,*' she swore at me.

I put my hands up in the hope it might calm her down. It merely gave her two more targets to aim at, as she slapped at them with surprising force.

'Ow!'

'*Cazzo,*' she repeated.

'Could you stop doing that, please?'

She swore once more, in a *Veneziano* that was beyond my powers of recall. I backed away further, into the office, where Gramsci sat on the desk, observing with interest.

'Can we please not do this? Look, you're frightening my cat,' I added, desperately.

She paused for a moment to look at Gramsci, who stared back at her with an expression on his face that suggested he should have tried something like this years ago.

She frowned. 'I don't think I am,' and lunged at me again.

And then Federica was behind her, to pluck the newspaper out of her hand.

There was silence, at last, broken only by Gramsci who, having decided that he'd seen everything of interest, plopped down off the table and padded from the room.

Lucia was breathing deeply, and reached for the newspaper again, but Federica snatched it out of reach.

'Okay, before I give you this back, two things. One, I live here as well and I'd prefer not to see my apartment trashed if it's all the same to you?'

Lucia flushed, but nodded.

'Secondly, if I give you this back, do you promise to stop attacking my husband? I know he can be annoying at times but, really, that's my job, not yours.'

She nodded once more, and reached for the paper.

Fede waved a finger at her. 'Uh-uh. Promise?'

'I promise.'

'Good. Here you are.' Lucia took it from her fingers, and I noticed that her hand was shaking, ever so gently. I smiled.

Fede glared at me. 'And I don't know what you've got to smile about, Nathan. Now, shall we all talk about this like sensible people?'

Lucia took a deep breath, and tossed the newspaper on to the table. 'There,' she said.

It was more than a bit ragged by now, but I smoothed it out as best I could. They'd done a very professional job, I had to admit. I rarely looked so good in photographs. Me, the *padre* and Giles Markham beamed out at the camera above the headline 'Now the English are helping.'

Moved by the recent scenes of terrible devastation in the city,

*philanthropist Giles Markham has pledged new efforts for res-
toration work throughout the Centro Storico. Tomorrow, he
launches a fundraising drive from the crypt of San Marco, in
the company of the mayor and the Patriarch. More than enough
for one week, you might imagine. But he took time out from
his schedule yesterday to help clean up the Anglican church of
St George's. Here we see him in the company of padre Michael
Rayner and His Excellency Nathan Sutherland, British Consul
in Venice and a long-standing friend to the city.*

'So,' said Lucia, 'what do you think about that?'

I rubbed my chin. 'Well, it's very gratifying to be addressed
as "Excellency", but they've got that bit wrong. I don't have
a title.'

'And the rest?'

I read further. 'Blimey. They're suggesting he might even
be nominated as Venetian of the Year.'

'Yes. I saw that.' She swore under her breath again. 'What
do you think about that?'

'Well, I don't think it's quite on, to be honest. After all,
I've been here a lot longer than he has.'

Lucia raised the newspaper but Fede, as gently as possible,
caught her hand and lowered it. 'I think it might help to be
serious, Nathan,' she said.

I took a deep breath. 'Okay.' I picked up the paper again,
and scanned through the rest before dropping it back on to
the desk. 'You want me to be honest? It's a bit shit, isn't it?'

Lucia leaned in towards me. 'You know how much work
we did yesterday. We'd been working until midnight the
night before. Alessio and Bruno cleared all the crap out of
your church. And this prick turns up, doesn't even get a mark

on his suit, and suddenly he's the saviour of Venice. Yeah. I think "a bit shit" covers it.'

'You're right. It's not fair. And I'll sort it. I'll get them to print the full story, maybe tomorrow. But I'll call them, I promise.'

She shook her head and drew in a great, shuddering breath. Behind all the bravado and bluster I could see she was almost on the verge of tears. Having so much to say and finding it hard to physically get the words out.

'It's not about that. Don't you get it by now, it's not about that? Don't you understand how hard it is to be young in this city? Every year, there are fewer and fewer of us. One day, everybody will have left for the mainland. One day, it'll be left to one of us to lock up for the final time.

'My dad says that the worst of it is that we've lost our self-respect. We've sold everything off. Nothing counts any more except milking tourists for money. That's all the city exists for now. To be looked at by tourists. That's all *we* exist for. Like those shitheads in Piazza San Marco the other day, enjoying their day out in Veniceland. So, what's left for us now, eh? *Carnevale's* not for us any more. And now even our disasters aren't.

'We don't want your pity. Do you get that? All we want is for you to start treating us like grown-ups. Enough with being patted on the head and "Poor Venice" this and "Poor Italy" that.'

'I understand,' I said.

She shook her head. 'No you don't. You don't at all.' I thought she was about to speak some more, but then her phone buzzed.

'*Papà*?'

I heard a voice on the line, but was unable to make out the words. Lucia rolled her eyes.

'I'll be home soon, *Papà*.' She raised her eyes in order to stare directly at me. 'I'm just speaking with this really dumb English guy. But I'm finished now.'

She hung up the phone and slid it into her back pocket. And then she turned and left, clicking the door shut behind her. It was the quietest thing she'd done since she'd arrived.

I sighed. 'Bugger.'

Fede put her arms around me. 'What it is to be young, eh?'

'I feel like I've let her down.'

'Not your fault. How were you supposed to know that Giles Markham was going to use the occasion to get himself in the papers?'

'I suppose I should have thought that he wouldn't miss an occasion for publicity.'

She gave me a hug. 'As I said. Not. Your. Fault. She'll calm down.'

'I wouldn't be so sure.'

'Well, I am. I remember being her age. You think you can change the world, and then it turns out that you can't. So you decide to be angry with it instead. It'll pass. You must remember what it was like?'

I thought about it, and shook my head. 'No. Even in my teens I breezed through life with the same cheery insouciance.'

She ruffled my hair. 'Come on then. Let's do lunch at the Brazilians. From what you were saying it sounds like Ed could do with our money.'

'Now there's an idea.'

I was about to take my coat off the back of the door when the doorbell rang again.

'There we go,' said Fede. 'That'll be Lucia, wanting to apologise.'

'No, it'll be Lucia having remembered there was something she'd forgotten to shout about to me.' I sighed and pressed the entryphone. '*Chi è?*'

There was a pause. 'Is that Nathan Sutherland?'

There was no mistaking the voice. '*Padre?*'

'Yes. Sorry, your accent's too good. I thought for a moment I was in the wrong place. Can I come up?'

'Actually we were just going for lunch. Why not come along with us?'

'I've got a better idea. Let me buy you lunch. I think it's the least I can do. And besides, there's something I need to talk to you about.'

Chapter 39

'You know, Nathan, when I offered to buy you lunch I would have been happy to take you somewhere other than the pub downstairs.'

'Believe me, *padre*, it's what we wanted.' I lowered my voice. 'And Ed's having a bit of a hard time of it, so it's practically your Christian duty to be here.'

'Is it? Oh right. Do you mind if I pass on one of those Negroni things though? I had one – at least I think it was one – at your wedding reception.'

'You didn't enjoy it?'

'I did at the time. The next day I thought it was the very distillation of evil. No, a small beer will be fine for me, thanks.'

'Sure.' I looked at Fede. 'Usual?'

She nodded.

'Okay. One small beer and two spritz Camparis, Ed.'

'Coming up.' He smiled. He was looking happier today.

'How are things?'

'Could be worse. The other day was a bloody miracle. Another ten centimetres and we'd have been flooded again. The only downer is the fridge. The insurance won't cover it. *Forza maggiore.*'

'Ah, sorry, man.'

He shrugged. 'It's okay. Could have been a lot worse. There's places round the city in a far worse state than we are. Anything to eat?'

I picked out some *tramezzini* and *polpette* from the cabinet and took them back to our table. Then I went back for our drinks. I became aware that the *padre* and Fede were staring at me.

'What?' I said.

'Nothing. Nothing at all,' said Fede. Then she nodded at my plate. 'You plan on sharing any of that with us?'

'Oh. I assumed we'd do our own thing. I thought if I picked you anything out it'd probably be the wrong thing and I'd end up having to swap.'

'Do I do that?'

'Yes. Yes, you do.' I bit into one of the *polpette* and made a yummy sound. 'These are good, you know? You should get yourself one.'

She sighed and got to her feet. 'Father Michael, can I get you anything?'

'Oh, I'll just have whatever you're having.'

'*Baccalà mantecato* and a small octopus on a stick.'

He paused. 'Okay. I'll have whatever Nathan's having.'

She returned with two plates. 'I can't believe you were going to let Father Michael go hungry.'

'I wasn't going to let him go hungry. I just didn't feel confident in my ability to pick out something he'd like. Otherwise he'd be sitting here staring at an octopus on a stick, and wondering how to be polite about it.'

Rayner coughed, gently. 'Married life treating you well then?'

We both smiled.

'Absolutely, *padre*!'

'Couldn't be better!'

'So,' I said, 'lunch aside – which is very kind of you – what's all this about?'

Rayner sighed. 'I take it you've seen the newspapers?'

'I've seen one of them. Sort of. Lucia came round and hit me with it multiple times.'

'Ah.'

'On the other hand, the Ambassador was positively purring when I spoke to him this morning.'

'Hmm. Similarly with the bishop. Which is strange. I never really think of him as being a particularly purry bishop.' He shook his head. 'I'm sorry about the young woman though. That Markham chap turned up and, well, just kind of seemed to take over.' He paused. 'And then there was all that business about "we should keep in touch".'

'Oh. Do you think he'll become a regular?'

'I very much doubt it. But that's not what he meant. No, he has it in mind to raise substantial funds for us. Very substantial.'

'Replastering the wall?'

'Replastering the wall. And the exterior. Resurfacing the floor. Repairing and resealing the stained-glass windows. And I got the impression he'd probably have the organ restored as well.'

'Wow. Well, that's fantastic. No wonder you've got a nice purry bishop.'

'"Fantastic,"' he repeated. 'Yes. You'd think so, wouldn't you?'

'It is good news, though? Right?' I said.

'Maybe. But I'm starting to wonder.' He sighed. 'I got a phone call yesterday from Don Giovanni at the Zitelle.'

I almost choked on my spritz. 'You what?'

'Don Giovanni at the Zitelle.'

I laughed again. 'I'm sorry. I'd never thought about this before, but Giovanni's a bit of an unfortunate name for a priest, isn't it? I mean, you'd think if his parents had had ambitions for their son in that area they'd have chosen a different name, no?'

I hummed a bit from the *Champagne Aria*, and then became aware that both Fede and Rayner were giving me a hard stare.

'Sorry,' I said.

Rayner looked at Fede. 'I'm beginning to understand,' he said. Then he looked back at me. 'Anyway, I have the pleasure of knowing Don Giovanni,' he glared, 'from the Ecumenical Council. And he, like His Excellency the Ambassador, my bishop and your young friend, was also looking at the newspapers this morning. And what he read inspired him to give me a call.'

'And?'

Rayner said nothing.

'Sorry, *padre*, maybe I shouldn't have asked but is this like asking you to break the seal of the confessional or something?'

Rayner sighed. 'Not exactly. It was something said to me by a friend. But, I suppose, he didn't say that I shouldn't pass it on. All he said to me was that I should be careful.'

'You what?'

'Be careful. That's all he said. Apparently the Zitelle also received some money from the Markham Foundation in the past. Don Giovanni told me that, well, it hadn't worked out quite as they'd have hoped.'

'That was all he said?'

'I think that was as much as he felt comfortable saying. The church of the Zitelle is very close to where Markham lives. I imagine it would be awkward if he found out that the priest of his local church – a place for which the Markham Foundation has raised substantial funds – had been telling stories.'

I finished my small octopus and looked sadly at the bare cocktail stick.

'That was mine, you realise? said Federica.

'Ah. Sorry. I'll get you another, promise.' I turned back to Rayner. 'So why are you telling me this, Michael?'

'Because I don't want to commit myself and my congregation to a lengthy period of matched fundraising if it's not what it appears to be.'

'Oh, I see. You want me to investigate?'

He winced. 'Don't call it that. But it would be nice to know exactly what it is I'm supposed to be careful of.'

'I understand.'

'And I knew I could count on you to be discreet, Nathan.'

'You certainly can, *padre*.'

'Actually, no. What I mean is I can count on Federica to be discreet.'

My face fell, but Fede smiled and patted his hand. 'You certainly can, Father Michael.'

Chapter 40

Even in November, less than a week after the greatest floods in half a century, the Rialto *vaporetto* stop seemed as busy as ever.

Fede and I crammed ourselves on to the Number 1. She shuffled around as best she could in order to face me, glaring at a tourist who refused to remove his rucksack.

'Why are you looking so happy?' she said.

I was going to gesture around the cabin, but didn't have sufficient space to move my arms. 'It's all this,' I said, turning my head to my left and then to my right. 'As much as we might complain about it, this is normal. That's what we need right now. Standing on an overcrowded boat is normal.' I chuckled. 'It's the city healing itself.'

The area around San Zaccaria was still a chaos of broken masonry from the effects of the flood, but all the boat services seemed to have been restored. We jumped on the next boat out to Giudecca, passing by San Giorgio Maggiore where two divers were investigating the anchorage of the pontoon. The sight of them in the grey, choppy, freezing-cold water made me shiver.

'Are they doing that everywhere?' I said.

Fede shrugged. 'I don't know about everywhere. But all the stops in the open lagoon, I imagine. The Sant Elena pontoon has disappeared completely. So has one at Zattere.'

After San Giorgio, the boat passed by the barracks of the Guardia di Finanza, past the homes of Giles Markham and his more glamorous neighbour and on to the *vaporetto* stop near the small, unloved church of the Zitelle. Lying between two of Andrea Palladio's greatest works, the church of the Redentore and San Giorgio Maggiore, it never attracted as much attention as its bigger, whiter, more Palladian neighbours.

It may or may not have been the work of Palladio himself. Nobody was quite sure. No evidence existed that he had ever been involved with the design, and construction did not begin until after the great architect's death. And so the church of the Zitelle – the centre part of a convent that had once given shelter to those unfortunate young women not wealthy enough to possess a dowry – would always be followed by the disclamatory suffix '*attributed* to Andrea Palladio'. Mass, now, was only celebrated on Wednesdays and Sundays, and part of the convent had been converted into a luxury hotel. The church of the Zitelle, like many in Venice, would one day – perhaps very soon now – close its doors forever. Just like Venice itself, I thought, and gave myself a mental slap for being so downbeat. Not the time, Nathan, not the time at all.

We were the only ones to get off the boat. 'Do you know, I don't think I've ever been here before?' I said, and promptly fell flat on my face.

I heard shouting from behind me, and then two sets of arms were around me, hauling me to my feet.

'*Signore*, are you okay?'

'Are you hurt, *signore*?'

I nodded. 'I'm fine, thanks. At least I think so.' I bent over, resting my hands on my knees. The wind had been knocked out of me and I breathed deeply, as my head spun.

'*Signore*, it's very dangerous here.' One of my rescuers rested his hand on my back. 'Look.' The edge of the *fondamenta* near the pontoon was slick with green algae. 'All along this stretch. The water's been high all year and this,' he cursed under his breath, 'is the result. Easy to get hurt. Be careful.'

'I will.' I took another deep breath. 'And thanks again.'

The two men walked off together, one of them sliding his shoe against the algae-slick stone and shaking his head, as if to indicate just how dangerous it was.

Fede rubbed my arm. 'Are you okay? Seriously?'

I nodded. 'Hell of a shock though. I could have gone in. How do I look?'

She smiled. 'A little whiter than usual, but that'll pass.' She put her hands on my lapels to adjust my coat, and then brushed me down. 'I think you've got away with it.' Then she looked back to the edge of the *fondamenta* and her expression changed. 'I don't come to Giudecca often, you know. But it never used to be like this.' She looked out upon the Giudecca Canal and shook her head. Then she shivered and pulled me closer to her. 'Every year, the water rises. It's getting worse.'

I hugged her. 'Come on. Let's go and look at a crumbling church. That'll cheer us up.'

I walked inside and immediately turned around. 'Mass still going on,' I whispered.

She checked her watch and gave a wry smile. 'Must be a long sermon.'

I shrugged. 'To be fair, there's a lot to talk about at the moment.'

I stepped back, and looked upwards at the church. Flanked by two bell towers, with a tympanum about the facade it looked – just about – Palladian enough.

'Did Ruskin ever come here?' I asked Fede.

'I don't think so. Even if he did he'd probably have been very rude about it. He didn't have much time for Palladio.'

'What did he say about the Redentore, again?'

"Contemptible under every point of rational regard."'

'Mmm. Yeah. He was a man of strong opinions, you'd have to say.'

'Oh, he was.'

'He's got a stained-glass window in St George's, you know. One of the things Markham's promising to restore.' She was about to reply when I heard movement from inside. 'Here we go, sounds like they're finishing.'

A congregation of perhaps twenty, mainly elderly, people filed past us.

'More than I'd expected,' I said.

'It's been a difficult time. It might have brought a few of the waverers back to the fold.'

'You ever been here before?'

She shook her head. 'First time.'

'Wow. There's a church in Venice you've never been into?' She squeezed my arm. 'Oh, you'd be surprised.'

The interior was smaller than I had expected, reminding me that much of what we could see from the outside was not, in fact, the church itself but rather two wings of the convent of which it had once formed a part. Nevertheless, if it inevitably lacked the grandeur of its bigger, more imposing neighbours, it was still a pretty little place, even in the greyness of the winter light. An appealing but neglected church, overlooked by Ruskin and not even important enough for Jan Morris.

Federica looked around, nodded, and then walked up to the altar, crossing herself as was her habit.

'Seen anything you like?' I said.

'A couple of things.' She pointed to the painting above the altar. 'Francesco Bassano. *The Presentation of the Virgin in the Temple.*'

'I'll never understand how you just recognise this stuff, you know.'

'Well, you start to recognise things. What's that horrible band you like?'

'Hawkwind?'

'No. Not them. The other one.'

'Goblin?'

'No.'

'Jethro Tull?'

'That's them. You'd recognise them from just a few notes, wouldn't you?'

'Well, yes. But there aren't many flautists in rock music. That makes it easier.'

'And there weren't many painters who used colour in quite the same way as Francesco Bassano. It's like a fingerprint. Once you know about it, it's hard to miss.'

'So Francesco Bassano is Jethro Tull?'

'If you like.' She grinned. 'Of course, what really made it easier to identify was reading the Wikipedia page on my phone.'

'Oh.' My face fell. 'And I thought you were so brilliant, as well.'

'Brilliant enough. But not quite enough to identify a painting I've never seen by a minor artist in a church I've never been into.'

A gentle cough came from behind us.

'*Signori*?'

We turned to see a tall, thin priest looking down at us from the altar steps.

'Don Giovanni?' I resisted the temptation to boom out the words like the *Commendatore* at the beginning of the penultimate scene of Mozart's opera.

'I am. Mr Sutherland?'

I took a step backwards. 'I'm impressed.'

He smiled. 'It's not that clever really. Father Michael said you might be paying me a visit. And so,' he spread his arms wide, 'an English accent in a church that nobody visits on a grey and wet day – well, I assumed it was you.'

'I'm still impressed.'

He chuckled. 'Well now, I'd have looked rather silly if it hadn't been you, of course. Father Michael said you might want to ask me some questions.'

'Yes.' Federica, I noticed, was no longer standing beside me but was next to the wall of the nearest chapel, trailing her fingers over the surface. She held her hand up to us, wiggling her fingers. I could see that they were damp, and flecked with white plaster. 'That's not good,' she said. 'So when did you get that done?'

Don Giovanni sighed. 'Come with me.'

***

Don Giovanni and Federica had been perched over a file of technical documentation for what seemed a considerable time. Finally, Fede removed her glasses and nodded.

'Okay,' I said. 'So what is it? What's the problem?'

'The rendering used on the interior wall. It's not the type recommended by the *Soprintendenza*. Technically, it might actually be illegal, but I'll need to check on that.'

Don Giovanni shook his head. 'I don't understand, *dottoressa*.'

'The rendering that's been used on your interior walls. It's not right for this environment. Oh, it might work somewhere like Sardinia with zero per cent humidity, but here? You're lucky it's lasted as long as it has.'

Don Giovanni frowned the frown of someone who was about to ask an awkward question but would prefer not to.

'Are you sure, *dottoressa*?'

I winced, but Federica's response was merely to replace her spectacles on her nose, the better to look over the top of them at Don Giovanni.

'I'm sure,' was all she said, her tone just a little bit too light.

'I don't understand,' said the priest. 'What's happened here?'

'I don't know, *padre*. Who was managing the project?'

Don Giovanni shrugged. 'Mr Markham, I believe. He told me he likes to be hands-on.'

'Evidently.' Fede looked at me and nodded. 'Okay, *caro*. Anything you'd like to ask the *padre*?'

I shook my head. 'I'm not the right person to be asking questions about this sort of thing. But thanks for your time, sir.'

'A pleasure.'

Fede smiled at him. 'It's been lovely to look around here. It's delightful.'

He gave an apologetic shrug. 'I'm afraid you're not seeing it at its best. Come back in six months.' He paused. 'Mr Markham has plans for restoring the floor.'

'Oh, does he? Does he now? Well, that sounds like something we shouldn't miss.' She nodded at him. 'Thank you again, *padre*.' She linked her arm in mine and steered me out of the church and on to the *fondamenta*. We waved at Don Giovanni, who smiled and nodded at us, prior to disappearing inside.

Fede stepped back and raised her head to stare up at the church. 'Thank you, *caro*. That was worth coming out for.'

'Oh good.'

'Yes. Not the most beautiful of churches, of course, but full of interest.'

'And what about – you know?'

'Well, right now I'm thinking of ways that Mr Markham might have got permission to use an illegal rendering on the interior walls.'

I looked to my right, and smiled. 'Well now. Why not ask him yourself?'

She frowned, and then her expression cleared as she saw what I was looking at. 'Oh.'

Dressed in a tracksuit and sweating profusely, Giles Markham was jogging down the *fondamenta* towards us.

'Good afternoon, Nathan,' he panted.

'Good afternoon, Giles. This is my wife, *Dottoressa* Federica Ravagnan.'

'*Piacere, dottoressa.*'

He was still jogging on the spot and becoming alarmingly purple-faced.

'You don't have to do that, you know.'

He looked confused for a moment, and then smiled. He stopped jogging, and I waited until his breath seemed a little less laboured.

'Better?'

'Much.' He was still gasping a little, but his face had assumed a more healthy colour. 'That's two laps of Giudecca finished.'

'Wow. How far is that?'

'About six kilometres, or so the app tells me. Too many at any rate. But I think I'm feeling the benefit.'

I tried not to stare. Markham, I thought, could only be a few years older than me, yet he did not seem to be particularly benefitting from feeling the burn. A dreadful thought struck me that perhaps I might be looking into my own future.

'What brings you over to Giudecca, Nathan? I'm sorry, if you wanted a chat could we make it some other time? I'll be fit for nothing after all this. Maybe after our presentation this evening?'

'Oh, don't worry, I'm not here on official business or anything like that. No, we just wanted a look around the church.'

If Markham was fazed at all, he didn't show it. 'Oh yes?'

'I've never been there before,' said Federica.

'Really?'

'No. I'm not over on Giudecca very often. When I was growing up, it seemed like the end of the world. So it was lovely to see it at last.' She paused. 'A shame that the plaster-work's crumbling.'

Markham smiled. 'I know. The problem is there's not very much that can be done about that.'

'Well, there can be. You just need to be sure you use exactly the right materials. The *Soprintendenza* would know all about that sort of thing.'

Markham nodded. 'Well, I'll be sure to ask for advice next time.'

'Next time?'

'Of course. If it's not been done correctly, I'll put it right.'

'That's good of you,' I said. 'Another fundraising campaign?'

He nodded. 'If that's what needs to be done.' He smiled again. 'Okay. I think I can make it back to my apartment without keeling over. You might have saved my life again.' He jogged backwards a few steps. 'Be seeing you,' he said, then turned and – slowly – jogged the remaining yards to his home.

Fede linked her arm in mine, and patted my hand. 'You know, *caro*, you don't have to do the *dottoressa* thing every time you introduce me.'

'Too much?'

'Just a little.'

'It's just that I'm very proud of you, you know.'

'Why, thank you.' She reached up to kiss my ear.

'*Dottoressa* Federica Ravagnan. Something of an expert in the field of the effects of humidity and brackish water on stucco. Not to mention mosaics. I think it's something to be proud of. And I tell you what . . .'

'What?'

I looked along the *fondamenta* to where Markham was fumbling with his keys in the gate.

'I bet I know who Giles Markham is going to be Googling just as soon as he gets inside.'

Chapter 41

A Doge's lot, in the early centuries of *La Serenissima*, was not always a happy one. Yes, you might technically be the supreme magistrate and governor of the Republic of Venice, wielding power from the Palazzo Ducale itself, but you also stood a reasonable chance of being overthrown, exiled, tortured, assassinated or any combination thereof.

And such was the fate of Pietro IV Candiano, twenty-second Doge of Venice. Like many such Doges of the time, he'd had both his good and bad points. He'd banned the slave trade with Byzantium, for example. On the other hand, he'd also destroyed the city of Oderzo, made war against Ferrara and blinded the Bishop of Torcello. In 976 the Venetians, sick of economic hardships brought about by his foreign policy, decided they'd had enough, set fire to the Ducal Palace, killed the Doge and his young son Pietro as they fled, and threw their bodies into a nearby slaughterhouse.

Setting fire to the *Palazzo Ducale* however, was not without its – possibly predictable – consequences, as the blaze quickly spread through the city, destroying over three hundred buildings. Amongst them was the Basilica dedicated to St Mark, the city's Patron Saint, and where the body of the Evangelist had lain since its theft from Alexandria in 828.

We might imagine, then, that awkward conversations were had and that quite a lot of explaining needed to be done.

Mark, however, seems not to have borne any grudges and in 1094 – during the construction of the third basilica on the site – he made his presence known to Doge Vitale Faliero by, apparently, extending his mummified arm out of a stone pillar, from wherein his remains were found to be intact. Today, his relics lie in a sarcophagus under the high altar. But in Faliero's day, the Evangelist was placed in a newly constructed chapel in the crypt beneath the Basilica.

It proved impossible to prevent it from flooding, however, and in 1604 it was sealed off, it was believed, forever, the miasma of fetid water and stale air giving it an unhealthy and unpleasant atmosphere. Reopened in 1899, it now served as the final resting place of the Patriarchs of Venice. The opportunity to visit it, therefore, was something of a privilege; although the company of a millionaire philanthropist, the mayor of Venice and the Patriarch himself was, to say the least, a little intimidating.

Federica had made sure I'd worn my smartest jacket and a non-offensive tie, although the effect was a little offset by the Wellington boots that would be necessary in the still-flooded crypt.

A few days earlier and we would have been chest-deep in water. Even now, boots were barely enough. Yet there was still a magic to this place. The blue-grey of the marble flooring shimmered under the surface of the water, whilst the overhead lights picked out the pink and white stones of the vaulted arches. And there, atop a stone altar, beneath the final resting place of the Evangelist, stood a shimmering green-blue crucifix in Murano glass. There was a ruined, yet magisterial beauty to it.

Markham patted me on the shoulder. 'Magnificent, isn't it?'

I could only agree, and nodded.

'I believe you know his *Eccellenza Reverendissima* the Patriarch. And our wonderful mayor, of course.'

'I've met them both. Briefly. I'm not sure if they'll remember me.'

'Oh right. Well, the format is that both of them will say a few words and then they'll pass it over to you, to introduce me. And then we'll take a few questions from journalists. Okay?'

'Absolutely fine.'

'Good man.'

I scarcely recognised the Patriarch without his work clothes. He was dressed in a thick Gore-Tex jacket, a large pectoral cross the only concession to his day job. Vestments, to be fair, would have been impractical in the water. He nodded and smiled at me, either remembering me or at least being polite enough to pretend that he did. The mayor gave me a curt nod of the head. Then he turned to the Patriarch, and laid his hand on his shoulder. His *Eccellenza* was unable to prevent himself from flinching slightly, but smiled as best he could.

'I need to get back to Mestre as soon as possible after the broadcast, *Eccellenza Reverendissima*. But perhaps we might consider something in the future? Perhaps a live service from the Basilica. Faith is a great help to people in days like these, I'm sure you agree.' His *Eccellenza* smiled, yet again, and nodded.

I looked down at the water pooling around our ankles. Was it me, or had it got visibly greasier?

Markham checked his watch, and then steered me in the direction of the altar. 'I know what you're thinking,' he said, lowering his voice.

'You do?'

'"Faith is a great help to people." Well, I'm sure it is, but a little bit of money to help them open their shops and clean up their houses might be an even greater help.' He clapped his hands together. 'And that's what I'm going to do. This is just the start, Nathan.'

'It is?'

'Absolutely. I think we should do a similar event, perhaps at the Salute. Maybe a third, at the Redentore. Tomorrow, I'm speaking with the *Times* and the *Telegraph*, *The Art Newspaper*, BBC News and Channel 4 News. And with a bit of luck, we might be able to get the Discovery Channel interested, but that's for maybe six months down the line. But that doesn't matter. That'll just give things a little bit of a kick, just when interest is starting to tail off.'

I blinked. 'You can just – do – stuff like this?'

He looked surprised. 'Of course. If you know the right people.' He grinned. 'And if you say to them, come and stay in Venice in one of my apartments for a month, it's surprising how accommodating they can be.'

'I can imagine. Well, perhaps not in my apartment. They'd need to like cats for one thing.'

The cameraman and the sound man made some last-minute checks, and then the director gave us a thumbs up.

'*Signori*, are you ready?'

Markham waved his hand at him, and spoke a few words in bad *Veneziano*. The director looked confused. Markham sighed, and repeated himself in English, perhaps a little too loudly. 'We'll just be five minutes. Okay?'

The director shrugged and turned his back.

Markham swore under his breath. 'I'll never understand this. You have a go at speaking their language and pfft! And I'm trying to do them a favour here.' He shook his head. 'Silly to get angry though. I mean, look at all this. How many people in this city have ever had this space to themselves, eh? How many people in the world, for that matter?'

'I wonder if Jan Morris ever came here? Or John Julius Norwich?'

'Probably. But not on an occasion like this.' He clapped his hands together again. 'It really is magnificent, isn't it?'

I could only agree. But, magnificent as it undoubtedly was, it was also bloody cold, and my toes were freezing inside my boots. I couldn't stop myself from shivering.

Markham noticed. 'Come on then. I think it's time we got started. Thanks for all your work here, Nathan. It'll help. I mean it. I'll give Maxwell a call, tell him how brilliant you've been.'

I bristled, just ever so slightly, at Markham's conviction that I should be pleased at this, as if he were passing a good report on to my line manager for my six-monthly appraisal. But then I forced a smile on to my face. In Markham's world this was simply what you did. He was trying to be nice.

'Thank you,' I said.

'No worries. And then perhaps afterwards we can head off to a bar and find something to take the chill out of our bones.'

'Good idea.'

'. . . I'd just like to repeat how very honoured I am to be here, as a representative of Her Majesty's Diplomatic Service and to assure you of our friendship and support in the months and years to come.' Ambassador Maxwell, I thought, would be proud of me. 'And with that, I think it's time to hand over to Mr Giles Markham, head of the Markham Foundation.'

I smiled and stepped to one side, as Markham moved forward, beaming at the cameras.

'Ladies and gentlemen, *signore e signori*.' He turned and bowed his head in the direction of the Patriarch. *'Eccellenza Reverendissima*. Mr Mayor. And Mr Sutherland. Honoured as I am to be here tonight these are not the circumstances, of course, which one would have chosen.

'We all know, of course, what has happened in this city over the past ten days. I think it's safe to say that no one who has been here during this terrible period is likely to forget it.'

He bowed his head for a moment. 'We know, of course, of those people who are still unable to return home. Of shops, bars, hotels, restaurants that are still unable to open despite the best efforts of the mayor and his people. But I wonder, perhaps, if we might start with a few moments of silence in memory of those who died last week.'

He closed his eyes and lowered his head, clasping his hands in front of him.

There was no sound except for the frantic clicking of cameras, and the splashing of water by photographers jostling for the perfect shot of Markham, his head bowed in respect. Fair play to him, I thought. He really knew how to work a crypt.

He opened his eyes again, and slowly straightened up.

'I'm not here to ask for money. I am here, purely and simply, to offer whatever help I can. Because this city is precious to me and to many throughout the world. Venice, I'm sure you all know, will not be left alone or abandoned in the weeks, months and years to come.'

Clever, I thought. Don't ask for money. That might be seen as vulgar. Just go on television, get your name out there on the news and then – then what? Wait for people to start offering help, or money, or both. Yes, it was clever. Giles Markham, I thought, was now a shoo-in for Venetian of the Year.

Another camera flashed in front of my eyes, dragging me back to reality. Markham's speech, it seemed, was drawing to a close.

'I haven't been in this city that long. But I am proud to call myself a Venetian. Because this is a city that endures. This is a city that survives. This is a city that is loved. It will endure this, it will survive this. And that love will carry us through this. Thank you.'

It would be untrue to say the crowd went wild. The Patriarch, for one, did not look like a man used to excesses of emotion. But he nodded appreciatively, whilst the mayor stepped forward to shake Markham's hand. '*Grazie, caro mio.*'

'Now I wonder if our friends from the press have any questions?'

A reporter raised a hand. 'Luca Fabris, *Corriere della Sera*. Mr Markham, you spoke of how loved this city is throughout the world. What can people do to help?'

Markham smiled. 'Thank you, Luca. What I'm imagining is a series of long-term projects. What's happened to the city can't be undone overnight. So the immediate problems are to get people back into their homes and to get the shops open again; and the mayor and his team are doing a fantastic job with that. What I'm looking at – and what I'm sure other charitable organisations will be looking at – is funding projects to restore what's been damaged. And so, really, what better place for an appeal like this than the crypt in which we're standing? My appeal, really, is on behalf of those institutions in Venice – either religious or secular – who might be in need of a hand-up. You'll notice I said a hand-up not a hand-out. That's an important difference. If you do have work that needs to be done, please get in touch with any of the Venice-based charities and organisations – and I'll include my own in this – and we can discuss what we're able to do in terms of fundraising. This isn't going to happen overnight. I know things take time. But I assure you, we are in this for the long haul.'

Fabris nodded. 'Thank you.'

'Any other questions?'

'Roberto Bergamin. *Il Gazzettino*.'

'Good evening, Roberto. What's your question?'

'*Signor* Markham, we're all very moved by your speech tonight, I'm sure. It's very humbling to meet someone – a non-Venetian – who loves this city so much.'

Giles smiled, and bowed his head.

'My question is simply,' and now it was Bergamin's turn to smile, 'how can people be sure that any donations they make to the Markham Foundation will be used wisely?'

The smile vanished from Markham's face, but only for a moment. 'Well, the process of fundraising is necessarily long and complex, but we have a proven track record – as indeed do all the Venice-based charities – of working closely with our partner organisations in order to ensure that all donations are used for the maximum benefit of the city. Any further questions?'

'Yes, just one.' It was Bergamin again. 'You mentioned a proven track record. Does the Markham Foundation *have* a proven track record of delivering quality projects?'

Markham shook his head, with more than a touch of annoyance. 'Yes, of course we do, but I don't want to spend time now on going through individual projects. Perhaps we might move on to some other questions?'

People were turning to stare at Bergamin, but he continued unperturbed. 'Mr Markham, your organisation funded a restoration of the church of the Zitelle, is that right?'

'That's right, of course, now—'

'The work carried out involved the use of inferior building materials. Cheaper building materials. And so the restoration is already crumbling away. So how can viewers who think they might be inclined to donate to your organisation be sure that their money is going to be used correctly?'

There was silence in the crypt, apart from the continual flash of cameras.

Markham stared at Bergamin. And then he slowly turned to me, his eyes boring into mine.

I shrugged and mouthed the words 'I don't know this guy!' at him.

He turned back to face the press, the dazzling Markham smile reappearing as if by magic. 'Okay. Thank you for your questions everyone. I think we'll finish there.' And, with that, he detached his microphone, as the director made a 'cut' motion.

There was an awkward silence. The Patriarch stood there, resplendent in pectoral cross and wellies, examining the floor. The mayor leaned over and whispered something in his ear. The two of them nodded at each other, and then at Markham, before making their way to the back of the crypt and up to the main body of the Basilica itself.

Markham stared after them, and then shifted his gaze back to his audience. Then the questions burst out, machine-gun like.

'*Signor* Markham, is there any truth in this?'

'*Signor* Markham, can all the money collected by your organisation be accounted for?'

'*Signor* Markham, have there been any complaints from Don Giovanni at the Zitelle?'

The little man who'd asked the original question had pushed himself forward. '*Signor* Markham, is there anything you'd like to say?'

I saw Markham twitching, bouncing ever so slightly on the balls of his feet. The atmosphere in the crypt was hot and humid due to the TV lights, and I could see his face was flushed with a fine sheen of sweat.

'*Signor* Markham. Anything you'd like to say?' the little man repeated. 'Our readers will be most interested.'

I saw the punch coming before Markham threw it, and I hurled myself at him to stop him.

'No, Giles!'

'Get off me, Sutherland.'

The two of us toppled into the water, but Markham was the first to get to his feet, grabbing the reporter by his collar and pulling him towards him as he balled his fist.

I threw myself towards them again, stretching out an arm in order to block Markham's punch whilst pushing the reporter back with my other hand.

I grabbed his arm. 'Giles, this isn't going to help anyone.' He wrenched his arm first one way and then the other, until he succeeded in elbowing me in the face. The shock made me loosen my grip, and then he was on the reporter, tumbling both of them back into the water. He had him by the throat, and pulled back his arm to punch him. I grabbed him by both arms and hauled him back.

'Let me go, you bastard.'

'Do you promise to stop punching him?'

'No.'

'Then I'm not going to let you go.'

I was finding it surprisingly difficult to keep hold of him and wondered if bench pressing also formed part of his new fitness regime. The reporter pulled himself up out of the water, dripping wet and with real anger in his eyes.

'You arrogant little English prick.'

'No, Giles!' I shouted again, but it was too late. He wrenched himself free, and punched him full in the face; and the little man would have toppled into the water again if I hadn't been there to catch him.

We heard shouting and the sound of footsteps from behind us, and two burly, armed, security guards ran into the crypt.

'*Cazzo,*' someone swore.

Markham stood there, breathing deeply, and glared at me, shaking his head. He tugged at his collar, loosening his tie, and then, without a backward glance, splashed his way through the crypt and up the stairs to the Basilica.

Part Three

Fallen Angels

Chapter 42

Fede dropped her copy of *Il Gazzettino* down on the breakfast table.

'I've got to say, *caro*, that it's quite a good photograph of you.'

Gramsci leapt up on the table, and snuggled himself down on top of the paper. I pushed him off and he landed with a thud, scrabbling away furiously at my trouser legs before stalking off.

There I was in glorious, if slightly blurry, colour. Her Britannic Majesty's Honorary Consul in Venice, standing in the crypt of St Mark's Basilica, desperately trying to hold two people apart, as Giles Markham, one-time shoo-in for Venetian of the Year, tried to punch a reporter in the face.

I had to admit, it was a good photo.

I put my head in my hands. 'Oh Christ.'

Fede patted me on the back. 'It's not so bad, *caro*. It'll be forgotten about within a couple of days.'

I raised my head. 'Do you really think so?'

'Of course. A fight involving a millionaire philanthropist and the British Honorary Consul in the crypt of the most holy site in Venice . . . this time tomorrow, everybody will have forgotten all about it.'

I gave her a withering look. 'So. You don't really think so.'

She hugged me. 'I'm sorry, *caro*, I'm just trying to make you feel better. What were the police like?'

'They were surprisingly nice about it. Considering.'

She ran her hands through my hair. 'What's this? There's something stuck here.' She tugged away, trying to comb it out with her fingers.

'Ow!'

'Don't move! I've nearly got it.'

She held it up to me. A fragment of plaster from the crypt.

She smiled. 'Well now, I wonder how many other people are waking up this morning to find a piece of one of the holiest sites in Christendom stuck in their hair?'

'Should I take it back, do you think?'

'I don't know. Maybe you'd get in trouble.' She placed it on the mantelpiece, and then kissed me on the cheek. 'There we go. Souvenir.'

The phone rang, and I looked at the number.

'Oh shit.'

I considered not answering it, but then braced myself.

'Naaathan . . . good morning . . .'

Fede, kindly, had made me a cup of coffee during what had passed for my conversation with Ambassador Maxwell. I closed my eyes, and breathed in the vapour, feeling my senses coming slowly back to life.

She let me sit there, in silence, for a few moments.

'So,' she said. 'Is he cross?'

I opened my eyes and nodded. 'Just a bit.'

'Oh dear.'

'I mean, I managed to calm him down a little. Pointing out that I was actually the one trying to *stop* the fight. I think that played quite well. Trouble is, I think he's a bit jealous that he wasn't actually there himself. He does like the bright lights, does Maxwell, even when it ends in a fight. Or a murder.

'Anyway, it seems I've gone viral. There's quite a lot of international press interest in Venice at the moment and two Brits having a fight in a crypt must seem like all their Christmases coming at once. I'm in *the Sun*, apparently.'

'Is that good?'

'That depends on your point of view. What was the headline again? Oh yes, "*Battling Brit Punched in the Gondolas*".'

She frowned. 'But that doesn't make any sense.'

'It doesn't have to make sense. It's British tabloid humour.'

'I don't think I'll ever understand that.'

'I'm not sure I do.' A thought came to me, and I looked down at my phone in expectation. 'I wonder if they'll want to speak to me? Or you?'

'Me?'

'Oh yes. They'll want to speak to the Battling Brit's Sizzling Italian Wife, I'm sure.'

She giggled. 'Do I sizzle? Really?'

'You're an Italian woman. To the British tabloid press, you all sizzle.'

'Oh, don't spoil it.' Then she laughed again. 'But come on, you must admit this is a little bit funny.'

I smiled. 'Yeah. Okay, it kind of is.'

The entryphone buzzed. 'That'll be them now, I imagine. They're probably all outside. *La Repubblica*. The *Corriere*. *La Stampa*.'

The phone buzzed and buzzed again. 'All right, all right, I'm coming. Don't all rush at once. And no autographs.'

'Sutherland?'

I couldn't place the voice. 'Yes, who is it please?'

'It's Giles Markham here, Sutherland, now let me in.'

'Giles?'

I heard him hammering away. 'Let me in, Sutherland, or I swear I'll knock this bloody door down.'

'Okay. Okay. One moment.' I buzzed him up, and heard him thundering up the stairs. I scarcely had time to open the door before he was pushing at it, banging it into my face and sending me staggering backwards into the wall.

'Ow!'

'You son of a bitch, Sutherland.'

I threw my hands up. 'Giles. Giles. Calm down.'

He pushed me back against the wall once more. 'Bastard!'

'Mr Markham. How nice to see you again,' said Fede. She was leaning on the table, her hand resting on the morning paper.

He jabbed his finger at her, his face turning an unhealthy shade of purple. 'And you! You bitch!'

'Steady on, Giles,' I said, and then wondered if 'Steady on' was the appropriate response to someone calling my wife a bitch.

He snatched the newspaper up, and jabbed at her with it, each time finishing about an inch from her face. 'What do you have to say about this,' he half shrieked, 'you . . . *bitch*!'

Fede didn't even blink. 'Are you finished?' she said.

'Am I finished? I've not even started yet you—'

'Bitch?' she finished for him.

He stood there, breathing deeply, his face flushed and only a few inches from hers.

'Mr Markham, will you just hear me out?' He looked on the verge of shouting once more, but she closed her eyes as if in pain, and he stopped. 'First of all, this is the second time I've been threatened by an angry person with a newspaper in the last week and I'm getting tired of it. Secondly,' her eyes snapped open, 'if you so much as touch me, I will hit you. Understood?'

Markham stepped back, breathing deeply.

'Why did you do it?' He looked around the flat, and then forced out a laugh. 'Money, is it? Wouldn't surprise me. I mean, look at this place. You couldn't swing a cat in here.'

Gramsci miaowed.

'Well, you could try it,' I said. 'But I wouldn't recommend it. And perhaps we should just rewind the conversation a bit?'

'You told him, didn't you? That bastard journalist.'

'Giles, I promise you I'd never even seen the man until last night.'

'Mr Markham to you!' Finger jabbing recommenced. 'I've already made a formal complaint to the Ambassador. I expect he'll be in touch very soon.'

'Actually,' I said, rubbing my ear, 'we've already had that conversation.'

'Good. That makes me very, very happy. And as for you,' he turned to face Federica, 'I can make things difficult for you. Don't be surprised if work starts getting thin on the ground. The mayor's a good friend of mine.'

Fede yawned, and sat down at the table and attempted to smooth out the crumpled newspaper. 'God, I need a cup of tea,' she said, almost to herself. Then she looked up at Markham. 'Well, I suppose if he's such a good friend, you should give him a call. In fact,' she brightened, 'why not do it now?'

Markham flushed.

'Or perhaps,' Fede continued, 'you've called him already? And perhaps he wasn't available? Is that it?' She folded her fingers together, and rested her chin on them. 'Because if there's one thing I know about the mayor, it's this: he's only interested in being associated with winners. Restoring the crypt of San Marco – good. Fist fight under the eyes of his *Eccellenza* the Patriarch – not so good.'

'I'll ruin you, you bitch!'

'"You'll never restore art in this city again"? Well, maybe. Is it worth repeating that neither of us spoke to that journalist?'

Anger having failed, he tried pomposity, the last resort of a man who'd found that money really couldn't buy him everything. He lowered his voice to a whisper.

'My father gave his life to this city. And that's what I'm doing. Giving my life to it. That's all I've ever tried to do. And I will not let anyone – anyone – destroy that. Or I tell you what, Sutherland, I will bloody destroy *you*.'

And with that, he turned and left, slamming the door behind him.

There was silence for a moment, and then Fede turned to me. '"Steady on",' she said. 'Did you actually, genuinely, say "Steady on"?'

'Sorry. So. What do we do now?' I said.

Fede patted me on the shoulder. 'I guess, *caro mio*, we take the bastard down,' she said.

Chapter 43

'So what do we know? What do we actually know?' said Fede.

'We have Don Giovanni and the church of the Zitelle. We know they used the wrong materials on the interior walls.'

'Okay. I wonder if we could make that stick, though? This is Venice. It's the sort of thing that gets kicked around the courts for years before they decide that nothing can be proved and, even if it could, it's far too late to do anything about it now.'

'Maybe so. Well then, there's what Terzi said to me. Jenny had found a number of projects that either weren't finished or weren't completed satisfactorily, and money raised that seemed to be unaccounted for. And if Markham knew that Jenny knew, that would be a motive for murder.' I scratched my head. 'But I don't really understand how the guy can leave a trail of failed projects and not be picked up on it.'

Fede shrugged. 'Think about the church of the *Pietà*.'

'How do you mean?'

'How long has the facade been under repair?'

I tried to remember. For almost as long as I'd been in the city, the facade of Vivaldi's church had been behind scaffolding and *maxipubblicità* for – amongst other things – designer sunglasses, Aperol and expensive pants.

Fede saw me struggling. 'Exactly,' she said. 'After a while nobody even notices any more. The only big project anyone cares about is MOSE. Everything else is just going quietly under the wire.'

'Okay. That's possible. But,' I rubbed my forehead, 'why would he do this? It seems like a complicated way to scam some extra money, and by a man who's already rich.'

Fede shrugged. 'There are people like that in Italy. I expect it's the same everywhere. However much they have, it's never quite enough. Somebody else always has a bigger yacht, a bigger apartment . . .'

'Almost as if they were compensating for something?'

'Exactly.'

'Okay. So, let's assume that this is what Markham is doing. Apart from Terzi and Don Giovanni, then, who else do we have who might know something?'

'That journalist. From last night. He'd got that story from somewhere, and I doubt Don Giovanni is the kind of man who leaks stories to the press. I think you need to speak to him.'

'You think he'll want to speak to me?'

'Well, you did try to stop him from being beaten up.'

'Tried and failed, to be exact.'

'No matter. It might have been worse if you hadn't been there. I'm sure he'll speak to you if you ask nicely.'

'Okay. That's worth a go. Let's have a look at that paper again.' I picked up the *Gazzettino* and scanned the front page. 'Roberto Bergamin. That's the guy. Okay, I'll give him a call.'

I was about to take out my mobile when the entryphone buzzed again. I sighed. 'I suppose I'd better get that.' I picked it up. 'Giles, if you've come back to shout at us some more please don't bother. Just speak to my lawyer, eh? When I get one, that is.'

I was about to hang up when the speaker crackled. 'It's not Giles, Mr Consul.'

'Lucia?'

'Can I come up?'

'Depends. Are you going to hit me with newspapers again?'

She muttered something that might have been no and so I buzzed her up. She looked tired, and flushed from the cold.

'So. What brings you here?'

'I thought,' she took a deep breath, 'well, I thought I maybe ought to say sorry. About last time.'

'Oh right. So, what, did your dad tell you to come around and apologise or something?'

She scowled. 'Look, I don't have to be here, all right? I didn't have to do this. I've got better things to do. And—'

'And.'

'Well, yes, I told him what happened. And, yes,' she muttered, 'he did kind of tell me to apologise.'

'Oh right. Well then, apology accepted.'

'Just like that?'

'Just like that. Coffee?'

She shook her head. 'Not now. There's something that I need to ask you. Something to show you, really. I was thinking about that English prick the other day.'

'You mean Giles Markham, international businessman and philanthropist?'

'Yeah. That prick.'

'Okay, I was just trying to avoid any confusion.'

'The one you punched yesterday.' She grinned. 'That was kind of cool though.'

'I didn't punch him. The camera angle makes it look worse than it was.'

'Anyway, I was thinking about that article in the *Gazzettino*. If I was you, I'd tell your mate the *padre* to be careful. There are other things I've heard as well.'

I cocked my head to one side. 'Okay. I'm hearing this more and more. Go on.'

She shook her head. 'No. It's easier if I show you. Then you'll get a better idea.'

'Okay. I'm intrigued. Does it involve going out into the cold and wet?' She nodded. 'Oh hell.'

'Do you need me as well?' said Fede, in the tone of voice that suggested she very much hoped not.

'Nah, it's okay. Mr Consul here was saying you'd had a tough week.'

'Oh good. Thanks.' She turned to me. 'I'll call the *Gazzettino* and see if I can get that journalist to speak to you.'

Lucia smiled. Actually smiled. 'All right then. Let's go.' She looked at Gramsci, atop his tower of literature, and tickled him under the chin.

'Nice cat,' she said.

Gramsci purred.

'What are you looking at?' said Lucia.

I'd stopped to look at the building next to the Conservatorio, a crumbling *palazzo* that the casual visitor would pass by without a second glance. Palazzo Moro, where I'd once pushed a lit cigarette into a forged Bellini.

'That,' I said, nodding at it.

She shrugged. 'They say it's being turned into a hotel. We don't have enough of them, it seems.'

'Really?' I chuckled. 'He'd have hated that.'

'Who?'

'The ex-owner. A man called Arcangelo Moro.'

She shook her head. Before her time, perhaps. 'Come on, we're wasting time.'

She led me through the monumental entrance into the Palazzo Pisani a Santo Stefano, better known as Venice's *Conservatorio Benedetto Marcello*. In a city not short on great composers, they'd bestowed the title on Marcello, the man who'd set the first fifty psalms to music before deciding that perhaps that was enough to be going on with, and had moved on to other projects, such as being governor of Pula and chamberlain of Brescia. He'd also found time to illegally marry one of his students. Yes, he'd packed a lot into his fifty-two years and so, then, might be forgiven for never getting round to the remaining one hundred psalms.

'So here we are,' she said, 'the *biblioteca*.'

It was hard to make out what it might once have looked like. The chequerboard pink and white floor was almost obscured by trestle tables stacked with books. People, everywhere, were hunched over manuscripts, interleaving the pages with what looked like sheets of blotting paper.

Lucia walked over to a tired-looking woman, who got up from her work and hugged her.

'*Ciao*, Prof.'

'Lucia. I told you to take a break, *cara*. Come back tomorrow.'

Lucia shook her head. 'I brought someone to help. A friend of mine.'

A friend. My goodness.

The *professoressa* smiled politely at me, but then turned back to Lucia and the two of them chattered animatedly in *Veneziano*. I couldn't quite pick it all up but it seemed that the *prof* was making the reasonable point that there were already a number of volunteers and perhaps there was no need for another well-meaning but totally unskilled little helper.

'It's okay,' she said, 'I can show him.'

The *prof* nodded and smiled at me again. 'Thank you,' she said, 'it's greatly appreciated.'

Lucia sat me down at a table. 'Did you catch any of that?' she said.

'My *Veneziano* is terrible. I got about half.'

'Well, I told her you weren't a grief tourist and that you genuinely wanted to help.'

'Oh, that's kind. Thank you.'

'And I said you'd been living in Venice a long time and were feeling a bit useless.'

'Well, yes. I guess that's true as well. I mean apart from investigating the murder of a British citizen, I've got literally nothing on my plate at all. So now I've got soggy books to, er, do something with. So, what do I do?' I looked at the hundreds of volumes lined up on the tables. 'And where do we start?'

Lucia cast her eyes over the ones nearest to us, and then smiled. 'Maybe this one.' As carefully as she could she pulled over a folio of heavily water-stained pages. 'You might like this one.' Carefully, ever so carefully, in order to avoid tearing the waterlogged manuscript, she turned over the front page.

I looked at the frontispiece. *Vivaldi. Concerto for Strings in G minor.*

'Wow.'

'I think it's number RV156.' She could read the surprise on my face and shook her head. 'Look, don't get confused by the Siouxsie Sioux act. I do know about this stuff, you know?'

'Sorry. It's just I've never met anyone who could catalogue Vivaldi by RV numbers before. I don't even know if I've heard this one. What's it like?'

'Pretty much like RV155 and RV154 to be honest.'

'Ah yes. The old joke that the Red Priest didn't so much write five hundred concertos as write the same one five hundred times.'

'That's unfair. Well. A little unfair. Come on, let's get started.'

And so we sat there and interleaved every page with a sheet of absorbent paper, ready to be boxed up and sent to an agency in Bologna who, it was said, could restore it to something resembling its original condition.

We moved on to RV157 and would have started on RV158 but both of us were tired by then. Lucia tapped me on the hand.

'Come on, Englishman. That's enough for one day. Time for you to go and cook lunch for your wife.'

I yawned and stretched. 'Oh good.'

I smiled and nodded at the *professoressa*, and we made our way outside.

'You know, I have to say that was a bit of a privilege. Just sitting there and working away on something that had been touched by the sacred hand of Tony Vivaldi.'

'It's a *conservatorio*. That's what it's for. Conserving things. There's a clue in the name.'

'So then. Why did you ask me along?'

'Volunteers are useful right now.'

'No, that's not it. There's no shortage of volunteers and I imagine that some of them, at least, have some idea of what they're doing. Unlike me.'

She reached into her coat and took out a packet of MS. She offered me one and I shook my head. 'Given up.'

'Oh. Do you mind?'

I shrugged. 'Go ahead.' I never failed to be amazed by the number of young people that smoked in this country. Walking past a school during the morning break was one way of assuring yourself of passively smoking your required amount for the day. It was one of those things that made it so bloody difficult to give up.

'So,' I repeated. 'What was all that about?'

She dragged on her cigarette, then exhaled, slowly. 'I was thinking about the other day. With that circus outside your church.'

'Hmm, it's not exactly my church, you know. It's just that my pal works there.'

'Whatever. Anyway, all that crap with the press, the cameras, the stories in the newspapers. What did it actually achieve? Nothing. It's just a photo in the *Gazzettino* and then, *pfft*, that's it. I thought you'd be interested in seeing stuff that actually gets done. You know, things that don't get you on the front of newspapers but actually make a difference.'

'Oh right,' I said. 'So it was all about making me a better person?'

If she noticed the sarcasm in my voice she didn't let on. 'Exactly.'

'Well, thank you for enlightening me. You know, there's one thing I don't understand about the *Conservatorio*. One very obvious thing. That's one of the greatest collections of musical manuscripts in the whole of Europe. All of them irreplaceable, almost beyond price and terribly, terribly fragile. In a city which floods several times a year. What the hell are they all doing on the ground floor?'

She dropped the butt of her cigarette, and walked on without bothering to stub it out. 'They were upstairs in the past. On the mezzanine. But there's so many of them the floors won't support the weight any more.'

'You're kidding?'

'And this is where your Mr Markham comes in. He pledged money – a lot of money, I understand – to reinforce the floors. Two years ago.'

She paused.

'I had a talk with the *professoressa* about it. This is money we're still waiting for. It keeps being promised, and then we're told it's been delayed for some new bureaucratic reason. And it never, ever arrives.'

I nodded. 'Well now. It seems that Mr Markham's business empire really is worthy of a bit of investigation, doesn't it?'

'It does. Now, you remember that favour I asked you? I'm calling it in.' She grinned. 'I think you'll find it useful.'

Chapter 44

'You *what*?' said Fede.

'Erm, well, we kind of needed a favour off Lucia and so—'

'We?'

'Well, Dario was there as well.'

'So "we" meaning "you" then.'

'Meaning me. Yes. I needed a favour off Lucia. You see I need somebody to have a look at Terzi's phone and laptop and Lucia's pal is a bit of a wizard at this sort of thing, it seems and so—' I paused.

'And so?'

'And so, well, he's the bass player in her band and they're playing a benefit gig for the city tonight. The idea is to try and raise money for people who've lost stuff. Given that insurance isn't likely to cover much. It's a nice thing to do, really.'

'Oh, it is. Now tell me again what sort of band it is.'

'Well, they're playing at Laguna Libre, and we haven't been there for ages, so perhaps we might even have dinner there or at least a spritz and—'

'What sort of band is it, Nathan?'

'They're – well, they describe themselves as the only Death Metal band in Venice.'

'Uh-huh. The only Death Metal band in Venice. Well, there's a fun way to spend an evening.'

'Oh, come on, it might not be so bad.'

'What's their name then?'

'Toxic Disposition.'

'Oh.'

'Apparently they used to be called Nekronomikon, but it turned out there was a band of the same name in Germany.'

'Oh, I see. Well, I can imagine there'd be all sorts of fighting over royalties and the like.' She rubbed her forehead. 'Oh God. Do we have to go? Do *I* have to go?'

'Yes you do. For one thing, I think she's genuinely sorry about having a fight with us the other day and she's trying to make it up. Secondly, it sounds like they haven't sold many tickets. And thirdly – and I really am prepared to beg if need be – please don't make me go on my own.'

'Don't you like this sort of thing?'

'Not really, no. And let's be honest, even if Hawkwind were playing, I've reached the age where I'd appreciate a nice sit-down as opposed to being in the mosh pit.'

'The what?'

'The bit in front of the stage where the young people jump around. I believe that's what they call it. Look,' I pleaded, 'this is Lucia's way of helping. You spend every day salvaging manuscripts at the Querini Stampalia. Lucia spends her days with the Mud Angels and her evenings playing with the only Death Metal band in Venice.'

'And we're doing this just so you can get some information off the bass player which will no doubt enable you to go off and do something at best irresponsible and at worst dangerous.'

'Yes. Yes, I think that's pretty much hit the nail on the head.'

She shook her head, but then smiled at me. 'Well, come on then. I'll see if I can find my blackest dress and something suitably spiky. How about you, have you got anything suitable to wear?'

'I've got an old Goblin T-shirt.'

'Oh, that's nice. That'll remind Lucia of her dad. And, who knows, perhaps we'll enjoy it.'

'You look nice,' I said.

Fede made to kiss me, and then thought better of it. 'Thanks.'

'The black lipstick's a nice touch.'

'Do you think so? It's not really black. I just kind of mixed up whatever I could find.'

'It's nice. Very appropriate.' I paused. 'That's actually quite sexy, you know?'

'Why, thank you.' She paused. 'You won't be expecting me to wear this all the time, will you?'

'Oh. Well, not if you don't want to. But you never know, perhaps we'll both turn out to have a taste for Death Metal?'

'Who knows. Let's keep an open mind, eh?'

I pointed to my T-shirt with its image of a red, batwinged imp, grinning grotesquely as it sawed away on a violin. 'I bought this when I saw them ten years ago. I can't remember which version of the band it was, though, if it was Official Goblin or Unofficial Goblin.'

'There's more than one?'

'At least two. Musical differences. Would you like me to explain the history?' There was silence for a moment. 'You wouldn't, would you?' She shook her head. 'Anyway, what do you think?'

'Well, you certainly look the part, *caro mio*.'

'Oh good.'

She patted my stomach. 'It's just a little bit snug, I suppose.'

'It's ten years old. It's shrunk.'

'Oh absolutely. But don't worry, you'll look fine.'

'Surprisingly sexy?'

'Don't push it.'

Laguna Libre was comfortably the hippest place on the Cannaregio Canal, but not so much so that I felt out of place. It had opened a few years previously and served, variously, as a bar, restaurant, art gallery and music venue. I'd visited a few times, most recently for an exhibition of works by a not-very-good artist of my acquaintance. The food was good, the Negronis better and if the music wasn't always to my taste, well, it was usually good enough to make me wish that we lived just that little bit closer in order to drop by more often.

Over the years they had hosted piano recitals, string quartets, jazz and blues nights and the occasional folk singer. They had, however, never hosted anything like Toxic Disposition before.

Lucia smiled out at what remained of the audience. 'Thank you all. We'll be back in about twenty minutes.'

Fede and I clapped, although I had no idea if anyone heard us. Like ourselves, I assumed everybody's ears were still ringing.

'So,' I said, 'what do you think?'

Fede shook her head. 'Louder,' she said.

I repeated myself but she shook her head once more. 'Spritz?' I said, making a drinky-drink motion.

She nodded, and I made my way to the bar. By the time I returned, Fede had been joined by Lucia and Mauro the bass player.

Lucia smiled. 'So, what do you think?'

'It was,' I searched for a relatively neutral word, 'cool.'

She punched my arm. 'You're a terrible liar, Mr Consul. It's okay. You can be honest. We won't be offended.'

I put my head in my hands. 'I'm sorry. I really am. I'm just too old for all this.'

'Well, thanks for coming anyway. We really needed people to come along. There's not much of a Death Metal scene in this city.'

'It seems not.'

'We were hoping to get a residency but,' she shrugged, 'I don't think it's really their thing, you know? Anyway, that's not why we're here right now. Mauro, this is Nathan and Federica.'

Mauro nodded. 'Nice T-shirt,' he said.

I turned to Fede. 'See. I told you. I'm down with the kids.'

'My dad really likes them,' Mauro continued, which wiped the smile from my face. 'So, what did you think about the words?'

'The words?'

'Is our pronunciation okay?'

'I think so.'

'Good. You would tell us though? It's just that English is the language of metal. We need to get it right.'

In all honesty I hadn't realised they were singing in English at all. 'Right. Oh, I see. Well, I don't think there's any chance of people misunderstanding you.'

He grinned at us, reached into a bag slung over the back of his chair, and took out the laptop. 'Now then, let's have a look at this, eh?'

'That'd be great.'

'It took a while. It was soaked through. You're lucky the battery didn't go up. But I've done what I can. A lot of it's quite well protected. He's been using Tor for one thing.'

'What's that?'

'It's an anonymity network. It's open-source, and works via a volunteer overlay network using onion routing.'

I blinked. 'You sure you're a musician?'

He laughed. 'It means you can search the internet anonymously.'

'Oh right. And so this Tor thing is illegal?'

He shook his head. 'Not at all. The only illegal thing is what you might use it for.'

'Such as?'

'Deep web. More specifically dark web.'

I shook my head. I was about to speak but Fede cut me off. 'He got his first smartphone just over two years ago. It might be best to assume that he doesn't know about any of this stuff.'

'Oh right.' He looked confused. 'Two years? Seriously?'

'Yes, seriously,' I said. 'I'm sorry, I'm a middle-aged man. I still buy CDs for Christ's sake. I own VHS video cassettes.'

'What?'

I waved a finger at him, 'Ah-hah, not so funny now, is it? So come on then, tell me about this Thor thing.'

'Tor.'

'Whatever. Tell me about Thor and the dark web. I'm assuming it's not the title of a superhero film.'

He stared at me, unsure as to whether I was joking or not. 'Okay. Think of the internet like an iceberg.' He put his fingers together in the shape of a triangle. 'Right at the top you've got the surface web. Stuff you can search for. Now underneath that you've got what we call the deep web. And this is everything that's out there that isn't indexed. Stuff which, for whatever reason, can't be found by conventional search engines.'

'Illegal?' I said.

He waved a finger at me. 'Not necessarily. For that sort of thing, you need to go to the dark web. The nasty bottom layer of the whole internet. And to look at that without attracting the attention of the police, you need to use something like Tor.'

'Okay.' I sipped at my spritz. 'What do you mean by nasty?'

'Anything. Buying and selling drugs. Guns. Terrorism. And, well, worse stuff. You know what I mean?'

I nodded. 'Yeah. I think I know what you mean. So tell me – what was the owner of that laptop looking for?'

'That's the thing. Nothing that you'd think was that bad.' He took out a sheaf of papers. 'I printed out the most interesting pages. Look at this.'

He slid them across the table to me. Fede craned to look over my shoulder.

'Albrecht Durer,' she said.

Mauro smiled. 'Strange, isn't it? Why use the dark web to search for a dead artist? But this is the thing – I think he was actually looking to buy or sell something.'

Fede riffled through the file. 'Okay, so he's been looking at auction prices for works by Durer over the past five years. Nothing illegal in that. Some of the sites he's used are subscription only. Again, nothing illegal in that.' Then she laughed. 'Hang on, look at this. Gottfried Lindauer.'

I shook my head. 'Who?'

'Nineteenth-century artist. Interesting life. Born in Bohemia, fled to New Zealand in order to avoid being drafted into the German army.'

'The other side of the world? He wasn't taking any chances, was he?'

'But the most interesting thing about him is this: a painting by him was stolen back in 2017. And later that year, rumours started to spread that it was being offered for sale on the dark web. With payment via Bitcoin.'

'And was it?'

She shrugged. 'I don't know. Most experts seemed to agree it was a fraud. What do you think, Mauro?'

'I'm not sure. But even if it was a fraud, it might still have given people ideas.'

'So why would you do something like this?' I said.

Fede tapped her fingers on the sheaf of papers. 'Perhaps if you don't know what you're doing?'

Mauro shook his head. 'No. This guy knows what he's doing all right.'

'I don't mean the technology. Think about it. What if you have something valuable you want to sell, but you don't know how to sell it? Seriously. If you have a piece – and let's say it's by Albrecht Durer – how would you go about selling it?'

'An auction house?' I said.

'Sure. Only two problems there. One is that the taxman is going to want his cut.'

'And the second?'

'What if you've acquired it illegally? Then you've got a problem. So, you could try selling it via organised crime groups. Problem is, that involves dealing directly with some very unpleasant people. Or, perhaps you could try selling it via the dark web. Which – if it is possible – would be safer and you might not have to get shot.'

'Which means?'

'Which means, *caro mio*, that someone has found themselves with a valuable work of art and simply doesn't know how to get rid of it.'

I turned to Mauro. 'And could this have attracted someone's attention?'

He nodded. 'He's been careful, but not that careful, in covering his tracks. Hell, it took me less than a day to follow his path.'

'A work by Albrecht Durer,' said Fede. She nodded to herself. 'Yes. That's something that'd be worth killing for.'

Lucia looked at her watch. 'We're due to go back on in five minutes. Mauro, tell them about the phone.'

He nodded, and placed it on the table. 'Looks like a regular handset, doesn't it? But it isn't. It's an EncroChat phone.'

This time, even Federica had to shake her head.

'He got hold of this via the dark web, using a forum called *Dread*.'

'Oh, that sounds harmless enough,' I said.

'Switch it on like this,' he pressed the power button, 'and you get a standard Android screen. But switch it on like this,' he held down the power and volume buttons together, 'and it takes you to the EncroChat login.'

'So what is it?'

'It's an encrypted communications protocol. It was supposedly developed for celebs afraid of having their phones hacked. In reality, it's used almost exclusively by crooks. And the thing about it is this: there's a "panic button" mode. If you put in a certain PIN, everything on the phone is erased. And that's what's happened here. There's no way of getting anything back on this, I'm sorry.'

'So we have a laptop with a secret web browser. A phone with all the data erased. And a rare book about Albrecht Durer. All in a briefcase on Terzi's boat.' I smiled. 'Whoever was on that boat wasn't trying to steal it. They wanted to dispose of it. Ending up in the canal was exactly what they wanted.'

'Terzi himself?' said Fede.

'It's got to be. Jenny Whiteread is found dead in his shop, to which she has a key. He knows, at some point, the story will get out that he had some kind of relationship with her. So at some point the police are going to be around, asking questions. Perhaps searching his flat. And then his boat. Any sort of evidence needs to be got rid of. He's only unfortunate in that any sort of crap washed up at the side of the canal has been piled up by the Mud Angels. And, in this case, little Emily mistakes it for Daddy's briefcase and passes it on to us.

'The questions are: where is the Durer, if it even exists? And who, exactly, has Terzi been speaking to?'

Mauro grinned, mirthlessly. 'Anybody you speak to via

the dark web or an EncroChat phone is, by definition, someone you don't want to be speaking to.'

And on that cheerful note, Lucia and Mauro returned to
the stage for the second half.

Chapter 45

My ears were still ringing the next morning when I made my way out to Mestre. It had been some time since I'd last needed to visit. Ever since Dario, Vally and Emily had returned to Venice itself there'd been fewer and fewer occasions when I'd needed to go there. I'd covered for my counterpart on *terra-ferma* for a couple of weeks earlier in the year, when he'd been away on holiday, but that had been a job that I'd mostly been able to carry out over the phone.

It was rare for British residents in Mestre to have need of the services of the Honorary Consul. As for those visitors who ended up there by mistake, and who found themselves with a view of Via Piave instead of the Grand Canal – well, they were more likely to get robbed on a *vaporetto* than waiting for a bus in Mestre.

Dario and I had kept up our tradition of beers at Toni's bar for a few months but eventually gave up. There was no shortage of decent places to drink in Venice and it seemed a little desperate to go out to Mestre and sit in the cold listening to the rumble of traffic, just for old times' sake. So the visits became fewer and fewer, Toni's expression became just that little bit more wistful every time he saw us, and eventually we just decided to stay in Venice itself. The two pint glasses that Toni kept behind the bar for our personal use would soon be packed away forever.

Roberto Bergamin's apartment block was a few doors down from the bar, sandwiched between a newsagent and a mobile phone repair shop that promised to unlock any brand of phone (perfectly legally, probably) within five minutes.

I thought about stopping at Toni's but decided against it. It was a chilly day, and an icy pint of beer didn't feel like it would hit the spot. Besides, there'd have to be a slightly awkward conversation with Toni, and I'd feel disloyal to Dario.

Federica had told me that Bergamin had been guarded but would at least agree to meet me, as long as it was at his apartment and not at the office.

I rang the bell.

'*Chi è?*'

'*Signor* Bergamin. I wonder if we could speak. My name's Nathan Sutherland.'

There was a pause for a moment, and then the door clicked open. 'Third floor.'

Three floors. Not too far to climb. Not too far at all. On the other hand, there was a lift. They were a rare thing in Venice, working ones even more so since the events of a week ago, and so I decided to treat myself.

Someone had sprayed the words '*Napoli Merda, Forza Juve*' on the interior and I wondered why someone who lived in Mestre would take the time to express their disapproval of a football team 700 kilometres to the south and admiration of one 500 kilometres to the west. But perhaps I just didn't understand football very well.

The lift jolted to a halt, and the doors shuddered open.

'*Signor* Bergamin?'

'You?' Bergamin was standing in the open doorway to his apartment.

'Yeah. Me. We met the other night.'

'You tried to punch me, you son of a bitch.'

I raised my hands, slowly, in an attempt to show that no punching, on my part at least, was going to be involved. 'If you'll let me explain. I was actually trying to stop you from getting hurt.'

He rubbed his jaw. 'Didn't do a very good job then, did you?'

'I'm sorry. Giles Markham is surprisingly tough for an international businessman and philanthropist.'

He scoffed. 'Philanthropist? That's what we're calling him now?'

'Call him anything you want. But can we talk about this?'

He rubbed his jaw once more and then nodded, slowly.

'Okay. Looks like you'd better come in.'

He stepped aside to let me in. I noticed that the wall outside his flat had been sprayed with another *Napoli Merda* logo.

I raised an eyebrow. 'Neighbours with strong opinions, eh?'

He sighed. 'Not them. It's not such a bad place here, but kids have realised it's easy to break in. You just buzz every apartment in turn until someone gets bored and lets you in. Then they spray the walls, if you're lucky. And if you're not, well,' he knocked on the wall, which responded with a hollow sound, 'you could punch your way through these if you really wanted to. I've been lucky so far.' He turned his back. 'Come on then, if you're coming.'

The apartment was small, and sparsely furnished, save for a framed Venezia FC football shirt hanging on the wall.

I nodded at it. 'You a fan?'

He smiled. 'That's from 2017. The year we got promoted to Serie B. I covered the last game. The whole squad signed it.'

'Nice.'

'I wasn't even supposed to be there. The main football reporter came down with food poisoning on the day of the match. So the editor just called round anyone who could get there in time. And that was me.'

'Bit of luck, eh?'

'You need that in this job. Being in the right place at the right time is what it's all about. Otherwise you're cooling your heels in Mestre and you get a call telling you to haul your arse over to Castello or somewhere because someone's bag's been stolen. You get used to filing reports with photos of empty seats outside restaurants, with a caption reading "Bag stolen here".'

'But now things are going better, I imagine?'

'What do you mean?'

'Well, now you get invited to cover a broadcast from the crypt of San Marco in the company of the Patriarch and the mayor. I imagine that's a pretty good gig to get.'

'You might think so. Apart from being punched.'

'You've probably been syndicated in the nationals. *La Stampa, Repubblica,* the *Corriere.*'

He nodded. 'Yeah. It's been good.'

'Might get you out of working for a regional newspaper. Might even get you on to one of the nationals.'

'It could do. If I play my cards right.' He yawned. 'What's your point here?'

'Well, it's just that I'm feeling part of your success. Given that I was on the front page of the *Gazzettino* seemingly involved in a fist fight with you and a wealthy English philanthropist. And my boss – well, my sort of boss – is very cross about it. It doesn't look all that good, really. People come to the Consular service looking for a bit of help and, well, if said Consul has been on the cover of a newspaper with the headline of *I pugilisti* – well, he's worried that it might hit confidence in the institution. Just a bit.'

He nodded. 'Okay, I'm sorry about that. But it wasn't me that came up with the headline.'

'Sure.' I smiled. 'But given that I really did try to save you from a beating, I wondered if you might do me a favour.'

His eyes narrowed. 'What sort of favour?'

'Well now, I'm just wondering why you chose that particular moment to ask Giles Markham some very awkward questions.'

He chuckled. 'Hey, can you think of a better moment?'

'Absolutely not. A bit of theatre, and what an audience! *Complimenti*. But what I'd like to know is where you got this information from. About Markham, about his foundation and about funds that are going missing.'

Bergamin wagged a finger and grinned at me. 'A journalist doesn't—'

I cut him off. 'Reveal his sources. Yes, I know that.' I sighed. 'Okay, Roberto, it's like this. I've got a priest in Venice who says that the restoration of his church was a botch job. I've got stories of big projects in the city where the money's never quite materialised. And more than that, I've got a young British woman who's been murdered. So I need to sort this out. And if Giles Markham's got anything to do with it, this story is going to be big. *Repubblica* and the *Corriere* will be beating a path to your door. So, again, I want to know – where did you get your information from?'

He nodded, and reached for a packet of cigarettes. He offered one to me, but I shook my head.

'Given up.'

'Okay. Wish I could. Hope you don't mind if I do.'

'Go ahead.'

He took a lighter from a wooden bowl on the table, filled to the brim with business cards.

'It started about three months back. Just one at first. An email claiming the restoration of the church of the Zitelle had been carried out using substandard materials.'

'Uh huh. So what did you do?'

'Well, I did nothing. It was a hotmail account. No name, just a stream of random letters and numbers. You get a few of those. Cranks. People with a grudge. So I just let it go. And then, maybe a month later, I got another email. A different address, but I figured it was the same person. This time, it was about the *Conservatorio* and a project to strengthen the floors so they could move the archive upstairs. And I looked at the figures involved, and I looked at the names of some of the people who'd given money, and I started to think it might be worth my time. Because there's some famous people on this list. That English actress who's moved to the Giudecca, you know her?'

I nodded. 'I know who you mean.'

'She's put up a lot of money. I figured she might be interested if she found out that money hasn't been used yet. Still,

I thought I'd wait just a little bit longer. But then came the flood. Now everyone in Italy is looking at Venice. Hell, everyone in the world is looking at Venice. And so when I heard that Giles Markham was going to be making an appeal for funds from San Marco, well, I figured I couldn't sit on this story any longer. So when I got the chance to be part of the press conference, well,' he grinned, 'you know the rest.'

'Oh, I do. I do. So tell me, Roberto, was your editor pleased?'

'He was! That photograph of you is everywhere, you know?'

I closed my eyes and rubbed my forehead. 'Oh Christ.'

'But on the other hand, this Markham prick is threatening to set his lawyers on us. And it seems like he's not a guy you want to piss off.'

I raised my head. 'I imagine not. So, is there anything else you can tell me about him?'

He shook his head.

'This is important, you know?'

'I know.'

'In that a British subject is dead and it might – just might – be linked to the Markham Foundation.'

'Yes, I know that.' He grinned again. 'But if anyone's going to find this story out, it's going to be me, and I don't need a sidekick. Sorry. It's a career thing.'

I screwed my eyes shut, counting to ten. When I opened them he was still grinning. I took a deep breath. 'I'm going to appeal to your better nature here.'

'I'm sorry, my friend, but I haven't got one. It's nothing personal.' He reached for his lighter again, rooting around in the bowl in front of him.

And then I saw it. A business card. A business card with the five angel's heads.

He must have caught the expression on my face and reached out to snatch it away, but I was too quick for him. I grabbed it and leapt to my feet, brandishing it in his face. He snatched at it once more but I pulled back my hand.

I turned the card over 'Dr Jennifer Whiteread. Angels in Venice,' I read. 'Well now, Mr Roberto Bergamin, I wonder what you're doing with this?'

'Give that back. That's my property. It's to do with work, that's all.'

'Of course. Of course.' I held it out to him, but then snatched it out of reach at the last moment. 'Except, of course, I wonder if the police will be interested.'

He laughed, but there was a slightly manic edge to the laughter. 'What's it got to do with them? I can talk to anyone I like.'

'Of course. It's just that poor Dr Whiteread is now dead. And she worked for the Markham Foundation. Which you've been seen and heard asking questions about. So I think anything you know about her might be of interest to them.'

I stretched out my hand, and he snatched the card away. 'Come on, Roberto,' I said. 'Let's be friends. Let's talk.'

He sat down, and rubbed his jaw once more.

'Okay,' he said. 'Let's talk.'

'It might take some time. Perhaps coffee would be good as well?'

Chapter 46

Bergamin returned from the kitchen with two steaming cups of coffee and a fresh packet of cigarettes.

'I just need to go and dig out this article, okay?' he said. Then he reached into the bowl, scooped up a handful of business cards and let them fall slowly from his fingers. He leaned in towards me.

'There might be a few things for you to read there, if you get bored. As you seem so interested.'

I nodded and smiled and reached for my coffee.

Roberto left the room, and I took the chance for a better look around the flat. How old was he? Not quite thirty, in a country where most young men stayed at home with their parents until they were safely married off. And now here he was, working for the *Gazzettino* and living in his own apartment. He'd done well for himself, it seemed. And now he might be sitting on an actual scoop; something that might get him noticed nationally.

I got to my feet and walked over to look out of the window. It was only the third floor, but we were higher up than felt strictly comfortable to me, and the floor-to-ceiling windows didn't help. The view looked out upon the heart of Mestre.

Not the suburbs, with their parks and gardens, but the town centre with its grey high-rises that stretched away into the distance.

'Shithole, isn't it?' said Roberto. I started, not having heard him come back in.

'I think that's a bit harsh,' I said. 'Mestre's got its charms.'

He rolled his eyes. 'I won't be here much longer. Leastways, I hope not.'

'Moving to Venice?' I said.

He laughed. 'You've got to be kidding? Who lives in Venice any more? The place is a mausoleum with the tourists as the living dead, shuffling around and giving the illusion that there's actually something going on there.'

Roberto Bergamin's youthful optimism, it seemed, had been knocked out of him at an early age.

'Here we go then,' he said, proffering a sheaf of papers.

I sat down, and began to read.

Dr Jennifer Whiteread is thirty-four years old. As a consultant with the Markham Foundation she's a new – and very welcome – addition to the ranks of British expats in Venice. Her new book The Angels of Venice *will be published next year. 'Call me Jenny,' she says as she crosses her long, slim legs under her while we sit and chat about her latest project.'*

I stopped reading, and put the paper down. 'Progressive,' I said.

Bergamin looked slightly embarrassed. 'It's what the readers expect.'

'Dr Whiteread,' I catch myself just in time, as she frowns at me, but with just a hint of a twinkle in her brown eyes, 'I'm sorry, Jenny. Tell me about The Angels of Venice.'

She smiles. 'Well now, there have been a lot of misconceptions about this. It isn't a scholarly book about art history. It's not meant for academics, and it was never meant to be. What it is, is simply a visual history of the angelic in Venetian art.'

'Do you mean like a coffee-table book?' I ask.

She smiles. 'Well, I think it would look good on a coffee table. And if it encourages people to look further, then I'd be delighted. The trouble is that – as a culture, in Britain at least – we've lost the ability to read paintings. In a post-Christian age, we have to work harder to understand them. If we don't know what they mean – or at least what they meant – then what are they to us except very pretty wall decoration? And that might be enough, but I do think we owe it to ourselves to try and read them more deeply. Now I'm not saying my book will necessarily allow you to do that, but it might at least be a step along the way. And if that happens then, as I said, I'd be delighted.

'I remember back in the 1990s, there was this marvellous woman on television. Sister Wendy Beckett. Now I was very young, but I remember watching her, and every week she'd introduce me to something beautiful. I think I was more than a little bit in love with her. I quite wanted to be her. In some ways I still do.'

'A sort of sexy Sister Wendy,' I say.

She frowns for a moment, but then breaks into a smile. 'I hope that's not going to be the headline! But what was so marvellous about her is that millions of people who'd never dream of picking up a book by Ernst Gombrich, for example, would tune in to watch this little middle-aged nun every week. Isn't that wonderful? And so I do hope, in some small way, that The Angels of Venice *might do something similar.*'

'Including television?'

'Well, that would be marvellous, but I know that sort of thing is very difficult to achieve these days.'

'Tell me about the Markham Foundation,' I say.

'Well, I was working in London – and I've got to say I really wasn't very happy in my job – and I fell over running for my bus one morning. And who was there to catch me but the lovely Fulvio Terzi?'

'He sounds ever so gallant,' I say.

'He absolutely is.' She laughs. 'Amongst many other things. And before I knew it, he said Giles Markham might be interested in speaking to me.'

'How did you find him? He sounds as if he might be a little intimidating.'

'Well, I admit I was a bit worried about that. But he's the sweetest man. The loveliest, gentlest man.'

'So what is your role with the Foundation?'

'Spending other people's money! No, seriously! The purpose of the Foundation is to raise money in order to provide funds for restoration work. And it's all being done in the name of Giles's father. I really do think that everything he does is in memory of him. His father would be so proud, I know.'

'So if I'm a priest, for example, and my church is crumbling away, I just send you an email asking for money?'

'It's a bit more complicated than that. Every application has to be properly costed. Otherwise I could just be throwing money away. More than that,' she laughs,' I'd be throwing other people's money away. And even though I said Giles is a lovely man, I don't think I'd last too long in the job if I did that. So we need to see, for example, an architect's report or something like that.'

'And what might a typical project look like?'

'There literally is no such thing! But I think it's important to stress that we're not always dealing with the most high-profile works here. Nothing like Titian's Assumption in the Frari for example. Because these works will always get sponsorship. Save Venice and Venice in Peril – don't get me wrong, they do an incredible job – will always be able to raise money for works like that. They have an international appeal. But if, for example, someone has a work by Francesco Bassano that they think could really benefit from some work – well, that's where we come in. We're there for the little guys – not the ones who'll attract attention in boardrooms in New York or London – but those artists and buildings that kind of slip through the cracks. They deserve some love as well. There's nothing that isn't interesting in this city!'

'So how many of you are working on this?'

'Just Fulvio and myself. Giles always thought it was important to have a Venetian on the team. That this shouldn't be seen as a vanity project for a rich Englishman – oh God, he'll read that and be so cross with me. But it's true.'

'Have you ever disagreed on projects?'

'Sometimes.' She nods. 'Sometimes I think, yes, that would have been a nice job to work on. But occasionally Giles thinks I'm getting too far away from the original purposes of the Foundation. Projects that have been just a little bit too glamorous, a little bit too high-profile. And I have to say he's always been right. Well, nearly always.'

'And does it leave you much free time?'

'Not as much as you might think. Fulvio's got so many other projects, you know, as well as the Foundation and his bookshop. And I need to spend time on my book, of course. Oh, and I really *do need to make more time for my lovely boyfriend, Matthew. He's been so patient.'*

'Your boyfriend? Is he involved in the art world as well?'

She laughs. 'My goodness, no. He does – and has done – almost everything else though. At the moment he's writing a children's book about a cat who lives on a gondola. He's very excited by the idea.'

'So do you both feel like Venetians now?'

'I'd be delighted to be considered an honorary one. But, sadly, we won't be here forever. The plan was always just to have the most wonderful year over here and then to go back to Britain. I'm sure we'll be back frequently though.'

I smile. 'But what is Giles Markham going to do without the face of his Foundation?'

She laughs. 'He'll still have lovely Fulvio.'

'I'm not sure he'll look quite as good on the cover of a glossy magazine,' I say.

'Now you're teasing me. And Fulvio would look just lovely on a cover.'

'One final question then, Jenny. Do you believe in angels?'

The smile never leaves her face. 'I always answer that question in the same way. I don't believe in God. But, yes, I do believe in angels.'

There's no sign that she might be joking.

'Seriously?'

'Absolutely. I see them everywhere. There's even one living downstairs from me. But that's another story for another time.'

'And with that, the interview is over. Dr Jennifer Whiteread, I conclude, has more than something of the angelic about her herself.'

Chapter 47

I put the interview down, feeling ever so slightly soiled. But if you could see beyond the casual sexism – and, to be fair, that was a pretty big ask – I wasn't quite sure exactly why Bergamin, or his editor, had considered this so controversial.

'I don't understand why this was never published,' I said.

Bergamin raised an eyebrow. 'No?'

'No. Unless your editor's a woman, I suppose.'

He laughed. 'Like I said, it's what the public want. What do we usually have on the cover of the Sunday supplement? A hot actress. A model. Maybe a sportswoman as long as she's in a swimsuit. And then one week we decide we're going to be a bit classy. So we get an art historian. Now we can go to Ca'Foscari and get a seventy-year-old with bad hair and bad teeth. Or,' he shook the papers at me, 'we get someone who looks like this. Who do you think is gonna shift more papers? Which one would you buy?'

I shook my head. 'Christ,' I said.

'You gonna tell me this doesn't happen in England?'

I smiled, sadly. 'No. I'm not.'

'Okay then. So you understand?'

'No, I don't. Why did you pull it? As you said, she'd look

good on the cover.'

He leaned back in the chair. 'Because there's a bigger story here.'

'Do you want to tell me about it?'

'No.'

I sighed. 'Roberto. A young woman is dead.'

'I know. And I'm sorry. Really, I'm not a bastard. But there's a big story here and I'm going to be the one to break it.'

'Break it, then. Break away. I don't give a damn about the story. I'm not going to steal it from you.'

'How do I know that?'

'Because my name is Nathan Sutherland, her Britannic Majesty's Honorary Consul in Venice. I have a job with a pretty cool title which ultimately means nothing. In my spare time I translate lawnmower manuals, drink too much and, according to my wife, have regrettable taste in music. I am not interested in writing and I am not interested in stealing your scoop. All I am interested in,' I took a deep breath, 'is finding out why a young British woman was found dead, floating face down in a pool of filthy water. Because I want to be able to tell her dad that his little girl will be going home soon. And by the time I put him on a plane back to the UK I want him to have something that at least resembles a bit of closure.'

He shrugged. 'Ah, you're doing that appealing to my better nature thing again.'

'I am. Come on.' I grinned. 'It's in there somewhere.' I wasn't 100 per cent convinced of that, but I continued. 'I don't give a damn about your story. You can keep that. If I'm right, people will be queuing up for it. Anything else I find,

I'll pass on to you. I promise. But tell me, please – why did you pull that story?'

He closed his eyes and nodded, slowly. 'Okay. I'll tell you.' Then he wagged his finger. 'But you go to anyone else with this, I'll break your balls. Understand?'

I nodded. 'I understand.'

'Good.' He reached into his pocket and took out his mobile. 'This is the last part of our conversation. After she thought we'd finished. There were still a couple of other things I wanted to ask her. Off the record.'

'And you recorded her?'

He shrugged. 'Sure.'

I shook my head.

He glared at me. 'You want to hear this or not?'

I nodded.

'Okay then.' He tapped at the phone, and then placed it between us before leaning back in his chair.

'Okay, thanks for that, Jenny.'

'That was all right, I hope.'

'More than all right.'

Jenny laughs. 'And you're not really going to use that quote are you – the Sister Wendy one, I mean?'

'Not if you don't want us to.'

'Thanks. I know it's a bit of fun and all that, but still . . .'

'No problem. Listen, there's just a couple more questions I'd like to ask you if that's okay?'

'I thought we'd finished?'

'It won't take long, I promise.'

'Well. Okay then.' Jenny laughs again.

'Can you just take a look at these?'

Bergamin paused the recording. 'At this point I showed her the printout of the emails I received.'

'Can I see them?'

'No. You don't need to.'

I shrugged. 'Okay. Go on then.'

Bergamin tapped away at his phone again and I suddenly wondered if he'd been taping me all this time as well. Then, after a long pause, I heard Jenny's voice again, quiet now and uncertain.

'I don't understand.'

'You've never seen these before?'

'No.'

'Have you ever heard stories like this before? About Giles Markham?'

'No.' She sounds visibly upset now. *'And now I should be going.'*

'Please Jenny, Dr Whiteread, just read them through once more.'

'I don't need to read any more of this.' Her voice is rising now, angry, yes, but also on the verge of tears.

'Okay, that's fine, that's fine. I understand.' Bergamin's voice is conciliatory. Then it hardens, just ever so slightly. *'But you understand that I'll have to do something with them.'* He chuckles. *'It's my job after all.'*

'No, please.'

'Signorina,' no Jenny now, no Dr Whiteread, *'these are two allegations about misuse of funds by the Markham Foundation. A project at the* Conservatorio *that's still at the planning stage after several years. And restoration work at the church of the Zitelle that was carried out with substandard materials.'*

'*Both those projects began long before I started work for Giles. Before Fulvio started, even.*'

'*Of course, of course.*' *He chuckles.* '*I'm not blaming you. But a lot of people are going to want to read about this. So I just want to know – completely off the record – did you send me these emails?*'

'*No.*'

'*Of course. Of course. It must be* signor *Terzi then?*'

There's silence on the recording.

'Signorina?'

Jenny blows her nose.

'*I heard,*' *her voice is shaky now,* '*from the priest at the Zitelle. It's so close to the Foundation's office that I used to see him quite a lot. One day he mentioned to me that the restored plasterwork was already starting to crumble away. He wasn't – he wasn't trying to be unkind or anything. I think he just assumed it was the sort of thing that would happen in Venice. With ever more regular flooding. That sort of thing.*

'*And so I mentioned it to Fulvio. This was months ago now. He told me not to worry about it. He said he'd check it out just to be sure everything had been done correctly.*'

'*And then?*'

'*And then he said, a couple of weeks later, that yes, there did seem to have been some sort of mix-up with regards to materials that had been used. And that, yes, work at the* Conservatorio *was still nowhere near starting.*'

'*So you think he sent me those emails?*'

'*I don't know.*' *Jenny is crying now.* '*But I don't know who else might have done.*'

'*So why,* signorina, *would Fulvio Terzi send anonymous emails to a journalist?*'

'*I don't know. Unless—*'

'*Unless?*'

She stops crying and takes a deep breath. 'Unless maybe he wanted some hold over Giles.'

'*Mm-hmm. And do you think that's likely?*'

She blows her nose again. 'No.' There's strength in her voice again now. 'Because Giles Markham is a good man. Fulvio Terzi is a good man. And both of them have done more for this city than a nasty, muck-racking piece of shit like you.'

Bergamin laughs. 'Okay. Okay. Don't be cross. It's not me who's stolen hundreds of thousands of euros. Anyway, you've been very helpful. Grazie, signorina.*'*

'*Fuck you.*'

There's the sound of a door slamming, and of Bergamin chuckling away. 'Goodbye, sexy sister,' he mutters.

The recording came to an end and I looked at Bergamin in disgust. He looked back at me as if to say that he knew exactly what I was thinking and didn't care.

'Christ,' I said, shaking my head. 'What a mess.'

He nodded. 'Looks like it.'

'So what are you going to do now?'

'That depends on what you're going to do.'

'For the moment, nothing.'

'You know, you English have that lovely expression – *keeping your powder dry* – well, that's what I'm going to do. Just for the time being. Because this story is going to be big.'

'I understand.' I got to my feet. 'Okay. I suppose I should say thank you.'

He grinned. 'A pleasure. Just remember what I said about breaking your balls. I don't want to wake up tomorrow morning and find those shitheads at *La Nuova* have got the story.'

I shook my head, wearily. 'Trust me, Roberto. I've no more interest than you in seeing that happen.'

I opened the door.

'Oh, just one more thing, Roberto.'

'Yes?'

'Are you single by any chance?'

I closed the door behind me without waiting for his answer, and made my way downstairs, and back along Corso del Popolo to the bus stop.

'Nathan! Hey, Nathan!'

I turned around to see Toni waving at me with a big grin – a big hopeful grin – on his face.

'You got time for a beer?'

I smiled, but shook my head. 'Sorry, Toni. I need to get back to Venice.'

His face fell. 'Right now?'

'Sorry. I'm kind of busy at the moment.'

'No time for even one beer? I've still got your special glass. It's been a long time.'

I sighed inwardly and then forced a smile on to my face. 'Okay. Sure I've got time, Toni.'

So I sat there and drank a freezing-cold pint for old times' sake, listening to Toni chatter away about how it wasn't the same since Dario and I had left. And I thought about Roberto Bergamin's interview with Dr Jennifer Whiteread, and anonymous emails about Giles Markham that might just have been sent by Fulvio Terzi.

Chapter 48

'Are you sure you need me here, Nat?' said Dario.

'I think so. I mean, I'm not imagining *signor* Terzi is going to be difficult. All I want to do is ask him why he's dripping poison about Giles Markham into the ears of anyone who'll listen. And then, maybe if there's time we'll talk about trying to sell works of art on the dark web.'

'And if he doesn't want to talk?'

'Nothing we can do. He hasn't actually done anything wrong as far as we know.'

'So what happens then?'

'Well then, Dario, we go for a beer.'

I pressed Terzi's bell once more, but he was either not at home or simply refusing to answer. I was about to give up when an elderly woman with a shopping trolley almost as big as herself elbowed me out of the way, and opened the door. I gave Dario a quick nod, and we tailgated her in.

She turned around and glared at us, suspicion in her eyes.

'Can I help you?'

'Well, maybe I can help you?' I pointed at her enormous trolley. 'Could I give you a hand with that?'

She put a protective arm around it. 'No.'

'Oh. Okay. I'm here to see *signor* Terzi.'

She narrowed her eyes even further.

'It's about a boat. Well, about his mooring, really. I wondered if he might want to rent it to me.'

She laughed. 'Oh, now I understand. Well, good luck with that. He won't let that go to anyone. Not to Venetians. And certainly not to foreigners. You're wasting your time like all those others.'

'Someone else has been round?'

'All he seems to do these days is fight with people. Shouting all the time. I'm sick of it.'

'*Signora*,' I rubbed my chin, 'who's been round? It might be important.'

She scowled, but then she looked down at her shopping trolley, and tested its weight. Then she looked up into the stairwell.

'Perhaps you can help me with this, after all,' she said.

Dario grinned. 'After you, *vecio*.'

I dragged the trolley up the last of the fifty-seven steps that led to the *signora*'s apartment and stood there panting for breath.

She opened the door to her flat and pulled her shopping through, as if not trusting me with that final step.

'So then,' I gasped, 'tell me about Terzi's visitors. Please.'

She shrugged. 'Hmmph. It started over a week ago. *Stranieri* calling on him at all hours. Englishmen.'

'Okay. Do you remember what they looked like?'

'No. I don't go spying on my neighbours!'

'Of course not. But if you came out to see what all the noise was about and looked downstairs that wouldn't be spying, would it? That would just be being a concerned neighbour.'

'Well, it's difficult to say.'

'One of them is quite a young man. Glasses. Longish hair. The other one's older, maybe about my age. Grey hair. Maybe about my build?'

She nodded. 'I can't be sure. But it could have been.'

'Did you hear what they were shouting about?'

She shook her head. 'I don't speak English.'

'But you're sure they were English.'

'Of course. They shouted like Englishmen.'

'"Shouted like Englishmen",' I repeated. 'Okay, thank you, *signora*. You've been very helpful.'

'Are you going to shout at him as well?'

'I promise we won't,' I smiled.

We made our way back down to Terzi's apartment, and rang the bell. There was no answer, and so I tried once more. Then I rapped on the door.

'Fulvio,' I called out. 'It's me. Nathan Sutherland.'

There was no answer.

'Fulvio, if you're there, let me in. We need to talk.' I waited, but there was no response. 'I know about Bergamin. We need to talk.'

Dario sighed, pushed me aside and hammered on the door. '*Signor* Terzi, are you there?' he bellowed.

'Oi!' The cry came from upstairs. 'You promised you weren't going to shout.'

I looked upwards. 'I'm sorry,' I called back. 'We'll come back another time.'

I heard a 'Hmmph!' and the sound of a door slamming. I sighed, and we made our way downstairs.

***

'So what do we do now, Nat?'

'I'm trying to think this through. Terzi told me he hadn't even let Blake in when I saw him the other day. It seems he was lying. And Markham's called on him as well. So what were they shouting about?'

Dario shrugged. 'Terzi might have been screwing Blake's girlfriend. That's a pretty good reason to shout at him.'

'And Markham?'

'From what you were saying, Terzi knew Markham was up to something dodgy. That's another good reason. Anyway, where now?'

'He could be at his bookshop. Which I can check on the way home. Or out on Giudecca with Markham – which would be a problem as Markham won't speak to me. Or he could just be out doing the shopping. But we can check his boat out.'

We made our way back through the *campo* and over the bridge to the Rio de San Zan Degolà. 'That's it,' I said, pointing at Terzi's boat.

Dario whistled. 'Nice.'

'You ever thought about getting one?'

'Yeah, maybe now that Emily's a bit older. It'd be fun. Hey, we could all go out together.'

'That'd be cool.' There was still no tarpaulin fixed to the boat, and so we jumped down on to the deck.

'Fulvio,' I called out. 'Are you there? It's Nathan Sutherland. Could we talk?'

There was no answer. I reached for the door to the cuddy, and then snatched my fingers back. It was warm to the touch and, as I looked, I could see smoke curling from under it.

'Christ almighty.' I stumbled backwards, banging into Dario. As I looked around, I could see a crowd starting to form on the *fondamenta*.

A city built *on* wood and largely *of* wood. Nothing frightens Venetians as much as fire.

I reached for the cabin door again but Dario held me back, screaming at me. 'Get away from there, Nat. Don't touch it!'

'Terzi could be inside,' I shouted.

'You open that door you maybe cause a backdraught.'

'We've got to try.' I yanked at the door. 'It's locked.'

'There'll be gas cylinders in there. Get the hell away.' He dragged me backwards, up on to the *fondamenta*. 'Run.'

I shook his hand off and turned to look back. Thick, black, choking smoke was now belching out from the cabin door. I saw the crowd falling back as people screamed and frantically shouted into mobile phones.

Dario grabbed me once more. 'Run, you stupid bastard.' He hauled me back as far as the bridge; and then we heard the whomp of an explosion and the windows exploded outwards, showering glass across the *fondamenta* as flames tore through the boat.

Above the screams and the roaring of the fire we could already hear the sirens of the *Vigili del fuoco*.

'Okay, Nathan,' said Vanni. 'Tell me what happened.'

'It's straightforward enough, Vanni. I needed to talk with Terzi. He wasn't at home. So I thought I'd see if he was on his boat.'

'And as soon as you got there you realised it was on fire?'

'Yep. Fortunately Dario was there to stop me doing

something really stupid.'

'Okay.' He set the Newton's cradle in motion. 'Can I ask why you needed to speak to him?'

'That business in the crypt of St Mark's. I'm pretty sure Terzi had sent compromising information about Markham to that journalist.'

'Pretty sure?'

'It could only have been him or Jenny. Compromising information relating to the way money from the Markham Foundation is – or is not – being distributed. You've seen the photos from St Mark's. Markham's got a hair-trigger temper. He punched that reporter live on camera. He came round to our apartment yesterday and threatened both of us.'

Vanni stopped the cradle ticking away. 'He threatened you?'

'He actually threatened to destroy me, to be precise.'

He rubbed his forehead. 'You didn't think about calling me?'

'I thought I could sort it out myself.'

'Oh Christ, Nathan.' He shook his head. 'Well, now you've seen the bloody consequences, eh?'

I bridled. 'That's not fair, Vanni.'

'Isn't it? We're still waiting for the pathologist's report on Fulvio Terzi. And given the state of the body that's going to take a hell of a lot of time. I tell you what, I hope to Christ the smoke got him before the flames did.'

'You think Markham did it?'

He shrugged. 'We can't be sure. But from what you've said he's certainly of interest.' He took the cap off his pen. 'So, come on then. Tell me everything you know about him. Let's start with that journalist. Have you spoken to him?'

'I have. This morning.'

'And?'

'And he told me he'd break my balls if I told anyone.'

'Nathan, *I* will break your balls, right here, right now, if you don't tell me.'

I looked into Vanni's eyes. He set the Newton's cradle in motion again, with a CLACK that made me wince.

And so I sat there and told him everything.

Vanni nodded. 'Okay. I think that's all we can do for now. Thank you, Nathan, that's been very useful.' He put the cap back on his pen. 'I just wish you'd come to me with this earlier.'

'Vanni, you were happy to think Jenny's murder was just a random break-in.'

He nodded, slowly, and sighed. 'We were. And maybe we got it wrong. And I'm sorry for that.'

'I can go then?'

He nodded. 'Sure.' He reached across the desk to shake my hand, as if to indicate no hard feelings. As we shook, he gripped it harder, pulling me towards his side of the desk. 'And stay away from Markham, you understand?'

'I understand.'

'I'm serious, Nathan. We can't do anything until we have a pathologist's report. Maybe not even then. But this is a man who's threatened you. This is a man who might have murdered two people. He might even have set one of them on fire.' He gripped my hand even harder. 'So you stay safe, okay? Let us get on with our job. And stay the hell away from Giles Markham.'

Chapter 49

Giles and Fulvio have been on edge all day. Giles keeps coming down to the office and seems disappointed to see you there. Eventually, he asks Fulvio out for a coffee. They just have some 'admin issues' to discuss and admin, of course, is something you don't need to worry your pretty little head about.

But now you're home again. All you want is a hot shower, a glass of prosecco and not to have a row. But immediately you notice that Matthew's bottle is half empty, both figuratively and literally. He scowls at you, and the forced smile fades from your lips.

'Hi,' you say.

He nods. You kiss the top of his head and, at least, he doesn't flinch too much.

'So how has your day been?' you ask.

He shrugs. 'Not good.'

Of course. You force yourself not to sigh. 'I'm sorry. What's the matter?'

'I'm finding it difficult to write.'

There will, of course, be no series about cats on gondolas. Matthew has other plans. Bigger plans.

'I'm sorry,' you repeat. The question is coming. Any moment now.

He refills his glass. 'I think we should at least talk about this.'

This time, there's no holding the sigh back. It's been a shit day. All you want is a shower, and a lie-down, and to close your eyes. Matthew, however, has scheduled in A Row.

'Matthew, we've been through this. I'm not sure there's much more to say.'

He drains his glass and refills it. You suspect he's getting drunk on purpose. 'Fulvio tells me a woodcut by this Durer guy sold for half a million quid at Sotheby's. That's for a woodcut. He said he couldn't even imagine what an original drawing would go for.'

Fulvio. He's been talking to Fulvio.

'It would go for a lot, Matthew.' You can't keep the tiredness out of your voice. How many times have you had this conversation by now?

'So,' he laughs, mirthlessly, 'what are we waiting for? This is a life-changing amount of money.'

'Because it's not right. Because she doesn't want to sell it. When she dies it's going to go to the city. Doing otherwise would break her heart.'

Matthew is breathing more deeply now. It's not to calm himself down. It's to show you how angry he's becoming. He's about to speak but you cut him off. 'No. There's no more to be said, Matthew. I don't want to hear about this again. And if you've been talking about this with Fulvio, well, I want you to stop.'

He screws his eyes tight shut. 'I. Am. Just. Trying. To. Make. Things. Better.'

You mimic his voice. 'Getting. A. Job. Would. Make. Things. Better.'

'I've got a job, remember.'

And then, suddenly, you see no point in holding it in any

more. 'Pretending to be a children's writer is not a job, Matthew. Pretending to be a photographer is not a job. Pretending to be a party organiser is not a job. Yes, you have a job, and that job is sponging off me and my dad. And you know what? You're very, very good at it.'

He looks at you in disbelief. 'You fucking bitch.'

You close your eyes, and breathe deeply. It's done now. There's no going back. You feel relief flooding through you.

'Matthew, this isn't working any more. It's not fun any more. It hasn't been for quite some time.' You open your eyes. 'I'd like you to move out by the end of the month.'

He shakes his head, and then he smiles. His old Matthew smile. The fun Matthew smile. Thinking that will change your mind. 'Come on, Jen. This is just a silly argument. Everybody has them. Look, we'll go out, we'll have a few drinks and grab a bite to eat and we'll forget all about this. Eh? What do you say? Come on?' There's a wheedling, whiny quality to his voice that, perhaps, has always been there.

'No, Matthew. I'm serious.'

'You can't do this.'

'It's my name on the lease. So, yes, I can. If you want, I'll even pay for your flight back to London.'

'Where am I going to go? Have you thought about that?'

'You've got friends there. They'll put you up. Or why not ask Fulvio if you can sleep on his sofa for a while? Given that you seem to be getting on so well?'

He swears again, finishes his drink and storms to the door. He turns and looks you up and down, smirking, in a way which is no doubt supposed to be intimidating. And then he's gone, slamming the door so hard the room shakes.

You slump into a chair, and lean your head back, breathing deeply. It's done now. You can begin again. Everything can begin again now.

Chapter 50

Fede slipped her arms around my neck.

'So. How are you feeling?'

I patted her hands. 'Not great. I can't help thinking about Terzi. God, imagine realising what was happening . . .'

She hugged me. 'So try not thinking about it. When you were last there he was telling you that he needed to service the space heater. That he was worried about carbon-monoxide poisoning. So perhaps he just forgot about it and fell asleep. There was some sort of accident and he never knew anything more. *Zio* Giacomo always used to tell me how careful you had to be on a boat. Wood, gas canisters and enclosed spaces. Electrical fires. It can all happen so easily.'

'But why lock the cabin door?'

'Perhaps he was worried about his safety if he left it unlocked.'

'Do you believe that, Fede? Because I don't. I think Markham found out that Terzi was leaking damaging material to the press, confronted him – and then locked him, hopefully unconscious, in a burning cabin.'

She hugged me again. 'I like my version better. But, no, I don't really believe it. I think you're right.'

'Well, I suppose Vanni will let me know when they find anything out.'

'And so you're going to do just what he says? Which means not going near Giles Markham?'

'Hang on, what happened to the "*let's take the bastard down*" Federica of a couple of days ago?'

'That was when Giles Markham was merely a corrupt businessman skimming off funds from his own charity. Today he might be somebody who locked a man inside a burning boat. That changes things.'

I yawned. 'You're right. But there is something I can do.'

'There is?'

'The drawing by Albrecht Durer. And *Angels for an angel*. There was something in Jenny's interview with Roberto Bergamin. About believing in angels. About actually having one living downstairs. So I'm going to talk to that old woman.'

Fede nodded. 'I suppose there's no way I can talk you out of this?'

'It's an elderly, blind woman. Trust me, I've got this . . .'

I waited outside the apartment block on the Calle del Cimitero, shivering, and wishing that I still smoked so it would at least look as if I were doing something other than loitering with possible bad intent. I forced myself not to look up at *Signora* Masiero's window in case I saw Oksana staring back at me or, worse, the *signora*'s sightless eyes.

Eventually I heard the front door opening, and I ducked behind the corner. I heard footsteps splashing through the water, but heading away from me. I risked a look. It was Oksana, her shopping trolley sending water spraying up from the damp stone, heading in the direction of the shops. I hadn't noticed anywhere open. If she was shopping for food, she'd be forced to head further afield. Good. That should give me all the time I needed.

I waited until she was out of sight, and made my way back around the corner. I buzzed the bell marked *Masiero* and waited.

'*Chi è?*' It was the old woman's voice, light and wavering.

'*Signora* Masiero. My name's Nathan Sutherland. I'm a friend of Jenny's.'

'*Che bello.*' I could hear the delight in her voice and hated myself for the lie. 'Come up, please.'

The door clicked open, and I made my way upstairs. I could hear her moving inside, slowly shuffling her way towards the door, and then the bolt was pulled back and the door opened half an inch.

She stared out at me with her milky eyes. 'From Jenny. What a lovely surprise.' She closed her eyes for a moment and smiled, and looked almost beautiful as the years dropped away. 'You must come in. Please.'

I followed her inside, as she made her way back into her front room, her right hand gently trailing along the wall. Then she stopped, as if mentally reassuring herself of where she was, and took two steps forward. She reached down with her hand, finding the arm of her chair, and then lowered herself into it.

'Could you close the door, my dear?'

I nodded, and then remembered I needed to speak. 'There we are,' I said, and clicked it shut.

'Thank you. I'm probably being silly, but Oksana says

I need to be careful. Although I really am old enough to remember when you could leave your doors open.'

'That must have been nice,' I said.

'Different times, my dear. Different times.' She looked sad for a moment. 'Jenny's no longer here, is she?'

How much could she possibly know? She might have spoken to Blake. 'No,' I said.

'A shame. I'll miss her. But she told me she'd have to go back to England at some point.' She paused, and then looked in my general direction. 'Is that where she is?'

'She – well, she'll be going back to her dad's. At some point.'

'Lovely. I hope she'll write.' She giggled, almost girlishly, and again I could see the years falling away. 'Oh, I know what you're thinking, but Oksana always reads my letters for me.'

'Does she now?' I said.

'She's very good that way. Even though it must be boring for her. So Nathan – it is Nathan, isn't it?'

I nodded, still forgetting that she couldn't see me, and corrected myself. 'It is.'

'Nathan.' She pronounced it the Italian way, with a short *a*. 'A lovely name. And you must call me Isabella. And so, how do you know Jenny?'

I hadn't been prepared for this. *Signora* Masiero might have been old and blind but she was by no means simple-minded, and I cursed myself for my assumptions. 'I'm the British Honorary Consul in Venice, *signora*.'

'I see. How lovely. Like Mr Rutherford was.'

'He was my predecessor, yes.'

'Such a nice man. An English gentleman, I always thought. So is that how you know Jenny?'

'That's right.' That, at least, was a half-truth.

'The Honorary Consul. The original Nathan was a prophet at the court of David, you know? He was the one who took him to task for committing adultery with Bathsheba. That can't have been an easy conversation. I expect you often have to tell people things they'd rather not hear, Nathan?'

I smiled, remembered she couldn't see me, and turned it into a chuckle. 'Yes. Sometimes.'

'And you're interested in art?'

'I think perhaps that's an obligation if one lives in Venice.'

She laughed. 'You'd be surprised. I don't think Oksana has ever set foot inside the Accademia in her life.' Her expression changed, became sad. 'Did Jenny tell you about the angels, Mr Sutherland?'

'I understand that was her passion.'

'She told me she was writing a book about them. And that made me sad. Because, of course, I'd never be able to read it.'

I took a deep breath. 'Angels were her absolute passion, as I said. So much so that I think she might have found something wonderful. Is it true that you have an original drawing by Albrecht Durer?'

She smiled. 'That's correct, yes. *Four Angels. Four Avenging Angels*, to be precise. It was probably the preparatory drawing that he made for his woodcut on *The Apocalypse of St John*.'

'That's amazing. Incredible.'

She must have picked up on the doubt in my voice. 'And so you're wondering how this mad, blind old woman in her tiny flat in Castello could possibly have an original work by Durer?'

I shook my head. 'No, no, that's not what I mean.'

She cut me off. 'Don't lie, darling. It's important to tell the truth. That's why I liked Jenny so much. She wasn't afraid to tell me if she thought I was being a silly old goose.'

'I'm sorry. Really.' I took a deep breath. 'Okay then. So tell me. How could you possibly have a work like this?'

'Well now, Mr Sutherland, my family haven't always lived in this apartment. The story has it that back in the sixteenth century, our family lived over near Rialto, by the church of San Bartolomeo. Where the Germans all lived, near the Fondaco dei Tedeschi. And one day a handsome young German arrived, looking for a place to stay. He had a commission from the German community, he said. A commission for an altarpiece, no less, in their *chiesa*. But, unfortunately, until the commission was complete, he would be short of money. He wondered if, perhaps, my family would accept a work by him in lieu of bed and board. And that's what he did. He gave them the preparatory sketch for *The Four Avenging Angels*. A piece that's remained in my family for generations. For five hundred years.'

I couldn't really think of the words, and so settled for what I hoped was a suitably reverent 'Wow.'

She laughed, a lovely fragile little chuckle. 'Wow, indeed, Mr Sutherland. But that's the very story my father told me, when he showed it to me for the first time. And it was the very story that his father had told him, and his father before that.' She paused, and shook her head. 'But it's almost certainly nonsense. Our handsome young Albrecht Durer was already famous throughout Europe by the time he arrived for his visit to *La Serenissima*. I don't think he'd have had many problems in paying for a roof over his head, and some bread and cheese at night.'

'Oh, what a shame. It's a lovely story though.'

'It is. But the drawing, of course, is what's important. It's a miracle it's survived. Father kept it hidden in the attic during the war, under a pile of newspapers. He was terrified that the Nazis would hear of it. Can you imagine, the honour in taking a work by the great Albrecht Durer back to the Fatherland? So that's where it stayed, all those long months of the occupation. We were lucky that it wasn't destroyed by water, or eaten by rats. But somehow it survived. And we've kept it here, ever since.'

She sighed. 'I don't know how many times I've looked at it in my life. There was a time that I knew every shading, every whorl of his pen from memory. And one day, I realised my sight was fading. One day, I realised, I would look at it and the patterns would no longer resolve themselves into shapes. And one day, not long after, I would not see them at all.'

'I'm so sorry, *signora*. I can't imagine how that must have felt.'

She shrugged. 'There was nothing to be done, of course. Sometime I think the most terrible thing in life is not the fragility of the human body, but its resilience. The will, somehow, keeps driving us on, when the body should have crumbled away long ago. But there we are. The unbearable must be borne.'

She placed her right hand on the table in front of her, moving her fingers lightly over its surface, until they came to rest on a scuffed leather document folder.

'But then Jenny came. She just knocked on the door one day and said she'd heard this incredible story about us and wanted to know if it was true. Well, Oksana was suspicious at first. I think she wanted to throw her out. But I thought she seemed kind. And, after all, they were neighbours. So I took her in and she sat down. And I opened up this folder and showed her the angels.

'She became my eyes again. She'd sit with me for hours, talking about Durer and his angels. And she'd describe them to me. All those lines started forming themselves into shapes in my mind. Until I could see them again. Yes, I think you could say there's something angelic about her.'

'That's so wonderful,' I said.

'The last time I saw her was the night before my birthday. The night of the *acqua granda*. She was upset when she left. Perhaps it was the thought of leaving Venice that was making her sad.'

Her birthday. *Angels for an angel*. A lovingly painted card for a woman who would never be able to see it. But that didn't matter. Because the two of them would sit down together, and she would describe it all for her.

She made to speak, then looked uncertain for a moment. 'Mr Sutherland, could I ask you something?'

'Of course.'

'Would you do the same for me? The drawing. Just describe it to me.'

'*Signora*, I'm very flattered. But I'm not like Jenny. I'm not an art historian or anything like that.'

'That doesn't matter. Sometimes it's good for us to see things through the eyes of others. And that's what you'd be doing.'

'Well then.' I smiled. 'I'll do my very best.'

She patted her hand along the table in search, I guessed, of mine. I laid my hand against hers, and she squeezed it.

'Thank you.' She reached for the document holder, and slid it across the table to me. 'You'd better open it. I can do it myself, but I worry so much about damaging it when I pull it out.'

'Of course.' I unzipped the wallet, and reached inside. There was a thick red folder inside that I took out and opened up. Inside that was a Manila envelope. And within that, under a sheet of protective tissue paper, lay Albrecht Durer's study for *Four Avenging Angels*. I ran my fingers gently, ever so gently over the surface, wanting to prolong the moment. And then, equally gently, I eased it away.

There was nothing underneath except for a blank sheet of paper.

Chapter 51

I stared at the blank page, shaking my head in disbelief. Then I picked it up and turned it over. Nothing. I looked inside the wallet, and turned it upside down.

Nothing.

I looked up to see Isabella staring sightlessly at me, but with a quizzical expression on her face. She was expecting me to start describing it to her. Or at least to have expressed some degree of excitement or admiration at having under my fingers something that vanishingly few members of my generation could ever have seen or even imagined.

'My God,' I said. I could think of nothing else to say.

Her face relaxed, and took on that serene, beautiful expression again. 'It's so lovely, isn't it? Just think, Mr Sutherland, how few people have ever had the privilege of seeing that.'

I struggled to find something to say. What should I do? Could I try bluffing my way through it and describe it as best I could from memory? Should I be honest with her or did that risk her suddenly being reduced to hysterics? Or even accusing me?

Oksana saved me from having to make a decision by choosing that moment to arrive back home.

***

She looked at me, then down at the table, then back into my eyes. The fingers on both her hands twitched.

'Oksana, this is Mr Sutherland. He's a friend of Jenny's.'

Oksana laid her hand on Isabella's shoulder, and stroked it, gently. '*Signora*, you know what I've told you about letting strangers in when I'm not here.'

'He's not a stranger, Oksana. He's a friend of Jenny's.'

The younger woman turned to glare at me again.

I decided not to mention that we'd already met. Not in front of Isabella. 'I'm the British Honorary Consul in Venice, *signora*. My name's Nathan Sutherland.'

'I don't understand, sir. What could the Honorary Consul have to do with us?'

Isabella smiled at her. 'He came to see this lovely thing. And to describe it to me. Just as Jenny did.'

I looked down at the blank sheet on the table and shook my head, once more, in disbelief. I raised my head and was about to speak, but Oksana waved a finger at me and then put it to her lips; silently shushing me.

'Can I offer you a coffee, Mr Sutherland?'

I nodded, before remembering that I needed to speak for Isabella's benefit. 'That'd be lovely. Thank you.'

'Come through to the kitchen then. *Signora*—?'

'Yes, Oksana?'

'We'll just be a couple of minutes. I'll make you a cup of tea.'

Oksana turned the radio on. Bland Europop played. She looked back towards the living room, and turned the volume up slightly, before turning her attention to filling the Moka.

'So now you know,' she said, spooning coffee into the pot. She screwed the top on to the Moka with what seemed like excessive force. Either the gasket was perishing or she was imagining my neck in its place. She set it down on the stove and turned the gas on, clicking away with an electric lighter that failed to catch until it suddenly burst into flame with a *wummph*. She snatched her fingers away, but not before the flames caught them and she swore.

'Oksana?' Isabella's voice came from the living room.

'I won't be long, *signora*.'

She reached over to the radio and turned it up just a little higher. Then she folded her arms and looked me up and down. 'So now you know,' she repeated.

'What do I know, Oksana?'

'There is no drawing. There are no angels. There never were.'

Jenny Whiteread. Fulvio Terzi. Dead for a blank piece of paper.

I shook my head. 'That can't be true.'

She stepped towards me, her eyes flashing and her finger jabbing towards my chest. There were, I could see, any number of sharp objects hanging from hooks on the wall. I was also aware that she was standing between me and the only exit. She nodded in the direction of the living room. 'This is why she shouldn't have visitors. It only upsets her. First that stupid English girl. And now you.'

'I'm not here to upset her. I'm just here to find out the truth.'

'Like the English girl who thought she was doing a good thing? Coming down here almost every night. Talking with the *signora* for hours.' She poured out a cup of coffee, swearing again as she slopped it over the side of the cup, and pushed it towards me. 'But it wasn't a good thing, was it? It just left her more confused than ever before. And it wasn't lovely little Jenny that had to look after her and calm her down afterwards, was it?' She jabbed her thumb towards herself. 'It was me. Always me.'

'But that picture must have existed at some point. She was convinced of it. How on earth did she find you?'

'She told me she'd telephoned every Masiero in Venice. Had they always lived in the city? Did their family come from the Rialto area? She told me about the research she'd done and the books she'd read. And when she heard all this, the *signora* no longer felt like a silly, useless old woman. She felt important again. Because of her. Because of the English girl.

'Lovely *Jenny*,' she almost spat the word out, 'even wanted to rent the apartment upstairs. She looks like she's got money, you know? She could be living somewhere better than that. But she just wanted to be near the *signora*. So, she could come down every night and talk to her. Talk to an old blind woman about a picture that doesn't exist any more. If it ever did.' She tapped her forehead. 'She has good days and bad days, you know? You're here on a good one.'

'I'm sorry. It must be tough.'

'It's my job. It's what we do.' I heard Isabella calling from the living room. Oksana rolled her eyes and sighed, deeply. 'One moment, *signora*. I'll make you a green tea.'

I sipped at my bitter coffee, and closed my eyes as I tried

to gather my thoughts. Asking for sugar, I thought, might not be a smart idea.

Jenny Whiteread had pursued a dream from Nuremburg to Venice and found nothing more than a blank sheet of paper. And she had still been a good enough woman, a kind enough woman, to sit every night with a confused old lady and talk about a non-existent drawing. I didn't know much about her. But, from the little I knew, it made sense.

Fulvio Terzi, though . . .

My eyes snapped open.

'No,' I said.

'I don't understand, *signore*.'

'I'm saying no. It doesn't make sense. Yesterday, a man called Fulvio Terzi was burned to death on his boat. He'd been trying to sell a previously unknown work by Albrecht Durer on the dark web. He'd even set himself up with something called an EncroChat phone for extra security. You don't go to that sort of trouble without at least making sure that the thing you want to sell actually exists. So why are you lying to me, Oksana?'

She sighed, a little too theatrically. 'I'm not lying. You can believe what you want, *signore*.'

I nodded towards the living room. 'Perhaps we should check with the *signora*.'

She leaned forward and hissed at me. 'How many times do I have to say this?' She tapped her forehead. 'She's old and muddle-headed.'

'Well, I'm not so sure about that. I'll be interested to see what her reaction is.' I paused. 'Perhaps she'll want to call the police?'

Oksana said nothing.

'So, let's just see what she says, shall we?' I made to move past her, and then paused, as if I'd forgotten something. 'By the way, what's your immigration status here, Oksana? I imagine that's the first thing the police will be checking.'

Her face flushed with anger, but I could see the fear in her eyes.

'You wouldn't.'

'Try me,' I said, hating myself for what I was doing.

'You prick. You bastard.'

I could only agree. I told myself I was only bluffing, but it was still a shit thing to do. 'Oksana, I'll be honest with you. I don't give a damn about Albrecht Durer or any undiscovered drawings of his. But I do care about the death of a British National. And that's what I'm investigating. So talk to me. Please.'

She said nothing, but she screwed her eyes closed in order not to look at me.

'You sold it, didn't you?'

She nodded. Then her eyes flashed open, and she jabbed a finger towards the living room. 'Not a word,' she hissed. 'Not a word.'

'I promise. But just tell me why?'

'I said she has good days and bad days, didn't I?' Her voice was hoarse, and her eyes red. 'This is a good one. They're not all like this. And I am tired of this filthy job. *Badanti* get paid almost nothing in this country. I haven't seen my husband in two years. With a little money I could go home, see my family, start over again.' She lowered her voice, and hissed at me, jabbing a finger into my chest. 'She has a drawing that she can't even see! Where's the harm in it?'

'It wasn't yours to sell. There's the harm. But go on. How much were you offered?'

'Ten thousand euros. That's a lot of money in my country.'

'And who offered you that? It can't have been Jenny. I don't believe that. Fulvio Terzi, then?'

She shook her head. 'No. It was a British man. The young man upstairs. He said his name was Blake.'

Chapter 52

I made my way upstairs as quietly as I could and pressed my ear against the door of Blake's apartment. No sound came from inside. I tapped, gently.

'Matthew?'

There was no answer.

'Matthew. It's Nathan Sutherland. I need to speak to you.' I tapped at the door once more. 'Okay, I'm going to count to five. And then I'm going to call the police. One. Two. Three . . .'

Reaching five seemed anti-climactic. I considered starting again, or perhaps making it ten. But there was no light under the door and no sound came from inside. I was pretty sure he wasn't there.

No matter. I knew where he'd be.

I was the only one standing outside on the boat to Zitelle. The *marinaio* kept looking at me as if wondering why I should choose to inflict the wind and rain on myself; but I had found it hard to settle inside the cabin, as the *vaporetto* slid through the lagoon with agonizing slowness.

The *cortile* of Markham's palazzo was fleetingly illuminated by the pale moon, picking out the moss-covered *vera da pozzo*. The windows of his apartment were darkened, but I could see light shining from inside the office. I made my way up to the *loggia*, the only sound being that of my own footsteps on the ancient stone. And then I paused as, from within, I heard the sound of someone gently crying.

The heavy bronze door scraped and juddered across the floor as I pushed at it, and the crying abruptly ceased.

'Hello, Matthew.'

'Nathan?'

Matthew Blake, his face bruised, scratched and wet with tears sat behind Terzi's desk. Giles Markham lay on the floor, half buried under a pile of papers and books that had been pulled from the shelves. I dropped to my knees and uncovered his face, bloody from the deep wound in his throat. Next to his body lay a broken bottle of J&B, its jagged edges covered in blood.

I looked up at Blake.

'Tell me what happened, Matthew.'

'This was an accident, Nathan. I swear it was.'

I nodded. 'Okay,' I said, keeping my voice as neutral as possible.

'We had an argument. It got out of hand.' He pointed to his face. 'He attacked me first. You can see that, can't you? I was defending myself, that's all.'

'An argument?' I said.

He nodded. Then he looked down at Markham's body and screamed as he pounded on the desk with his fists. 'Stupid bastard. You stupid, stupid bastard.'

'I know what you were arguing about, Matthew and I know where it is. If I find it, do you promise to calm down?'

'You know?'

'I do.'

'Then you tell me where it is right now, Nathan.' He reached into his jacket and took out a small revolver. He levelled it at me, his hands shaking almost as much as his voice. 'Tell me.'

I raised my hands. 'Put that down, Matthew. There's no need for anyone else to get hurt.'

'Tell me,' he repeated, as his hand continued to shake. 'Everyone's trying to cheat me, Nathan. Everyone's trying to screw me over. Everyone thinks good old Matthew is the useless boyfriend. But no more. I'm the winner now.'

'Just put it down, eh, Matthew? Come on. I'm not going to cheat you. What would I want with it anyway?'

He nodded, and took a deep breath, placing the gun down on the desk. 'All right. But I'm watching you.'

I nodded reassuringly, and dropped to my knees again, combing through the debris on the floor until my fingertips brushed the edge of a photo frame.

'Here we are,' I smiled, as I got – slowly – to my feet. I ran my finger over the glass. 'It's cracked, but hopefully no harm done.' I turned it over in my hands. 'Simple clip frame,' I said as I eased the back off. 'Easy to conceal something behind it.

'Terzi was worried about being searched by the police. So much so he dropped everything he thought might be incriminating into a canal. But what to do with the drawing itself? He'd have been afraid to keep it at home. And so, he put it here, on his desk at work. Behind a simple photograph of angels. I wondered why he'd been so possessive about it, the first morning we met.' I slid out the fragile sheet of paper from behind the image of Reynolds's *Angel's Heads*. 'Here you are, Matthew. Careful now. Don't grab. It's ever so delicate.'

Blake hunched over the image for a moment, breathing deeply. And then he leaned back in Terzi's chair, half crying, half laughing. I wondered if I should make a grab for the gun, but decided against it. I'd never used one in my life and wasn't sure if this was the right time to start. It might be safer to get him talking.

'So, come on then, Matthew. You've won. You're the winner now. Tell me all about it.'

He rubbed his eyes, and sighed. 'It all started as a bit of a joke at first, you know? Jen told me about this drawing she'd found. Valuable, she said it was. Then she told Terzi, and he told Markham. And we started thinking, there's an old lady living right downstairs from us with a precious work of art that she can't even see. I mean, talk about a victimless crime.

'Jen spent so long looking for it. I think she must have called every Masiero in the phone book. And then, when she found the right one, she even rented an apartment in the same building. Just to make it easier to go and sit and describe paintings to a blind woman. I mean, seriously?

'It was like a gang coming together, you know what I mean? Markham was the one who could put some money up front. Terzi was the fixer, the guy who knew about technology and how to get in touch with people who might buy stuff like this. He fixed us up with those EnchroChat phones for extra security.' He picked up the gun, weighing it in his hand. 'He even got hold of this. On the dark web. Just in case we ran into the wrong people. We felt like we were in a heist movie together. It just seemed like a bit of fun at first.'

'And then, like all the best heist movies, the gang started falling out with each other. So, what was your role, Matthew?'

'I was their man on the ground. I was able to find out what was going on behind *signora* Masiero's door. And when I found out her carer was some penniless woman from some godforsaken place in the Eastern Bloc . . . well, the rest was easy.

'But we knew we had to get Jen onside. We knew we didn't have much time before she discovered what we'd done. So, Terzi phoned her and just suggested she came round to his bookshop. Just for a little chat.'

He looked straight into my eyes and raised his voice. 'That's all it was supposed to be, you understand? Just a little chat.'

Chapter 53

You're running again, but slowly, as if in a dream. And you're falling once more, but this time the sky, like the water pulling at you, is dark and grey.

The cold water knocks the air out of your lungs, and you gasp for breath. You pull yourself to your feet once more. There's nobody to be seen anywhere. Nobody is venturing out on a night like this. Not if they have any choice.

And so on you run, dragging your tired limbs as fast as you can.

You remember the telephone call. 'Jenny, it's Fulvio. Please come to the shop right now. We need to talk. It's important.'

Guardian angels. Dark angels. Fallen angels.

On you run. Because you're the angel now. You're the avenging angel.

You trip once more and you're about to fall and you scream with the sheer frustration of it all. And then arms are around you, steadying you, pulling you upright.

'Signora?'

Your vision is blurred by both the rain and your tears, but you recognise the voice. You blink the wetness from your eyes. You don't know his name, but he has the bookshop near Fulvio's. The one in the Street of the Assassins.

'Signora,' he repeats. 'Are you all right?'

You nod.

'You shouldn't be out on the streets tonight, signora, it's going to be very bad. Go home as quick as you can.'

You try to speak but the words will not come and you wrench out a half-scream. He drops his hands from you and steps back in alarm, afraid you've misunderstood his intentions.

'I will kill him for this,' you sob. 'If he's done this, I will kill him.'

And on you run, without looking back.

The Calle de la Mandola is deep under water now, and you force yourself to walk slowly so as not to fall again, breathing deeply to get some air into your lungs. Be calm. Be calm. Think clearly.

You try to put the key in the lock but your hands are shaking. The door swings open at your touch and you step inside. Into the dark.

The three of them are there.

Markham is leaning back against the desk, his arms folded.

Matthew is turned away from you, nervously dragging on a cigarette.

Fulvio steps forward, his arms open and a broad smile on his face.

'Jennifer. Thank you for coming, cara mia. We just want to talk to you. That's all. Just talk for a moment.'

'Fulvio, if you've done what I think you've done, I'll never forgive you.'

Matthew turns around. Guilt is etched on his face.

'Jen. Babes. We need to talk.'

Terzi nods at Markham, who moves to lock the door.

Chapter 54

Blake ran his hands through his hair and laughed. 'We were trying to calm her down. That's all we were trying to do. Calm her down. I just stood there listening to this stupid fucking *bitch* who'd dragged me out to Venice and then dumped me. And now she was going to ruin everything else. Then I saw this crappy glass paperweight on Terzi's desk and . . . well, I just picked it up . . .

'We just stood there. Looking at her lying in the water. Realising that this whole thing wasn't a game any more.

'Terzi seemed to know what he was doing. He forced the door of the safe as best he could, to try and make it look like a break-in. He took the card and money from her purse. Wiped down the paperweight and dropped it into the water. Then he told us to put the emergency PIN into our EnchroChat phones to wipe everything. Everything else, he told us, he'd be sure to get rid of.

'He took the drawing as well. Well, of course he did. Like I said, he seemed to be the only one who knew what he was doing.'

'There's one thing I don't understand,' I said. 'Why Markham? What was in it for him? He was a wealthy guy.'

Blake laughed again, and there was a manic edge to it now. 'Except he really wasn't. Terzi discovered that Daddy's money was all in a trust. It could only be used to fund projects in Venice. He couldn't touch it. He was living month to month, just like the rest of us.'

I nodded. 'Okay. So that explains the ever-delayed projects and the ones done on the cheap. It was a way of money laundering. Turning his father's money into something he could use. But then, of course, Terzi had discovered this months ago. He started leaking information to the press. About how Jenny had discovered something that wasn't quite right about Markham's affairs. Which directed suspicion towards Markham and away from himself. Every day, just buying himself a little more time to dispose of the drawing. But then, let me guess, Markham suggested you could just split the money down the middle if only Fulvio could be removed. Removed by you, of course?'

He nodded. 'He's good at getting people to do what he wants.'

'Including murder? But, of course, he'd seen you kill Jenny. That gave him a hold over you.'

'It wasn't murder. He just wanted me to scare Terzi. That was all. Things – well, things just got a bit out of hand.'

'You locked him inside a burning boat, Matthew.'

'It wasn't supposed to go that far. Just scare him, that's what Markham told me.' He leaned across the table towards me, his hand twitching above the gun. 'I needed the money, Nathan. Jen had thrown me out. Her dad's cut me off. I don't even have the cost of a flight back to the UK.'

'Well, now you have it. You're the last man standing. It's

all yours. Albrecht Durer's study for *Four Avenging Angels*. Something only a handful of people have ever seen. You should feel privileged. It's just that – well, I'm wondering what you're going to do with it?'

He looked at me as if talking to an idiot. 'What am I going to do? Sell it, of course.'

'Sell it.' I paused. 'How exactly are you going to do that, Matthew?'

'There are people who'll pay good money for this.'

I shook my head. 'There are very, very bad people who will pay very little money for this. How are you going to find them? And what will you do if you do find them?'

Blake shook his head. I continued. 'You see, I can just about believe that Terzi – a man who'd spent his life dealing in rare books and works of art – had found a way to do this. Maybe on the dark web, using Bitcoin. Or maybe he just knew the right – or the wrong – people. I suspect it wouldn't have worked. If it were that easy then people would be doing it already. But it was at least some kind of a plan. But you – what are you going to do? Seriously, where are you going to find people who'll give you more than ten per cent of what this is worth? And how are you going to stop them shooting you in the head a minute later?'

'I'll find someone.'

'No. You won't. The only people who'll be interested in this are crooks who'll use it as collateral against drugs or weapons. You're not part of that world, Matthew. You're not a gangster any more than you are a children's author. The chances of you making any money out of this are even less than they are of you writing a best-seller about a cat living on a gondola. That's not the person you are.'

'Oh, Nathan.' His voice was shaking now but whether with rage or with fear I was unable to tell. 'Tell me what sort of person I am.'

I shrugged. 'I think you're weak. I think you're greedy. I think you have a staggering sense of entitlement. But you're not alone in that. In some ways you're just like Markham. But I do think that maybe, just maybe, you might be a person who could be persuaded to do the right thing.'

'Meaning?'

'Pick up the phone. Call the police. Tell them everything. Take responsibility and give Bill Whiteread a bit of closure.'

He took a deep breath. His eyes flickered to the gun for a moment, and I cursed myself for not having tried to seize it. 'So, what'll happen?'

'Article twenty-two of the Penal Code. Life imprisonment. Which means, with good behaviour, that you could be out in twenty-one years.' I looked him up and down. 'You'll be, what, mid-fifties? Plenty of life still ahead of you. Time enough to start again.'

'I can't do that. I just can't. That's too much to ask.'

'What's the alternative, Matthew? The rest of your life on the run? It'll be nasty, brutish and short, running from place to place trying to hock that drawing for a pittance to anyone who'll take it off you. But if you pick up that phone and make that call, you've got a chance. A better one than poor Jenny Whiteread ever had, at any rate.'

He put his head in his hands and sighed. Then he raised his eyes, and looked directly into mine while he picked up the gun.

'There's another solution, of course,' he said, levelling it at me.

'Another body?'

'If there has to be.'

'It won't work, Matthew. Too many people know too much. My wife. My best friend. The bass player of the only Death Metal band in Venice. You can't kill us all.' I nodded at Markham's body. 'And that must have made a hell of a lot of noise. Your neighbours must have heard. Hell, Elton John's probably on the phone to the police as we speak.'

He was crying again, the tears streaming down his face, and the gun twitched and jerked in his hand. Again, I thought about reaching for it. No. There was every possibility he'd shoot either me or himself by accident.

He rubbed the back of his hand across his forehead, and then swept his hair back, breathing deeply.

'The police. I'll tell them it was an accident. You can get me a good lawyer, can't you? And it was an accident. I didn't mean to kill anyone. Please, Nathan.'

I shook my head. 'You locked Fulvio Terzi in a burning boat. You killed Giles with a broken bottle.' I kept my voice as calm as possible. 'You can believe it or not, Matthew, but I really am trying to help you. Because there are only two ways out of this. One of them has you walking out of the gates of Santa Maria Maggiore in twenty-one years. The other involves sad little notices in the British press about a UK citizen found dead under a bridge in Milan, or Rome or Naples. If you even make it that far.'

'I can't. I just can't.' He choked the words out in between his sobs. Then he took a deep breath and nodded, as if at peace with himself once more. 'As you said, Nathan, I'm not that sort of person.'

Before I could move, he had positioned the gun against his temple. His hand twitched one, twice, a third time. Then he squeezed his eyes shut and pulled the trigger.

The shot echoed around the room, and then Blake slumped over the desk; dark, sticky blood pouring from his head and over Albrecht Durer's *Four Avenging Angels*.

'Christ,' I said. 'Oh Christ.' I turned away and breathed deeply, trying not to vomit. And then I reached for my phone and dialled Vanni's number.

Chapter 55

'He lived for four hours, they told me,' said Vanni, shaking his head. 'But he was too badly injured. So, how are you feeling, Nathan?'

'Kind of okay. I guess. It's not something that anybody should have to see, though.'

'I can imagine. You know, you could just have telephoned us straight away and we would have sorted it out.'

'And then what would have happened?'

'Oh, I imagine we'd have shot him. Or he'd have shot himself anyway. From what you were saying, it doesn't sound as if there would have been any outcomes other than bad ones.'

'I don't think there were, Vanni. Although I still think he didn't really mean to do it.'

'Perhaps not. A shot from a small-calibre revolver through the side of the head?' He shook his head. 'It's not like the movies, Nathan. In some ways he's lucky he's dead.'

'There were lots of things he didn't mean to do. I think he'd convinced himself that he didn't really mean to kill Jenny. Or Terzi. Or Markham.' I sighed. 'Yes, there were any number of things he didn't mean to do, but he did them anyway. So, what about the drawing?'

Vanni shook his head. 'Not good. It's soaked in blood. In more ways than one, I suppose. It's still, I imagine, of enormous interest. Possibly even more so to people who are into – *that* sort of thing. But as to whether it could ever be cleaned. *Boh.* That's something for other people to answer.'

'Does Isabella Masiero have to know about this? Really? She doesn't even know it's gone.'

'It's her property, Nathan. She's going to have to know at some point.'

'It seems so unfair, Vanni.'

'That's because it is, Nathan.'

I sighed. 'I've just thought. It's going to be my responsibility to have the two of them repatriated. Blake and Markham.' I shook my head. 'That feels . . . weird.'

'Can't anyone in Rome or Milan help you?'

'Possibly. But that will involve all sorts of awkward conversations with the Ambassador. So it's probably easier if I just do it myself.' A thought sprung to my mind. 'Thank you for not making this an awkward conversation, by the way.'

Vanni smiled. 'There was no need for it to be. Given that you were honest with us.' Then he leaned in just a little closer, and his smile flickered for a moment. 'You were honest with us? Weren't you?'

'Ah, you know, Vanni, I had a moment there. When I had a chance to grab the gun. I thought of Jenny Whiteread, and of a blind woman holding her precious folder with a single blank sheet of paper. And I thought, I could just shoot him. Say it happened in the struggle. Nobody would know. And if they did, would anybody blame me?'

'So what happened?'

'I've been asking myself that, Vanni. And I'd like to say that I wouldn't have been able to live with the guilt. But, you know, I think I'd have got over it. No, at the end of the day I just didn't have it in me.'

Vanni smiled, properly this time. 'Nathan, I don't think you're the kind of person who would shoot an unarmed man, no matter how much of a bastard he might be. Just as well, really. It would make our relationship with the British diplomatic service a little strained.'

'And what about you, Vanni? What would you have done?'

He leaned his head to one side, as if thinking, and then grinned. 'Why don't we go for breakfast, and I'll think about it in the meantime?'

'Oksana has gone home, they tell me. I'm sorry I never got the chance to say goodbye.' She smiled at the young Romanian woman who had let me in. 'This is Ecaterina. She's going to be with me from now on.'

'Pleased to meet you, Ecaterina. I'm Nathan.' She smiled back at me.

Isabella Masiero's expression changed, and she looked sad for a moment. 'Perhaps Oksana was lonely. It must be difficult, being in a strange country with only an old woman for company. I never asked her very much about herself. I should have done.' She smiled. 'Well then, I must try harder in the future. I'm glad you've come back again, Nathan.'

'Well, there was something I had to give you, Isabella. From Jenny. She would have given it to you herself but, well, that's not possible now.' I took out the card. 'I suppose you could call it a birthday card but I think it's more than that.

She painted it herself, in watercolour. She called it *Angels for an angel*.'

Isabella said nothing, but slid her hand across the table, searching for mine. So I sat there, and talked about Sir Joshua Reynolds and *Angel's Heads*. And, however imperfect it might have been, I described them to the sightless woman who smiled and held my hand throughout.

Chapter 56

'So, Ed,' said Fede, 'can I ask the big question? Namely, are you staying?'

Ed refused to meet my gaze, and I looked down at my shoes in despair.

'Because if you really are going to leave then I'm going to have to persuade my husband not to sink all of our savings into this place and do a job which, frankly, he would be rubbish at.'

'I'm not so sure I'd be rubbish at it,' I began.

'You would be terrible at it. There is nobody else in the city less equipped to run a bar than you. And if I thought, for an instant, that you were serious about this I would be moving back in with *Mamma*.' She turned back to Ed. 'So, you see, quite a lot rests on your decision.'

Ed quit trying to look serious. 'Ah, I decided about a week ago. Of course I'm not going.'

I looked up from my shoes. 'You what?'

'I'm staying.'

'You decided a week ago? Why didn't you say anything?'

'Well, you seemed to be really busy and, besides, I wondered if maybe I'd be destroying your dream and so I never really seemed to find the time.'

'You never found the time? You never found the time for the guy who helps you move fridges in the middle of the night? You never found time for him?'

Ed turned to Fede. 'Am I being the bad guy here? Seriously, am I the bad guy?'

Fede rubbed her face. 'Can we not do this? Can we not just skip to the manly hugs stage? Please?'

I sighed. 'You're staying, Ed? Really?'

He smiled, and nodded. 'Yeah. It didn't take much thought really. Just think about the city over the past few weeks. You and Fede coming to help me out in the middle of the night. All those students, the Mud Angels – little more than kids. People coming in from Mestre to help. And more than that – every day in the paper, there'd be messages from all over the world. This city matters to people, you know? Maybe they've only been here once. Hell, maybe they've never been here at all. But it matters to them. There's a love for the old place and that's not something you can easily turn your back on.'

'Wow. That's beautiful, Ed.'

'And also my cousin's a bit of a dick. I didn't think I'd be able to work with him.'

'Ah. Right.' I paused. 'Should we do the hug thing now?'

He grinned. 'I reckon we should.'

He made his way around the bar, and gave me a bear hug almost Dario-like in its intensity. I returned it as best I could, and looked over his shoulder to where Fede was smiling at us.

'Negronis all round then?'

'Absolutely.' I paused. 'On the house?'

He grinned. 'Don't push it!'

***

'You know,' said Lucia, 'you don't cook too badly for an Englishman.'

'Thanks. I think.'

'I wish my dad cooked. But he's kind of a traditional Italian guy. Grew up in a house where the women did all the cooking.'

'Ah well, I grew up in a house where no one did the cooking. That was an incentive to learn.'

Fede topped up our glasses. 'Bring him round next time, Lucia. I'll cook him my signature dish. Maybe that'll inspire him.'

'What's your signature dish?'

'*Pasta e fagioli alla Bud Spencer*. Well, I say it's my signature dish. It's really my only dish.'

Lucia frowned. 'Who's Bud Spencer?'

Fede and I looked at each other. Then I laughed. 'Damn, you're making us feel old.'

'You are old. Well, not my dad old. But kind of old.'

'Not helping! And shouldn't you be back home right now, or does your dad let you stay up late on Fridays?'

Lucia grinned at us. Then she ran her hands through her Siouxsie Sioux hair and looked serious, as if she'd just remembered something. 'What's going to happen now? To the young British woman, I mean?'

'There'll still need to be an inquest into her death. Even though everyone involved seems to be dead. So it'll be a while yet until we can send her home.'

'I'm sorry. That must be horrible for her dad.'

'It is, yes. I hate using the word "closure", you know. But at least, maybe, he's got that now. He's going back to the UK tomorrow. I promised him I'd see him off on the *Alilaguna*. Just to say goodbye.'

'I wonder if he'll ever come back,' said Fede.

'I hope so. That he'll come back in the summer and walk the streets Jenny used to walk and maybe start to understand why she loved it so much.' I shook my head. 'Poor Jenny. She came to Venice to find angels.'

Fede patted my hand. 'Are you getting morose, *caro mio*?'

I nodded. 'Just a bit.'

'Well, don't. Forget about Markham, and Terzi and Blake. They're just crooks and we have them everywhere. There are good people in this city as well.'

'You're right.' I smiled. 'There's you, of course. And Dario. Oh, and agressive girls who dress like Siouxsie Sioux and have too many dark clothes.'

'Oh thanks,' said Lucia. 'If I wanted to be insulted by an old man, I could have stayed at home.' She looked at her watch. 'I should be heading off, you know?'

'I was only joking about your dad,' I said.

'I know. But the band are rehearsing tonight. We're playing tomorrow again. Be great if you could make it.'

She let us wait for a few seconds, with our faces frozen in horror, before laughing. 'I'm joking. You don't have to.'

The relief must have been palpable on my face and she gently clonked me across the back of my head as she got to her feet.

She leaned over to hug Federica. 'Bye, Fede.'

'Bye, Lucia. Drop by any time you're in the area.'

'I will.' She turned to me and hugged me as well. 'Bye, Nathan. Oh, and my dad will be in touch.'

'Oh yes?'

'Yeah, he wants to come around and check out your record collection.'

Chapter 57

Morning.

I'd lain awake for some time. Gramsci had woken me early, demanding food, and I'd been unable to drop off again. Federica was fast asleep beside me. I got out of bed as quietly as I could, in order to avoid disturbing her, and went to fix myself a coffee.

As the Moka bubbled away on the hob, I went through to the living room, opened the window, and craned my head outside. A grey morning, with a pale sun struggling through the clouds. But dry. And, at the moment, Venice would settle for dry.

One day, of course, the waters will win. But not yet. Not today.

My phone buzzed. A text message from Bill Whiteread.

I nodded to myself, and then checked the time. I went through to the bedroom, and kissed Fede on the forehead. She murmured sleepily, and then pulled the duvet over her head. I got dressed and made my way downstairs.

The streets were still quiet at this hour. Bill was the only passenger waiting at the Sant'Angelo stop, a heavy wheelie bag at his side.

'Hello, Nathan.'

'Morning, Bill.'

'Come to see me off?'

'I thought I should.' I shivered under my jacket. 'It's a cold day. I should have wrapped up better.'

He smiled. 'You need to look after yourself. It's a wonder you haven't caught your death.'

'Well, a lot of my wardrobe's going to need a proper dry-clean. I'm running out of winter clothes, to be honest.'

Bill checked his watch and then leaned out of the pontoon to look up the Grand Canal.

'Going to the airport, then?' I said. 'You could have gone straight from Fondamente Nove.'

He smiled. 'I wanted to say goodbye. And, besides, I felt like one last walk through the city.'

'You didn't feel like staying on for a bit?'

He shrugged. 'I could have done. It seems Mr Markham's paid me up for a couple of weeks. But, really, what would I be staying for? There's nothing to keep me here now.'

'I understand. Do you think you'll ever come back?'

'I think so. But not for a while.' He sighed. 'This was Jenny's favourite place in the world, after all. But I think Venice and I need a break from each other for the time being.'

We stood in silence for a while. Then he checked his watch again and leaned out of the pontoon once more. 'It's coming now,' he said.

'Okay. All the best, Bill. I hope everything goes as well as it can.'

'Thanks, Nathan. For everything.' He paused. 'What's going to happen now?'

I shrugged. 'I don't know. I really don't know. Italian justice moves very slowly. And there's a lot to investigate. But Jenny, we can hope, will be home soon. Oh, and I imagine this story is going to run for some time. You might find the press will be taking an interest in you.'

He shook his head. 'I'm not sure I've got anything I want to say to them.'

'I understand. Just be aware, that's all. I imagine they'll be calling me as well.' I sighed. 'That's not going to please the Ambassador.'

The pontoon rocked gently with the arrival of the *Alilaguna* boat. The *marinaio* laid a gangplank down, and Bill wheeled his bag on board. He gave me a little salute, and smiled.

'Goodbye, Nathan.'

'Goodbye, Bill. *Buon viaggio.*'

I waited until the boat had pulled away from the stop, then turned and made my way back along the *calli* to Campo Sant'Angelo. The *edicola* was already open and I stopped to buy a newspaper.

'How are things?' I said.

The man in the kiosk grinned. 'Everything's still wet and it stinks of damp. Just like the city. But it's good to be back.' He pointed at the rubbish that was still piled up in the middle of the *campo*. 'That's just about all that's left, you know? One more load for *Veritas* to take away and the place will feel like normal again. Those kids were out here again this morning, cleaning up. When I was a student you wouldn't get me out of bed until midday.'

I smiled. 'See you tomorrow, then.'

'*A domani.*'

I walked back in the direction of Calle de la Mandola and the Street of the Assassins. The city, slowly, was coming back to life. Maybe Ed would be open? Maybe Fede and I should go there for breakfast? Maybe . . .

'*Oi!*'

The cry dragged me out of my daydream.

'*Oi!* Englishman!'

I turned to see Lucia standing, arms folded, in front of a pile of waterlogged furniture.

'If you want to make yourself useful, you could always help with some of this, you know?'

I grinned, tucked my newspaper into my back pocket, and went to give her a hand. In Venice, at least, angels come in many forms.

Glossary

a domani	see you tomorrow
acqua alta	the phenomenon of seasonal high tides in the Adriatic Sea and Venetian lagoon leading to periodic flooding of areas of the city
acqua granda	a name coined for the exceptional flooding that hit the city in 1966 and 2019
amaro	literally 'bitter'; typically a herbal *digestivo* such as Campari
baccalà mantecato	an iconic Venetian dish of stockfish beaten with milk and olive oil to a light, fluffy consistency
bacino	the San Marco basin, typically used to refer to that area in front of Piazza San Marco, where the Grand Canal and Giudecca Canal merge
badante (pl. badanti)	a caregiver, or in-home nurse

biblioteca	library
caffè corretto	a coffee 'corrected' with a shot of alcohol, usually grappa
calle (pl. calli)	a narrow street, alley
campanile	the bell tower of a church
carta d'identità	ID card
cazzo	expletive (relatively strong!)
centro storico	historic centre. In Venice this is typically used to refer to the main area of the city and not the outlying islands
chi è?	literally 'who is it?', a common question when answering the entryphone
chiesa	church
chiuso	closed
complimenti	congratulations
conservatorio	conservatory
cortile	courtyard
CPSM	Centro Previsioni e Segnalazioni Maree – the system providing meteorological and tidal information for Venice
dimmi	tell me

Eccellenza Reverendissima	Most Reverend Excellency, formal title of address for the (Roman Catholic) Patriarch of Venice
edicola	newspaper stand
fondamenta	typically the street alongside a canal
Il Gazzettino	a daily newspaper of Venice and the Veneto
giallo	Italian dark crime fiction, so called because of the yellow (*giallo*) covers or page edging on the cheap paperbacks associated with the genre
MS	a brand of Italian cigarettes, sometimes blackly referred to as *Morte Sicura* ('certain death')
magazzino	a cellar or storage room
marinaio	here, the conductor aboard a passenger boat
Mondadori	an Italian publishing house
MOSE	*MOdulo Sperimentale Elettromeccanico*. A system of barriers installed at the inlets of the Lido, Malamocco and Chioggia that can be raised or lowered to protect the city from the effects of *acqua alta*. Hugely over-budget, behind schedule and mired in scandal, the system was finally used for the first time on 3 October 2020.

moto ondoso	the wake created by boats travelling through water. The increase in size and power of boats travelling through the Venetian lagoon has steadily increased the size of these wakes, leading to increasing damage to the structure of the city.
nonno/nonna	grandpa/grandma
paratia	a solid metal barrier which can be dropped into two brackets fixed to the doorframe, with the intention of minimising the amount of water that floods into your property during *acqua alta*
passerella (pl. passerelle)	here, temporary walkways erected throughout the city during *acqua alta*, allowing the pedestrian to walk above the flooded streets
piacere	a pleasure
polpetta	meatball
porta blindata	reinforced door
previsione	weather forecast
Querini Stampalia	a Venetian cultural institution, housing an archive, a library and a museum
Questura	main police station

RAI	the Italian state broadcaster
sandolo	a traditional, flat-bottomed, Venetian rowing boat
se non ora quando?	if not now, when?
sestiere	Venice is divided into six *sestieri* or neighbourhoods
signorile	noble, refined, gentlemanly
Spencer, Bud	Italian actor, much beloved for his partnership with Terence Hill in a series of comedy Westerns
straniero	foreigner
tabarro	the classic Venetian cloak
tesoro/caro/cara/vecio	terms of endearment
terraferma	the mainland
terrazzo	typical Venetian flooring, made of marble or granite chips set in concrete and polished until smooth
tramezzino	the traditional Italian-style sandwich; triangles of white bread with the filling typically heaped up in the middle
vaporetto	the style of boat used in the public transport system in Venice

vera da pozzo	the wellhead around a well, frequently beautifully decorated, and a common feature of streets and *campi* in Venice
Vigili del fuoco	the fire service
Veritas	the organisation responsible for refuse collection in the city
zio	uncle

Acknowledgements

Over the course of those terrible weeks in November 2019, many young people – some students, some still at school – took time out of their own lives to help with clearing the city of the mountain of detritus left behind by the flood. Shops and private houses were cleaned, the elderly and infirm were checked up on, food was delivered to those who felt unable to go out. After seeing some photographs of a group of Mud Angels in *La Nuova,* I realised that a number of them were ex-students of mine. I am, of course, enormously proud of them all.

I have taken some liberties with the timeline of events in the weeks following the *acqua granda*. Nevertheless the events of the night of 12 November, and the effects on the city, were as I describe.

The church of the Zitelle has sadly been closed for some years now, except for the occasional exhibition. On a happier note, however, although the church of St George's was flooded there was no long-term serious damage as detailed in the story.

To all my lovely readers – thank you so much for your continued support and good wishes. This would not be happening without you!

I finish, as ever, with my thanks to my agent John Beaton; to Colin Murray; to Krystyna, Zoe, Jess, Andy and everyone at Constable, and – of course – to Caroline. It's become something of a cliché by now to mention her incredible reserves of patience, but it is nonetheless true!

Philip Gwynne Jones, Venezia 2021
www.philipgwynnejones.com

*Read the next book in Philip Gwynne Jones's
thrilling Nathan Sutherland series . . .*

The Venetian Candidate

To tell the truth is a revolutionary act

Battered by floods and crushed by overtourism, the city of Venice faces an uncertain future. The election of a new mayor, therefore, has never felt more important.

As the candidates jostle for position and alliances are made and promises broken, Andrea Mazzon, a controversial writer and historian, emerges as a strong candidate.

Nathan Sutherland, meanwhile, has more important things on his mind as he investigates the case of an elderly British academic who has disappeared, while also researching the fate of his grandfather during the Great War. The trail leads to a remote Commonwealth war cemetery where, under the ice and snow, Nathan makes a discovery that links the terrible events of a century ago with the electoral campaign in La Serenissima. A campaign that might ultimately set the victor on the road to the Senate – and on the road to murder . . .